THE HOUSE PARTY

THE HOUSE PARTY

A NOVEL

RITA CAMERON

WILLIAM MORROW
An Imprint of HarperCollins*Publishers*

THE HOUSE PARTY. Copyright © 2022 by Rita Cameron. All rights reserved. Printed in the United States of America. No part of this book may be used or reproduced in any manner whatsoever without written permission except in the case of brief quotations embodied in critical articles and reviews. For information, address HarperCollins Publishers, 195 Broadway, New York, NY 10007.

HarperCollins books may be purchased for educational, business, or sales promotional use. For information, please email the Special Markets Department at SPsales@harpercollins.com.

FIRST EDITION

Designed by Leah Carlson-Stanisic

Library of Congress Cataloging-in-Publication Data has been applied for.

ISBN 978-0-06-321806-2

22 23 24 25 26 LSC 10 9 8 7 6 5 4 3 2 1

FOR SEAN

THE HOUSE PARTY

APRIL

2008

1

The texts started going out at noon on Friday: There's a party at the house going up by the river. Can you get beer? Make it a keg. Just our crew, no kids. Are you holding? You up for a Philly run? Park on the road—no cars by the house.

A backpack hummed against a chair leg, the phone inside set to vibrate. Will O'Connor sat in the back row of his calculus classroom. He slipped his hand into his bag, glanced down at the screen, and then flicked his eyes back to the board.

Plans were made and the slouching students stirred, their eyes drifting to the windows. It was April, but it was warm, and graduation for New Falls High was only six weeks away. Final projects were just about in, and these last weeks of classes didn't really matter for the seniors. The students knew it, and the teachers knew it. The lessons were halfhearted and geared toward showing movies whenever possible. In any case, the kids who were going to college already had their acceptances, and their places in the class of 2012 were secured with Daddy's check. And the kids who weren't going to college never worried about it too much anyway.

Will watched through the window as a few of his friends slipped out of the cafeteria doors and hopped into a car that would head down I-95 to a neighborhood in North Philadelphia, about an hour away. They knew a block there where they could buy coke just by rolling down the car window, like picking up fries at the McDonald's drive-thru. Booze was even easier—they could just get a keg at Mason's in

town, where Mr. Mason barely looked at their fake ID's before handing them a tap.

The bell rang. Only two more periods to go. Will slung his backpack over his shoulder and walked down the hall to his AP history
class.

At five o'clock there were already a few cars parked near the house
on River Road. It was a mix of the pricey and the practical, just like
the town itself: a late model BMW, a handful of beat-up Civics and
station wagons, and an open-top Jeep.

New Falls sat on the outskirts of the Philadelphia suburbs, nestled
into the rolling hills of Hart County. The town, originally an old ferry
crossing, was inseparable from the river that bordered it, and over the
years it had tried on and shed a few different personalities: artists' col-
ony, tourist attraction, and suburban outpost. In the hills around town,
sprawling horse estates sat side by side with tree farms.

More recently, clusters of affordable townhomes and high-end
housing developments had begun to encroach on the open fields. The
houses' reclaimed wood floors and wrap-around porches mimicked
the old farmhouses they replaced, and the neighborhood names, like
Deerfield and Quail Ridge, evoked the local wildlife even as they
drove it away. In theory, New Falls was within commuting distance of
both Philadelphia and New York City, but the closest highways were
nearly thirty minutes away, making the town feel either pleasantly
secluded or isolated, depending on your perspective. The families that
had been there for generations were spoiled by its peace and beauty,
and the highly ranked public school provided a good education to the
children of doctors and landscapers alike.

It was a town where everyone, if asked, claimed to be middle
class, whether they had a Mercedes in the garage or a tractor they
could barely afford to keep running. This attitude was evidence of
the town's Pennsylvania Quaker roots: a belief in the importance of
equality and humility, even where it didn't actually exist. New Falls
prided itself on retaining its character, and it was true that if you
squinted, the town looked much as it had a hundred years ago. But

the house going up on River Road was new, and different—a sign not of suburban sprawl, but of money and style, trickling down from New York.

The sleek contemporary sat just north of town, shielded from its neighbors by several acres of wooded waterfront on either side. It was long and angular, with walls of glass along the back and a wide deck that wrapped around to a firepit. It resembled a series of boxes, each opened like a gift toward the river. Inside, the rooms were light and airy, with expanses of white walls and a pristine, almost featureless white kitchen. A black metal staircase seemed to float unsupported up to the second floor. In the back, the deck dropped off and the carpet of grass ran right to the river's edge, where it met stone steps that descended straight into the water.

There were a few girls sitting there now, their bare feet dangling in the water. Halfway between the house and the river was a pool, the concrete poured but not yet filled with water. Two boys were using it as a half-pipe, the wheels of their skateboards hissing up and down the curved walls. The local skaters could sniff out newly built pools as if they had a divining rod for waterless ponds. Or maybe one of the kids' uncles worked for the concrete company.

The work on the house was almost finished. The floors and walls were in, and most of the kitchen appliances. There was only detail work left: wires protruded where lighting fixtures would go, and an empty space in the cabinetry, like a missing tooth, waited for the refrigerator. Expecting to start work again on Monday, the contractors had left some of their tools behind—drills, floodlights, a sander.

Will and his brother Trip passed the line of cars along the road and pulled down the driveway, the gravel crunching under the tires of Will's pickup truck.

"I might head home early," Will told Trip as they got out. He hadn't been planning on coming at all. He had track practice early the next morning and AP exams coming up in two weeks.

"I got you," Trip said, pushing back the hair that hung over his eyes and giving Will his signature lazy smile. "We'll just have a few drinks and then head home."

"Sure," Will said, rolling his eyes. His brother wasn't exactly known for taking it easy on Friday nights. Or on any other night that offered itself up for a good time.

The girls sitting by the river stood and walked up to the house, carefully drying their feet in the grass before stepping inside. They'd been best friends since elementary school: June Jeffries, Maddie Martin, and Rosie Mendoza. All three wore short shorts and tank tops and had long hair hanging down their backs.

June had always been the ringleader of the group; even she thought of herself without irony as the queen bee. She was tall, with black hair and lips that seemed to be permanently pursed. Her confidence had carried over into her academics: she made straight A's, led half the clubs at school, and was headed to the honors college at Penn State in the fall. Maddie was pale and delicate, a blonde with translucent skin and faded blue eyes. She was quieter than her friends, constantly drawing in her notebook and occasionally showing her work at the art collective in town. And Rosie had a quick smile, a cascade of sun-streaked brown hair, and big eyes with thick black lashes. She tended to follow June around, when she wasn't working at her father's restaurant, and she'd be joining her at Penn State in the fall. They were all pretty, regularly and effortlessly devastating the boys at school with their long limbs and clear skin, no need to try too hard.

Rosie began mixing drinks, dumping out half a jug of cranberry juice and topping it back up with vodka. She tightened the lid, shook it, and started pouring into plastic cups. Trip walked up behind her and squeezed her waist, causing her to squeal.

"How about one of those for me?" he asked. She made a face, but poured him a drink. Trip took the cup and pulled himself up to sit next to Maddie on the kitchen counter. He casually draped an arm over her shoulders, and she let him. They hung out with Trip mainly because he was Will's brother, and because he held a sort of elder-statesman position among the high school crew. But at twenty-one, his act was getting less cute, and a string of arrests for drunk driving and pot possession meant that he wasn't going to be working anywhere but his parents' farm anytime soon. The girls put up with him, but they weren't going to date him.

The door opened again and Hunter Finch walked in. June slid off the counter and kissed him, while Trip clapped and whistled. Rosie blushed and looked away. Hunter and June had been going out for almost a year, although Hunter didn't attend the local high school like the rest of them. His father, a real estate developer, had serious money and sent Hunter to Collegiate Prep, a private school in New Jersey. If high schoolers could be a power couple, then they were it: she was smart and he was rich, and they seemed to make sense, even if they didn't get to see each other all that often.

Will O'Connor slapped Hunter on the back. The Finch estate shared a property line with Will's family's farm, and the boys had grown up together, playing in the fields between their homes. They'd stayed friends despite going to different schools, and that fall they would be together again—at Princeton. Will had worked hard for it, and he had a merit scholarship from a local foundation that would pay the tuition his family was expected to cover, even with the generous financial aid. He could still hardly believe it was happening. Hunter was a shoo-in, despite his shaky academic record. His father was an alumnus and a generous donor.

"How's the other half living, man?" Will teased.

"They're doing it right," Hunter replied, pulling from his pocket a ziplock bag filled with a dozen white pills. "Should we get this party started?"

"Hell yes." June stuck out her tongue, and Hunter put a tab of ecstasy on it. Rosie followed suit, and Hunter popped two.

Maddie met Will's eye. They were going out, although they hadn't put a label on it. Will smiled and shrugged. "I'm cool," he said. "Early practice tomorrow." Maddie hesitated for a moment, and then shook her head. "No thanks," she said.

"C'mon, Maddie," Hunter said. "I thought you wanted to try it." He held the pill out to her. "Just because Will doesn't know how to have a good time doesn't mean you can't."

"Don't let me stop you," Will said, holding up his hands.

Maddie stared at the baggie. "Maybe I'll just try half," she said, then stuck out her tongue like June had. Hunter placed the whole pill on her tongue.

"Hey!" she said, but she'd already swallowed. Hunter just laughed.

"Don't worry," he said. "I'll take good care of you. You're going to love it."

Will headed for the door. "C'mon, man," he said to Hunter. "Let's go throw the ball around before you're too stoned to do anything but roll around in the grass."

They tapped the keg and filled their cups. Someone plugged in an iPod and speakers, and a few kids set up a table using sawhorses and plywood from the garage. Soon a beer pong game was going strong, with Trip O'Connor landing his balls without fail. Kids were hanging out in the kitchen and on the deck. Will came back inside just in time to see his brother arc a perfect shot into his opponent's last cup. Trip's opponent, who looked like he was about fourteen, gamely tossed back the beer, and then stumbled away from the table. "Lucky shit," the kid slurred. "I mean, lucky shot. I'll get you next time."

Trip laughed. "Drink some water!" he advised the kid's retreating back.

Will looked into Trip's cups. He'd only had to drink half of his beers, but he already seemed a little toasted. Will checked the time on his phone—they'd only been there for an hour.

"Had enough?" Will asked Trip, already knowing the answer. His brother lived for this kind of thing.

"Are you kidding?" Trip asked. "I can't quit while I'm ahead. Come on. I need a partner."

Will watched as Trip arranged the cups and poured fresh beers. Some kids from school wandered over and began to do the same on the other side of the table. "I have track practice in the morning," Will reminded his brother. But even as he said it, Will was already bouncing the ping-pong ball off the table, testing out its spring. He loved any kind of competition, and beer pong was the sport of drinking.

"Consider this carb-loading," Trip replied.

Will grinned, giving in. It was almost the end of senior year. How many more nights like this would there be? He watched his brother make his first shot, and then he closed one eye, focused, and sank his own ball. Trip slapped him on the back. "Team O'Connor!" he roared, and Will echoed him: "Team O'Connor!"

Will and Trip kept playing, showing off for the girls who were watching. Some kids from New Jersey arrived with more beer. The music got louder. The kids who'd gone to Philly for coke finally got there, looking wired, and set up shop in the upstairs bathroom. Word went around that you could get two lines for five dollars. Will slipped upstairs and did a quick line—just one, never more—to keep himself sharp.

On his way back down, he could hear Kanye's *Graduation* album blasting as all the seniors cheered, feeling like the music was made just for them. Kids were dancing now, stealing glances at their reflections in the sliding glass doors. *And yes barely passed, any and every class*, they chanted, laughing. Will looked around for Maddie, but she must have been outside. A girl he recognized from school started pulling on his hand, leading him toward the group of dancing kids. He followed her and she smiled at him and then began to dance, her body rolling with the music. Will automatically put his hands on her waist, but he was relieved when the beat picked up and she turned to bounce between him and some of her friends. He wasn't quite drunk enough not to feel self-conscious. *Welcome to the good life,* the kids sang along, and Will slipped away, feeling good, feeling like he wanted another drink.

He pushed past the crowd, which had somehow doubled over the past hours, and grabbed a Solo cup and a bottle of Jack Daniel's from the kitchen. Through the window, he spotted Hunter on the deck and went out to join him. Hunter lit a cigarette and handed one to Will, who knew there was no more telling himself that he was going home early. There was nowhere else he wanted to be right now. He'd worked so hard all year, loading up on APs and making National Honor Society and captain of the track team, while pulling fifteen hours a week at his family's farm. He'd even volunteered as an umpire for Little League. He had everything under control. This was clearly going to be the party of the year. He didn't want to miss it.

Will stood on the deck smoking with Hunter as the sun slipped behind the hills and the river at the edge of the lawn turned a deep, glassy blue. A few kids plugged in the contractor's floodlights and went into the woods to look for kindling for the firepit. From the house they heard the synthetic throb of a Katy Perry anthem as the shadows of the dancing kids flickered across the deck. The girls were rolling hard now, wrapping their arms around anyone and everyone, shouting to them that they loved them.

Will took a last long drag on the cigarette, an American Spirit. It was too strong for someone who didn't usually smoke, and he coughed, feeling lightheaded. Hunter laughed at him, and when Will smiled, his face felt numb from the booze and the coke that was still racing through his system. "Do you think we'll miss this?" he asked Hunter.

"No way," Hunter said. "Next year is going to be epic. Thank god you're going to be there, Will. I wouldn't want to go without you."

"You're getting sappy, man," Will said, laughing. "I think the ecstasy must have hit."

But Hunter grabbed Will's arm, shaking his head. "No, seriously," he said. "I couldn't have cared less about going to Princeton until I found out you were going too. Princeton has always been my dad's thing. I was kind of dreading it, to be honest. It's going to full of rich pricks—you'll see. But it'll be cool, because we'll be there together."

"You're a rich prick," Will said.

Hunter smirked. "I need you to keep me humble."

They tapped plastic cups and Hunter stood up. "I'm getting a refill," he said as he started toward the door. "You?"

"I'm good," Will said. He turned to watch the scene around him. Someone had lit a fire in a trash can near the pool, and a tall skinny kid had set two ends of a tree branch on fire and was dancing, whipping the flames through the darkness as he spun. A speaker on the deck was playing nineties rock, an incongruous mash-up with the

techno beat coming from the kitchen. Will saw June and Rosie playing on the steps by the river. He frowned. They were in up to their
knees, and he knew the water couldn't be more than sixty degrees this
time of year. He walked down to the river, thinking that they were
so fucked up that they'd have hypothermia before they even noticed
it was cold.

Will called to the girls, but they were laughing and splashing each
other, oblivious to his voice. He sighed as he kicked off his shoes and
waded in to pull them out. Back on the lawn, he dropped down onto
the grass beside them. "Where's Maddie?" he asked, looking around.

Rosie and June just giggled as they laid on the grass. "Seriously,"
Will said, sitting up. "Was she with you? Did she go in the water?"
He pulled June up and tried to get her to look at him, but her eyes
were unfocused.

"She's *your* girlfriend," June slurred. "You should know where she
is." June made a kissing face and then slumped against him.

"For Christ's sake, June. You only took one pill," Will said, helping
her to her feet. "Okay, you and Rosie go up to the house. See if you
can find Hunter. It's time to go home. I'll look for Maddie."

Will scanned the water, but he didn't see any sign of her. His heart
was beating hard. Had she been in the water? He walked up and
down the edge of the river, calling her name and trying not to sound
as panicked as he felt. He knew that he was drunk, and he couldn't
tell if that was making him more or less worried than he should be.
He jogged over to the pool, where a bunch of kids were taking turns
dropping in on their skateboards.

"Yo, has anyone seen Maddie?" he asked.

A couple of the kids laughed. "Oh yeah, man, I saw her," said a boy
that Will didn't recognize. "Whoever moves in here is gonna need
curtains."

Will looked up at the house. "What the fuck are you talking
about?" he asked. But before the boy could reply, Will was already
making his way back to the house, where he could see a group of boys
on the second-floor deck.

Will pushed through the throng of kids in the kitchen, then took the stairs to the second floor, two at a time. He jogged down a corridor and found the door that led out to the deck. A few boys were standing in a huddle against a sliding glass door at its far end. They were laughing and whistling, and one was taking pictures with his phone.

Will shoved them aside. Through the glass he could see Maddie. She was lying on the floor, with her shirt pushed up and her jean shorts around her knees, her white lace bra and panties visible. A guy was on top of her, kissing her, his hand under her bra. Will felt himself grow hot, and then nauseous. "Who is that?" he asked, and the kids around him shrugged. He banged on the door, but neither Maddie nor the boy reacted. He couldn't be sure, but it didn't even look as if Maddie was awake. He tried the glass door, but it wouldn't open.

"It's locked, bro," one of the boys said. "Else I'd be in there myself." The other guys cracked up.

Will felt a rush of adrenaline, as if he was about to hit the kid. But he didn't have time for that. He went back into the house, his heart pounding, and ran along the hallway. He tried the inside door, but it was locked as well.

Will raced back downstairs. He rummaged through the tools in the kitchen, looking for a screwdriver. He couldn't find one, so he grabbed a hammer instead. He climbed the stairs again, and the boys standing by the window backed off, watching him and waiting to see what he was going to do.

Will looked at the hammer in his hand and then at the glass door. He had to get Maddie out of there.

Everything that followed seemed to happen very slowly, the night stretching out into the early morning, the music and the drugs coming in and out of focus, carrying them along. But later they would remember it happening too quickly to stop, like a pileup on the freeway. Nothing to do but brace yourself for impact.

Will took a deep breath, drew his arm back, and let the hammer fly. The glass door shattered into pebbles, cracks spreading from the point of impact and then shards falling quickly with a sound like rain.

For a moment the roar of the party stopped, and the only sound was the dissonant music, echoing from the bare walls and floors of the house. Then someone gave a loud whoop. The shrill explosion of a beer bottle breaking was greeted by cheers, and then there was more breaking glass as people began to rocket bottles from the upstairs windows and decks. Someone turned up the music, drunken conversations resumed, and the party lurched forward into the night.

2

The pounding was in his head, not on the door. No, scratch that, it was both. Hunter rolled over and pushed his palms against his eyes. "What is it?" he called out.

The door opened and his dad walked in. Dominic Finch was big: linebacker shoulders in an expensive suit. He leaned against the doorframe, filling the space, and checked his watch, also expensive. "Are you going to stay in bed all day?"

"Maybe." Hunter yawned.

"It's almost noon. And what about the two girls asleep on my sofa?"

Hunter closed his eyes, trying to conjure the memory of what he'd done last night. The nights tended to run together, even when he hadn't drunk to the point of blackout, and at first he drew a worrying blank. Then he remembered the party, pushing his way through the dark and crowded house, music echoing against the bare walls and floors. And then, as he stepped outside for a cigarette, the sound of police sirens, distant but getting closer. The next thing he remembered was weaving home in the BMW, not quite able to see straight, with June and Rosie passed out in the back seat.

"Your mom is pretty upset," his father was saying. "There's a scratch all the way down the driver's side door of her car. And there was mud in the back. How did that happen?"

Oh, fuck, the BMW. A brand-new six series, borrowed without permission, since he'd totaled his own car a few months before. Hunter winced. "Stepmother," he muttered, stalling for time.

Dom Finch sighed. "That's Lindsay's new car. She said that she told you that you could borrow it, but she didn't expect it to come back damaged inside and out."

She'd covered for him, at least a bit. That surprised him. Hunter thought fast. "We, uh, went kayaking on the river after school. It turned into kind of a late night—there was a bonfire." He sat up in bed, warming to his story. "I didn't realize how muddy it was. Maybe I scratched it on a branch by the boat launch?"

"Kayaking?" It was clear that Dom didn't buy it, but he was looking at his watch again. He seemed even more distracted than usual. "Look, Boy Scout, I have to go. I have meetings in New York all afternoon. Make it right. Drive June and her friend home, then take the car in and get the paint taken care of. It won't kill you to take responsibility for something. And apologize to Lindsay. I really don't need this shit right now. I have my hands full with work."

"It's Saturday," Hunter said. He was surprised by how childish he sounded. Why did he care if his dad was working on the weekend? The man hadn't built one of the most successful real estate businesses on the East Coast by sitting around the breakfast table with his kids on the weekend. Hunter cleared his throat. "Whatever. I'll deal with the car."

Dom sighed. "Hunter, I know I haven't been around much lately. We're having some hiccups with the financing for the new Brooklyn waterfront properties. It's unusual enough that I feel like I should go up there and look everything over myself, take a few people out to dinner, try to feel out what's going on."

Hunter's window began to rattle. The helicopter was coming in to land on the tennis courts behind the house.

Dom glanced out the window, then back at Hunter. He seemed to be assessing how much more time he should take talking to Hunter, and how late that would make him for his meeting. He blinked, the calculation complete. "I gotta go. I'll be back late. Don't forget about the car."

"See ya."

Hunter laid back in his bed, thinking. He suddenly remembered the sound of breaking glass and cheering. Fishing around in the tangled sheets for his phone, he scanned his texts, but there was nothing from Will. Had they all left together? He dialed Will, but the call went straight to voice mail. He put the phone on his nightstand and, as he rose, noticed his sneakers on the floor at the foot of the bed, wet enough that the balled-up socks inside them appeared to be soaked as well. What exactly had happened last night?

Hunter slipped down a set of back stairs that led to the kitchen, hoping to avoid his stepmother while he went to wake up June and Rosie. The house was old and full of odd passageways and funny turns. It had been pieced together over the last two centuries, each family adding on to the original stone structure until it became a rambling mansion, nestled between a pond and an overgrown orchard. It had character, his father liked to say. It was nothing like the gleaming house clones that Finch Properties built up and down the coast in mazes of cul-de-sacs. Those houses always made Hunter feel off-kilter, each one of them almost the same, but eerily different. A closet where you expected a bathroom, or the kitchen a mirror image of what it should have been.

Hunter shuddered, and then steadied himself. It was just the comedown from the ecstasy, he told himself. All of the dopamine drained from his brain.

He heard the little kids' voices before he made it down to the kitchen, but it was too late to turn around. They would have already heard him on the creaky steps, and he didn't want Lindsay to think that he was too scared to face her. Even if he was.

Jack and Grace, four-year-old twins, were eating lunch at the kitchen table, a portable DVD player open in front of them. Lindsay sat across from them, her hands wrapped around a mug of tea and her face a blotchy mess. When the kids heard Hunter come in they looked up at him quickly and then stared back at the screen so hard that Hunter was sure they weren't paying the least bit of attention to it.

"Hey, uh, sorry about the car," Hunter said sheepishly.

"I don't care about the car," Lindsay snapped, too quickly. She had clearly been going over this conversation in her mind all morning. She walked it back. "I mean, I do care about the car. But what I really care about is your father waking up to a bunch of girls sleeping on his sofa and the car parked halfway off the driveway, all scratched up. And of course I'm the one that he gets . . ." She was about to say "pissed at," but she was always careful about her language in front of the kids. She steadied her voice before she spoke again: "I'm the one he gets upset with. It looks like I don't know how to run my own house."

It was right on the tip of his tongue: It's not your house. But he felt bad for her, and for his half siblings, who were now staring down at their plates.

"Look, I'm sorry. It was a late night." He gave Lindsay half a smile, inviting her into his circle: You're young, you get me. This strategy had worked for a little while. When he woke up with his first real hangover, she rolled her eyes and made him a big breakfast. But at some point she had gotten older, or maybe his act had just gotten old. It didn't help that Dom tended to blame anything that went wrong at home on her. The honeymoon was over, and it was clear that she was looking forward to Hunter going away to college in the fall with outright glee.

Hunter made a last-ditch attempt at peace. He gave both the kids a tickle and they giggled, their heads bobbing in unison. "Hey, guys, want to play hide-and-seek later?" he asked. "Now!" they both shouted, and Hunter laughed. "Later, later. Eat your lunch." Out of the corner of his eye, he saw Lindsay's face soften. This was his chance. He made for the door.

"Lindsay, I've got to go out. Can you tell June and Rosie to text me when they get up?"

"You're leaving them here?"

"I'm taking the car in."

He was out the door and halfway across the lawn before he heard Lindsay at the door behind him. "You forgot the keys!" she shouted. And then, fainter: "You're just like your father." He pulled up the hood of his sweatshirt and kept walking, pretending not to hear.

Hunter cut through the woods at the back of the property and picked up the dirt road that led to the O'Connor Family Orchard. He passed the white clapboard house where the O'Connors ran their stand on the weekends, selling cider and baskets for U-pick berries or apples, depending on the season. Inside, he could see Mrs. O'Connor standing behind the counter in a white apron, smiling and chatting with the customers. The locals came in early for the best fruit. At this time of day, it was mostly city people, from New York and Philadelphia.

He caught her eye and waved. Mrs. O'Connor had always been good to him, and even more so after his mother started having her problems, disappearing for longer and longer stretches, before she disappeared for good. Mrs. O'Connor checked in on him without prying, and she was one of the few people who could ask him how he was doing and get a real answer. A few times, he'd even come by the orchard when he knew Will was out at a meet or practice, just to hang around while she worked. This morning she met his eye, but instead of giving him her usual quick smile, she frowned and turned back to the line of customers waiting at the counter.

Hunter continued past the stand and the tangle of old farm equipment. The ranch house with mustard-colored siding where the O'Connors lived was tucked behind the barn. Hunter rapped on the side of the screen door, knowing better than to let himself in. He was greeted by a chorus of howls and nails clicking against the linoleum as the O'Connors' two Dobermans barreled toward the door. They'd never liked him.

Neither had Mr. O'Connor, who followed the dogs at a more measured pace. Unlike Will's mother, Will's father had always regarded Hunter with suspicion, if not outright hostility. He came to the screen door, but he didn't open it. He stood behind the door with his arms folded as the two dogs jumped and growled at his sides, their spittle catching in the screen. "Sit!" Mr. O'Connor barked, and the dogs obeyed at once, resting back on their haunches and giving Hunter the side-eye.

Will's father was wiry, like his son, with short-cropped gray hair and matching stubble on his chin. His shirt, open at the neck, showed a sliver of the SEMPER FI tattoo inked on his chest.

"Hello, sir," Hunter said. Mr. O'Connor was the only person

Hunter ever called sir. Not that he had been asked to—it just popped out of his mouth one day and stuck. Mr. O'Connor only grunted. "Is Will around?" Hunter asked.

"So," Mr. O'Connor said, as if he hadn't heard Hunter. "You weren't at this party in the woods last night?"

Hunter ran his hand through his hair, trying to piece together what might have happened, trying not to give anything away. Mr. O'Connor's narrowed eyes told him that Will must have gotten caught. By the cops, or just by his dad, Hunter wondered. He decided to play dumb. "Party?" he asked.

Mr. O'Connor just kept looking at him, not buying it, but, like Hunter's own father, not bothering to call him on it. Hunter got this a lot, from teachers and from other kids. Even once from a local cop who had pulled him over doing nearly eighty miles an hour down a back road. The guy had him nailed. He took his time administering the sobriety test, leaning against the car and enjoying Hunter's stoned attempts at balance, while his partner ran Hunter's license. "Now spell marijuana backward," he demanded, snickering when Hunter only made it through the first two letters. But when the partner came back, pointing at the license and whispering something Hunter couldn't hear, the cop's face tightened. Hunter, high as he was, knew the drill when he saw it. *That's Dominic Finch's kid. There's no real problem here, right? Just call the family to come pick him up.*

"Look," Hunter said, emboldened by Mr. O'Connor's silence. "Is Will here? I need to talk to him."

"Don't you fuck this up for him," Mr. O'Connor said quietly, his eyes never leaving Hunter's face. "He's going to college next year."

Here we go, Hunter thought. Mr. O'Connor always treated him as if he and Will were competitors instead of friends, and like Hunter had entered the contest under false pretenses. "I know he is," Hunter said. "Princeton." He couldn't help himself: "So am I."

"Uh-huh," Mr. O'Connor said, his voice using those two syllables to make it clear that he thought only one of them deserved that honor.

They stood there, the screen door between them and the silence like a game of chicken. Just then Trip came around from the back of the house, his face stubbly like his dad's, carrying a large crate of half-frozen apple cider for the shop. He gave his dad and Hunter a wary look, and then motioned to Hunter to help him with the crate. Mr. O'Connor disappeared back into the house without a word, and Hunter took one end of the crate.

"I think I'm growing on him," Hunter said. "He seems happy to see me."

"Your timing could be a little better."

"He knows about last night?"

"Sort of," Trip said.

"What the hell happened? I left with June and Rosie when I heard the sirens. Did you guys get out of there?" Hunter felt no shame in admitting his hazy memory to Trip, who he knew had plenty of half-remembered nights of his own.

Trip motioned to Hunter to put down the crate. "Things got pretty hairy there at the end, huh? Glad you got out. We were walking up River Road to get Will's truck when the cops picked us up. I parked up there after we unloaded the booze so that we wouldn't get parked in, and there were a couple of other kids who were also leaving at the same time. The cops saw Will toss a beer can into the woods, so they gave him a ticket for underage drinking and insisted on calling the folks to pick us up. Our dad kept asking Will about drugs, and if you were there, but he couldn't get anything out of him, so he sent him to bed. He woke us up at dawn to start work, and now he's got Will out there raking the apple field. Oh, and the parents took his phone, so don't text him."

"Shit, I'm sorry." Hunter recalled passing the cops on River Road as he'd headed home. He remembered glancing at the clock on the dash and seeing that it read 1 a.m. just as two cop cars passed him, their lights flashing. "I must have left right before they got there," he said. "Did they write you up?"

"For what? I'm twenty-one, and I wasn't driving yet, so no DUI. Honestly, I think they just wanted to get everyone out of there and go home."

"But what about the house?" Hunter asked. "There must have been fifty kids there."

"Dude, that's the crazy part," Trip said. "I don't think they even saw it. We were up on the road when they stopped us. I mean, shit, I was sweating bullets. If they'd seen the house we would have been completely fucked. Trespassing, breaking and entering? I don't even know. But one of the cops asked if we were drinking in the woods, and someone said yes, and that was that. Real detective work." Trip laughed. "Sometimes I think they're just going through the motions."

Hunter frowned. "Someone's going to find it, though." He remembered walking through the kitchen, an inch of water on the floor from a clogged sink. It was starting to come back to him—his wet shoes. "Things got pretty out of control."

Trip lit up a cigarette—hand rolled, of course, part of his thing. "Whatever," he said, as if that was an answer. "Whose house is it, anyway? No one from around here. It's probably just some builder doing it on spec, trying to make a quick buck." He looked at Hunter and winked. "No offense."

"Yeah, I guess so," Hunter said, thinking that Trip was taking this way too lightly.

"But when whoever is building that house sees it, they're going to want answers. The cops will put it together that you guys were down there. Who else got caught?"

"A couple of girls from the high school. They seemed young— maybe sophomores? You shoulda seen it. They were all crying, and they practically had the cops comforting them. A few other kids I didn't know, probably from Jersey. They won't know who we were. Look, the cops can think whatever they want, but they can't really put us at that house. They missed it. The important thing, if anyone asks questions, is that everyone stays cool and plays dumb. We'll just stick to the story. We were drinking in the woods, and that's it. I'll get Will to talk to the kids from school. If we stick together, they can't prove anything."

"Maybe," Hunter said.

"Definitely," Trip replied. "It could have been anyone. It could have been the guys working on the house! Besides, it'll clean up okay."

Hunter felt, at the edges of his memory, something lurking, something that he couldn't quite put his finger on.

"Hey," Trip said, his tone suddenly more serious. "Did you hear anything about Maddie? I was wondering about her. After . . . you know. I heard some of her friends took her home."

Hunter looked up sharply. "No," he said. "I took June and Rosie home. What happened to Maddie?" Again, something tugged at his memory.

"Don't tell me you didn't see the fight?" Trip said. "After Will . . ." He stopped abruptly.

"After Will what?" Hunter asked.

Trip stubbed out his cigarette. He seemed to be thinking it over. "I don't know," he said finally. For a moment, the normally so-cool-he-was-almost-catatonic Trip actually looked flustered. Then he grinned and shook his head. "Look, it was a crazy party. Who knows what all happened." He paused. "But don't, you know, mention to anyone that I was there," Trip added. "Just keep quiet about it, and it will all blow over."

Hunter watched as Trip hauled the crate back off the ground. He was showing the effects of last night, with bloodshot eyes and a clammy sheen of sweat on his brow. Hunter hoped that Trip was right, and that this would all just blow over, like the river sweeping away the beer cans after one of their usual parties in the woods. But Trip's confidence did nothing to soothe Hunter's anxiety. Trip may have gotten them into and out of plenty of sketchy situations over the last few years, but something about this one felt different. If only, Hunter thought, he could remember what it was that had left him with a sense of dread that only seemed to sharpen, even as his hangover began to lift.

3

On Monday morning, Jake Tillman glanced at his watch and decided he had just enough time to stop for a decent coffee on the way to the office. He knew it would be the only one of the day—the coffee at the district attorney's office was always cold, but still somehow managed to taste burned.

The day was already in full swing at the coffee shop in downtown New Falls. A group of men in their sixties, all fit if a bit paunchy in their matching spandex biking gear, clomped around in cycling shoes, taking their coffees outside for a postride chat. Inside there were half a dozen people in line, mostly moms in yoga pants with expensive strollers, sure to order complicated latte creations that would hold up the line. Nobody, aside from Jake, looked like they were on their way to work. How did people do it around here?

Coffee finally in hand, Jake swung his briefcase over his shoulder and walked the two blocks to the Hart County Courthouse, which housed the prosecutor's offices. In a town of brick rowhouses and window flower boxes, the courthouse, with soaring concrete arches and a wall of glass, struck an odd contrast. But what was fresh in the sixties was fading now, and Jake always felt that the fluorescent lights and linoleum floor made his position as an assistant district attorney in a small, wealthy town seem dreary rather than dashing. During his days at law school down at Temple University, he'd imagined himself in an office with parquet floors and brass fixtures. Maybe even a bar cart. The reality of public service had turned out to be a little different.

After passing through the metal detectors in the lobby, Jake took the elevator to the second floor. He slid his key into the door, but the handle moved freely beneath his hand. Someone had beaten him in.

"Is that you, Jake?" called a raspy voice. Donna, assistant to the head district attorney, Hal Buckley, was sitting at her desk outside of Hal's closed office door.

Jake looked at his watch. "Don't tell me Hal's here this early."

Donna glanced at the planner on her desk. "Hal has meetings off-site this morning. He won't be in until after lunch."

"Sounds like tennis and lunch at the club to me."

Donna smiled. "It's good to be the boss."

"It certainly is."

Donna glanced at the paper under Jake's arm. "You're not going to need that. The news came to you this morning. Jimmy's waiting for you in your office."

Jake perked up. "Something interesting?"

"I'll let him tell you. He's practically salivating."

Jake went down the hall to his office, where every surface was covered in three-ring binders and case files filled with the usual small-town problems: drunk driving, petty theft, domestics. Detective Jimmy Murray was sprawled on a chair in the middle of the mess. "Counselor," he said, nodding.

"Detective. To what do I owe the pleasure of your company? If you've got another DUI for me, you can add it to the pile." He flicked his thumb at the stacks of documents.

"Oh, I got a few of those, and some drunk and disorderlies for you too; the usual Monday morning assortment. But that's not why I'm here. You won't believe this shit." He tossed a slim folder onto Jake's desk, but he launched into the story before Jake could open the file.

"So, Friday night, I get a call about a bunch of kids down by the river making a ruckus. Typical end-of-the-school-year stuff—we break up parties down there every spring. I head down to River Road, throw on the sirens to smoke 'em out, and sure enough, a few kids start coming out of the woods, running for their cars."

"High school students. What a collar." Jake smirked.

"Hold on, hold on. So, we round up half a dozen kids—some of them were pretty wasted—and we start collecting ID's. A couple of them I already know; a few have Jersey licenses. One dumbass was actually still holding a beer, so he gets an underage-drinking ticket, and we start calling parents. But basically it goes down like usual: the parents show up, we give a little lecture, and everyone goes home. Typical Friday night."

"And?"

"And I go home and crawl into bed with my wife, take the kids to Soccer Tots in the morning, and I don't think about it again all weekend. Until six this morning. That's when we get a call from a contractor working on that new house going up by the river. You seen it? It's the all-glass one, looks like a spaceship. Anyway, the contractor goes over to open up the house for the painters, and finds the place completely trashed. He calls it in as vandalism, and Officer Cruz and I go down to check it out. Guess where it is? Less than a quarter mile from where we found those kids on Friday night."

Murray took out a digital camera, and Jake leaned in to look as he pulled up photos on the grainy screen. The first one showed a kitchen, or what was left of it. The doors were torn off the cabinets, the fixtures were gone, and the walls had been punched through and tagged with looping swirls of spray paint. The next picture showed a wooden deck with a charred hole in the center. Murray scrolled through pictures of broken windows, pools of water, and cigarette burns in the floor. The last picture showed a toilet, broken in half and lying on its side on the deck.

"It looks like they have plumbing issues," Jake said, taking the camera to look closer. "Among other things."

Murray winced. "We completely fucking missed it. By the time the contractor got there, the whole place was flooded from the faucets running all weekend. We counted a dozen broken glass doors, walls all punched in, and piss everywhere. I've seen squats down in the city that looked better. The chief is pleased as hell, of course."

Jake was still scrolling through the photos. "They really did a number on this place. And you're sure it was kids? Where are the owners?"

"They haven't moved in yet. The contractor is calling them. I'm sure I'll be hearing from them shortly."

"You really think kids did this?" Jake asked again. "It's pretty extreme."

"I'm not ruling anything out, but the whole place stunk like beer. They tore a mirror off the wall; looked like cocaine residue all over it. We'll send it to the lab. If adults around here are throwing this kind of party, we've got bigger problems than just this house. But it was most likely high school students. They must have gotten all jacked up and lost their fucking minds. Anyway, I'm on the hook for missing it on Friday night. Chief said I had to bring it down to you, make sure we do it all by the book, since we're dealing with teenagers here. Everyone I sent home on Friday night was eighteen or under. And these aren't punks. These are rich kids, or most of them are, anyway. When the parents realize that there are going to be charges, they'll lawyer up."

Jake glanced down at the picture of the wrecked kitchen. "What kind of kid would do this?"

Murray laughed. "I'm sure you got into your share of trouble when you were that age."

Jake shook his head, thinking of his own teenage years in a working-class part of Philly: Catholic school, a part-time job after class instead of sports, and always the vague suspicion that somewhere else people were probably having more fun than he was. "Not too much," he said. "Maybe a little drinking in parking lots and basements, that sort of thing. This seems different. But maybe I'm just getting old." He shook his head. "So, what's the plan?"

"First I'll check back in with officers who are still on-site, see what they turned up at the house. Then I'm gonna follow up with the kids we caught on Friday. Get the real story and see who else was there."

Jake opened the file folder Murray had given him and flipped through until he came to photocopies of the tickets that Murray had given out on Friday night, scanning the names to see if any of them were part of the regular rotation. "William O'Connor. We know him?"

"You're thinking of his brother, Sean O'Connor III, goes by the name Trip. He's been through here for possession and a few other things. He was on the road too, actually. But he's twenty-one, so I just sent him home."

"And William?"

"Never seen him before."

"Following in his brother's footsteps," Jake said. "Let's start there. Pull Trip O'Connor's record. We can probably put some pressure on him, if he's looking at distribution to minors. He won't want to take the fall for this if half the high school was there."

"With any luck, I'll have this all wrapped up by the end of the week, and the chief will forget I ever missed it."

4

Maja Jensen sat at her dining table, trying not to think about the pregnancy test in the bag on the counter. She sipped her tea—herbal, no caffeine—and paged through the *New York Times Magazine* without really seeing it. When she got to the last page, the crossword, she flipped back to the beginning and started again. She picked up her phone and refreshed her email, but nothing popped up to distract her. She thought about checking Facebook, but she wasn't in the mood for the baby picture landmines scattered among the status updates. It was 8 a.m. She still had an hour until she needed to be at Louis Faber, the gallery where she worked on the Lower East Side.

She closed her eyes and took a deep breath. There was no point in waiting. She was either pregnant or she wasn't.

In the beginning, before she started carefully tracking her cycle and marking the days that she and Ted were supposed to do it in red ink on the calendar, she bought her pregnancy tests in packs of four, which was cheaper and seemed to make sense. Like a scratch-off lottery ticket, she'd ripped the foil from each one, fully expecting it to be *the one*. But that was three years ago, when she was thirty-three, and still under the magic fertility number of thirty-five. Now she was thirty-six, almost thirty-seven, and she bought them one at a time, making the trip out to the Duane Reade only after Ted left for work. When the second, crucial line failed to appear on the stick, she would wrap it up in the bag from the drugstore and carry it down the hall of their building to the trash chute. She couldn't bear to leave it lurking in the trashcan, physical proof of her failure.

When they first started trying, it had been fun. Well, of course the trying had been fun, but so had the planning and the dreaming. It had given her and Ted something to talk about endlessly—a shared project. And as much as she hated to admit it, they'd needed something to bring them together.

Ten years ago, when they were first married, they hadn't had time to get bored. Ted was working like crazy, leaving each day for his new job at the investment firm Foxfield Barnes like he was heading into battle, and celebrating his wins in the market with round after round of drinks. And Maja was still painting, in addition to working as an assistant at the gallery. When she scanned the calendar on her Mac, it always seemed as if an endless stream of happy hours and gallery events filled every empty weekend. Back then, they were always grateful for the rare free day to spend together, just the two of them.

But after awhile, their state of constant motion had seemed to slow, as their friends had kids and moved to the suburbs, and opening nights at the gallery and office holiday parties had started to feel more like what they really were: work. Her friends complained about sleepless nights and stubborn baby weight, but Maja detected a hint of pride even in their complaints. And as she heard from them less and less often, she told herself that it wasn't personal. It was only natural that a couple would turn inward in those first tender years as a family. She imagined that it was like being young and in love: the outside world just ceased, for a time, to exist.

In the first year that they tried, everyone told her not to worry, that it takes time. That all she needed to do was relax. In the second year, the advice changed: it turned out that maybe she should be worried, and that she might want to see someone. Suddenly she was inundated with recommendations for fertility doctors, acupuncturists, and herbal supplements. Now, at the end of year three, she had tried multiple doctors and medications, and she avoided talking about it with friends as much as possible.

The next step was IVF, but Ted had drawn the line there. "If it's not happening," he said, "maybe it's not meant to be." It was one of the many platitudes about fertility that made her insane. He claimed that he was worried about the physical and emotional toll that it was taking on her, but she couldn't help thinking that, really, he had just lost interest. It was an unfair thought, she knew, but she could tell that he didn't feel the disappointment in the same crushing way that she did.

Now, instead of making a baby, they were building a house. Even without a baby, the one-bedroom apartment in Tribeca was feeling cramped. She and Ted had begun to bump into each other, knocking elbows as they brushed their teeth and stepping past each other awkwardly in the narrow galley kitchen. Although space was tight, they rarely fought. But when they did, she imagined that she could sense a current of resentment beneath the surface, like the rumble of the subway ten stories below their apartment. She blamed these arguments on stress, or work, or the tiny apartment, but she still felt unsettled afterward, even as they made up and promised each other that it meant nothing.

The last fight had been over whether Ted could take down one of Maja's paintings to hang a framed Yankees jersey—a gift from his father. Every inch of wall space in the apartment was filled, and it really wasn't an unreasonable request. But Maja had responded by wrapping all of her paintings in brown paper and putting them in their storage area in the basement of the building. They'd both apologized later, but the framed jersey still sat in the closet, the paintings remained in storage, and the walls of the apartment stayed empty. They needed to get out of the city. It was past time.

When they found a rarely available empty lot along the river in New Falls, an artsy little town just in commuting distance of New York City, it felt like a sign. It wasn't cheap—far from it—but it was everything they wanted, with plenty of privacy and space. They'd cashed in a big chunk of Ted's shares at Foxfield Barnes and paid cash. Five full acres, which seemed impossible to comprehend from their 750-square-foot rental. They always joked that if they lived anywhere besides New York City, they would feel rich, and now they did—or would, after the construction loan was paid off.

The architectural plans for the house, a sleek two-story contemporary with walls of glass to showcase the view from every room, were taped up on a window of the apartment, the perfect angles and proportions backlit by the morning sun. They'd splurged on a top-notch architect and high-end finishes, telling themselves that even though it was a stretch now, it would be worth it in the long run. The house felt like the one thing they had really gotten right, and in the excitement of meeting with architects and visiting kitchen show-rooms, it was easy not to think about the baby thing, or at least not to talk about it.

The baby thing. Maja glanced at the bag on the counter and decided she would rather know, either way. Besides, she would have to start walking over to the gallery soon, and she knew from experience it was a mistake to do the test at work, where she might burst into tears if anyone tried to talk to her. She picked up the test and took it into the bathroom.

When she finished, she slid the plastic cap back over the wet tip, a nice hygienic touch that only served to remind her that she wasn't a mother yet, no need to deal with anything messy or human. She put it on the sink and waited.

The liquid crawled across the plastic screen, darkening the absor-bent material as it went. It hit the first line, the control, which turned pink. All this told you was that you had managed to use the test properly; as in you didn't mess up peeing on a stick. Maja had gotten this part right every time. It was the next part, the second line that confirmed you had managed to create new life, that gave her trouble. She could barely look at it, but she forced herself to check.

There was nothing there. She didn't need to refer to the instruc-tions. She wasn't pregnant.

She looked into the bathroom mirror, letting it sink in. She'd de-cided that she would give it one more month before she broached the idea of IVF with Ted again, and somehow she had convinced herself that this would be the month that it finally happened. She'd visualized this moment: looking into the mirror, seeing a change in her face that meant that she was going to be a mother. Calling Ted and telling him to take the day off and come home.

Instead, she looked exactly the same as she had that morning: messy blond hair, cut in an asymmetrical bob, and big gray eyes filling with tears. A face so Slavic, with its tendency toward melancholy, that old-timers in Greenpoint, Brooklyn, where she grew up, would automatically speak to her in Polish, a language her parents had failed to pass on to her. The only difference she noticed today was that she looked older, or at least more tired, as she tried to blink back the tears so they wouldn't smear her mascara.

She tossed the pregnancy test into the trash bin and gripped the sides of the sink. She wanted to rip it from the wall. She wanted to scream. Why was this so hard? She had never come up against a challenge that she couldn't solve through hard work or creativity. But this was one problem she just couldn't fix. The frustration of it made her feel helpless, and a childish voice inside her insisted, *but I want it now!*

She pressed her palms against her closed eyelids and took a deep breath. She was an adult; she was in control. She could wait another month. *I trust my body*, she whispered, repeating one of the fertility mantras that an upbeat acupuncturist had given her. *It will happen when the time is right.* She tried to ignore the other voice in her head that wanted to make the counterargument: *You're not getting any younger. It's never going to happen.*

She swallowed, and the tightness in her throat told her that she'd successfully fought back her tears. A small victory. She would call Ted right away and tell him. It would save her from having to dread the conversation all day at work. She walked out to the kitchen to look for her phone.

It was already ringing, and with her mind on calling Ted, she picked it up without looking at the screen and said, "Ted? No luck this month, I'm afraid. I guess you'll just have to keep ravishing me." She tried to keep her voice light, but the joke sounded strained.

There was a long pause and then: "Maja?" It was a familiar voice, but not Ted's. "This is John."

"Oh!" The contractor. "John. I'm sorry. I thought it was Ted."

She definitely didn't want her contractor ravishing her, although it sometimes felt like she spent more time talking to John than to her husband.

"Look, Maja, has anyone called you or Ted? About the house?"

"Um, no, I don't think so. What's up?"

"There's a problem. There's been some damage."

Up until this moment, Maja had only been half listening to John. But now he had her full attention.

"Damage? But I thought we were almost finished. There shouldn't have been anything that major to do. There wasn't a flood, was there?" The house, situated on the river, was in a hundred-year flood plain. But everyone had assured them that there hadn't been a flood that high recently, and that the insurance would cover it if there were. "It didn't even rain this weekend, did it?"

"No, not a flood. At least . . . Look, Maja, I hate to be the person to tell you this, but it looks like some people—probably local kids—got into the house and threw a party."

"A party? That's . . . wow. How did they get in? Can we hire a cleaning crew?" She'd handled the aftermath of some pretty rowdy parties at the gallery, but usually an industrial cleaning crew could deal with any red wine stains or cigarette burns. The thought of people doing that to her house—her *dream house*—was hard to imagine. But at least it wasn't a flood. They'd clean it up and move on.

"I'm afraid it's a bit more involved than that," John said. "The police weren't too keen on me poking around this morning, but from what I saw there was damage to the walls and the floors, maybe from overflowed plumbing. Major glass elements were broken. We lost most of the fixtures. You're going to have to come down."

What John was saying made no sense to her. "The police? I'm sorry—it was a party?"

"Look," John said. "I gave the police your number, so I'm sure they're going to call. They can probably give you more details. For the moment, I'm going to call my guys off for a few days, until you decide what you want to do."

"What I want to do?" Maja repeated, unable to process what she was hearing. "Okay, thanks John. I–I'll call you back." She hung up, stunned.

For months she'd been monitoring herself for any signs that might indicate early morning sickness. And now, ironically, she finally felt the bile rising in her throat. A wave of nausea caused cold sweat to break out all over her body, then sent her hurtling down the hall to the toilet.

5

There was a lot of activity in the high school parking lot for a Monday morning. Usually it was quiet, with kids yawning as they threw their backpacks over their shoulders and hurried in, trying to make it before the first bell. But this morning everyone had gotten there early. Will saw a group of girls, with Maddie at the center, as if the others had formed a wall around her. She was wearing jeans and a black sweatshirt, even though it was warm out. Her pale hair hung down over her face, and her eyes were puffy, as if she'd been crying. The image of her, passed out while that dude pawed at her, flashed across Will's mind, and he flushed with both anger and embarrassment. Rosie whispered something in Maddie's ear, and Maddie looked right at him, her expression unreadable. He quickly looked down and pretended to be busy examining his shoes, then headed inside.

He'd thought about nothing else all weekend. He could still hardly believe that he'd broken that window. It had shattered just like they did in the movies. But he hadn't had a choice. He couldn't have just left her in there. And what were they going to do—call the cops? He tried to imagine that call: Hi, there's a bunch of drunk teenagers in a house that doesn't belong to us, and we'd like some help with the situation, please.

From the moment he'd thrown the hammer through the window, nothing had felt real. It was as if they'd unleashed a monster: kids who'd been dancing moments before kicking holes through the drywall; a girl falling from the counter where she'd been dancing, taking the cabinet door with her; and the heady fumes of spray paint as the vast white walls were transformed into a psychedelic mural. And then he and Trip slipping out of the party and cutting through the dark woods toward his truck.

They were walking along River Road when the flashing lights slowed and pulled up behind them. Will's heart was beating so hard it felt like a drug, making him dizzy. He heard Trip whisper in his ear, his voice thick: "Stay calm. Don't say anything." It wasn't reassuring. At the last second, he tossed a beer can he was holding into the trees.

This is it, Will thought at that moment. I finally went too far. He loved to party and have a good time, sure. But he'd never overdone it the way a lot of kids did around here. He was always careful never to get hooked or get caught, and he never blew a school deadline. That had been the key—getting good grades, being an athlete and a leader. He'd learned that by watching Hunter's family and their wealthy friends. If you took care of business, no one seemed to mind if you had a little too much fun once in awhile. And until now he'd always managed to have it both ways: work hard, play hard. Not like his brother. Trip couldn't just smoke pot—he had to sell it too, and get caught in the process. And it was never just a few beers, like Trip had promised. It was always eight or ten, and then shots. He loved Trip, but even he thought that Trip took things too far.

Faced with the cops, Will's instinct was to tell them everything. If he could just explain to the officer what had happened, he'd thought, how things had gotten out of control, couldn't they find a way to make it right? He hadn't meant to hurt anyone.

Trip knew him well, and he read in Will's loosening shoulders and rising hands the instinct to explain, as the cop put down his radio and started toward them. Trip leaned over one more time and whispered, "I could do serious time for this. Please be cool." Will's mouth went dry. He stared at the cop, waiting.

In the end, the officer barely asked them any questions. He rounded up a couple more kids who crashed noisily through the woods behind them, and collected everyone's ID's. It was quiet, and every time the police radio crackled to life, Will startled. He was sweating and trying not to sweat, which just made it worse. Finally the cop wrote Will an underage-drinking ticket, told them to quit partying in the woods, and called their parents. Will kept waiting—for someone to mention the party, for the cops to notice the music that he could still hear, coming faintly from the house. But it seemed the cops didn't know. For them, it was just a routine stop.

Trip, still on alert, watched his brother. His jaw was tight, and his hand was on Will's arm. "Be cool," he whispered one more time. Then he looked up and shielded his eyes from the oncoming headlights. "Here comes Dad."

On the ride home the car was silent, the five-minute trip excruciating. At home, his father spat questions at a rapid clip, but Trip did most of the talking and eventually Mr. O'Connor sent them both to bed like little boys.

He woke Will up early Saturday morning to stack crates. Coach would be pissed that he was missing practice, but this wasn't the time for Will to argue with his dad. Working in the warm barn, Will sweat out his hangover quickly. The anxiety was harder to shake. He spooked at every sound from outside the barn, sure that it was the police arriving to arrest him.

He was also sensitive to the brewing storm that was his father. There was nothing quick and clean about Mr. O'Connor's anger. It always built slowly, as if he savored it and didn't want to rush it. While they waited, Mrs. O'Connor and the boys tiptoed around the house, tense and jumpy.

It was elbows on the table at dinner that night that set it off. Mr. O'Connor had served in the marines, and he couldn't stand sloppy manners. When he started yelling, it was all the usual complaints: Will was careless, he was entitled, he thought the world owed him something. Running around with the Finch boy had given him the mistaken impression that he was a rich kid too. Well, he wasn't.

Will kept his eyes on his plate and let his father's anger wash over him. Repeated exposure had taken some of the sting out. At this point, his father would usually retreat into what Will thought of as the brooding phase, and everyone would tread carefully, trying not to provoke him. But this time the storm seemed to clear the air rather than muddy it.

Mr. O'Connor leaned back in his chair with a sigh. "Look, Will, you're not a bad kid." His eyes were careful to avoid Trip, who had sat silently through the whole thing, waiting for his turn, which hadn't come. "I know you work hard. You're just blowing off a little steam. I get it. But there's a lot on the line here, and when you have a lot going for you, you have a lot to lose. You're going to college next year. Not just college. Princeton." He shook his head, as if he still couldn't believe it. "You worked hard for this. And you earned it, unlike a lot of kids around here." Thinking about Hunter, Will knew. His dad had a real chip on his shoulder about him.

His father was staring at Will's hands, and Will looked down and noticed the two split knuckles on his right hand. There'd been a fight, just before they left the party. He had a hazy memory of crashing through a screen door, his fist connecting with the other boy's jaw. His father didn't comment on it, though. He never minded the boys fighting.

"All I'm saying is," he went on, "you've got to be careful. You have a scholarship. Only one kid in the county gets that scholarship every year, and they chose you, Will. Without that money, there's no way we can cover the family contribution. Not with all of the expenses that have piled up for the farm this year. We just can't take on any more debt right now. There are a lot of kids around here that could take it or leave it. You're not one of them."

"I know, Dad. It was stupid," Will admitted. "I was just blowing off steam, like you said. It won't happen again." Will gave his father a weak smile as he thought to himself, *Dad would shit a brick if he had any idea what actually went down.*

After he'd broken the glass door, he hadn't known what to do. The boy assaulting Maddie had taken off into the house as soon as the glass shattered. Will kicked the remaining glass from the frame and stepped into the room. He tried to shake Maddie awake, but her eyes were closed and she was mumbling, not making sense. To his relief, a few girls followed him into the room and took over. He'd felt useless and embarrassed watching them coax her awake and pull down her shirt, and so he'd taken off to look for the kid, leaving Maddie to their care.

Will had waited all weekend for the cops to show up at his door. But somehow they hadn't. By the time he'd gotten up for school this morning, he'd started to half-believe that all he'd done was get caught drinking in the woods. No big deal, as Trip had said. And then there was Maddie in the school parking lot, and seeing her made the whole thing suddenly feel very real. Will took a deep breath.

"Yo, what's up man?" An arm hooked around his shoulders, and Will jumped. It was Brendan, a junior who ran on the JV track team. "I heard you got picked up on Friday night! Bad luck. Raging party, though."

"You were there?" Will frowned. "I didn't see you."

"Hell yeah. Hey, I heard you were the one who put a hammer through the window. That shit was awesome."

"Oh, yeah? I don't know. It was a crazy night. I don't really re-member," Will lied. He didn't know this kid very well. Why was he talking so loudly?

"Anyway," Brendan said, "cool party. How did you find that place?"

"I just heard about it," Will said. "Like everyone else." He felt a prickle of fear. Were people saying that *he* had planned the party? "Look," he said, "it's probably best not to talk about it."

Brendan looked confused. "You get in trouble? I heard that they haven't found the house yet."

"Yeah, no, that's right." But hearing Brendan say it out loud made Will realize that if they hadn't found it yet, they would. Everyone must be talking about it, and it's not like they'd cleaned up before they left. Like it would have even mattered. The anxiety that he'd felt all weekend sharpened and intensified. Once again Will wondered if he should come forward and admit what had happened. Wasn't it better to be honest instead of waiting to get caught? But it was impossible. Trip had warned him not to discuss what happened at the party with anyone, even Hunter. You never know, he'd said. And his father had scared him by reminding him that his scholarship, awarded by the Hart County Union Club, might be on the line if he got into legal trouble.

The bell rang. "I've gotta get to class," Will mumbled. He walked down the hall, searching the faces of the other students as he passed. Was it his imagination, or was everyone looking at him? Any one of them might have been there, and any one of them might tell.

Maddie pulled up the hood of her sweatshirt and slipped into school just before the bell rang. She was also wondering if everyone was staring at her, but in her case, it seemed to be true. Well, maybe not everyone, but she was getting some curious looks. Even worse were the kids who saw her and then quickly looked away. Like Will had in the parking lot.

She focused on breathing, and on getting to her locker. Breathe in, breathe out. One foot in front of the other. It's not a big deal, she told herself for the thousandth time since she'd woken up on Saturday morning. There'd been plenty of drunken hookups at parties over the last few years. How was this any different?

But it felt different. The problem was, she didn't know exactly what had happened. This was hard to admit, even to herself. She'd stayed in bed all weekend, telling her parents that she was sick, and tried to put the pieces together.

The last thing she could remember clearly was sitting with June and Rosie on the stone steps by the river. The other girls were playing with each other's hair, buzzed from the pills that Hunter gave them. Maddie's heart was racing, but otherwise she wasn't really feeling the ecstasy. And then, all at once, it hit her so hard that her eyes nearly rolled back into her head. "Oh my God," she breathed, and the world around her suddenly slid into focus. She felt everything: her hair against her neck, the air filling her lungs, and the stone steps beneath her, still radiating heat from the afternoon sun.

She made a humming sound, and the vibrations traveled through her whole body. June was laughing at her. "There you go," she said, and she leaned over to rub Maddie's shoulders. At first it felt amazing, like she was melting into June's hands. But soon it started to feel too amazing, her nerves on overload. Her stomach felt funny, and she shifted away from June and got unsteadily to her feet. "I'll be right back," she mumbled, and made her way across the lawn and back to the house.

Now that it was dark, the house looked sinister, glowing like a jack-o'-lantern from the light of the contractor's lamps. The music was way too loud. She stood on the deck for a minute, trying to decide what to do. She held onto a railing, breathing hard and feeling as if the boards under her feet were heaving like the deck of a boat. She went inside to look for some water.

After that, her memories became disjointed and blurry: trying the locked handle of the bathroom door; looking in the kitchen for a clean cup. An arm around the small of her back—not Will's, but someone else's—holding her up on jelly knees as she leaned against the kitchen counter, and a coaxing voice in her ear, hard to hear over the roar of the party. The scent of cologne, mixed with cigarette smoke and the yeasty smell of beer, turned her stomach.

And then, one last memory, which made no sense in the context of her other memories: She lay on her back, with the full weight of a boy on top of her. It was dark and quiet, and he was kissing her, and then at some point, she was pushing his hands away as he pulled down her shorts. She remembered saying, or at least thinking, *Don't*. What had she been doing upstairs?

The next thing she remembered was being in the back seat of a car, her head on another girl's shoulder. The car stopped and the girl jostled her. "We're here," she said, and Maddie recognized her from her sculpture class.

"Where?" Maddie asked. Where were Rosie and June?

"Your house," the girl replied, getting out the car and holding the door open for Maddie. "Come on." She put her arm around Maddie and helped her to the back door, handing Maddie her purse and then helping dig her keys out. "Are you okay?" she asked, and Maddie just nodded. All she wanted to do was get upstairs and into bed.

The other girl paused for a moment, looking torn. "Do you want me to wake your mom up?" she asked.

"No, I'm okay," Maddie said, and the girl looked relieved.

"Thanks for the ride," Maddie remembered to say. And then she staggered upstairs and fell into a long, deep sleep.

When she finally checked her phone the next day, there were a dozen texts from Rosie and June asking her if she was okay, if she knew that boy, and if she wanted to talk. And that's when she knew that whatever had happened, it wasn't good.

How could she not know? She couldn't even remember what his face looked like. Had she wanted to make out with him? And how far, exactly, had it gone?

She got into the shower and stayed there for a long time, scrubbing her body with hot water and soap. When she looked down, she saw a fresh bruise on her left hipbone.

Stop it, she told herself as she spun the dial on her locker. *Stop thinking about it.* It had been such a relief this morning in the school parking lot when all everyone was talking about was the destruction at the party. After checking in with her, neither June nor Rosie mentioned what happened again, and Maddie was grateful. The big news was that Will's brother, Trip, had thrown a toilet out of the window, and that the police had ticketed some kids on the road but had somehow never shown up at the house.

Maddie managed to steady her hands enough to get her combination right. She swung the locker open and checked her reflection in the mirror inside. She looked tired, but not as bad as she felt. She just needed to get through the next couple days, and by the end of the week this would all be behind her. Some new gossip would come along to occupy everyone's attention and she could forget all about what had happened.

She closed her locker and was suddenly face-to-face with Olivia, a sophomore whose locker was next to hers. Olivia's eyes went wide.

"Oh!" Olivia exclaimed, looking flustered. And then: "I'm sorry, I just didn't think you'd be here today." Her face turned pink. "I mean," she backtracked, "of course you should be here if you want to be. Are you okay?"

That question again. For a long moment Maddie just stared at Olivia. She'd been kidding herself. Something bad had happened to her, and everybody knew. She took a deep, ragged breath, and walked away without answering. She was definitely not okay.

6

Maja arrived late at Louis Faber Fine Arts, the gallery where she'd been working since she graduated from art school. She'd started as an assistant, putting in just enough hours to cover her rent on an inexpensive apartment share in Bed-Stuy and still have time to paint. Now she managed the other assistants, hiring on recent graduates that reminded her of herself at that age: young women in carefully curated outfits meant to look thrown together, trying to mask their enthusiasm with a thin veneer of sophistication. Her boss, Louis, only liked pretty girls working in the gallery. He thought it helped close deals with his investment banker clientele.

The latest assistant, Yasmine, was already there, sitting at Maja's desk. "Sorry!" she called out, hopping out of Maja's seat. "I thought I'd get started on printing out the labels for the new exhibit."

"That's fine," Maja said, setting her bag down. "I'm sorry I'm late. There was an emergency at my house down in New Falls."

"No problem," Yasmine replied. "Louis called. I told him that you were on the phone with a client." She winked. "He said to tell you that he's staying down in Miami until tomorrow." Louis Faber also had galleries in Miami and London, and he occasionally left the New York location to Maja's care.

"Thanks," Maja said. "Actually, is there any chance that you can stay late this afternoon? I have to get the bus down there to see what's going on."

"I can stay till four," Yasmine replied. "But that's it. It'll take an hour to get home around that time, and I have to get ready for my big night." She smiled, looking both proud and embarrassed.

"Of course, your show. I forgot. Just lock up whenever you need to get going." Yasmine was showing her work that night at a café in Bushwick, and Maja had promised to make an appearance. Maja could remember staging her own first informal shows at friends' apartments, back when she was still painting, wondering if anyone would show up, pouring cheap Merlot for those who did, and drinking too much of it herself in her nervousness. Trying to calculate if the sales she might make would even cover the cost of the canvases and the wine.

"I'm sorry that I'll miss it," she said, "but don't worry, I know it will be great!"

Maja checked their voice mails, returned a few calls, and then left the gallery to Yasmine's care. As she hailed a taxi up to Port Authority, she made a mental note to talk to Ted about buying one of Yasmine's paintings as a show of support.

The bus to New Falls was halfway across New Jersey before Maja began to breathe deeply again. The Port Authority bus station, with its nauseating scent of ammonia and exhaust, was mercifully behind her. They'd left the highway and were now twisting along a country road bordered by crop fields, soybeans, maybe, she wasn't sure. She would have to learn. She could plant a vegetable garden behind the house, she thought. People did that in the country. She imagined herself in jeans and a straw hat, pulling things from vines and carrying them back to her kitchen, eating only what was seasonal. Then she laughed. This wasn't *Eat Pray Love*, and moving to Pennsylvania was more about searching for extra square footage than searching for new meaning in her life. Although she wouldn't object to a little inner peace to go with all that space.

Moving to New Falls had been her idea. Ted laughed at her when she first brought it up. She couldn't even drive! There'd been no need to learn, growing up in the city. College was only six subway stops away in Clinton Hill, and after she met Ted, he'd always driven on their weekend trips to the beach rentals they shared with friends. I'll learn to drive, she'd said, and Ted had pulled a look of mock horror and asked her if that was a promise or a threat.

Ted had grown up in the New Jersey suburbs and dreamed of New York City. He'd never considered living anywhere else. He watched his father do the long commute into the city for twenty years, and swore he'd never do the same. If he was going to work in the city, he was going to live there. Of course, he'd also sworn that he would never go into something as dull as banking. But after a hungry stint writing music reviews, that's exactly what he'd done, turning his father's connections into a well-paid investment banking job. It wasn't until recently, however, that he'd started making the serious money, paid out as bonuses. And now, at forty, it had been surprisingly easy for Maja to convince him to move back to the suburbs.

Before they'd even really decided to make the move full-time, the momentum of the house project took over, and they went with it, happy to be going with the current rather than fighting against it. It felt like one day they were looking through design magazines and interviewing architects, and the next thing they knew, they were spending weekends visiting stone warehouses and showrooms. Maja joked that she was using her art degree from Pratt more in working with the architect than she had in ten years of working at the gallery, where she spent most of her time putting together schedules and following up with buyers. And to her surprise, the frequent meetings and showroom visits weren't a chore. Instead, it was a little like dating again, and the thrill of the money they were spending on faucets and furniture was just as intoxicating as any cocktail on a Manhattan rooftop.

Maja glanced down at her phone, but there was nothing more, either from the police or from her contractor. When they'd called, the police had been vague—vandalism, trespassing, could she come into the station? After she'd spoken with her contractor, she'd called Ted to give him the news. Maja hated bothering him at work with house problems, but this couldn't wait.

When Ted picked up, his voice was thin and clipped. The markets were down, and rumors were already circulating about small bonuses, or no bonuses. Their conversation had gone much like the one she'd had with the contractor, with Ted taking her role this time. "The police? A party? How bad can it be? *Kids* did that?"

"We won't know anything else until we get down there," Maja pointed out. "I think we should go right away, to see what we're looking at. Maybe it's not that bad. I have Yasmine covering for me at the gallery."

There was a long pause on Ted's side. "Maja, I hate to ask you this, but can you start down without me? I need a few hours to wrap things up here. I'll rent a car and meet you there as soon as I can. Unless you'd rather wait and go together?"

Now the pause was Maja's. "Okay. Fine. Of course." Ted had been so consumed by work lately that it felt like she was often left to handle everything else. But she was anxious to see what they were dealing with, and she didn't want to wait. "I'll take the bus down."

"Thanks. I'll call you when I'm on my way. And I'll get us a room at that inn that we stayed at last time."

It was only after she hung up that she realized she hadn't told him about the negative pregnancy test.

They were getting close to New Falls, the bus rolling down into the river valley. As they crested the last hill, Maja could see the white steeple of a church rising above the green. They squeezed onto a narrow bridge and slowly crossed the river, and then they were there.

She spotted John, her contractor, leaning against his pickup truck in the gas station parking lot. He was about fifty, with thick gray hair, tan skin, and overalls. He nodded at her, not quite meeting her eye, and opened the passenger door. He didn't say much on the ten-minute drive over to the house, but then again he'd never been much for small talk.

They pulled down the long gravel drive that led to the house, and Maja got out and looked around. It took her about two minutes to realize that it was a disaster. Until this moment, she'd held out hope that the damage was mostly surface level. But this wasn't a matter of a cleaning crew and new paint. One whole wall of the living room had been formed from custom-made folding panels of glass, ten feet high. She'd imagined that in the summer they would slide them open, effortlessly creating the flow between indoor and outdoor living that all the design magazines raved about. Now the glass was gone, laying in glinting mounds.

The floor planks, carefully chosen for their width and grain, were already starting to warp from the water that had poured from open faucets all weekend. John had closed all the taps, but the flooding on the second floor was still seeping down through the light fixtures.

John walked her through the house, pointing out the damage as they went. The wall near the stairs was bubbled and damp. All of the drywall would have to be ripped out and replaced, he told her, after the studs were examined for water damage. Upstairs, the master bathroom had been literally torn apart. The toilet was missing, as was the mirror. Dirty footprints crossed the floor, and the sink was clogged with cigarette butts.

"Where is the toilet?" she asked, and John pointed, unexpectedly, out the window.

Maja followed John back down to the kitchen, at a loss for words. The appliances—splurges she had convinced Ted to buy—were filthy, the knobs and handles missing. A cranberry juice bottle lay on its side on the marble counter, a pink stain forming where its contents had spilled onto the white stone and had been absorbed. Hinges where the cabinet doors used to be hung at odd angles, ripped from the wood. She wrinkled her nose. Was that pee in the dishwasher?

Maja looked around, at the wreck of all of her effort, and felt sick. Her head was pounding, and if the kitchen counter she was leaning against hadn't been covered in something sticky, she would have laid her forehead against it. It was much, much worse than she thought it would be. Not just the damage, but the unexpected feeling of violation.

She had tried to create a place for her and Ted that would be so perfect that it would justify all of the work that she'd put into it. Not only into the house, if she was being honest with herself, but also into their lives together.

On the surface, each decision was aesthetic—questions of color, or texture, or scale. But it had never just been a house to her. The success of the house was going to be proof. Proof that, even without a child, her marriage was a real, solid thing. Proof that she had made the right choices; that even if she sometimes played second fiddle to Ted's career, she'd still built something beautiful out of her life.

If they could just wake up, she'd thought, and look out over the water, they could never be unhappy. Away from New York, with its constant distractions, she and Ted would have time to really be together. Over the last few years, between the pressure of Ted's job and their pregnancy struggles, they'd each retreated into their own private worlds. She'd believed that if she could design a house clever enough to withstand the hundred-year floods, it could protect her and Ted, and their life together.

And here it was, revealed to be nothing but a damaged shell, another thing that she would have to hold together through force of will. She looked over at John, and she could tell that he saw the damaged house only as a new set of logistical problems. She tried to listen to him, but she only caught snatches of what he was saying: ". . . water damage . . . pull out the floorboards . . . check the joists in the upstairs bathroom . . ."

He was asking her something about insurance. She didn't know the answer and shook her head, trying not to cry. Men could not handle crying. Finally she got the question out: "How much?"

John put his hands in the pockets of his overalls and looked around. "A few hundred?"

"A few hundred thousand? Are you kidding? I think we're already . . ." She was about to say that they were maxed out on the amount they could borrow, but she caught herself. She didn't want to spook him.

"It's just a guess. Like I said, I'll have to see what's going on underneath the surface. But most of the fixtures will have to be replaced. We'll be redoing a lot of the work that we did over the last few months."

"Okay." She took a deep breath. "Okay. But insurance should cover it, right?"

"Yeah, sure. Vandalism is usually covered by the builder's risk insurance."

Was it her imagination, or did he sound a little glib as he said this? No, of course the insurance would cover it. These things happened. Or did they? Well, they were certainly happening to her. Maja's mind went around in circles. She had to get out of the house. "Excuse me," she muttered to John, and walked out through what used to be a custom-made sliding glass door and onto the deck.

The view was still gorgeous. She squinted and the trash dotting the lawn disappeared. It was sunny, and the river, full of spring runoff, reflected the light, its surface a shifting mirror of trees and sky. She wasn't wrong—it was hard to be unhappy surrounded by this beauty. She took a deep breath. Putting the house back together was going to be difficult, but she could do it. She had to do it.

The sound of car wheels brought her back to the present. A police car was rolling up the drive. It pulled to a stop in front of her, and two men got out, one in standard blues and the other in a button-down shirt and tie. The uniformed officer had a thick mustache and mirrored shades and looked like a character from a seventies cop show or like he was about to rip his shirt off and start stripping. Surprise! This is all just a hoax, like an elaborate bachelorette party.

The patrol officer looked her up and down, and Maja felt very aware of her high-heeled boots and short dress. She had dressed for work at the gallery, her all-black ensemble as much a uniform for her downtown job as his badge and blue suit. But now she felt self-conscious, and she tugged her skirt down as if he was a high school principal who was about to call her mother to pick her up. As she did, the stiletto heel of her boot slipped between the boards of the deck and stuck there. Keeping a smile pasted on her face, she tried to wiggle it free without anyone noticing.

The man in the tie glanced at the notebook in his hand and then back at her. "Maja Jensen?" he asked. He pronounced her name like *Ma-jah*.

"It's actually pronounced *My-ah*. It's Polish." She'd corrected hundreds of people over the years, and she always tried to put people at ease about getting it wrong. She liked having a unique name. She used to explain to people that Maja meant "good mother," and add a little joke that her mother was clearly pleased with herself when Maja was born. But lately she'd been skipping that part.

"Mrs. Jensen," the officer said, sticking to her easier last name as he climbed onto the deck, his hand outstretched. As she leaned forward to shake it, her boot popped loose, and she stumbled forward into his arms.

"Steady there!" he said as he helped her catch her balance. He glanced at her shoes with a raised eyebrow, but didn't say anything.

"I'm sorry," she muttered, embarrassed.

"Don't be. Damsels in distress come with the territory. I'm Detective James Murray, New Falls PD." He was lanky and slightly slouching in his suit, with sunglasses and curly brown hair. His face was serious, but it looked like he might break into a smile at any moment. "This is your home?" he asked.

"It is. I mean, it will be. We're building it. I'm from New York." She cringed. Why had she said that? People here probably hated when New Yorkers came down and invaded their town. Police officers always made her nervous.

But the detective just smiled. "I'm sorry about the house," he said. "I guess this isn't quite the housewarming party you imagined."

Maja laughed. "No, it's not." She looked down at the red Solo cups that littered the deck. "I was thinking we'd use actual glassware. I just don't understand how something like this could happen."

"Looks like a party that got very out of hand. Could have been local kids, but it's too early to say for sure."

Maja nudged the butt of a half-smoked cigarette with her toe, and saw that it had left a welt in the wood as it smoldered to ash. "I've never seen a party like this. Maybe in the movies. You think kids did this?"

"Well, again, we don't have anything solid yet," Murray said. "But as a matter of fact, we picked up a few kids not far from here on

Friday night, up on River Road. We get a lot of the local high school students drinking beer down by the river, or in the woods, especially this time of year. It's like spring hits and they start their mating dance. Except instead of bird calls and feather displays, it's all about texting and who can get cheap beer." He glanced at her, checking to see if he was being too casual, and then continued: "This was one of the prime spots. Before your house was here, of course."

"You were here on Friday night?" Maja asked, confused. "John told me he found the damage this morning. Why wasn't I called on Friday?"

Detective Murray exchanged a glance with the other officer, and when he spoke again his tone was much more formal. "Yes, ma'am, that's right. No one was aware of the damage until this morning. On Friday night, we had no indication that there were additional youths in the area, and we had no reason to suspect there was anything going on at your house."

He sounded defensive, Maja thought. They were getting off on the wrong foot, and that was the last thing she needed. She sighed. "So, where do we go from here?"

"First one of my officers is going to need to speak with your contractor and get his statement. The guy who called it in?"

"That's John. He's in the house," Maja said. "I'm sure he'll be happy to help you." The officer nodded and went inside.

"And I'd like to ask you a few questions."

"Go ahead. I'm not sure how much I can help, though. I just got here."

Detective Murray flipped open his book and took out a little gold pen. Maja found it comforting that he was taking actual notes.

"How would you describe your relationship with your contractor?" he asked. "Any problems come up during the construction?"

"No, nothing. Everything's gone really well. I mean, there's always a few things that don't go as planned in this sort of process, and everything costs twice as much as you think it will, but John's been really on top of everything."

"Oh? What hasn't gone as planned?"

"Just, you know, it took awhile to get the building permits and then we had some scheduling issues. And somehow the wrong tile was ordered for the kitchen. But we got everything cleared up and worked out. There's no way he had anything to do with this."

"Okay. Now, I have to ask, is there anyone around here that might have a grudge against you or your husband, or who you would consider an enemy?"

"An enemy?" Maja asked in surprise. "No, we don't have any enemies here. We only know a few people here, actually." She paused. "It feels like someone here must hate us, though."

The detective nodded sympathetically. "Like I said, I had to ask. But this doesn't look like anything personal. Just kids getting out of control. This is a really nice town. Good people."

She didn't love the way he said that. It sounded dismissive, like he was excusing what happened. "My house—my *home*—has been destroyed," she said. "I don't give a shit if it was just kids. And I can't imagine they're good people."

The detective's face didn't alter, but a slight shift in his shoulders told her that his appraisal of her had changed. One sharp word and she'd gone from pretty victim to bossy bitch. Working at the gallery had made Maja an expert at reading people, especially men. She imagined the officers back in their squad car, cracking jokes about her. But she was on a roll, and she didn't care that her voice sounded haughty and shrill, even to her. "This is a crime. Can I expect that it will be treated as one?" Tears sprang to her eyes, and she quickly wiped them away, embarrassed at how emotional she was.

"Yes, ma'am. Of course." Detective Murray's perception had shifted again. She was no longer a bitch, just a hysterical woman. He knew what to do with that. He gave her a sympathetic smile. "I'm sure it's been a long day. Are you going back to New York tonight?"

She took a deep breath. "No. I'll be staying at the River Inn until we get everything sorted out here." She looked around. "My husband is supposed to be meeting me, but he isn't here yet."

"I can give you a ride. Oh, and here's my card. Call the precinct and they'll get a copy of the report to you. You'll need that for your insurance."

"Right, the insurance." She reached for the cigarettes in her purse that hadn't been there for five years, and then grabbed her phone instead. She glanced at the screen. Nothing from Ted yet.

John had finished with the police officer, and he was standing a few feet away, waiting for her attention. "So," he said, addressing both of them. "Can I get my guys in here to clean up?"

Maja and Detective Murray spoke at the same time.

"Yes, please do."

"No, not yet."

"Oh," she said, looking at Murray. "We have to leave it like this?"

"Just for another day or two. I want to make sure that we log any evidence before it gets cleaned up. But everything will be back to normal before you know it."

Maja reflexively looked at John for confirmation, but instead of meeting her eye, he shoved his hands in his pockets and pretended to be busy testing the broken boards of the deck with his foot. As he put his weight on one near the hole where the toilet had crashed through the deck, the board gave way beneath him with a pop, and he jumped back, narrowly avoiding falling through. At least she wasn't the only one who felt like they weren't on solid footing.

She thought about how the detective had said this was a prime spot for kids to drink before she'd built her house here, as if she'd somehow displaced them. She wondered if the detective had been one of those kids back in the day. Could she really trust him to look out for her best interests?

7

Detective Murray dropped Maja Jensen off at the River Inn, and then wheeled his car around and headed out of town toward the O'Connor place. There was no point in waiting; it would only give the kids time to get their story straight. He knew that Trip O'Connor had something to do with this, and he was sure that he could use the threat of Trip's previous record to get a few more names out of him.

Not for the first time that morning, Murray felt his stomach clench. He'd really blown it on Friday night. There was no other way to spin it. It was lazy police work, and he knew it, and the chief knew it. And soon the Jensens would figure it out too, when the shock over their house wore off and they started putting together the timeline.

If he'd bothered to call in an extra unit, tramp down into the woods, and check the waterfront, he could have rounded up a bunch of the partygoers then and there. He'd be in Tillman's office right now, working on the charges instead of being bawled out by the chief and playing catch-up and cover your ass all day.

The truth was that when it came to teenagers, there were a few unspoken rules in the New Falls Police Department, and that was where Murray had gotten tripped up. It wasn't that they got a free pass—those days were over. Parents expected, and seemed to accept, a certain amount of crackdown: tickets for speeding and underage drinking, and semi-annual roundups at parties in the woods. Parents were called and lectures were given, and once in awhile there was an actual bust for smoking pot, the records sealed and expunged when the kids turned eighteen.

But there was a line. This was a wealthy town, and a lot of the kids had bright futures ahead of them: scholarships, fancy colleges, and family businesses to run. A real record could derail all that, and no one wanted that, right? It was no secret that Chief Whitman was well connected. His family had been in Hart County since the beginning, and you saw their name everywhere: Whitman Quarry, Whitman Road, the Whitman Christmas Tree Farm. The chief played golf every Thursday with a mix of the old and new money in town, in the name of keeping up community relations, and the rank and file took their cues from him. Keep the peace, give lots of warnings, and bring the parents in early. It wasn't exactly a case of the customer is always right, but it was close. People paid plenty of taxes around here, and they expected good service.

But a house had nearly been destroyed. This wasn't an out-of-hand pool party, and it wasn't going to look good for the New Falls Police Department that they'd missed it. That *he'd* missed it. Now this was his problem, and he intended to deal with it.

When Murray parked in the lot at the O'Connor Family Orchard he spotted Trip right away, changing the oil on a tractor in front of the barn. This was not their first meeting. Murray had pulled him over two years earlier for erratic driving, and it hadn't been a surprise when the car stunk like a skunk. In the back he found an ounce of marijuana and the kicker, a small electronic kitchen scale. The amount of marijuana wasn't enough to rate, but the scale immediately made it intent to distribute. The O'Connors didn't hold any special place with the chief—they were what he called local yokels—so the charges stuck. The sentence had been suspended, however, since Trip didn't have any priors.

"Mr. O'Connor," Murray called, walking over to Trip.

Trip looked up from his work and frowned when he saw the detective. He wiped his hands on a greasy towel and stuck it in his back pocket. "Sorry, Officer. The farm stand is closed." He paused before adding, with a hint of a grin: "But my mom probably has some of her famous cider doughnuts in the kitchen."

Murray let it pass. He pulled his notebook out of his pocket and looked it over. "One DUI. One charge for possession. And that's just for Hart County. Anything else I should know about?"

Trip shook his head. "Did you come over just to reminisce about old times?"

"Is your brother here?" Murray looked back down at his notes. "William?"

Trip's face was guarded. "He's at school."

"When will he be home?"

"Later," Trip replied. "He's got track practice."

"Good party on Friday night?" Murray asked, but Trip didn't answer. "You guys did a number on that house," Murray continued, watching Trip for any sign that he knew what Murray was talking about. There was a flicker, just a slight tightening of Trip's jaw. He stared straight at Murray as he said, "I don't know what you're talking about." Then he blinked three times, and Murray knew he was lying. Now he just had to catch him in it.

Murray proceeded as if Trip hadn't said anything. "My guess is that you bought the booze. Is that why they still let you hang around?"

"You can keep talking," Trip replied, "but I don't know anything about it. You didn't have shit to say to me on Friday night."

"C'mon, Trip. I don't want to play games. I was there. You were there. I've got you." Murray leaned over the tractor, as if to have a look at the engine, then tried it out: "And your brother too, by the way." With a sideways glance Murray saw Trip stiffen, and he pushed on. "No record on your brother, though. He might pull through this without doing time, but I don't know. That's up to the prosecutor." He stood up and consulted his notebook again. "But not you, Trip. You fucked up. You're looking at corruption of minors, vandalism, breaking and entering. And then there's that pesky suspended sentence."

Trip didn't answer. He was working on the tractor again. Murray let him think it over for a minute. It was too easy, really, turning these kids. Murray tried not to think too much about whether he was wasting his time and talent with this small-town shit. He had a job to do here, and now it was more—he had to make things right with the chief.

It was Police Academy 101: keep quiet and the witness will eventually fill the void. Most people couldn't bear a long silence. Murray folded his arms and peered out through his shades at the orchard. Long rows of stunted apple trees, stretching as far as the eye could see. He counted under his breath: one, two, three . . . bingo! Trip was turning around. He was ready to talk.

"Look," Trip said, spreading his hands in a gesture of concession. "I don't know anything about a party in a house. What I do know is that there were a couple of kids drinking beer in the woods on Friday. Down by the river, same as when I was that age. And, yeah, Will was down there. But you already gave him a ticket, and he's in the doghouse here. He was humping crates all weekend for my dad. I only know because I picked him up along the road later that night. I told him he could call me anytime for a ride—I didn't want him getting into the same sort of trouble I did. He's a good kid. And that's when you showed up." Trip grinned. "That's the whole story. I was watching out for my little brother. Nothing else to it."

Murray nodded. "So you're saying that you weren't at the party. That you were just there to pick up your brother."

"Yup." Trip nodded. "From the woods. I don't know anything about a house."

"If that's your story . . ." Murray flipped his notebook shut. He could smell horseshit, and it wasn't coming from the orchard.

He was about to say as much to Trip when the screen door banged open and a woman Murray recognized as Mrs. O'Connor walked outside and joined them. Her brown hair was tied up in a bun, and she was wearing jeans, work boots, and a sleeveless top that showed the strength of her shoulders. He could see that she'd been pretty, but now she looked tired, her face freckled and lined from the sun.

"Officer," she said, her voice wary. "Is there a problem?"

"No, ma'am," Murray replied. No point in putting her on her guard. "Just asking around about a house party on Friday night. Seems like a few kids got a little out of hand. You hear anything about that?"

Mrs. O'Connor glanced at Trip, but she was already shaking her head. "No, I'm sorry. I don't know anything about it."

Murray fished around for a card and handed it to Mrs. O'Connor. "Well, if you do hear anything, feel free to give me a call. My direct number is on there. We're just looking for the responsible parties. We'd hate to see any good kids take the fall on this."

Linda O'Connor watched as the officer got back into his car and drove down their road, a cloud of pale brown dust in his wake. Then she turned to her son, who had his head back under the hood of the tractor. She felt a familiar twinge of disbelief. How was this lanky man, his back brown from working in the sun, her little boy? And how had that curious, charming child become this man? The charm was still there, but the curiosity seemed to be gone. For her firstborn she had imagined travel, college, and adventure. She had imagined him breaking hearts, but not hers.

Somewhere along the way he had gotten stuck. There was no specific event that she could point to. No clear division between the curly-haired boy who played soccer and climbed trees out in the orchard until well past dark, and the young man who lied to her with a smile, who was content to pass the weekends piling up beer cans, and who barely left the town, let alone the country. It was just a series of small things—some trouble at school, putting off applying to college—that had finally culminated in his arrest, and the realization, for her at least, that he wasn't just taking a break, or finding his way. He wasn't going to college, and he wasn't going to explore the world. This was his life.

Not that running the orchard was a bad life, but Trip seemed to take no particular pleasure in it. Rather, working here had simply been the easiest of all of his options. The orchard was her baby, her passion. It was what she had dreamed of when she was first married and living in cramped base housing while her husband, Sean, was serving in the marines.

The property belonged to Sean's grandparents, but it hadn't been properly tended to in decades. They'd visited once, and Mrs. O'Connor had fallen in love with the overgrown orchard and the tumbledown red barn. Rabbits bounded through the tall grasses and apples grew on the spreading, unpruned trees. The fallen fruit lay on the ground, and the aroma of the rotting apples smelled sweet to her, with the promise of fertile soil and rebirth. When Sean had a chance to leave the marines, she convinced him to use the money they'd saved to buy out his cousins' interest in the property and start the farm. Having grown up around farmers, he knew that a farm could break you. The only question was whether it would get your heart or your back first. But he loved her, and so he bought out the property against his better judgment.

Mrs. O'Connor sighed. In more than twenty years of parenting, the one thing that she'd learned was that you had to deal with the child right in front of you, not the one you wished they would be. And her disappointment with Trip—or her inability to understand him, as she liked to think of it—was now tinged with fear. Fear that whatever had gotten hold of him and rooted him to this spot might still lay in wait for her other boy. Will had always been a little less charming and not quite as handsome as his older brother, but he'd nonetheless quietly and steadily proved himself the more likely to succeed.

"What happened on Friday night?" she asked Trip. "I thought you said you were just hanging out by the river."

"Mom. We've already been over this. There's nothing to worry about."

"Nothing to worry about? Trip, I've got a police officer in my driveway. I'm worried."

"Well, don't be. Who knows what happened after Will and I left the river? But it can't be that big of a deal if all the cops did was call you and Dad." Trip flashed his crooked smile at his mother, and put his arm around her. "We're lucky to have you, mother hen."

Mrs. O'Connor felt annoyed rather than relieved by Trip's nonchalance, and she pulled away. "Trip, whatever happened, I want you to keep Will out of it. He has a lot going for him right now, and he can't mess it up. If there's any kind of trouble at school or anything, it might affect his acceptance at Princeton."

"Princeton." Trip let the word hang in the air for a minute. "I know. I know how important this is to him, and to you. Don't worry."

Mrs. O'Connor couldn't quite let it go. "It's not just Princeton. If anything happens to that scholarship, there's no way we can make up the difference. We just took out a big loan for all the new equipment. We won't be able to cover any additional loans. You'll look out for Will?"

When the kids were little, she was always so careful to treat them equally. They were constantly watching, trying to judge who got the bigger slice of cake, or who sat in the front seat of the car more often. She knew that it wasn't reasonable that she was more worried about Will right now. Whatever happened on Friday night, it seemed to her that the boys had been in it together. But fair or not, the consequences would be much worse for Will. She wasn't sure what, exactly, she was asking of Trip. But her sons were long past the point where she could ensure that life would be fair to them, and right now she needed Trip's help, whatever that meant.

Trip turned back to the tractor that he'd been working on. "I won't let anything happen to him," he said, his voice muffled by the hood.

Mrs. O'Connor put her hand on his shoulder, giving it a squeeze. "I'm counting on you," she said. "I know you'll do the right thing."

8

Detective Murray left Trip O'Connor to think it over and drove back
down River Road to follow up with the officers who'd stayed at the
house to survey the scene. He glimpsed the river through the trees,
running quickly from recent rain. There was more in the forecast
for the weekend. He made a mental note to request that an officer be
posted near the bridge in town over the weekend. Tourists who came
out from the city to tube and drink beer on the river often got themselves into sticky situations when the water levels rose.

He pulled down the driveway and saw two officers waiting for him
by their squad car. "Find anything useful?" he asked as he climbed out.

One of the officers beckoned for him to follow. "It looks like they
might have entered through the garage," he said, leading Murray over
to the door. Inside the door was a stack of standard-issue wine and
liquor boxes, printed with the names of wineries and distilleries. The
officer lifted a flap on one of them and showed Murray the shipping
label: MASON LIQUORS, STOCKTON, NJ. "It looks like whoever brought
the alcohol pulled into the garage to unload. There are tire prints in
the gravel that back that up."

Murray glanced over at an area of gravel that had been marked off
with caution tape. "There must be a lot of cars in and out of here in
the course of a day."

"The contractor said he parks his pickup over there, on the grass,"
the officer said, pointing to a muddy area near the trees. "According to him, no one has parked in the garage. We took pictures of
the tracks. Wide wheelbase, deep markings—it was a truck, maybe a

pickup. It's hard to say for sure, but my guess is whoever was driving hadn't taken their snow tires off yet for the spring."

"The garage was open?" Murray asked.

"The contractor said that it was closed. They'd just installed the door. It should have been very secure. He looked through the house for the opener, but he couldn't find it."

Murray frowned. "So the vandals knew right where to go, and presumably they had the garage opener." He sighed. "Are we looking at this the wrong way?"

"You're thinking it could have been the contractor?" the officer asked.

Murray thought about the older guy in overalls that they'd met that morning and shook his head. "More likely his crew. You spoke with him. What do you think?"

The officer shrugged. "He said his guys packed it up around four p.m. on Friday, and not much else. I got the feeling that he didn't want to say any more with Mrs. Jensen around."

Murray glanced at his watch. "I'll try to swing by and follow up with him tomorrow. I've got one more stop to make before I call it quits for the day. I want to catch up with William O'Connor before he has a chance to talk with his brother."

Jake Tillman was already waiting outside the courthouse when Detective Murray pulled up in an unmarked car. "Don't want to alert the kids," Murray explained as Jake slid into the front seat. Talking to Will O'Connor at school wasn't Murray's first choice, but he wanted to get ahold of him before he got home.

While he drove, Murray filled Jake in on his meeting Maja Jensen and the bullshit story that Trip O'Connor had given him. "I guess it's possible that the brothers already worked out a story, but that wasn't the impression that I got. Seemed to me like Trip was making it up as he went along. My best guess is that they decided to keep quiet about it, but Trip got nervous when I pressed him on his suspended sentence. He mentioned that his brother had track practice after school. We might be able to find him there."

"We need to be careful here," Jake said. "If we end up getting any-thing useful out of these kids, it needs to be by the book."

"Hey," Murray grinned at him, "we're just asking questions. We're going to follow up with the contractor's crew as well, but my money's still on the high school kids. Let's just see who knows what. When we know who we're looking for, we'll bring them in to the station, call the parents in, and make it official. Honestly, it's usually pretty easy with these kids. They all think they're hard. Who knows where they got that idea. Too many gangster movies, maybe, and too much money. But they hold up under questioning for about three seconds. In my experience, they turn tail the minute they sense real trouble. They want to convince you that they really are good kids, and they'll tell you almost anything while they're at it."

They pulled into the lot in front of New Falls High School, a sprawling, colonial-style brick building surrounded by sports fields.

Jake started toward the front door, but Detective Murray gestured for him to follow as he headed around the back of the school.

"You don't want to stop in at the office?" Jake asked.

"Not yet," Murray replied. "Let's keep it casual. Once we show up at the office, we'll show our hand. Right now we're just gathering information."

"Just keep it real casual, then," Jake advised him. "Nothing to in-dicate an interrogation, or that he's not free to leave."

Murray smiled and loosened his tie. "You got it, boss."

A few questions led them out to the track, where Murray spotted the kid he'd ticketed on Friday night warming up for practice. He looked at them warily as they approached, but he agreed to speak with them. They walked him a bit away from the other kids.

"Mr. O'Connor," Murray began. "Can I call you Will?"

"Um, sure," Will mumbled, and then more clearly: "Yes. Officer."

"Detective," Murray corrected him. "We're just checking in with all the kids we rounded up on Friday night, making sure that they understand how to address those underage-drinking tickets. I hope your dad wasn't too hard on you? He didn't look happy."

Will was surprised by this line of questioning, and he laughed nervously. "Well, he wasn't very happy. So, I, uh, just show up at court and pay the fine, right?"

"That's it. Easy. Now, just so I get everything right in my report, can you tell me one more time how you came to be standing on River Road in the middle of the night?"

For a minute Will didn't say anything. He seemed to be thinking it through. Jake knew, and Murray knew, that there was no real report, not for something the detective had initially considered so minor. Jake guessed that Will was trying to remember what the officer might already know.

Will looked down and kicked at the edge of the turf with the toe of his track shoe. "I was hanging out with my brother. Down near the rope swing. We had a few beers." He blushed a little as he said this, glancing up at Jake and Murray.

"Just you and your brother?"

"Yeah."

"What about those other kids? The girls?" Murray asked casually.

"Oh. Yeah. There were some other kids there, but we weren't really hanging out with them. They came later." Will's voice was pained. He seemed like a kid who wasn't used to lying.

"They came later, huh?" Murray asked, sounding confused. "That's funny, you know, because I just had a chat with your brother, and he told me that he was only there to pick you up. That you needed a ride."

Murray's words caught Will completely by surprise. For a minute he didn't speak at all, and Murray and Jake let the silence linger. Finally, with a sheepish look, Will tried to explain: "I must be mixing up my nights. Yeah, I think that's right. I was there, in the woods with some friends, and then Trip showed up to meet me. To take me home."

Murray flipped open his book and wrote something down. He didn't press Will on the time line. Instead, he asked, "Can you tell me who else was there?"

Now Will looked truly miserable. "I don't really remember," he mumbled.

"And you were by the rope swing? Nowhere else? Not, for instance, in a house?"

Will glanced up at them, his eyes going wide. Then he looked away. "Look, Officer, I really need to go," he said. "Coach is waiting for me."

Murray turned and looked at the track. The coach was indeed staring at them.

"Okay," Murray said, flipping his book shut. "Thanks for your help. We'll get back to you if we need to."

Will gave them one more worried look and then trotted off to join practice.

"He's covering for his brother," Jake said. "Too bad they didn't get their stories straight."

"It's funny," Murray said. "He's nothing like the brother. Not what I expected at all."

"So, what's the next step?" Jake asked.

"Now we really scare them," Murray said. "Let's start calling parents."

9

The River Inn wasn't technically on the river—it was across the street, in an old stone building at the edge of the town. It smelled like the river, though: damp and earthy, like mud and leaves. On her last visit, Maja noticed a place along the front wall of the inn where they'd marked the water level of floods dating back over a hundred years, with the highest one as high as her waist, and the most recent one fifteen years ago. Better control of the reservoirs upriver in New York had cut down on the number of the once-common floods.

Her room upstairs was sunny, with wooden shutters, window boxes filled with geraniums, and a handmade quilt on the bed. Maja unpacked, mostly out of habit. She put her clothes for the next day in the oak dresser and lined up her toiletries on the edge of the sink. Even though she was just staying for the night, she hated the feeling of living out of a bag. Ted never seemed to mind. He always left everything in his suitcase, digging through it for clean clothes and tossing the dirty ones back in at the end of the day, silk ties jumbled with damp running gear. She gave him a hard time about it, but secretly she liked it. It was a little breach in his otherwise perfect business-man's armor.

She picked up her phone and tried him, but the call went right to voice mail. She checked the time—4:30 p.m. The markets were closed for the day and Ted was probably on the subway, heading to pick up the rental car. She wouldn't have the police report until tomorrow, and there was no point in contacting their insurance company until she had all the information. It looked like she had some time on her hands.

The River Inn didn't have television in the rooms—apparently it was a point of pride, as it was mentioned on their website. She thought of calling her mother, but it would be late in Kraków, where her parents were helping her grandmother for a few months while she recovered from surgery. And besides, she'd avoided going into too much detail with them about the house project. In comparison to the one-bedroom apartment in Greenpoint where she'd grown up, and where her parents still lived, the house seemed shockingly extravagant. Without knowing exactly why, she'd always minimized the luxuries that Ted's job afforded them when she spoke with her parents.

She scrolled through her phone until she found the number for Aneeta Dhillon, one of the few people that she knew in town. Aneeta and Maja had worked together at the gallery ten years ago, and they'd been friendly, going out for the occasional drink after work. But Aneeta left the gallery after just a year, and Maja had been surprised to receive an invitation to Aneeta's wedding twelve months later. Ordinarily she would have declined—what was the point of trying to keep up a friendship that had already fizzled?—but a quick scroll through Aneeta's wedding website changed her mind. It was being held in a pretty riverside town, and there was a whole weekend of activities planned: a wildflower hike, tubing on the river, and cocktails at a historic inn.

Maja and Ted booked a room in town and made a weekend of it. When they weren't hanging out with the wedding party, they explored, ducking in and out of galleries and antique shops and laughing at the store that sold only Christmas ornaments, even in July. It felt like a world away from New York City, even though the drive was less than two hours. When they learned that Aneeta's new husband, Adil, made the commute to the city to work as an attorney at J.P. Morgan, the seeds were planted.

Maja and Ted started coming down to New Falls for regular weekends. But within a year Aneeta was pregnant and consumed with renovating a big house in town, and the visits became less frequent, and, to be honest, a little less fun. They'd still kept in touch, especially when Maja started looking for land in town to build a house.

Aneeta picked up on the second ring. "Hello? Maja?"

"Aneeta! I'm so glad that I caught you. How are you?"

"Fine! How's the house? Almost done?"

"Actually, there's a problem with the house," Maja said, her voice quivering. "Aneeta, can I come over?"

"You're in town? Of course, come over!"

"Thank you. It's just me—Ted hasn't made it down from the city yet. I'm staying at the River Inn. I'll walk over."

"Of course you will," Aneeta laughed. "You're still a New Yorker."

Aneeta lived about a half mile from the hotel, where the closely set houses of the village began to give way to the open acres that surrounded it. Her house was a perfect copy of the one from every Hollywood movie about family: a white colonial with all the trimmings—columns, shutters, perfect boxwood hedges, and a front door painted red. It wasn't the type of house that Maja had ever wanted for herself, but it did represent a sort of American dream ideal that had always fascinated her.

It was, Maja had to admit to herself as she walked through town, partly this fascination with the suburban, the solid and predictable, that made Ted so attractive to her. In college, Maja had dated boys who were, to one extent or another, not unlike herself: film students, boys in bands, and the occasional Polish boy, just for variety. After college it was a writer (bartender), a jazz musician (music teacher), and her former social psychology professor, which in retrospect was so messed up on both of their parts that she couldn't think about it without cringing. And then she met Ted.

He had come into the gallery with some friends who worked in banking, and who were looking for large works to decorate their new lofts. While the other guys looked at paintings, Ted, with his thick auburn hair and impish grin, looked at her.

For the first few years of their marriage, they were always adding new friends, always choosing between weekend invites, and always spending much more than they saved. It was a fun way to live in the city. Once Ted started his job at the investment bank, Maja no longer had to keep a running tab of the cost of each cocktail that she ordered, plus tax and tip, to make sure she could settle her tab at the end of the night. Now she could plunk down their credit card for an entire round of drinks without worry. Ted had even paid off her student loans, another thing she'd never mentioned to her parents.

Couples in New York could go on this way forever, Maja knew, entertaining and being entertained. New York City was like a year-round summer camp for adults, except instead of canoeing and songs by the campfire, there were hot yoga classes and drag brunches. Always something new, no need to get bored.

And yet, it had become sort of boring. Or maybe it was her, or Ted. Maybe they had become boring.

Her phone buzzed in her pocket, like a reproach to her thoughts. It was a message from Ted: I'm sorry, babe. Got stuck in a late meeting. On my way now. Her phoned beeped with a low-battery warning, and Maja turned it off and tucked it into her purse. He'd get there when he got there.

Aneeta was standing at the mailbox, waiting for her. "Helloooo!" she called out, her voice cheerful, with its slight British accent. Maja couldn't remember if Aneeta had actually grown up in England, or if she'd just attended boarding school there, or neither. In private, she joked to Ted that the accent was nothing but a put-on, like the waitresses at their neighborhood pasta place that faked Italian accents for better tips.

Maja followed Aneeta into the kitchen, where expanses of pale gray and white marble gleamed beneath matching cherry-red appliances in all the right brands: a shiny KitchenAid stand mixer, a Breville espresso machine. A flat-screen TV built into the wall was silently tuned to HGTV. Aneeta opened the fridge, which was paneled to match the cabinets, a touch that Maja always found both appealing and unsettling: the idea that a refrigerator that probably cost thousands of dollars was somehow gauche and had to be hidden. Aneeta pulled out a bottle of wine and smiled conspiratorially. "It's practically cocktail hour, right?"

Maja started to refuse, out of habit. She'd basically given up drinking since she'd doubled down on her efforts to get pregnant. She hadn't really missed these afternoon cocktail hours, which she thought of as the "white wine whine"—women commiserating over minor inconveniences to justify their afternoon wine habit. But today she had her own problem to complain about. "Close enough!" she said, as she accepted the generously sized glass.

To Maja's surprise, Aneeta took a bag of Cheetos out of the cabinet, poured some into a bowl, and set it between their wineglasses. "Is this why you had kids?" Maja asked.

Aneeta laughed. "I read an article in *Saveur* that said that the chicest cocktail snacks were the most effortless. They recommended Doritos, but I hate the way they smell. Apparently cheese platters make it look like you're trying too hard. Cheetos are my simple pleasure."

Maja had to hand it to Aneeta—she could even justify junk food as a lifestyle choice.

They sat down at the kitchen table, which was cluttered with papers, in contrast to the rest of the almost fanatically clean kitchen. "Sorry about the mess," Aneeta said, pushing some aside and placing the drinks in front of them.

Only two types of people apologized for their homes being messy, Maja thought. People whose houses really could use a deep clean, and people who were fishing for compliments on how neat and organized they actually were. "Thanks," Maja said as they clinked glasses. "And your house looks perfect, as always." And with that, she burst into tears.

Aneeta looked bewildered, and Maja quickly dabbed at her eyes. "I'm so sorry," she sniffed, taking a tissue from the box that Aneeta offered. "It's the house. It's a disaster."

To Maja's surprise, Aneeta laughed. "Oh, darling, construction is *always* a disaster, right up to the minute when it all somehow comes together! But you really should have used my builder. He's absolutely reliable."

"It's not that," Maja said, and she began to tell Aneeta about the party, and the police, and the house. When she finished, she looked up to see the incredulous look on Aneeta's face.

"Oh, Maja," she said. "That is . . . unbelievable. I am so, so sorry. Adil and I are here for you, whatever you need. Want to start with a Xanax?"

Maja laughed, for the first time that day. "No. Thank you, though. I think the wine took the edge off." She glanced down at her glass and saw that she had almost finished it.

"They think it was kids?" Aneeta asked, frowning. "*Local* kids?"

Maja shrugged. "The police officer said that they like to drink down by the river on the weekends. He seemed to think they might have broken into the house."

"This is a really nice town," Aneeta sighed, echoing Detective Murray's words. "But I have heard some things about the high school. Great SAT scores, but also a lot of partying." She lowered her voice, despite the fact that, except for her sons playing upstairs, they were alone in the house. "There was actually an overdose last year. Pills, I think. But that's what happens when you mix money with access. Most people here send their kids to the public school. It's all very democratic. But that includes a lot of families who don't, let's say, hold their kids to the same standards we might. It doesn't matter so much when they're little. We love the elementary school. But Adil and I have talked about looking at private schools when the boys are older. I'd hate to see them get mixed up with kids who aren't on the path to college."

Maja frowned, wondering how true that was. People moved here for the schools. "Aneeta, I don't want to start any rumors. I don't know if it was kids from the local school or not."

"Don't worry," Aneeta said. "I won't tell a soul."

While Aneeta took a snack up to the boys—carrot sticks, not Cheetos—Maja began to flip through the stacks of catalogs that were piled on the table. There were a few housewares catalogs, but mostly they were real estate brochures and Home Depot circulars.

"Hey," she said, when Aneeta came back into the room. "How's business?" In the last few years, Aneeta had gotten involved with buying up older properties, renovating them, and flipping them for a profit. It would have surprised Maja, except that investing in real estate seemed to have become a national pastime. As far as Maja knew, Aneeta's only prior experience was renovating her own kitchen. Which, admittedly, was gorgeous.

"Not bad!" Aneeta said. "All of that time watching HGTV has really paid off." She laughed, and Maja laughed along, thinking that the line sounded a little tired, like it had been trotted out one too many times at cocktail parties. "You should see some of the dumps that I've had to work with recently," Aneeta continued. "But after I put in a new kitchen and new paint, you'd never recognize them. So, believe me when I tell you that your house is going to be okay."

"I thought you were finding the properties through Adil's bank," Maja said.

"That was only one," Aneeta said. "J.P. Morgan doesn't usually hold that sort of loan, but these mortgages were part of some kind of bundle that the bank trades in. They went belly-up and the properties reverted to the bank. One of them was nearby, so we went to look at it. That's not Adil's job, obviously, but he was curious to see what the bank owned. You know Adil, he's such a lawyer right to the core. He was worried about liability. They were never expecting to have to foreclose, so there was no system in place to move the properties off of their hands. But they've closed out a lot of those loan products now. I get most of my properties at foreclosure auctions."

"There's a lot to pick from?" Maja asked.

"You wouldn't believe it," Aneeta said. "But I look for ones that haven't been renovated at all, out near Quakertown and Levittown. We fix them up, give them a more modern vibe, and put them back on the market. The whole thing takes maybe six months. We make a killing."

"Wow, that's so fast. But what about the homeowners? Do you ever have to kick them out of their houses?" Maja asked.

"Oh, no! They're always empty by the time I get them. I mean, these people buy houses that they just can't afford. I have no idea what they're thinking. They get in over their heads, and then they just *trash* these places. No maintenance, front lawns with weeds up to your knees. It's terrible for the neighborhoods, as you can imagine. The neighbors are usually so excited when we get them back in shape and back on the market. And they sell fast. I'm practically doing a public service."

"I can't imagine ever wanting to work on a house again after all this," Maja said. She felt a momentary prickle of something. Not jealousy, exactly. She had zero interest in flipping houses. And she had no expectation that working at the gallery would ever pay nearly as much as a job like Ted's. But hearing about Aneeta's success, despite her total lack of experience, gave Maja a familiar feeling of tightness in her throat, like the ache of an old injury. A feeling that she'd somehow been sidelined and had failed to reach her full potential. She'd always batted this feeling away, telling herself that she had more time, if that's what she wanted. She could always start painting again. And she'd talked to Louis about the possibility of his going in with her on opening an offshoot of the gallery in New Falls. "There's a lot of money down here," she'd told him, "and only so many paintings of covered bridges that people can hang in their big houses." He was thinking it over, but Maja couldn't tell if he would bite. And then here was Aneeta, running her own real estate business. Her accent might be fake, but the money sounded very real.

Maja sighed and downed the rest of her wine. "I feel like I can't make anything work right now," she said. "The house . . ." she trailed off. She didn't want to get into the baby thing. "It just feels like one step forward, two steps back. And on top of everything else, our lease on the apartment is up in September. The building is converting to condos. There's no way we'll be able to extend it."

Aneeta gave her arm a squeeze. "You're in shock," she said. "But this is just a setback. If I can get my flips fixed up in six months, I know you'll be able to get your house back on track by then. Now, I don't want to hear any excuses. You're staying for dinner."

Maja switched on her phone and saw that she had a series of missed calls and texts from Ted: I'm here. Where are you? Call me, I'm worried. She texted him back: Sorry. On my way.

"Thanks for the offer," she said, "but I have to meet Ted at the inn. It looks like I'll probably be down here at least through tomorrow. Can I take a rain check?"

"Of course," Aneeta replied. "We're here for you. Whatever you need."

Adil came home just as Maja was leaving, and she accepted his offer of a ride back to the inn. She was anxious to go over everything with Ted. She needed to hear him say that everything would be okay, and that they would get through this, somehow. But when she slipped her key into the lock and opened the door, she saw Ted laying on the bed, fast asleep. He was still dressed in his suit, and he had one arm flung over his eyes and his phone in his other hand. "Ted?" she asked gently.

He mumbled and rolled over onto his side, but he didn't wake up. He was such a deep sleeper; Maja envied him. She turned off the overhead light and went into the bathroom to take off her makeup and get undressed. Before she got into bed, she pulled off Ted's socks and slipped the heavy watch off of his wrist. He stirred again but didn't wake, and she crawled into the bed beside him. He put his arm around her and pulled her toward him, nuzzling his face against her neck.

"Hey you," he whispered.

"Hey," she said back, and just like that, her body relaxed, and any thoughts of what had happened during this long, long day seemed better saved for tomorrow.

10

Maja woke up on Tuesday morning with the confused feeling of finding herself in a strange bed. She had a single blissful moment, stretching out next to Ted, before she remembered why they were there. She felt a sinking in the pit of her stomach, like a dawning hangover, as she thought of the house.

They walked into town to have breakfast at the Blue Moon, a café tucked between the river and the canal. After they put their order in, Maja began to run through the details of the day before, and Ted listened grimly as she described the damage, the police investigation, and the contractor's vague estimates.

"A few hundred thousand dollars?" he said. "Are you kidding me?"

"John said he wasn't really sure yet," Maja said. "But I wouldn't be surprised if it was more."

Ted sighed. "It just sounds like a lot for party cleanup."

Maja shook her head. "Ted, it wasn't just a party. It was . . . I don't really know what to call it. The house is *trashed*. You have to see it."

For a moment it looked like Ted was going to protest, but instead he gave Maja a thin smile. "I'm sorry I couldn't make it down in time. Thank you for dealing with the police. I know I should have been here. Things at work just have me really stressed out. But I'm here today. Whatever needs to be done."

"The markets have been really jumpy, huh?" Maja asked, trotting out a Wall Street worry that she had heard repeatedly over the last few months, but only vaguely understood. As far as she could tell, the markets were always either up or down, and no matter what, everyone, or everyone they knew, still seemed to make money. She had a hard time buying into all of the anxiety that seemed to accompany these fluctuations.

Ted snorted. "Yeah, you could say that. Frothy, even. Dow's still up, so that's nice." Ted seemed almost to be talking to himself. "Something's going on, though. I can feel it. People at work look nervous." He gave Maja a searching look, as if she might have an answer. But everything she knew about finance she knew from him, so her face was only a reflection of his own confusion. "Credit has been hard to come by," he went on. "Home sales are down and foreclosures are up. I don't know. Things seem too flat. Too calm. It's what people aren't saying that worries me."

"Foreclosures? That's funny, Aneeta was just talking to me last night about foreclosures. She said Adil's bank had a few of them. I was surprised—I didn't realize that J.P. Morgan was the kind of bank that held mortgages. But aren't you in structured finance?" It was a term, like many related to Ted's job, that she used without really understanding it. Derivatives, swaps, futures, options. Ted liked to explain these things to her in detail after a few glasses of wine, but the nuances always faded for her by the next morning.

At the mention of Aneeta's name, Ted frowned. "Sure, but my products are tied into the real estate market. Aneeta mentioned foreclosures at J.P. Morgan? What exactly did she say?"

Maja was surprised. Ted almost seemed more interested in this than in anything she'd said about the house. "If you're curious about it," she said, "let's see if they can meet up for dinner tonight."

"Sounds good. So, what's the game plan?" Ted asked. "I already told the office I'm out all day. Shall I hunt down whoever did this and give them a severe beating? Maybe burn their house down?"

"I wouldn't mind seeing that," Maja said.

"I'm only half-joking," Ted replied.

"Let's go over to the house first," Maja said. "You have to see it to believe it. I had a message from the police last night—they have the initial report ready, so we can pick that up. Then I guess we start by filing the insurance claim."

"Can we call John and have him meet us there?" Ted asked. "Maybe he can give us some more definite numbers."

Maja nodded, but her throat suddenly felt tight. It was all so overwhelming. They had so much of their money tied up in the house. She'd never thought about what would happen if something went wrong.

"Hey," Ted said, putting his hand on hers. "I love you. It's going to be okay. We're going to get through this."

"What about the money?" Maja asked.

"The insurance will come through," Ted said. "In the meantime, we can float the expenses. Don't worry about that part. Just focus on the house. I'll worry about the money."

Maja wanted to tell him that it wasn't just the house that had her down. It was also the negative pregnancy test from the day before. She'd let herself get her hopes up too much, *again*, and she'd barely had time to process her disappointment. Everything she read told her not to frame it as a personal failure, but that's what it felt like. Like she wasn't holding up her end of the bargain. But Ted had enough on his plate right now. They could talk about it later.

"Let's do something fun this weekend," she said with forced cheerfulness. "Even if it's just ordering delivery and watching a movie in bed. I feel like we've hardly seen each other lately."

"Sounds great. We just need to get through this week first," Ted said. "Is it really only Tuesday?"

"It feels like it should at least be Thursday," Maja said. "Think we'll make it?"

"Hold fast," Ted advised, miming a sailor clinging to a ship's rigging in a storm.

Maja held up her own fists, mirroring his motion. At least, she thought, we're in this together.

11

Detective Murray pulled up in front of a small but impeccably neat Craftsman-style bungalow at the edge of town. A pickup in the driveway was emblazoned with a logo that read JOHN WILLIAMS, HEARTH & HOME BUILDERS. Murray knocked on the door, and John opened it, looking surprised to see the detective again. They sat on the front porch.

"Nice place you have here," Detective Murray began. "Very different from the house that you're building for the Jensens."

"I prefer a traditional style," John said. "Fits in better with the area, in my opinion. But my job is to build what the client wants. It's a real shame what happened at that house. We were nearly done, and I was looking forward to getting those last checks."

"I know Officer Cruz went over some of this with you, but just for my notes, can you tell me if you'd seen anyone hanging around the site recently who shouldn't have been there?"

John shook his head. "Just my crew. Once or twice a neighbor would get close enough to get a look—the neighbors are always curious when a new house goes up. A few times I noticed some beer cans down by the riverfront on a Monday morning."

"That didn't concern you?"

"It's a construction site." John shrugged. "The owners can put up security cameras if they want to."

"What about your crew?" Murray asked. It had occurred to him that a lot of guys working construction jobs in the area were just out of high school themselves. "Can we get a list of who's been at the site?"

"Sure," John said. "But it wasn't my guys. Most of them have been working for me for a few years, at least. They do their drinking in their own homes."

"You didn't seem very shocked when you called it in yesterday," Murray said, changing tack.

John frowned. "I don't like what you're implying. But no, I wasn't totally shocked. A house like that—it was a target. What do you expect when half the people around here live in mansions and half of them work landscaping jobs? But like I said, I build what the client wants. And I didn't like seeing my work destroyed, whatever you might think. I had nothing to do with that."

"Tell me about Friday afternoon," Murray said.

"It was a normal day. We were sanding the floors and putting in some of the light fixtures. I stopped by around three-thirty. I looked over what had been done, and then told the guys to call it a day. We were out of there by four."

"And the house was secure when you left?"

"It was."

"How do you think the vandals got access to the house?"

John gave a dry laugh. "You saw the place. They coulda walked right in through any of those broken windows. The house was secure, but a brick through the window will change that real quick."

"What about the garage door? I was told that the opener is missing."

For the first time since they started talking, John's face seemed to darken. "That damn garage door," he muttered. And then, more clearly: "It could be anywhere. It's a mess in there. Whoever broke in could have taken it with them."

Murray picked up on the defensiveness in the contractor's voice, but he kept his own tone even. "Did the garage door give you some trouble?" he asked.

"It just went in beginning of last week, but to be honest I shoulda waited. Custom glass and wood. It cost over ten grand. I ordered it on my account, and Mr. Jensen was supposed to reimburse me right away. I cashed the check, but it bounced. When I called Mr. Jensen, he said that it was some sort of mistake. That he just needed to move some money around, something about investments. I didn't want to hold up the construction schedule, so I went ahead and installed the door. It happens, you know. These are big numbers. I'd never had any issue with their payments before, so I didn't worry about it. I figured it would clear by Monday at the latest.

"You didn't say anything about that to the officer yesterday."

John looked uncomfortable. "I didn't want to say anything in front of the missus," he said. "I already got my hands full with her."

"You've had issues?" Murray asked.

"Eh, just here and there," John walked it back. "She had us redo a few things that I didn't necessarily agree with, but she's the customer. Women like that, they're sticklers; everything's gotta be just so. I'm happy to do it—so long as my bills get paid."

Detective Murray closed his notebook. "Thanks for your time," he said, handing John his card. "If you could get me that list of your guys who worked on the house, I'd be grateful. Gotta cover all our bases."

As Murray walked back to the car, he wondered whether he'd stumbled onto an actual conflict between the contractor and the Jensens, or if these were just run-of-the-mill construction issues. He'd been surprised to hear that the Jensens had bounced a check. Mrs. Jensen hadn't mentioned it, but then again, it sounded like she might not know. Was John Williams merely annoyed at the delay, as he'd said, or was he angry enough to turn a blind eye while his guys threw a beer bash in the new house? And where was the garage door opener?

12

On Tuesday afternoon, Maja and Ted sat across the desk of Assistant District Attorney Jake Tillman, Maja feeling as if she was at a job interview for a position she didn't actually want. Ted had suggested asking for a meeting, and she was a bit surprised when the DA agreed to see them so quickly. She was nervous going in, but Tillman was patient as he answered all of Ted's questions. In fact, he seemed almost excited about the case. Maja got the impression that this was the most interesting thing that had happened in New Falls in a while. It was like they were starring in their own reality TV show, pitched as *Cops* meets *MTV Cribs*.

After he ran through the process, Tillman gave them a copy of the police report, saving them a trip to the police station, and a printout labeled VICTIMS' RIGHTS INFORMATION.

Maja stared at the word "victim" for a moment before she spoke. "I've never been involved in anything like this. I feel like I should be doing something, but I don't know what."

Jake smiled sympathetically. "Right now we're still in the information-gathering stage. When we're ready to file charges, you'll get a copy in the mail. Or you're always welcome to call my office. What happens after that will depend on whether the perpetrators plead guilty or not. At that point, we may need an impact statement from you. But that's a ways off."

"The police told my wife that some kids were ticketed near our house on Friday night," Ted said. "It seems to me that they're the most likely culprits. Who were they?"

Jake nodded slowly. "Well, I can't discuss those specific charges, but I can tell you that the police are following up on every lead."

"If the police had followed up on Friday night, we might have avoided the most serious damage to our home," Ted said, his voice tense. He'd been worked up all day after seeing the house. Maja put a hand on his arm—she knew that they needed the prosecutor, and the police, on their side, and she didn't want Ted to fly off the handle.

But Jake seemed used to dealing with people thrust into extreme situations, and he took Ted's questions in stride. "I can assure you that the police department is doing everything in their power right now," he said.

"Thank you," Maja said quickly. "We appreciate what you're doing. It's funny—in the city, we were always on alert. But it never occurred to me to worry about something like this out here, in the country."

"Well, this is more of a suburb than the country, but we do have crime here, like anywhere else," Jake said. "An incident like this is unusual, though. It's not much of a welcome, is it? I hope it doesn't scare you off of New Falls. It really is a nice town."

"That's what everyone says," Maja said with a sigh.

Jake walked them to the door. "I'm sorry that this happened," he said again. "We're going to do everything in our power to make it right." He shook his head. "The parents need to open their eyes. You'd think that kids who have everything going for them would want to protect it, but it makes them feel invincible. Now they're going to get a taste of the real world, and I don't think they're going to like it."

Aneeta's table, set beneath an arbor in the backyard, reminded Maja of something from a cooking magazine. One of those spreads where a chef entertains their friends at home with a casual six-course meal that just happens to include a signature cocktail, pizzas pulled from backyard wood-fired ovens, and artfully arranged platters of stone fruits for dessert. The guests are always beautiful and boho, smiling as they sip wine from water glasses, a casual touch to show that this was all just thrown together. The host is relaxed in the pictures, never hovering over the stove or cursing when he remembers that he forgot to buy flowers for the table.

And there was Aneeta, laughing as she untied a pristine apron from around her waist and ushered Maja into the garden. The patio was Pottery Barn perfect, with wicker sofas and strings of warm white lights strung overhead, and Aneeta's two boys were kicking a soccer ball back and forth on the thick green lawn. The table was set with a silver champagne bucket and a cheese plate. What had happened to the Cheetos?

Aneeta popped the champagne and poured two glasses. Ted and Adil came out of the house, carrying tumblers of scotch, and they all clinked glasses. "I don't like the circumstances," Adil said, "but we're always happy to see you. To new neighbors."

"If we're ever able to move in," Ted said darkly.

Adil grimaced with sympathy. "Let me show you the new dock," he said, leading Ted down to the riverfront where he kept his kayak. The two little boys trailed behind them, leaving Aneeta and Maja alone.

"Ted's taking it hard," Aneeta observed.

"He's a day behind me on letting it sink in," Maja said. "Until you see the house, it's hard to believe that a party could cause that much damage."

"Here," Aneeta said, refilling Maja's glass. "Drink. What did your insurance agent say?"

Maja shrugged. "They're sending us some forms, and there's a deductible, of course. That's the first thing they tell you. But at least we got the process started. The police haven't told us that we can clean up yet, so we're in a bit of a holding pattern."

"What about work?" Aneeta asked. "Are you going back up to New York tomorrow?"

"I'll have to," Maja replied. "Louis is in Miami until Thursday, and we have an opening this weekend."

"He's lucky to have you," Aneeta said. "But please tell me that you aren't going to keep commuting once you move down here."

"Ted will be commuting every day," Maja said. "Just like Adil."

"Sure," Aneeta said. "But not on the weekends! It can hardly be worth the money . . ." She stopped abruptly, realizing what she'd said.

"It's okay," Maja said. "It's true." Maja was used to this. Of the couples that she and Ted were friends with, very few of the wives worked. They did charity boards, or they were working on a novel, or they were stay-at-home-moms-with-nannies. Or, like Aneeta, they dabbled in investing or real estate. But Maja had hung on to her job because she liked to keep her hand in the art scene—sometimes her job seemed like the last thread connecting her to her old life. But she had also hung on to it because it was easy. It may have been a little monotonous, but at least it was manageable. Unlike the banking and law jobs that many women she knew had given up, her job at the gallery had always allowed her plenty of time for other pursuits: painting, at first, and more lately the work that had gone into trying to get pregnant and building the house. Once they started trying for a family, she'd assumed that she'd work until she had a baby. But now she wasn't sure if that would happen.

"I haven't really decided yet," Maja said. "It is a long commute." For a moment, she debated whether to share with Aneeta the plan that she'd been hatching. "Don't say anything in front of Ted," she said, "but I've been talking to Louis about the possibility of opening an offshoot of the gallery in New Falls. There's a lot of money down here, and most of the art galleries here are very . . . regional. I think we'd do really well. Louis isn't totally on board, but I'm hoping that I can convince him. I thought that maybe he and I could go in on it together, as partners."

"I love it," Aneeta said. "It's exactly what we need here. Ted doesn't know?"

"He knows," Maja said. "He just doesn't like it. He thinks we already have our hands full. You know, the house, his job . . ."

"Kids?" Aneeta added with a wink.

"Maybe," Maja said. She saw the men coming up from the dock, the kids by their sides. She watched as Ted plucked the baseball cap off the older boy's head, holding it up playfully as the boy jumped for it. Maja felt an ache. They should have this, she thought. She should be able to give this to Ted. The taste of champagne in her mouth was suddenly sour.

She turned away so that Aneeta wouldn't see the tears that had sprung to her eyes, but Aneeta was focused on the boys. "Come on!" she called to them. "Special treat tonight. You get to picnic in front of the TV." She looked at Maja over her shoulder as she led the boys inside. "They'll be happier watching a movie than listening to us talk. You sit and I'll be right back out."

As they ate dinner, Maja described the destruction at the house and all the work she thought it might take to get it back in shape. She knew that she was being a bore, but Aneeta clucked sympathetically and Adil poured generous glasses of Japanese whiskey for Ted. They were outraged at all the right parts, even when Maja told them about waiting endlessly on hold with the insurance company and then getting cut off just as the line finally clicked to life.

Inevitably, Ted and Adil fell into a long discussion about the markets. For the people she knew who worked at investment banks, their job wasn't just a job. It was their passion, their hobby, and their way of life. Normally Maja would have been annoyed at another dinner conversation hijacked by work talk, but tonight she was grateful for the distraction, and even more grateful that Aneeta seemed to be following the conversation with interest. Maja was exhausted, and happy to half-listen while she leaned back in her chair, looking out at the garden.

Adil poured Ted another whiskey. Was that his fourth? Whatever, Maja thought. She'd had a fair bit herself tonight. What was the point of abstaining when she was never actually going to get pregnant?

"We've been dumping that shit at J.P. Morgan for six months," Adil was saying. "Frankly, my opinion was that we never should have been in the mortgage-backed securities market to begin with. Maybe ten years ago. Back then, at least you knew what you were getting. The ratings meant something. I've done the due diligence on some of these products, and you wouldn't believe some of the subprime shit that's packed into them. But nobody wants to hear it from the lawyer. The traders are too busy counting their bonuses."

Ted laughed, but it sounded forced, which caught Maja's attention. "I don't think there's a firm on the street who isn't doing these deals," Ted said. "Investors like the yields on the mortgage vehicles, and we're making bank on the fees. We're printing money. Or we were," he corrected himself. "There've been some liquidity problems lately. But the ratings are good."

"The ratings are bullshit," Adil said. "Those AAA ratings aren't worth the paper they're printed on. Have you ever stopped to think about it? Who do you think the customer is for those ratings? It's the bank, not the investor. You guys package up debt obligations you don't know the first thing about, slice them, dice them, and take them over to Standard and Poor's, where you pay them for a nice rating so you can market them in your funds. If you don't like the rating, you take your business down the street. It's in everyone's interest to push these things through. Have you ever looked, really looked, at the underlying assets?"

"They're mortgages." Ted shrugged. "We don't keep them on the books too long."

"A lot of those mortgages aren't what you think," Adil pressed him. "They're subprime, issued without income verification. They're based on these low rates that balloon after a few years. And it works as long as the real estate market is up. But the party won't last forever. Ask Aneeta—when she first started buying up foreclosures, she had to take what she could get. Now she has her pick of the litter. Buyers can't keep up. They're losing their homes left and right. And no matter how complex your investment vehicle is, at the end of the day, the income streams depend on people paying their mortgages. Or not." Adil shook his head. "You guys are so far in over your heads, you can't even see the tsunami coming for you."

Adil sounded a little worked up, and Maja tried to meet Ted's eye, to signal that it might be time to let them go to bed. But Ted was staring at the table, frowning.

"Well!" said Aneeta, standing up suddenly. "Enough work talk for tonight. Who's ready for dessert?"

"Me!" Maja said, relieved. She suddenly wanted the night to be over. Everyone seemed to have had one drink too many, and what had started as a fun evening had begun to make her feel uneasy. With everything that had happened this week, the last thing that Maja needed was for Ted to be even more preoccupied with work. Adil seemed to think that something very bad was about to happen, and Ted, Maja noticed, hadn't said much to contradict him.

13

Will had both of his windows open, and an old box fan shoved into one was doing its best to push the warm air around the room. It had been one of those spring days that seem to get hotter as the night goes on, a taste of the summer to come. He lay in the semidarkness, the nearly full moon illuminating the window.

The fan sat uneasily in the window frame, and its rhythmic whirl-whirl-tap as it vibrated against the screen kept time with Will's thoughts, which had cycled through his head in an unsatisfying loop since the night of the party. It was only Wednesday, but it felt like a lifetime since Friday night.

First there was his conversation with the police on the track at school on Monday. He hadn't expected them to show up there, and every time he played through his lame answers to their questions his face began to burn. The fact that they hadn't really challenged him on anything only made it worse. They knew he was lying, so why hadn't they said anything? By Tuesday morning, the news that the police had been called to the house was all over school. As the stories about who was there, and who had done what, raced through the halls, Will had started to realize that it probably wasn't a matter of *if* he would be caught, but *when*. He'd always enjoyed being the one who could get booze for parties, but now he wished he hadn't brought it.

This afternoon, when Will floated the idea to Trip that they should come forward—that it would be better to be honest with the police about their involvement rather than wait for other kids to do it for them—Trip insisted that they keep quiet. *I could go to jail for this,* he said. *I'm counting on you.*

Was it true that Trip could do time if they got caught? Will wasn't sure, but with Trip's suspended sentence, and the fact that he was probably the only person at the party who was over twenty-one, Will didn't want to find out.

What he did know was that if the police connected him to the house party, and he was charged, it would screw up everything with his admission to Princeton and his scholarship from the Union Club. This was the place, for the past several days, where his mind shied away, as if even thinking about it was bad luck. And then he would start again, going over his conversation with the police, looking for clues, trying to figure out how much of this was in his head, and how much was real.

He dozed for a minute before he was jerked back awake by the pull of his unfinished thoughts. The sound of the fan seemed to grow louder, and then he realized that it was actually an approaching helicopter, probably Hunter's dad flying in from New York. His head pounded. He felt a childish desire to climb out of bed and walk down the hall to his mother's room. He wanted to tell her everything, and to listen to her as she whispered to him not to worry, that they would figure everything out together in the morning. But he knew he couldn't do that. He wasn't a little boy anymore.

There was a tapping sound, and for one second, Will thought that maybe it was his mom, checking on him. He sat up in bed just as his window screen slid up. A face appeared at the window, and to his surprise, Will saw Maddie's pale hair lit up by the moonlight. She'd never shown up like this before, but in the next second she pushed herself up and over the windowsill. She slipped her shoes off and sat on the edge of the bed, not looking at him. She whispered something that he couldn't quite hear.

"Maddie?" he said, his voice hoarse.

"I can't sleep," she said, more clearly.

"Me neither," Will said. He moved over to make room for her to sit on his narrow single bed.

"Are you scared?" Maddie asked.

"Yeah," Will admitted. "We never should have been there. It was so stupid. I thought it was just going to be another beer bash by the river. I didn't actually think we were going to break into the house. And then—I don't know—for a while it seemed just like any other house party. But it got so out of control." He paused for a moment. He'd wanted to talk to her, but he hadn't been able to find the words. "I'm sorry about what happened."

Maddie leaned over and kissed him, and her face was wet against his. She drew back with a shuddering sigh. "Can I stay here with you?"

He put his arm around her and they lay down.

With her back to him, it was easier to talk. "I thought that you'd drowned in the river," he said, giving voice to the fear that he'd felt the night of the party. "When I couldn't find you."

Maddie was quiet for a moment, then said, "I wish I had."

"Don't say that," Will said and pulled her closer.

She was still crying, but quietly, and soon her breathing slowed, and he thought that she must be asleep. He knew that it would be trouble if his father caught them together in here in the morning, but he didn't care. He didn't want to be alone, and neither did she. Worrying about her felt easier than thinking about himself. He breathed in the clean scent of her hair, let his mind go blank, and finally fell into a deep sleep.

When Will woke up the next morning for school, Maddie was gone and the heat had broken. The sky outside his window was gray and the air smelled good, like it had rained overnight. He paused in the hall to listen for sounds of his father, but he had the house to himself. In the kitchen he poured a cup of coffee, added milk and a generous helping of sugar, and sat down at the table. There was a stack of mail arranged in his usual spot. On top was a thin white envelope from the county court. Will's hands grew clammy as he opened it, but it was just the summons for his underage-drinking violation. He wasn't sure what else he was expecting. He was pretty sure that the police didn't usually arrest you by sending a letter through the mail.

Underneath was a much thicker envelope, from Princeton. Will felt a thrill just looking at it. It reminded him of the day he'd received his acceptance. Standing at the mailbox at the end of the farm's long driveway, he'd known without opening it that he was in. They only sent the big envelope if it was good news. It had felt so satisfying, after all of the work and the waiting, to hold it in his hands. Almost too good to be true. And yet he had the letter to prove it to himself. He was in, and he knew that it meant that his life would never be the same.

He'd qualified for financial aid, but expenses on the farm varied widely from year to year, and the family contribution was still steep. After a few tense weeks, Will finally allowed himself to celebrate when he received a phone call letting him know that he'd been awarded the generous scholarship he'd applied for from the Hart County Union Club. The scholarship meant that he could actually afford to go, even if it would still be a stretch to buy the new laptop he would need, along with all the books. He was in, he was good enough, he was going to Princeton.

In New Falls, the high school students tended to sort into predictable postgraduation paths: the rich kids headed to fancy liberal arts schools, the kids of local farmers and contractors went to work for their parents, and everyone else went to state schools. His parents assumed that he would go to a state school—maybe even Penn State, perhaps with a stop at community college first to save some money. No one expected him to apply to Princeton, and the only people he told were his AP English teacher and his track coach. He had never in his life wanted anything more than he wanted this.

He'd been to the Princeton campus a few times, tagging along with Hunter and his father at an alumni barbecue and a basketball game, and once for the ribbon-cutting ceremony when the Finch Architecture Collection opened at the library. Will loved everything about it: the old buildings and the neat expanses of lawn, the carefully constructed feeling of something between a country club and a library. He watched as Dominic Finch greeted old buddies, introduced Hunter to their sons and daughters, and sang silly fight songs at the basketball game. Mr. Finch treated Will almost as a son on these trips, buying him and Hunter matching sweatshirts, resting a hand on each boy's shoulder. But of course Will wasn't his son, and Will was always keenly aware of this. He was smart enough to know that there was a world of difference between being invited to the barbecue and having your family name on the building.

It was impossible to know if he would have dreamed of going somewhere like Princeton if he'd never known Hunter. But once he had the idea, he couldn't let it go. He'd never been jealous of Hunter, not in any way that really mattered. Sure, sometimes it was tough to watch girls fall all over themselves in front of Hunter, or to hear about his travel plans when Will had to spend the summers working at the orchard. Hunter could blow off exams, or let his grades slide for a semester, and never sweat it. There was no question of where he would go to school, or who would pay for it. But Hunter had never held it over him. He was always generous, inviting Will when he could, everything paid for without question. He never made Will feel like he didn't belong in that world, or even that there was anything better or different about his life.

But even so, Will would have preferred to be able to pay his own way. And Princeton was his ticket. He would never say this to Hunter, but when his acceptance letter arrived, he had felt, for the first time, that he had something that Hunter didn't. Not the acceptance letter itself—there was no doubt that an identical one was waiting in Hunter's mailbox—but the sense of having earned it. He enjoyed the feeling for a moment, and then set it aside. He was going to college with his best friend, and that was what they clinked beers to that night, drinking in the woods between their houses.

That was a month ago, and it had felt like a sure thing. Now, well, he couldn't even think about it.

As he put his coffee cup in the sink, he heard a buzzing in the junk drawer. Glancing around one more time for his dad, Will grabbed his phone, which his father had kept since the night of the party, and flipped it open. The most recent text was from Hunter: We need to talk. Woods after school today? Will texted, OK, and shoved the phone back in the drawer.

14

The ravine between the Finch estate and the O'Connor orchard was where Hunter and Trip had been hanging out for years. It was just far enough from both houses that it escaped any sort of landscaping from either side, and the hollow along the seasonal creek made it a perfect place for the boys to play and shout undetected as kids, and later to smoke cigarettes and hang out with girls.

Hunter was sitting in what remained of the grand tree house project that he and Will had constructed in middle school out of old orchard crates and lumber scraps from Dom Finch's garage. It had been an all-consuming project, and in those days, before they had cell phones and twice-a-day sports practices, they would show up whenever they could, sometimes working on it alone and sometimes together, or with Trip.

At its peak, the tree house had been epic. They built it into the lap of a weeping willow that rose from the marshy bed of the creek, and the central platform branched into lookouts and escape routes that ran up the limbs, connected by haphazard ladders and rope swings. Every spring, the tree burst into bloom, hiding the tree house under a curtain of pale green leaves. It was their military command base, their X-Men mansion, and their detective agency.

Hunter had been so proud of his creation that one day, on a whim, he had dragged his father away from his desk and out to the woods to see it. Before they even got to the ravine, Hunter had begun to worry that it was a mistake to bring him there. Looking at the tree house through his father's eyes, he suddenly saw how slapped together the whole thing looked. But to his surprise, his father loved it. He spent a long time examining their design and asking Hunter questions about how they'd made it. Hunter was sure that his dad must have recognized some of the materials that he'd taken from the garage, but he didn't mention it. It had turned out to be one of the best afternoons he had ever spent with his father.

Not long after, Hunter's parents had begun to fight, and they seemed to operate at only two volumes: violent shouting or stony silence. Hunter spent more and more time hanging out at the tree house, and he suspected he wasn't the only one. Sometimes, after one of his parents' big arguments, he thought he could smell his dad's spicy aftershave in the air, and he would find stubbed-out Marlboro reds near the tree house, a brand that he knew his father secretly smoked, because he'd stolen a few out of the glove box in his car. His dad never said anything about it, and neither did he. And then his mom had taken off, and the tree house had seemed childish, and was no longer a place to pretend, but rather a place to escape to.

Hunter flicked his cigarette ash off the edge of the platform. June and Rosie were with him, sitting on a log and laughing together at something on June's phone. He'd brought June here plenty of times before, and he'd even brought Rosie once, before he started going out with June. He'd never said anything to June about it, and he got the feeling that Rosie hadn't either. Rosie was always tagging along with the two of them, and sometimes he could feel her staring at him. He liked her attention. He even encouraged it, when he thought he could get away with it. He didn't worry too much about June getting jealous—it would never occur to her that he could be interested in anyone other than her.

Hunter heard Will approaching through the woods. "Your dad finally let up?" he called out as Will climbed onto the platform and sat down.

"Oh, sure," Will said. "You know my dad. He's famous for taking things in stride. Actually, he's just busy. They're updating a lot of the equipment right now, and pulling out a bunch of old trees. Trip's been helping him out, so he's basically left me alone. What about you?"

"My dad wasn't happy that I scratched up Lindsay's car, but it was sort of hard to hear him over the chopper wings as he flew off to work," Hunter smirked.

"Hey, Will," June said, as she and Rosie climbed up the ladder to sit with them. "I heard that the police talked to you at school on Monday."

"Yeah. You?"

June shook her head.

"It's because I got that ticket on Friday night," Will said. "They know I was at the house."

"They know that you were on the road," June corrected him. "But they can't prove that you were at the party without some other evidence."

"Does having a lawyer for a father make you one too?" Hunter asked, and June stuck her tongue out at him.

"Whose idea was it to party there, anyway?" Rosie asked.

Will shrugged. "I heard about it from you," he said to June. "When you asked me to pick up the keg."

"People were talking about it at choir practice on Thursday," June said. "I don't know who actually planned it. I think some kids from school have been going down there to skate in the empty pool."

Will closed his eyes, trying to remember who he'd run into at the house. "When I got to the house," he said, "someone opened the garage. They told me I could unload the booze there."

"It doesn't matter who planned it," June broke in. "We were all trespassing."

"We shouldn't have been there," Will said miserably.

"Come on, relax," Hunter said. "There were so many people there. Everyone was wasted. They won't be able to prove who did what, or who was even really there."

They were all quiet, and Will just looked at him. "Things got really out of control." He pictured, for the thousandth time that week, Maddie lying on the floor as a few girls coaxed her half back to waking. Downstairs, in the chaos of the kitchen, he'd overheard a kid laughing about it, and Will grabbed him and punched him in the gut. The kid bent over, gasping, not used to taking a hit. But he'd recovered quicker than Will expected, and when he straightened back up he launched himself at Will, the force of his hit carrying them both through the screen door. Trip had seen them fighting and grabbed the kid. He pushed him against the deck rail, which wasn't fully attached yet, and it collapsed under the pressure, leaving the kid and the rail lying on the lawn. He was coughing and yelling insults, but he didn't get up for more.

Will tested the skin around his knuckles, which was healing but still sore. There was no way, between his breaking the window and fighting in the kitchen, that every kid who'd been at the party wouldn't know that he'd been there too.

Finally June said, "I'm worried, but Hunter's right. Everyone who was there has an interest in keeping quiet. At least we didn't write our names all over the walls. Did you see those kids who were tagging up the dining room?" She rolled her eyes. "If no one cooperates with the police, we might be okay. Just deny being there. Make them prove it. As far as we're concerned, we were hanging out in the woods and it's all an unfortunate coincidence."

"So that's our story?" Will asked. "End of year party at the rope swing?"

"Don't say anything if you don't have to," June said. "But if they ask, that's the story. I do not need any problems with my Penn State acceptance. I'm in the honors program, and there's no way I'm losing out on that and getting put in with the gen pop." She looked over at Rosie, who was also attending Penn State, just not in the same program. "No offense."

Rosie frowned. "I'm the first person in my family to even go to college," she said defensively. "So yeah, we've all got a lot on the line here."

"You're right," June said. "So we all look out for each other."

"What about Maddie?" Hunter asked. "Has anyone talked to her?"

Will kept quiet, not wanting to say anything about how she'd shown up in his bedroom crying the night before.

"She's not talking much," said Rosie. "I think she's really embarrassed. Who was that kid, anyway?"

They all looked at each other and shook their heads. "I've never seen him before," Will said. "But someone must know him. Hunter, did you get a look at him?"

Hunter shook his head. "I missed the whole thing."

"I think you're the only one," Will said. "Where were you?"

Hunter shrugged. "Who knows? Things got pretty fuzzy there."

"I can ask around at school and see if anyone knows who he was," Will said.

"Maybe it's better not to," Rosie said quickly. "I think she just wants everyone to forget."

"He didn't actually, um, hurt her, did he?" Will asked. He'd wanted to ask Maddie the night before, but he felt like he couldn't. Even now, he couldn't bring himself to say the word. Rape.

"I don't think so," said June. She looked embarrassed. "He was just feeling her up. But who knows what could have happened. She doesn't remember much."

"Let's hope everyone else was that messed up," Hunter said. "The less everyone remembers, the better."

"Hey," Will said. "That's not funny."

"I'm sorry," Hunter said, holding his hands up. "You're right. Look, we're all in this together. As long as we look out for each other, we can get out of this thing okay."

"That's what Trip says," Will replied.

"Well, he knows what he's talking about."

"You think so?" Will asked. He'd always looked up to Trip. When Will was a kid, no one seemed cooler, or smarter, than his brother. He'd followed Trip around like a lost puppy. But lately Will was beginning to think that Trip seemed a little lost himself. "I guess we'll see," he said. But he couldn't help thinking that it was easy for Hunter to take this in stride. Whatever happened, Will was pretty sure that Hunter's dad could buy his way out of it, the way he always had.

15

Detective Murray's first task of the day on Thursday was to stop in at the DA's office to catch up with Jake Tillman. Not that he had much to report. He had called around to the parents of all of the kids that they'd picked up on River Road, and, to his surprise, not a single parent had agreed to voluntarily bring their kids in for questioning, even when he described the destruction at the house party. As Murray saw it, he and the parents should have been on the same side. It didn't do any good for kids to get away with this stuff—it just encouraged them to push it further the next time. But these parents saw it differently. They seemed to think that their role was to protect their children from consequences rather than to guide them through their mistakes. It worked, he thought, as long as you had money for lawyers. As a cop, he knew the truth: the poorest people often paid the highest price for their crimes, and sometimes for the crimes of others.

At Jake's office, Murray accepted a cup of terrible coffee from Donna and told Jake about being stonewalled by the parents. "If we want to bring them in, we're going to need warrants."

"What about the contractor?" Jake asked.

"We can't totally discount the possibility that someone from his crew threw the party," Murray said. "I have an officer following up with his guys. Actually, we already turned up one interesting piece of information: Apparently they were leaving the garage door opener under the overhang on the deck so that when subcontractors stopped by they could have easy access to the house in case the regular guys weren't there. It's another question whether they used it to open up the house for the party, or whether someone else knew it was there. And I'm going to follow up with the Jensens about the check that bounced. But this doesn't look like an insurance money play to me. If that was the case, they'd just burn it down. My money is still on the high school students."

"What about the O'Connor boys?" Jake asked. "Anything there?"

"Nothing solid," Murray replied. "Not yet, anyway."

Jake got up from his desk and stood by the window. "I met with the Jensens. They're pressing us hard—especially the husband."

"They've called our office three times already for updates," Murray said. "They want to see arrests, and I don't blame them. But they have to understand that if we rush it, the case could fall apart. Right now, all we have are the tickets that I gave out on the road nearby."

"I don't get it," Jake said. "In a town like this, I would have expected that property destruction would be exactly the kind of crime that would get the community worked up. There are a lot of beautiful homes around here to protect. But I haven't heard a peep about it in town. It's like it never even happened."

"It might be different if it happened to a family from around here," Murray said. "But the Jensens are out-of-towners. No one here is going to put their kid's future on the line to do right by someone they've never even met."

Jake shook his head. "But we know those kids were there."

"Oh yeah, they were there," Murray agreed. "And I haven't run out of leads to try to prove it."

Murray's next stop was Mason's Liquors. Murray wasn't holding out much hope the owner would help him, but he wanted to check it off his list. He pulled one of the boxes he'd found at the house out of the trunk of his car and went inside.

Mr. Mason sat behind a long wooden counter stacked with wine bottles. Murray flashed his badge and Mr. Mason gave him a sly grin. "A little early in the day for drinking on the job," he said. "But who am I to judge?"

"It hasn't come to that quite yet," Murray said, playing along. "But give it a few hours." He put the box on the counter. "Recognize this?" He'd picked one of the boxes from a more obscure whiskey distillery in the hopes that Mr. Mason might remember packing it up.

"Sure do," Mr. Mason replied, and for a second, Murray's pulse quickened. "It's a whiskey box."

"Ask a stupid question," Murray said with a smile, staying cool. "Know who you sold it to?"

Mr. Mason waved his hand dismissively. "I reuse the boxes. Makes it easier for the customers to carry out big orders."

Murray tried a different angle. "I'm looking for someone who might have made a big purchase on Friday. Someone on the younger side." Murray was careful not to say underage. It was an open secret in town that Mr. Mason wasn't too picky about who he sold to. He'd gotten into trouble a few times with the cops on the Jersey side, but it wasn't Murray's problem today. Today he just wanted to find out who had supplied the alcohol for the party. If he found that, he'd be a long way toward making a case that would stick.

"There's always a lot of big orders on Fridays," Mr. Mason said. Murray thought back to the scene when they'd shown up at the house. "Absolut Vodka, Southern Comfort?" He listed off the bottles he'd seen strewn around the kitchen and smashed in the sink. "A keg too. Probably something cheap?"

Mr. Mason sighed and pulled a notebook out from under the counter. "If they got a keg, the name's in here. When they bring it back for the deposit, I cross it off. He pushed the notebook across the counter. Murray scanned the list of names. All of the names were crossed off, except for one: O'Connor.

"No first names?" he asked, and Mr. Mason shrugged. He pointed to a dollar symbol next to the name. "This means they paid in cash," Mr. Mason said. "And before you ask, yes, he had ID."

Murray pulled a printout of Trip O'Connor's mug shot from his last arrest out of his file. "Is this him?" he asked.

To Murray's surprise, Mr. Mason stared at it for a moment before shaking his head. "I don't think so," he said. "Shorter hair. More serious-looking."

Murray frowned. There were likely plenty of O'Connors around here, but Mr. Mason probably just didn't want to get involved. Then he had a thought. He showed Mr. Mason a photocopy of a clipping they'd pulled from the local paper. It showed Will O'Connor, along with the rest of the track team, after a regional win. Mr. Mason nodded. "That might be him," he said. "Can't say for sure. That's a pretty grainy picture."

It was enough for Murray. If they needed a better picture, they could get it. "Thanks for your help," he said. Finally, something he could work with.

As he left the store, Mr. Mason called after Murray: "Hey, if you find your guy, tell him to bring back my tap!"

16

Maja sat at the kitchen table in her apartment and stared at her to-do list, which was growing longer each day, with no corresponding cross-outs to balance out the load: Return call to Belltown Mutual Insurance, call contractor, get appliance orders in, check in with the DA. They were at a standstill with the house. A cleaning crew had come in to mop up the beer and piss, and sweep away the Solo cups and cigarette butts. But there was nothing they could do about the larger damage until the insurance company scheduled an adjuster to come out, and they seemed to be dragging their feet. She'd tried to broach the subject of writing the checks themselves until the insurance paid out, at least so that John could start ordering new materials, but Ted was adamant that they should wait. They were already on the hook for a ten-thousand-dollar deductible, and Ted was uptight enough about that.

Last night he'd come home from work looking exhausted and had snapped at her when she complained that she felt like she was doing everything.

"Maja," he'd said, not quite looking at her. "I'm working. You know, the job that pays all the bills, including all the bills for this house you wanted."

Maja's mouth had parted in shock. The comment was so unlike Ted that at first she could only stare. He rarely snapped at her, and when he did, he usually apologized immediately. But last night he'd just stared ahead in stony silence, eyebrows raised as if he was conducting some internal dialogue.

"I'm working too," she said. "Why is it that whenever one of us has to be flexible, it's always me? Sometimes I feel like your job is taking over our lives."

Ted gave a bitter laugh. "I'm doing the best I can. We are leveraged up to the hilt. I have no flexibility. None. I'm sorry, I know it's not fair to you, but that's the way it is. If you want the big house, I have to have the big job."

It was the trump card. Ted didn't have to remind her that her job still paid hourly, and didn't offer retirement saving, or a fancy medical plan like Ted's. He wasn't wrong—they needed his job. But she needed his help too. She hated feeling like she was begging him for his time. "I thought this was the house that *we* wanted," she said. "It's our house."

"You're right," he said. He sounded tired. "I'm sorry."

"It's okay," she sighed. "I know you're stressed about work." She'd walked over to him, and he'd wrapped her up in his arms. She didn't want to fight, but she couldn't shake the sense that she was constantly in the position of asking him for something: time, money, a weekend away, a nice sofa. It wasn't a good feeling.

Maja tried to marshal the energy and organization that she'd brought to pushing through their building permits, a task that had felt Herculean when she started. One step at a time, she thought, picking up the phone and dialing Belltown Mutual.

She entered her case number when prompted and waited on hold while she flipped through a show catalog that she was proofreading for the gallery. The music finally cut out and Maja heard Cindy, her assigned agent, typing into a computer on her end of the line.

"Okay, Mrs. Jensen, it looks like we have news for you! We've scheduled an available adjuster to come out, two weeks from now. I'm sorry about the delay, but as soon as we have the report, we can have the damage schedule drawn up, which will include the damage we've documented, as well as the estimates for repair," Cindy chirped.

"Does that mean I'll be able to start scheduling my contractor to start work again soon?"

"Very soon," Cindy assured her. "But I do have to let you know about one issue we're facing here," Cindy continued, emphasizing the *we*, as if she and Maja were in this together. "Belltown Mutual has determined that your contractor"—Cindy paused, and Maja heard the sound of typing again—"John Williams, Hearth and Home Builders, Incorporated, may be at fault in this matter."

"Wait," Maja said, her heart sinking. "That can't be right. This wasn't a construction accident. We were the victims of a crime. The police are saying that it was probably teenagers throwing a party. Vandalism."

"Oh, I know, terrible," Cindy commiserated. "Just terrible. But the issue here is the access to the house. The police report indicates that the perpetrators entered the house using a garage door opener that was left out by your contractors. You'll be getting a call from our legal department, but I can tell you that in these types of cases, there's usually a sharing of liability among several parties."

"I don't understand," Maja said. This was the first time she'd heard anything about the garage door opener. Had she missed that in the police report? "What happens now?" she asked.

"As I said, you'll be getting a call from our attorneys. Belltown Mutual will handle any case against Hearth & Home Builders, but we will need your help. Any details that you can remember will be useful."

An unpleasant thought sprang to mind: Yesterday, when she'd called to check in with Detective Murray, he'd asked her to confirm that she and Ted had bounced their last check to the contractor. This had been news to her, and she'd denied it at the time. Now she made a mental note to check in with Ted about it. "You want me to sue my contractor?" she said aloud. "I just can't believe that he would be so careless."

"I know this process can feel overwhelming," Cindy was saying, "but it's very common. Your builder carries insurance for just this type of situation. A legal case always sounds scary, but generally these things are worked out in settlements between the insurance carriers. I can't promise anything, of course, but your builder will know that this isn't personal."

Like hell he will, Maja thought. They would have to find someone new to put their broken, half-finished house back together. It was going to be impossible. Who wanted to take on a project like that? The tears she'd been holding back started to spill over. Why was she so emotional? She felt like the shocking fact of strangers violating her home was being lost in all of the bureaucratic red tape.

"Talk to your contractor," Cindy was saying. "This won't be the first time he's dealt with a situation like this. Well, maybe not *like this*, but with shared insurance liability. He'll understand."

"I'm on it," Maja said mechanically, adding CALL JOHN to the bottom of her to-do list, before realizing that it was already on there, near the top.

When she got off the phone with the insurance agent, she dialed Ted's cell to give him the update, but it went straight to voice mail.

Maja sighed and hung up without leaving a message. What she wanted to do was to climb into bed and pull the covers over her head. But instead she forced herself to dial John's number.

Despite Cindy's chirpy enthusiasm, John did not take the news that he was going to be sued well at all. "They're trying to pin this on my guys?" he said. "That's bullshit."

"They said something about the garage door opener being left out," Maja said.

John let out a short breath. "I don't know anything about that," he said. "We'll have to let the damn insurance companies figure it out."

His tone didn't give Maja much comfort. "In the meantime," she said, "I'm not sure if there's much we can do at the house."

"I'll have my guys board it up," John said. "Then I guess we'll see what happens."

"When this is all figured out, we'd still like to have you finish the work on the house," Maja said, trying to sound hopeful.

There was a long pause, and then John made a noncommittal noise before quickly getting off the phone.

When Maja hung up, she crossed out CALL JOHN from her to-do list, and then added a new item: ASK ANEETA FOR CONTRACTOR RECOMMENDATIONS.

17

When Will went into the locker room to change for track practice on Thursday afternoon, he saw three boys huddled together, laughing as they looked at a cell phone. One of the boys called Will over and said, "Check this shit out."

The boy holding the phone looked up, and Will saw that it was Brendan, the kid who'd asked him about the party in the parking lot on Monday morning. Brendan snapped his phone closed and told the kid next to him to shut up.

The kid didn't take the hint. "Dude, show him the picture!" he insisted, but Brendan shook his head. The other kid grabbed the phone, and Brendan tried to snatch it back, but he was too slow. Will grabbed it before Brendan could get ahold of it.

Will flipped open the phone and stared at the screen. He had an idea of what he was going to see—he'd already seen it, after all, the night of the house party. Even so, it was hard for him to look at the picture of Maddie passed out on the floor. Just looking at the picture gave him the same rush of adrenaline that he'd felt that night as he pushed the kid through the screen and off the deck.

Will looked up from the phone and found a target for his rage. Brendan was saying something, but Will wasn't listening. "You took these?" he asked, clenching the phone in his fist and stepping close to Brendan.

"No, no, man. Come on. I wouldn't do that," Brendan said. He sounded scared. He was caught between Will and the gym lockers, and his two friends were backing away.

"Then how'd you get them?" Will asked, his face almost touching Brendan's.

"What's she, your girlfriend or something? You know, your friend was all over her. I'm not the guy who did anything." Then, seeing the enraged look on Will's face, he said, "Look, I'm not the only one who has them. It's nothing personal."

"It's fucking personal!" Will yelled, and he swung at Brendan, catching him hard across his left cheek.

Brendan slid halfway down the lockers, clutching his eye. He let out a moan, and then he focused on Will with his good eye. The words made no sense to Will. His friend was all over her? He'd never seen the kid who'd hurt Maddie before in his life.

Before he knew what he was doing, he was punching Brendan over and over again, the phone still curled in his fist. It felt so good to hit him that he never wanted to stop. With each solid slam of his fist into flesh, the force that had been building up inside him unbearably over the last few days was finally set loose.

The locker room door banged open and Will's track coach ran in. He grabbed Will under his arms and dragged him, still swinging, to the showers. As the cold water poured down on Will, he took big gulps of air, trying to catch his breath.

"What is going on with you, O'Connor?" the coach shouted, shaking his head. He tossed him a towel. "Dry off. We're going to the principal's office."

Dr. Johnson sat on the edge of his desk, his arms folded. "You know," he said. "This is the first time that you've been in my office for a disciplinary matter in four years at this school. Not like your brother. He was in here all the time. It's a shame. He was a smart kid, but he made bad choices."

"Maybe I'm more like him than you think," Will said, feeling reckless.

"Maybe," Dr. Johnson said. "But I don't think so. I guess we'll see. At any rate, I should suspend you."

Will swallowed. A suspension would go on his record. It was the last thing he needed right now. "It was between me and Brendan," Will said. "It was personal. There's no reason why the school needs to get involved in our fight."

"It's not really a fight if only one person is doing the hitting," Dr. Johnson said. "That's just a beating."

Will couldn't argue with that. "What's going to happen?" he asked.

"I'll speak with Brendan, and then I'll decide," Dr. Johnson replied. "In the meantime, I'll be calling your parents."

"Great," Will said. Things were already tense at home. His parents were going to hit the roof when they learned he might be suspended.

Maddie heard Will had been hauled into the principal's office for fighting. She was leaning against the wall of the school when he came barreling through the front doors, letting them slam shut behind him. She jogged after him and caught up in a few steps. "Bad day?" she asked.

"Yeah," he answered. "How about you?"

"Same," she said. "Let's get out of here."

They hopped into Will's pickup and peeled out of the school parking lot. Maddie wanted to ask him what had happened, but it didn't seem like he wanted to talk. She could understand that.

"Where do you want to go?" he asked her.

"Anywhere but home," she replied.

"Same," he said. "Let's go out to the tree house. No one will be there."

He didn't say anything else, and she fiddled with the radio, running through the stations. Nothing good was on. From her purse she pulled an airplane bottle of Absolut that she'd taken from her parents' bar and downed it in two gulps. She winced, then pulled out a second one and did the same.

Will raised his eyebrows, but she turned away to stare out the window, and he didn't say anything.

As he pulled onto a road lined thickly with trees, a deer leaped out in front of them, its knobby legs sending it sailing across the road. It happened so quickly that Will didn't have time to hit the brakes.

The deer turned its head at the last second and stared at them with eyes that were wide and terrified. Will swerved hard to the right, and missed hitting it by inches.

"Dumb animals," he muttered.

Maddie put her hand on Will's knee. "That was close."

As soon as her hand touched his knee, he leaned over and kissed her. It was the first time he'd done that since the night of the party. He'd been so distant. She'd worried that he wouldn't want to touch her after what had happened.

Another car came up behind them and started honking. "Alright," Will said, hitting the gas. "We're moving."

Will parked the truck in the public lot for the orchard rather than pulling up to the house, and Maddie followed him into the woods behind the farm.

They climbed onto the platform of the tree house, and talked for a few minutes before Will kissed her again. "Is this okay?" he asked her, and she nodded.

It felt better to kiss than to talk. Easier. Thoughts tried to crowd in, but she pushed them away. As long as they were kissing, she didn't have to think. She'd wondered if she would be able to do this again, but it felt okay. She just wanted to feel normal. To be wanted. She kissed his neck, and then she pulled back from him. Her head felt hazy from the vodka.

"Do you want to?" she asked, leaving the question half-spoken.

"Maddie," Will said, and then there was a long pause. He drew her face forward and kissed the top of her head. "I want to. But is it a good idea?"

"What do you mean?" she asked. But she had a sinking feeling that she knew what he meant. She'd been right—he didn't want to sleep with her. She was damaged goods.

Will seemed to understand what she was thinking. "No. I mean, after what happened," he said. "Are you okay?"

Maddie was already pulling away. "Why does everyone keep asking me that?" she snapped. She felt close to tears.

"Because we're worried about you," Will said.

"Really?" Maddie asked. "Because it seems like everyone is a lot more worried about what happened to that house, and whether or not they're going to get caught and get in trouble."

"*I'm* worried about you," Will said. His voice sounded strained, too high. Maddie realized that he didn't want to be having this conversation any more than she did.

"I don't want people to worry about me. I just want things to go back to how they were," she said, gulping back a sob.

"Maddie," Will said, "maybe you should go to the police. What that kid did isn't okay. I could probably give the police a description if you thought it would help."

"No," Maddie said quickly. "They would know that you were at the party."

"I don't care," Will said. "I think they know anyway. Maybe it's better if we come forward. I wanted to, that night. Trip asked me not to say anything. But if it would help you . . ."

"No," Maddie said again. "I don't want to tell anyone. It's probably better to just forget it ever happened." It looked like Will was going to argue with her, and she suddenly felt as if she needed to get away. She couldn't bear the way he was looking at her—with pity. She stood and picked up her backpack. "I'm going to call my mom for a ride," she said. And then she jumped down from the tree house and took off through the woods, not turning to see if Will came after her.

18

∽

Detective Murray was just pulling into police headquarters on Friday when his phone buzzed. He answered, listened for a minute, and then let out a low whistle before dialing Jake Tillman's number.

"You busy?" he asked when Jake picked up.

"No, I'm just having a drink at the country club," Jake replied.

"With Hal?" Murray asked, surprised.

"No, I'm joking. I'm at the office," Jake said. "What's up?"

"There's a student at the high school who has something to report. The principal just called into the station. Want to head over with me to check it out?"

"See you there," Jake said.

They met in the parking lot. "This could be it," Murray said. "We just need one kid to talk and then they'll all start coming forward. No one wants to be the last kid left holding the bag."

Inside the high school, Jake noticed the plush carpeting and the slight smell of chlorine from the indoor pool. In the lobby there were groups of lounge chairs where kids sat typing on slick-looking laptops. Jake could imagine the well-stocked chemistry labs, the state-of-the-art gymnasium—all of the bells and whistles that the steep local real estate taxes could buy. Kids around here didn't need to go to private school. This practically *was* a private school.

Down the hall, the secretary ushered them into the principal's office. It was large, with shelves holding trophies and plaques lining the walls. The principal was a tall man, about fifty years old, with thinning hair and wire rim glasses. He sat behind the desk, his chin resting on his pressed-together fingers.

In front of him, a girl sat hunched over in her chair. She had a long ponytail and was wearing a T-shirt from a local 5K. She looked like she'd been crying, but now her eyes were dry and she was staring at her hands in her lap. Jake noted a woman sitting slightly apart from the others, against the wall, with a notebook in her hand and a concerned look on her face.

The principal shook hands with Jake and Murray. "Dr. Johnson," he introduced himself, and Jake glanced back down at the nameplate on the desk with a flicker of amusement: STEPHEN JOHNSON, PHD. That kind of doctor.

"Thanks for coming right away," he said. "I've heard some concerning reports today. Nothing to do with the school," he added quickly. "But concerning nonetheless. Olivia? Do you want to tell these gentlemen what you told me?"

The girl seemed to hunch over further in her seat, but she didn't say anything. Dr. Johnson cleared his throat. "Maybe I'll start. Olivia Park, here, is a sophomore in Ms. Grady's history class." Dr. Johnson gestured in the direction of the woman taking notes. "Olivia became very upset during Ms. Grady's class this afternoon. When she couldn't calm down, Ms. Grady sent her to the nurse, and Olivia told the nurse that there was an incident. Again, I want to be clear, it was not on school property, but it did involve one of our students. It seems that there may have been an assault." Dr. Johnson glanced over at Ms. Grady. "A, uh, sexual assault. Possibly."

At the principal's announcement, Jake and Detective Murray exchanged surprised glances. This wasn't what they were expecting.

Murray sat down in the chair opposite the girl. "Olivia? I'm Detective Murray. I'm an officer with the New Falls Police Department. Is there something that you'd like to talk to me about?"

Olivia finally looked up from her lap, but she didn't reply.

Murray tried again. "Did somebody hurt you?"

Before she could answer, Ms. Grady interrupted. "Excuse me, but shouldn't Olivia's parents be called? I mean, before she speaks to the police?"

Jake glanced at Murray, expecting him to be annoyed, but his face betrayed nothing but polite concern. He didn't take his eyes off of Olivia's face as he replied: "Of course, if you'd be more comfortable, Olivia, we can call your parents. But if there's something that you'd like to tell us without them here, that's also okay."

Olivia was already shaking her head. The idea that her parents might be called seemed to make up her mind. "Nobody hurt me," she said emphatically. "It was . . . well, it was another girl. From school. I saw, I mean I heard about it. She was . . ." Olivia paused, seemingly unable to find the right words, or unwilling to say them in a room full of adults and strangers. "She was sexually assaulted," she finally said, borrowing the principal's words. "Someone gave her some kind of drugs, and she was really out of it. It's all anyone's been talking about." She crossed her arms over her chest and stared at Murray, the principal, and Ms. Grady, almost as if she resented having to explain this to them, as if they should already have heard and done something about it. Just another failure of the clueless grown-ups.

As a prosecutor, Jake heard a lot of lies, and some truth, and he had learned that one was often embedded in the other. People lied for all sorts of reasons—to protect themselves, for attention, or simply because they wanted something to be true so badly that they started to believe their own inventions. Jake sensed that the girl was lying, but also that she was telling the truth. He wondered if she was trying to hide something more important to her, possibly, than the assault.

Detective Murray continued to question Olivia, but he wasn't getting much more out of her. She had become much calmer after she made her announcement. She seemed to feel that she had done her duty by alerting an adult, and she wasn't going to be pushed any further. But she absolutely refused to share the girl's name. Dr. Johnson sat back in his chair, took his glasses off, and rubbed his eyes. Jake could tell that he was already losing interest, now that it turned out that the girl sitting in his office had not been assaulted, and that he was listening to, at best, a secondhand story. No doubt he had heard a lot of gossip and hysteria in his years at the high school. He looked as if he wanted to wrap this up as quickly as possible.

Murray was making notes in his little book. "And, I'm sorry, where did you say this took place?"

"At the party," she replied, exasperated. Then her eyes went wide. "Oh, I don't think I actually said . . ."

"A party." Murray kept his voice even. "And when was this party?"

"Last Friday night," Olivia whispered, realizing that there was no point in trying to backtrack.

"Do you know who was there?"

This put Olivia in a tough spot. If she denied knowing anyone who was at the party, they would know that she was lying. But if she gave them names, she would be getting people into trouble. She looked out the window and didn't answer.

Murray pushed on. "Did this party happen to take place on River Road?"

Olivia's head snapped back around and she looked right at Murray. "Um, yeah. Maybe."

Dr. Johnson was fidgeting with a heavy metal top on his desk, spinning it and catching it before it spun off of his desk. Now he slapped it down midspin.

"Olivia, you are wasting this officer's time. You came to us to report an assault, but you won't tell us who was hurt, or where it happened. This is a serious matter, and I have to insist that you tell Detective Murray what you know."

Olivia immediately burst into fresh tears, and Murray looked annoyed. He had been getting somewhere with the girl.

"I didn't mean to make this a big deal," she whispered. "I was just upset. I'm sorry that I said anything." She bit her lip, and then seemed to make up her mind. "I wasn't there."

A lie, Jake thought.

"Can you tell me who *was* there?" Murray asked, not calling her on it. "If you can help us figure out what happened, or who organized the party, the police department would be very grateful. And I'm sure you'd like to get this over with and back to class."

The possibility of ending the interview worked on her. "I heard June Jeffries and Brendan Sullivan talking about it at choir practice," she said. "I don't know if they were there," she added. "But they were talking about it."

Murray wrote the names down in his book. Then he started running through the list of the names of the kids that he had ticketed on the road for underage-drinking, to see if Olivia had heard anything about them being at a party. Olivia shook her head at each one, looking at the floor. Already she seemed to regret giving up the names that she had. The last name on Murray's list was William O'Connor. At the mention of his name, Olivia looked up. "Will," she started, and then stopped. "I don't really know him," she said.

A bell rang, the loud electronic buzz startling everyone gathered in the office. Olivia looked hopeful, as if she might be about to be dismissed.

Murray stood up and reached into his pocket. He pulled out two of his cards and handed one to Olivia and one to Ms. Grady. He thanked Olivia for coming forward and told her that she could call him anytime, and that she should tell her friend the same. "Nobody gets in trouble for coming forward to report a crime," he assured her. Olivia slipped the card into her backpack and hightailed it out of the office.

"So that's it?" Ms. Grady asked, surprised.

Murray shrugged. "At this point, it's just a rumor. Hopefully Olivia will talk to her friend, and she'll come forward. In the meantime, we'll be speaking with other students to see if anyone knows anything. We'll see what we turn up." He consulted his notebook then turned to the principal. "Dr. Johnson, I'd like to have a word with June Jeffries and Brendan Sullivan. Do you know where we can find them?"

Dr. Johnson looked at Jake. "Are we on solid ground here? Legally? I mean, should I be alerting the parents?"

"I don't see an issue," Jake said. "Detective Murray here is simply seeking information about a possible crime. If it becomes necessary to take anyone into custody, we will of course contact the parents. But I don't see any reason to get them involved at this stage."

Dr. Johnson looked relieved. It was clear that he wanted this over and out of his territory as soon as possible. He looked at his watch. "It's last period. Ms. Grady, can you have the front desk pull the schedules for those students?"

Ms. Grady left and came back a moment later with two printed class schedules. Dr. Johnson consulted them and then took a yearbook down from the shelf and began to page through it. He pointed to a black-and-white headshot of a pretty young woman wearing pearls. "This is June Jeffries. She's a senior. You can find her in the cafeteria. Study hall. And here is Brendan Sullivan." Dr. Johnson indicated a kid whose face was still holding on to its baby fat under curly dark hair. "He's a junior. Looks like he should be in the technology lab."

Dr. Johnson glanced at his watch again. "Now, gentlemen, I'm afraid that I have parents waiting to meet with me. If there's anything else I can do . . ."

Jake and Murray thanked Dr. Johnson and Ms. Grady for their time, and left the office.

"This complicates things," Murray said to Jake. "Think she was telling the truth?"

"A version of it, at least. She didn't give us much to go on."

"I think we can use it, though," Murray said. "Kids might be more willing to talk to us if they think we're just investigating an assault, and not the party itself. Starting with June Jeffries."

In the cafeteria, Jake scanned the room, looking for June. His eyes lit on a familiar face, a slender girl with dark brown hair who was sitting at a computer. She looked surprised to see him, and gave a little wave. He waved back, wracking his brain. Of course, it was Rosanne. Or Rosie, that was it. Her dad owned the restaurant where Jake ate dinner a few nights a week. She waited tables, and he had seen her studying there, her books propped up on the bar. He had assumed that she must be a college student.

Murray followed his gaze.

"She waits tables at Al's," Jake explained.

"Oh, right, I think I've seen her there," Murray replied, then pointed to a girl reading a magazine, her long black hair spilling over it like a curtain. "Hey, there's our girl." June Jeffries was wearing a T-shirt and shorts that were so short Jake couldn't help wondering if schools had given up on dress codes. He spoke to the study hall proctor in the hallway, who then called June over. Her manner was polite, and she frowned in a way that was meant to convey that she understood the seriousness of their presence, if not the reason. "What can I help you with?" June asked, biting her lip and sounding concerned.

"We're investigating a possible assault of a student," Murray explained. "We're looking for anyone with information. We were told you might be able to help us," he added, the fib meant to keep her at ease.

June was quiet for a moment, as if she was thinking. "Who told you that?" she finally asked, surprising Jake with her question.

Detective Murray knew better than to take it further. He pivoted. "What were you up to last Friday night?"

"I don't remember," she replied. Too quickly, Jake thought. He watched as she swallowed hard and looked off to the side.

"You don't remember where you were last weekend?" Murray pressed.

Now she smiled, meeting Murray's eyes again. "I'd have to check my planner. It's the end of senior year. It's a really busy time."

It was one of those statements that was both so innocuous on its face, and so ludicrous when you really considered it, that Jake's interest was immediately aroused. A sharpening in Murray's voice told him that the detective felt the same way.

"There was a party on River Road. A lot of kids were there. Does that jog your memory?"

Jake wasn't sure exactly what he was expecting, but it wasn't what happened next. The polite concern dropped from June's face, and she pursed her lips and looked them both over, her face registering her disregard for what she saw.

"This isn't an interrogation, is it?" she asked, placing her hands on her hips. "Because I know my rights. And I have a right to an attorney."

Murray held up his hands and smiled, unruffled. "Slow down. We're just trying to find out if someone hurt one of your friends. You don't have to talk to us, but we sure could use your help. Too many of these crimes go unreported."

"That's right," June said, making up her mind. "I don't have to talk to you. I think I'd better call my lawyer."

"Your lawyer?" Murray asked. Jake almost laughed, but he managed to turn it into a cough.

"Yeah," June said. "My dad. He's a lawyer. In New York. And I think he's going to be very interested to hear that the police are questioning students without their parents present."

Before Jake could open his mouth to assure her that she could call a parent if she'd feel more comfortable, June had already turned, tossed her hair, and marched back into the cafeteria without another word.

"That went well," Jake said, shaking his head.

"It's a start," Murray said. "Innocent teenagers don't immediately demand to speak with their lawyers."

The technology lab, Jake noticed, was top-notch, with long rows of shiny silver Apple computer screens lining the desks. The back half of the large room was filled with what would have been called shop equipment when Jake was in school, but was probably called engineering equipment now. The instructor was involved with a group of students at a table who were huddled over a machine that looked like a cross between a vacuum cleaner and a robot.

Brendan was typing away furiously at one of the computer stations. He looked just like his yearbook photo, except for the blue-black shiner under his left eye.

Jake spoke with the instructor, who seemed dubious about letting them pull Brendan out to the hallway. But just then one of the kids working on the robot vacuum thing lit a blowtorch, and the instructor waived them away impatiently, turning back to his students.

In the hallway, Brendan immediately started to sweat, his dark curls sticking to his forehead. Jake could feel Murray tense, like a dog that had caught a scent.

Murray hadn't even asked him a question before Brendan started speaking. "Is this about the fight?" he asked. "Because Will started it. He sucker punched me."

"Will O'Connor?" Murray asked, and Brenan nodded.

A fight made sense, Murray thought. It would explain how some of the damage at the house had occurred. "That must have been some party, huh?" Murray asked.

"What?" Brendan said with a frown. "No, I had nothing to do with that fight. Will O'Connor jumped me in the locker room. Here, at school."

Murray was thrown, but only for a second. "But there was a fight at the party? The one on River Road?" He went out on a limb: "Word is you were there."

"Oh, man," Brendan muttered. And then again, this time a little higher, "Oh, man."

Jake and Murray exchanged looks. Jake almost felt bad for the kid. It was too easy.

"The place got trashed," Murray said. "We're looking at trespassing, vandalism, and I'm not sure what else." He turned to Jake. "This is Assistant District Attorney Jake Tillman. He'll be handling the charges, so it's up to him, but it's not looking good."

Brendan looked miserable. "Who said I was there?"

Detective Murray shrugged. "That's just what we heard. Is it true?"

Brendan was shaking his head. "I have a pretty strict curfew," he said.

Not willing to lie, Jake thought. But also not ready to tell the truth.

"Your parents keep a pretty tight leash, huh?" Murray said. His voice was friendlier now, understanding. "How old are you, anyway?"

Brendan looked close to tears. "Seventeen."

Now Murray was all smiles. "Seventeen! Well, there you go. If it turned out for some reason that you were there, that's the magic number."

Brendan looked hopeful. He was drowning, and Detective Murray had thrown him a rope. "It is?"

"Sure. You're under eighteen—still a minor. The courts usually go easy on juveniles."

The mention of the courts was the last straw. A few tears slipped through his dark lashes, and he turned and quickly wiped them away.

"Of course, there *are* other options," Murray went on, as if he hadn't noticed. "We could use some help figuring out who was responsible. I mean, you didn't plan this party, did you? It wasn't your idea, right?" Brendan shook his head furiously, and Murray kept going: "You seem like a good kid, Brendan. If you can help us figure out what happened, maybe we can forget all about this."

Brendan winced, but he repeated Murray's words—"forget all about this"—and he seemed to be thinking. He was about to speak when the instructor stuck his head out of the classroom door.

"Brendan," he said. "I need you back in the classroom. It's your team's turn with the blowtorch." He frowned at Murray and Tillman. "If you need to speak to this student further, I suggest that you contact his parents. I'm happy to give them a call right now if it would help."

All of the color drained out of Brendan's face. Murray knew that if the parents were called at this moment, the kid would deny everything.

"I think we're finished," Murray said.

Brendan started to follow his teacher back into the lab, but he turned at the last minute, one hand gently testing the swollen flesh under his eye. "You should ask Will O'Connor what happened to those big glass windows," he said. "And his friend. Some rich kid. He was handing out ecstasy like it was candy. A lot of the girls were real messed up thanks to him."

Murray perked up. "You know that kid's name?" he asked, but Brendan just shrugged and disappeared back into the classroom.

"Will O'Connor," Jake said as they walked back out to the parking lot. "Now, there's a name that just keeps coming up. Think this was his shindig?"

"That certainly would be convenient, since we've basically got him at the scene with that underage-drinking ticket," Murray agreed. "But the fact is, we still haven't heard much more than rumors. We need something solid if we're going to make any of the charges stick."

"The kids are protecting one another," Tillman said. "Think they can keep it up?"

"All we need is one kid to come forward," Murray said. "Let's keep the pressure on. Someone will break."

19

On Monday morning, Jake printed out his notes on the house party case and slipped them into a manila folder, along with the pictures from the scene and photocopies of the underage-drinking tickets.

It was unusual for Hal to call a meeting at this point in a case. That was one thing Jake admired about Hal—he trusted his deputies, and, as he liked to say, he let them have their head. Every year he cherry-picked a few cases to handle himself, or to follow closely. Even the staid Hart County served up an occasional dead body or unexplained fire. But for most of the run-of-the-mill incidents—hit-and-runs, domestic violence—Jake ran his own cases. If Hal wanted to meet now, while the investigation was still ongoing, he must consider the case serious. And Jake agreed. Something about this one bothered him.

When Jake entered Hal's office, Hal and the police chief, Bob Whitman, were already deep in conversation. The chief was wearing a dark uniform suit and tie, but Hal was in his full DA regalia: tweed suit complete with vest, pocket square, and round horn-rimmed glasses. He liked to dress the part of the country lawyer.

"Come on in, Jake," Hal boomed. "I was just telling Bob here that he's lucky to have you on this case. That you'll know exactly how to handle such a delicate matter."

"Chief," Jake said, nodding. Delicate wasn't exactly how he would have described the case, but he guessed that Hal was referring to all of the kids involved. It was going to be tricky separating out responsibility and charges between the kids who would be routed to juvenile court and those, like Trip O'Connor, whom they could fully charge as adults.

Chief Whitman offered up his hand for a shake, and Jake took it. "Tillman. Didn't I see you at the country club last week? You played in the Union Club charity tournament, didn't you?"

Jake laughed as he sat down across from the chief. "No, afraid not. My golf is a bit rusty. I don't think I've been out since law school."

Jake was ready for the small talk to be over. He knew, though, that if he was serious about aiming for Hal's job at some point, he should probably suck it up and start getting in good with the chief. Even if that meant investing in some golf clubs.

"Here," Jake said, handing copies of his file to Hal and Chief Whitman. "I'll run through what we have so far, and then we can discuss the possible charges."

Hal took the file, but didn't look at it. Jake started anyway.

"I've been working closely with Detective Murray. He's still interviewing possible witnesses, but we do have a few people we can pin near the scene, and a possible ID on who bought the alcohol." Jake was doing his best to glide over the fact that they still had very little evidence to connect anyone directly to the party. "As far as charges go, once we identify the organizers, I'm thinking it will run the gamut: criminal trespass, corruption of minors, vandalism, criminal mischief. We might be limited to trespass for some of the kids, but we're still working on getting the full picture. And of course we'll recommend restitution payments. Hit these kids—and their parents—where it hurts: the pocketbook."

Jake had Hal's full attention now. "Criminal mischief? That's three and a half to seven. That's a serious charge."

Jake frowned. Neither Hal nor Chief Whitman had opened their files yet. "It was some pretty serious destruction," he said. "Have you seen Murray's report? We're talking probably half a million in damage."

"I spoke with Detective Murray," Chief Whitman said. "In fact, I've asked him to back off a bit. I had an earful from Mike Jeffries,

June Jeffries's father. Does that name ring a bell? He's an old friend. He called my office and said his daughter had been interrogated at school. Said she was so upset she had to stay at home the next day to deal with the anxiety of being ambushed in the hallway."

Jake snorted. He couldn't help it. He had a clear memory of June Jeffries coolly lying to them and then pulling out the my-dad-is-a-lawyer card before they could challenge her on it. The thought of that girl needing a mental health day was rich. But the chief didn't look happy, and neither did Hal. This was not going how Jake thought it would, and he had a moment of uncertainty, wondering if they'd gone too far by visiting the school.

He leaned back in his chair. "Hey, I was there, and everything was by the book. There was a report at the school that a girl was assaulted at a party—sounds like the same party—so Murray asked a few questions. It was definitely not an interrogation."

"An assault?" Hal asked, obviously hearing about it for the first time.

Jake winced. This would muddy the waters, and Murray hadn't turned up any further information. "Just rumors so far. We don't even have a name to go with the victim, so there's not much we can do until someone comes forward."

Hal sighed and traded looks with the chief. "Alright, this is how it's going to go. No more visits to the school. If Detective Murray needs to talk to any kids, let's do it in their living rooms, with the parents there. Murray knows, the chief spoke with him." Hal finally glanced down at the file. "Trip O'Connor. That kid's a punk. And also not a kid anymore, so let's concentrate on him. It's a shame—the parents are nice people—but that boy is just bad news. Let's look at the brother too—William? Local yokels, right, Bob? As for the rest of these kids, it sounds to me like a year-end party just got a bit out of hand. I'm assuming that the majority of the charges will be for simple trespass." He flipped through the file until he reached the list of kids that had been ticketed on the road. He raised his eyebrows. "I know a few of these names. They're good kids, but they made a mistake. Let's not rock the boat."

Jake couldn't believe what he was hearing. "Hal, all due respect, but have you seen the photos? This was a lot more than a mistake. We're not talking about a few beer cans left in an empty house. They threw a toilet through a window."

Jake couldn't be sure, but he thought Hal might have stifled a laugh. He was shaking his head. "Terrible. Like I said, we're not going to look the other way here. Where it makes sense to bring full charges, I want you to do it. But for most of these kids, let's keep it quick and light."

"A slap on the wrist?" Jake asked, his voice sarcastic.

"Exactly," Hal replied, either not noticing Jake's tone, or deciding to ignore it. "This isn't a case that looks good for anyone. Not for us, going after a bunch of kids. Not for the police department, which, sorry, Chief, missed it in the first place." The chief shrugged, and Hal went on. "None of us comes out of this case looking like a hero. If it was some punks from the city, maybe, but not with local kids."

Wow, Jake thought. Hal was actually saying the quiet part out loud. If it was kids from the city—Black kids was what he meant—they'd be all over this case. But these kids from the suburbs, who'd had every advantage, whose parents had the police chief on speed dial, were going to get to walk. "But what about the Jensens?" he asked. "Their home was destroyed."

For a second, Hal's face looked blank, and then it registered. "The homeowners. Out-of-towners, right? Have they come in yet?"

"Yes, I met with them. They're not going to be satisfied with trespassing charges. They're devastated—they're basically going to have to rebuild."

"Terrible. Like I said, let's deal with this as quickly as possible, so that they can move on with their lives. I'm sure that's what they want." Hal closed the file. "Thanks, Jake. Keep me in the loop."

Jake walked back to his office, his face burning. Why did he feel like he was somehow in the wrong for putting together a case against these teenagers? These *criminals*, he corrected himself. He had the uncomfortable feeling that he'd been told on, and in a way he had, with June

Jeffries's father calling the chief to complain. Once again, the entitlement of these kids, and their parents, blew him away. Instead of being concerned that his daughter might be involved in a crime, the father was upset that the police had even spoken to her.

It was clear to Jake that Hal wanted no part of the case. He may have been worried about how it would look to his golf buddies and their kids, but Jake knew there were plenty of people in Hart County who would resent the idea of a bunch of rich kids destroying a home and getting away with it. Not for the first time, Jake thought that Hal might be ready for retirement. He seemed out of touch. But if Jake was able to push the case forward on his own, and get a big win, it could be huge for his career. Maybe even a flagship case, if he decided to run for DA down the road. Jake shook his head. He was getting ahead of himself. Without Hal's support, it would be very difficult to bring serious charges. But it was certainly an idea.

That evening, Jake pulled up a barstool at the counter of Alejandro's Diner, threw his jacket over the back of the seat, and arranged his newspaper and his cell phone in front of him. He didn't need to look at the menu—he ate here two or three nights a week, and he rotated through a few favorite dishes.

The girl behind the counter—the owner's daughter whom Jake had noticed at the high school—poured him a glass of water.

"So, what's it going to be?" She closed her eyes as if trying to divine the future. "Steak salad, side of black beans, no red onion?" She opened one eye and glanced at him. "Nope, I've got it. Chicken tortilla soup, green salad. Am I right?"

Jake laughed. "Soup it is. I love your dad's chicken soup."

"I know. It's really good. I like it with habanero sauce—you should try that. It was my mom's recipe. It always makes me think of her."

Jake realized that he had never seen Al's wife in the restaurant. He hadn't thought to wonder about it. "Oh," he said awkwardly. "Well, it's a great recipe."

She scribbled his order on her pad. "I'll just run this to the kitchen."

Jake flipped to the back of the town's weekly paper, where the police blotter was printed. There was a short item about vandalism at the house, but nothing about the kids that Detective Murray had ticketed on the road. The town was small enough that almost everything made it onto the blotter. Even cars colliding with deer could make it in if it was a slow week, especially if they went through the windshield. Incidents involving minors were generally not included, however. Jake turned back to the front page, but there was nothing else about the party, as he had expected.

The girl came back from the kitchen. She placed a bottle of home-made hot sauce in front of him and refilled his water.

"I saw you at school on Monday," she said. "I didn't know that you were a police officer. You're never in uniform. Are you a detective?"

Jake smiled. "I'm not a police officer," he said. "I'm an attorney for the county. No uniform. Unless you count the tie."

"What were you doing at school?" she asked as she set him up with silverware.

"It's Rosie, right?" he asked her. She nodded and he went on. "I was there with the police to help gather information. There was a party last week, and a house was destroyed. We were there to see if anyone had information that could help us find the people responsible." He watched her face, wondering if she knew anything. Her name hadn't come up in any of Murray's interviews.

"I saw you talking to June," Rosie said.

Jake waited, but she didn't say anything else. "Are you two friends?" he asked.

She shrugged, and Jake thought she looked a little uncomfortable. "Sure. I've known her forever. Let me grab your dinner."

When she came back, Jake handed her his card, and one of Detective Murray's. "Listen, Rosie, if you hear anything at school that you think Detective Murray or I might need to know, you can always call us. We're investigating the vandalism at the house on the river, but there may have also been other crimes committed there." He paused for a moment and watched her face, which was hard to read as she wiped the counter with a damp towel.

"I'm usually working here," she said. "Even on the weekends."

"I know," Jake said. "But if there's anything that you hear that you think we should know, you can always give us a call."

The door behind the bar swung open and Alejandro himself came out to the counter. "Rosa," he said to his daughter, "you get back to your homework. I'll cover the counter." Then he turned to Jake. "Hey, my friend," he greeted Jake. "Long week?"

"You know it," Jake said, and Al reached into the case below the counter and pulled out two cold bottles of Heineken. "I won't tell if you don't," Al joked, as he popped the caps. Only the fancier restaurants in town had the pricey liquor licenses required to sell alcohol. "It's not a crime if it's on the house." Jake winked, and took a long and very welcome drink.

"So, what's the word on that house that got destroyed?" Al asked him. "I had a customer in here last week told me every window was kicked out. Teenagers?"

Jake hesitated. "I shouldn't say too much, but it wasn't just the windows. They kicked in the drywall, tore the cabinet doors off, the works. This wasn't collateral damage. It was like the people at the party *wanted* to destroy it. It's hard to understand."

Al whistled. "No respect," he said. "Some of these kids, they got no idea. They never had to work a day in their lives. You know, I used to have some of them come in here after school. They'd order coffee, or something to eat. They weren't loud, and they always paid. But they'd steal stuff. Dumb stuff—the saltshakers, the silverware. It was nothing anyone would want. At first I thought I was imagining it, but I watched them, and the girls would just slip stuff into their purses."

Jake looked down at the silverware. The most you could say for it was that it was serviceable. "Why do you think they did it?"

"I'll tell you why," Al said. "They're bored. It's like a game to them. When you're given everything, nothing has value. All you have are these little thrills."

"So what did you do?" Jake asked. "Kick them out?"

Al shrugged. "That doesn't fly around here. You make a scene, you're going to have angry parents in here. Nasty reviews on Yelp. It's not worth it. But I told all my employees that when they come in, you give them the to-go forks, and clear the vases off the table when you take their order." He gave a dry laugh. "I guess I'm lucky they didn't break in here and throw a party. But they're not all bad. Rosa's friends are nice kids. It just comes down to how they're raised."

20

The School Board meeting for May was the last one of the school year, and it was usually sparsely attended. Tonight, however, parents were pouring into the auditorium.

Dr. Johnson was not entirely unprepared for the turnout. For the past two weeks the school office had been fielding a steady stream of phone calls from concerned, and sometimes irate, parents. They wanted to know why their kids had been questioned by the police at school, who was supplying their underage children with alcohol and drugs, and what the school intended to do about it. The call from June Jeffries's father had been a particularly unpleasant conversation, and Dr. Johnson saw that he and his wife, Kim, the head of the PTA, had arrived early and were sitting in the front row of seats.

At the back of the auditorium, Dr. Johnson saw Jake Tillman, the assistant DA who was working on the case. He was speaking to a blond woman who sat in the seat next to him. Dr. Johnson didn't recognize her. She looked like she'd gotten lost on her way to an off-Broadway performance and instead wandered into a PTA meeting by mistake. Tillman was pointing discreetly to a few of the parents in the rows ahead of them, and the woman followed his gaze and frowned. Dr. Johnson wondered if she might be the person who owned the house, who he'd heard was from out of town. If she was, she was about to get a pretty real look at her new neighbors.

The board president had been briefed by Dr. Johnson and the chief of police on the matter, but he had no wish to take a public stand at this point. He called the meeting to order and glanced down at his notes.

"As usual," he said, "we will reserve the first thirty minutes of the meeting for public comments. Please remember to state your name and address for the record, and keep comments limited to three minutes per person."

Kim Jeffries was first in line at the microphone that was set up in front of the stage, of course.

"Our kids are under extreme pressure, academic and social," she said into the mic. "They are trying their best to navigate a difficult world. And I, for one, think that school should be their *safe space*." She paused to look around, eyebrows raised, as the other parents nodded. "Instead, it's become a place where they can be pulled out of class, willy-nilly, to be grilled by the police. These are *children*. We should be protecting them, not trying to trick them into talking to the police about things they know nothing about, and without their parents present. The school didn't so much as contact the concerned parents *before or after* this incident. The administration has a duty to protect these students, and they have failed. Completely." She turned and looked right at Dr. Johnson. "I think we all know there is a certain element in New Falls that is unfortunate, but unavoidable. In a rural area like this, there will always be a segment of the population that isn't as focused on . . . let's just say, *success*. If the police can't deal with that, that is an issue for another meeting. But to drag our children, our students, into it . . . it's shocking."

Dr. Johnson had to hand it to her. Her husband might be the successful litigator, but Kim Jeffries had the crowd of parents eating out of her well-manicured hand. In a few quick sentences, she'd offered up to parents worried their kids might be at fault a host of alternative villains: the school, the police force, and the "rural element," by which he assumed she meant anyone who was more focused on paying their mortgage than paying for SAT prep.

"New Falls High has always had an excellent reputation," Mrs. Jeffries continued. "But I'd like to remind the board, and the administrators, that a school is only as good as its students, and its families. Many families in New Falls that could easily send their children to private schools make the choice to send them here. I've always considered it a good thing for the community, and a good thing for my daughter, to support our local public school. But the school's reputation could change very quickly if parents can't be assured that their children are safe here."

Dr. Johnson glanced at his watch. Kim's three minutes were almost up, thankfully.

"The school needs to take responsibility for involving our kids in this sordid business," she concluded. "We expect an apology, and we expect that this will never happen to another innocent student. Thank you."

Mrs. Jeffries returned to her seat to enthusiastic applause. But Dr. Johnson also noticed more than a few people who were sitting with their arms folded or whispering angrily to each other.

There were, in Dr. Johnson's opinion, bigger issues at play here than a few disgruntled parents. First was the shocking nature of the property crime. He'd seen the pictures, and although it was like nothing he'd seen before, he had no doubt that at least some of his students had been involved. There'd been enough gossip at the school that some of it had bubbled up even to him. And he'd worked with teenagers long enough to know that where there was gossip, there was probably guilt.

The next parent was at the mic, and Dr. Johnson heard a saying that always rubbed him the wrong way: "Kids will be kids! We need to look at this in context." Dr. Johnson worked hard at keeping his face neutral. The excuse that kids will be kids made sense when a toddler drew on the walls or yanked a toy out of another kid's hands. It did not apply when teenagers ripped out a stranger's appliances and punched holes in their walls. The second issue that concerned Dr. Johnson was the possible assault that had been reported. He'd failed to dig up any more information about it at school, and the police didn't seem to have found anything either. And yet he sensed that something had indeed happened.

Now Linda O'Connor took the mic. Dr. Johnson had sat through plenty of meetings with her, back when her older son, Trip, was at the school. He'd been a bright boy, but he couldn't stay out of the office for ditching school and goofing around. It had taken awhile for Dr. Johnson to realize the younger brother, Will, was an entirely different story.

"We have a lot of parents up here blaming the school, saying that their kids are good kids who are being unfairly targeted by the police," Linda said. "We even had one parent up here who wanted to blame the 'rural elements' in town, whatever that means. I know it can't mean the hardworking people who grew up here, and worked the land and the shops here, well before our real farms were replaced by oversize house farms." She paused and there were a few whoops from the audience. "If anything is to blame here, I, for one, think it's the culture of wealth and entitlement that seems to have taken over our town. It's a dangerous thing for kids to think there are no consequences and to take no responsibility for their actions. There are a lot of kids in this town with a lot of money and time on their hands. We can't protect our kids from the real world, and we shouldn't try."

As Linda finished, Kim Jeffries rose to her feet: "We all know when there's trouble in town, your son Trip is usually at the center of it!" she yelled, and the room went quiet. "Why don't you take responsibility for raising a hoodlum, if that's so important to you?"

The board president was banging his gavel, and Mike Jeffries tugged at his wife's arm, urging her to sit. Linda O'Connor stood still in front of the mic. The room had started to buzz again with voices. She took a deep breath. "If either of my sons were involved, then they will come forward," she finally said, almost in a whisper. "But I hope they were not."

Before she could sit, a man from the audience stood to speak without waiting for the mic. "Linda's right," he said. "These kids are out of control. I had a boy put his car right through my fence, and the parents asked me why I didn't have reflectors up! These rich kids think they can do whatever they want, and their parents go right along with it. Well, it stops here."

"You're blaming rich people?" another woman called out, her voice incredulous. "You mean the people who actually pay taxes in this town? Success is not a crime."

Dr. Johnson quickly made his way down the aisle and grabbed the mic, patting Linda on the shoulder sympathetically. The crowd was talking loudly as Linda returned to her seat, and Dr. Johnson cleared his throat a few times before they quieted down.

"Okay, folks, let's get down to business. I'm really glad to see all of you here. Like I always say, when we are all engaged in our kids' education, we all have a chance to learn. I know emotions are running high tonight, but I want us to focus on what's important here: the safety and best interest of our students."

The crowd nodded. No one could argue with that.

"I'm going to bring District Attorney Hal Buckley up onstage." At these words, a murmur went through the room. "Hal is also the parent of a student who graduated from New Falls High School, and he has agreed to give an update on the police investigation into the house party. As to whether or not students will face consequences at the school level for their involvement, I'm not able to speak to that at this point. It is, however, always a possibility."

Hal, who had been waiting off to the side, came up onto the stage and took the mic. "Thank you, Dr. Johnson. I do appreciate this opportunity. Don't forget, I also attended this fine school. But that was so long ago that they probably didn't keep written records back then." This got a nervous laugh from the crowd. Everyone seemed to be sitting on the edge of their seat.

"Now, this is an unusual situation we have here, and our office generally does not publicly discuss an investigation at this point. However, I know that we have a lot of concerned, involved parents here in New Falls, and I want to personally assure you that the school, the police force, and the district attorney's office are handling everything in accordance with all of our rules and procedures. There is no indication that the person or persons throwing the party had any right to be there. Several local youths were ticketed nearby in conjunction with underage-drinking. In addition, evidence taken from the house indicates that the party was mainly attended by local high school students, from New Falls and the surrounding area."

Hal continued. "No charges have been filed yet. However, the police are actively investigating leads. Now, here's the important part: I want every parent here to talk to their child about this incident. Whether or not your child was involved, this is an opportunity to impress upon them the seriousness, and the possible consequences, of what can start out as typical teenage behavior. If you believe that your child attended or was involved with planning this party, I encourage you to come forward. Our office, and the police department, are committed to finding solutions here for everyone, but especially for the homeowners. I know that if any of you were in their shoes, you'd want the same. Thank you so much for your time. I won't be taking any questions tonight, but if you would like to discuss the matter further, my door is open. Goodnight."

Hal shook hands with Dr. Johnson and then exited through the stage door. Dr. Johnson saw Jake Tillman and the woman with him get up and head out the back of the auditorium. The temperature in the room had noticeably cooled, and the parents no longer looked so sure of themselves. In fact, many of them looked downright concerned. Good, thought Dr. Johnson, now we're getting somewhere.

On the sidewalk outside of the school, Maja released a breath she hadn't realized she'd been holding.

"That was tough," Jake Tillman acknowledged. "But it's good that you came. Now you can see what we're up against. Communities like this, when they sense an outside threat, they close ranks."

"I'm not a threat," Maja said. Her heart was still racing. She wasn't sure what she'd expected, but it hadn't been a debate over how fairly the *kids* were being treated. "I thought I was the victim here," she said, thinking of the handout Jake had given her.

"When it comes to kids, anything that puts their futures on the line is a threat," Tillman said. "Detective Murray's job is to convince them that it's more dangerous for them to stay silent than it is for them to come forward. Give it a few more days. At least a couple parents will decide that their odds are better if they come in and cut a deal for their kids. I know it feels like this is taking a long time, but this isn't a case to rush. There are a lot of people in town who'd like to see this whole thing swept under the rug. If we bring the charges before we have the evidence to support them, the case will fall apart pretty quickly."

Maja trusted what Jake was saying, but it had still been tough to watch her future neighbors get more worked up about the investigation than they were about the damage to her house. Jake had encouraged her to bring someone for support, but Ted was working and Aneeta had given her a thin excuse. Maybe her son actually did have a cold, Maja thought, or maybe she just wasn't ready to align herself with Maja in a town that had clearly already taken sides.

She quickly said goodbye to Jake, anxious to get away from the parents streaming out of the school. Walking back to the inn, she felt conspicuous, as if she didn't belong there. Several people had given her questioning looks at the meeting, and Maja imagined they knew who she was. It was unsettling. This town, which had seemed so perfect on the surface, was starting to look a lot darker when she peeked underneath.

21

Linda O'Connor walked into the Giant supermarket and pulled a crumpled list from her pocket. Even in the midst of what felt like a slowly unfolding disaster for her family, everyone still had to eat dinner.

Walking through the produce section, she automatically stopped by the "grown local" section to check on their produce. The Giant was good about promoting local farms, and even though they didn't make much profit on it, Linda considered it good publicity—a reminder to people in New Falls that there were still businesses like hers to support. Twice a week she had Will drive down a few cases of whatever they had on hand: apples from cold storage, bouquets of cut flowers in jam jars, and berries when they were in season.

Will—every time she thought of him her chest grew tight and she tasted foreboding like metal in her mouth. He was a teenager, so of course he wasn't normally very talkative, but in the last few weeks he had grown almost surly. He was still showing up for all of his shifts at the orchard, but aside from that she rarely saw him. He'd been staying late at school, as far as she knew. But she didn't really know, and that was the problem. Neither of her sons told her anything anymore, and the police hadn't been back since the day Officer Murray spoke with Trip out by the tractor. Trip had claimed that they weren't involved in the party. But as she thought about the late-night call from the police, summoning her husband to pick the boys up on River Road, Linda's mouth went dry. As desperate as she was to believe her sons, it would have to be quite a coincidence.

Linda absentmindedly plucked a fading flower from one of the bouquets that Will had set up on the stand and looked at her grocery list. Pasta, Cliff Bars, orange juice, and frozen pizzas. Fuel for two young men who always seemed to be standing in front of the fridge, looking for their next meal. Feeding them was one of the few remaining things they allowed her to do for them. She tried to concentrate on pushing her cart through the aisles, trying not to worry about what was going on with Will. When he needed her, she told herself, he would come to her.

She was still making her way through the produce section when she saw June Jeffries's mother coming toward her. Linda stopped short. Kim hadn't noticed her yet, and Linda took half a step, ready to abandon her cart and make a run for it. But it was too late. Kim looked up and they locked eyes.

Linda watched as Kim's face flushed. Well good, Linda thought. She should be embarrassed. She put her hand back on her cart, thinking that she wasn't going to be driven out of the supermarket by Kim Jeffries, of all people. Kim may have humiliated her at the school board meeting, but that didn't mean that Linda had to stoop to her level. Linda summoned all of her self-control and nodded stiffly at Kim. She would be polite but distant.

To her surprise, Kim didn't ignore her, but instead came barreling down the aisle like she was about to use her shopping cart to mow Linda down. Then she stopped abruptly in front of Linda, eyebrows raised, as if she expected Linda to say something.

Taken aback, Linda tried to maneuver her cart around Kim, muttering, "Excuse me," but Kim pushed her cart farther forward, blocking the way.

"Well?" Kim said, in the officious tone of voice that she used as PTA president when she was strong-arming an unsuspecting mother into making a donation or volunteering for field day.

Linda felt her own face growing red. She fought off a surge of anger, and she gripped her cart tightly, trying to maintain her calm. "What do you want, Kim?" she asked, her voice strained.

"I want to know if your son is going to come forward and admit to organizing this party," Kim said, her eyes bright. "Or if he's going to let the police continue harassing innocent children. You had a lot to say about responsibility at the school board meeting, but I haven't seen much action from your family."

"You're talking about Trip?" Linda asked. "What makes you think he organized it?" She was angry, but she was also honestly curious. Did Kim know something that she didn't?

Kim put her hands on her hips. "Where exactly do you think the kids around here get all their alcohol?" she asked. "Your son. Supplying alcohol to minors is a crime, you know." As she spoke, her tone grew louder, and the other shoppers were starting to pay attention.

"Yes, I know," Linda said, keeping her voice quiet. "But I seriously doubt that my son is supplying alcohol to all the teenagers in New Falls. Your daughter, for instance, seems bright enough to manage to get into her own trouble." She gave a dry laugh, which seemed to enrage Kim.

"My daughter has *nothing* to do with this," she hissed, her eyes bright.

A nearby shopper had stopped to listen, pretending to squeeze avocados for ripeness as she tilted her head to listen. A couple standing near the bananas was watching them, and Linda recognized them as customers at the orchard. The woman gave her a little wave. "Everything okay?" she asked, and Linda smiled tightly and nodded, hoping that they would move on.

She tried to keep her voice steady as she spoke. It was one thing for Kim to cause a scene in the grocery store, but Linda was a local business owner. She couldn't afford to do anything to damage her reputation in town, especially in a store that carried her produce. "If your daughter had nothing to do with the party," Linda said, "then how do you seem to know so much about it?"

Kim took a sharp breath. "I hear things," she said. "My husband golfs with the police chief once a month." She stated this fact like it was a threat.

"Kim, this is getting out of hand. June and Will have been friends for years. Our family is not the enemy here. If the kids got themselves into trouble, we can deal with it. Kids make mistakes. It's not the first time, and it won't be the last."

"You know, I let my daughter hang around with Will against my better judgment. He seemed like a polite, hardworking boy. Nothing like his brother, who—and I know that you don't want to hear this—was trouble from the start. I heard about his arrest for dealing marijuana last year. But I can see now that I made a mistake, and I take responsibility for that. You want to be open-minded, but when it comes to your children, you can't be too careful. Research shows that who teenagers hang out with can have a bigger impact on their futures than their grades."

Linda couldn't believe what she was hearing. "Will is going to *Princeton*," she said. "I can't believe you're saying he's a bad influence. But while we're on the subject of who our kids are hanging out with, you, Kim, seem only too happy to let June hang out with Hunter Finch. There's no trouble Will or Trip have gotten into that Hunter hasn't done or worse. But I suppose it's okay because his family has money and his father plays golf at your club. Is that right? You're a hypocrite, and if you think you're going to pin this whole thing on my sons, you'd better think again!" Without realizing it, her voice had grown louder and louder until she was yelling. There wasn't a single person in the produce section who wasn't staring at them now.

Kim stepped back, her hand on her chest, as if Linda had lunged at her. "Ask your sons," Kim said, as she turned on her heel and began to walk away. "You seem to be the last person around here to know what's going on."

Linda could feel the other shoppers' eyes on her as she released her grip on the shopping cart. She'd been holding on so tightly that her hands tingled as the blood rushed back into them. She left her cart where it was and walked back toward the entrance, avoiding gazes as she went. She suddenly remembered the night, not even a month ago, when she and Kim and a few other parents had all gathered at Hunter's house to take prom photos of the kids in front of the Finches' pond. The girls looked so grown up in their gowns and updos, while the boys looked somehow younger in their ill-fitting tuxedos. Kim had congratulated her on Will's scholarship, and Linda had suggested poses for June and Hunter's pictures based on ones that she'd seen at the many engagement photo shoots that took place at her orchard. They weren't friends, necessarily, but they'd certainly been friendly. Though now she could see that Kim had only tolerated Will, and her, out of a flimsy notion of "open-mindedness." It hadn't taken much to go from sparkling-cider prom night toasts to a shouting match in the produce aisle.

In the parking lot, Linda sat in her car and thought about the day that Will told her he'd gotten into Princeton. She hadn't even known that he'd applied. She remembered feeling like it was too good to be true, and she felt as if she'd been holding her breath ever since, waiting for the other shoe to drop. Now she let out a long breath and her shoulders slumped into the worn seat of her car. Kim Jeffries was a bitch, she thought, but she was right about one thing: it was time to find out if her boys were involved in that party, before everyone else in town knew something she didn't.

22

Maja was getting a taste of what it would be like to commute between New Falls and Manhattan. It had been two weeks since they'd learned about the house party, and she'd already been back and forth three times. First to make sure the house was secure after John had it boarded up. On Friday she'd gone down to sit in on the school board meeting. And then yesterday she'd taken another day off of work—much to Louis's growing annoyance—to meet with several new contractors recommended by Aneeta. Maja hadn't been wrong about John—aside from one last invoice for work he'd done right before the party shut everything down, she hadn't heard a word from him after she gave him the news that her insurance company was trying to split liability with him.

The meetings with the new contractors lacked the excitement of her early discussions with John. Walking them through the damaged house, she saw only potential pitfalls rather than possibility. The first contractor seemed overly optimistic, and the second one was too concerned with taking on liability from the work that was already done. The third person she met with actually specialized in restoration work, putting houses back together after floods and fire. He seemed like the most promising of the bunch, a fact that drove home for Maja how badly the house had been damaged. Hiring a new contractor felt a lot like diving back into the dating pool after a bad breakup: The contractors said all the right things to her, but she knew there was a good chance that it would all just end in disappointment and recriminations.

By the time she'd finished her meetings, Maja was exhausted, and she gratefully accepted an offer from Aneeta to stay for dinner and go back to New York in the morning. Ted hadn't minded, which wasn't a surprise. He'd been so preoccupied. He'd barely said a word about work, and whenever she'd suggested that they make dinner plans with friends, or meet for a drink after work, he'd begged off. He'd never put in the call that he'd promised to make to the stone yard to see if they could match any of the materials they already had, and he'd even forgotten to take in his dry cleaning, which he was always on top of. Maja knew whatever was going on at work had him stressed, and she was trying to give him space. Most of the nights they'd spent together over the last two weeks were in front of the TV, zoned out on HBO shows.

Maja was tempted to stay in New Falls for the day and stop by the police station. She hadn't heard anything from them in a few days, and she wanted to see if they were any closer to filing charges. Not knowing who it was who had broken into her home, in such a small community, was a weird feeling. But she couldn't miss another day of work.

After coffee with Aneeta, she walked into town to catch the bus back up to the city. There was a group of commuters huddled together at the gas station, sipping coffees and eating donuts from a shared box that sat open on the bench as they waited for the bus. Maja stood a little apart, watching them. They looked like they'd known each other for years. Would she and Ted be a part of that group one day?

One of the women caught her eye and waved. "Morning!" she called out. "I think I've seen you on the bus a few times. Donut?"

"Thanks," Maja said, walking over. She wasn't usually a sweets person, but even from a few feet away she could smell the warm scent of cinnamon and apples. The woman handed her a napkin and she plucked a donut from the box.

"We get them once a week from O'Connor Orchard," the woman said. "Fred lives nearby and picks them up." She gestured toward a middle-aged guy and he raised a hand in greeting. "It makes commuting a little sweeter," she said, smiling. "I'm Cathy. Are you new to the commute?"

"New to town, actually," Maja said. "I haven't moved down yet. I'm building a house here." She shook the woman's hand. "Maja Jensen."

"Oh," the woman said, her eyes going wide. "You're not . . ." She didn't seem to know how to end her sentence. "Was it your house that . . ."

"Got trashed?" Maja finished her question. "That was us."

"Oh, honey, I am sorry," Cathy said. "That's terrible. I heard that half the high school was there."

"You're probably right. Although I don't know much about what actually happened. I'm sure you've heard more about it than I have," Maja said, shaking her head. "The police keep putting us off. I know it's tricky, because there are minors involved, but it's been frustrating. And we haven't heard a word from the families. No one has come forward."

Cathy raised her eyebrows. "Well, that I'm not surprised about. My kids are grown and off on their own now, but back when they were at school here, I remember being blown away by the lengths some parents went to. Every kid was special—do you know what I mean? Travel sports teams, private SAT tutors, the works. If parents weren't happy with a grade, it was never the kid's fault. They had no problem marching right into school and demanding a retest or whatever they thought they deserved. A lot of the parents work on Wall Street, and they bring home that zero-sum, grab-whatever-you-can mindset. Someone's kid is going to win, and it better be theirs. If they didn't get into a prestigious university, it was the end of the world. But do you know what the funny thing is? I swear half of those kids ended up back here after college. No skills to make it in the real world."

The man who supplied the donuts wandered over to them, and Cathy introduced him. "Fred, this is Maja Jensen. She's building the house where that party was," Cathy said. "On River Road. You must have heard about it. Terrible. She's moving down here from New York."

The warm smile on Fred's face seemed to freeze. "Ah," he said. "Yes. Terrible."

At the same time, Cathy seemed to realize something and stopped midchatter. After an awkward moment of silence, Fred nodded stiffly to them and stepped back to the group.

Maja looked at Cathy questioningly, but she just gave a little half smile. "Not everyone is a morning person," she said, peering down the street as the bus slowly made its way toward them. Maja glanced over her shoulder at Fred. He was the right age to have kids in high school, she thought. She didn't recognize him from the school board meeting, but there'd been a lot of parents there.

On the bus, Maja chose a seat by herself near the back. She felt unsettled as she thought about her soon-to-be neighbors. Once she and Ted moved, she realized, awkward meetings like this could happen at any time. It was a small town, and a lot of people were bound to know kids who'd been at the party, or their parents. Maja had just assumed that people would feel bad for her, or angry on her behalf, as Cathy had been—at first. It had only dawned on her, after the school board meeting, that others might feel very differently. Like Cathy said, people were willing to go to great lengths where their kids were concerned.

When they arrived at the Port Authority, she made her way downtown to their apartment so that she could get changed before work. She didn't need to be at the gallery until noon, so she stopped on her way and picked up a few groceries. There was something that she needed to talk with Ted about tonight, and she thought that cooking his favorite meal couldn't hurt.

By the time she got home, it was nearly ten-thirty. She dropped her bags on the kitchen counter, glanced through the mail piled there, and then headed back to the bedroom to change. As she rounded the corner, she ran right into Ted and let out an involuntary scream.

"Holy shit! What was that?" he asked, alarmed.

"I'm sorry!" she said, laughing and catching her breath. "You scared me. What are you doing here? I thought you'd already be at work."

They walked into the kitchen and Maja noticed that Ted was still in his boxers and hadn't shaved yet. "Everything okay?"

He busied himself with boiling water for coffee. "I'm feeling a little under the weather. I thought I'd just go in late."

"I thought things were crazy at work right now. You told me that you didn't have time to meet with the new contractors."

"They are," he said irritably. "If it's so important to you I'll go right now. You can make your own coffee." He banged the coffee press so hard on the counter that Maja was surprised that it didn't break.

"Hey!" Maja exclaimed. "That is the second time that you've snapped at me lately. I don't care what's going on at work. You can't talk to me like that."

He started to brush by her, but she put her hand on his arm. He shook it off, but he stopped and sat down at the kitchen table. He rubbed his eyes, and when he looked up at her, Maja saw that they were bloodshot, with dark circles underneath.

"You don't look great," she said more softly. "Maybe you should head back to bed."

Ted shook his head. "No, I'm sorry. I don't know what's wrong with me." He leaned his head against her arm, and she felt, in the weight of his head, how tired he was. Normally this would have softened her, but she was still feeling shaken by his sudden anger.

She waited for him to say something else, to explain, but he just sat there for a minute and then got up and headed down the hall. She heard the shower start.

Maja waited for a minute, took a deep breath to calm herself, and then followed him into the bathroom. She perched on the toilet seat. It was steamy, and she could only see the outline of his form through the fogged glass.

"Look," she said. "I know things are really busy at work right now. And I want to give you space for that. But I'm also having a tough time, dealing with the house on my own. I'm trying to take as much stuff off of your plate as I can, but I need to feel like we're a team here. We are, right?"

For a minute there was just the sound of the water, and then he said: "I'm sorry. I've been checked out. I know that it isn't fair to you. There've been some things lately . . . I'm worried about money. I'm worried about the house. I'm not sure I realized how much we're spending. But I know it's just temporary, and that you're doing a lot right now too. I promise I'll do better."

Maja wanted to believe him so badly that she was willing to ignore the slightly monotonous tone of his voice, which made it sound as if he was reading lines that he didn't really mean. He's tired, she told herself. I'm probably really touchy right now too.

As Maja stood up, she noticed the wrapper from the pregnancy test she'd taken two weeks earlier wedged behind the wastebasket. It had never made it to the trash chute, but Ted hadn't asked about it anyway.

She felt a flash of irritation. Sometimes it seemed as if she was the only one who still cared whether they had a child or not. It was she, after all, who had to think constantly about the day-to-day work of what she should and shouldn't put into her body, how it was feeling, and whether or not it was doing what it was supposed to do. Maja took a breath. She knew that she wasn't being fair. She'd been so sensitive about her failure to get pregnant that it wasn't surprising Ted wouldn't bring it up.

"Hey, babe, there's something I need to talk to you about tonight," she said. "Want to meet here after work?" Even though things were strained, she'd made up her mind to speak with Ted about the possibility of doing IVF. It wasn't ideal, she knew, to bring it up while they were already dealing with so much. But it could be a long process, and the sooner they started, the better.

"Sure," he said. "See you at seven." He drew a heart with his finger in the fog on the shower glass. She smiled. He used to leave messages for her that way when they were first married, since he was usually up and showered before her. At the time, it drove her crazy because she was the one who kept the shower glass clean. Now she realized that she had missed it.

Maja went into the gallery for a few hours, and she was relieved that it was quiet, since she wasn't exactly in the mood to be charming.

Most of the people who wandered in were tourists rather than serious buyers, and she used the time to catch up on her inbox.

After work, Maja prepped dinner—Ted's favorite, French onion soup, even though it was wrong for the season. The scent of the slowly caramelizing onions was overwhelming in the small kitchen, and she opened the sliding glass doors to their tiny balcony to bring in some fresh air. She put a bottle of wine in the fridge and made a quick salad dressing. Between the commute and work, she was beat. She had a few minutes until Ted would be there, so she laid down on the sofa and closed her eyes.

She must have dozed off, and when she awoke, the room was dark and cool. She sat up, feeling groggy, and closed the balcony doors. She flipped on the kitchen light and looked at the clock on the stove. It was almost nine. The onions in the pan were congealed and smelled metallic. Ted said he would be here at seven. What the hell was going on?

She flipped open her phone to check for a message, but he hadn't called. While she scraped the onions into the trash she tried his number, which went straight to voice mail.

Maybe he'd gotten caught up at the office. But if that was it, there'd be no reason not to call. Her second, clichéd thought was that he was having an affair. Had she missed it somehow? She'd been preoccupied with finishing the house and trying to get pregnant. If she was honest with herself, she'd been so involved with her own stuff the past year that she hadn't been paying much attention to what he was doing.

But Ted just didn't seem like the type. Is that what all wives thought? She took a deep breath. It was probably just work. And she had said that she would give him space to deal with it. She sat on the couch with a magazine to wait, but she couldn't concentrate. Whatever was going on between them, they had to figure it out. She grabbed her jacket and her keys and headed out the door.

She saw him in the very first place she looked: Reilly's Pub, on the corner of their block. He was pulled up at the bar with his back to her. There was a woman with long red hair and a skirt suit sitting to his right. Maja was still, watching them, but in the next moment, the woman leaned over and spoke with a man on her other side. Ted was alone. For a minute, Maja just stood there, her heart beating hard. Is this what men did when they were planning to leave their wives? Drink beer alone in pubs? But maybe he did this all the time. She often worked evenings at the gallery. Was this totally normal for him? Besides, if he was sneaking around, he wouldn't have come to their regular spot.

"Hiya, Maja," the bartender called out in his usual singsong greeting, and Ted turned around. He didn't look surprised to see her.

"What are you doing here?" she asked him. "You said you'd be home hours ago. I made dinner." She wasn't sure what she hated more right now: the nagging way her voice sounded, or the fact that he'd put her in this position.

"I'm sorry, babe," he said. "I should have called you."

"Ted," she said apprehensively. "You have to tell me what's going on. I'm worried. Is it work? Or . . . is it me? I honestly don't know what to think. You're scaring me."

"It's not you," he said. "I love you. It's . . ." He paused for a long moment, as if he was thinking something over.

Maja wasn't sure if she wanted to hear what Ted was about to say or not.

"You know how hard I've been working," he started, and Maja sighed with relief.

"If it really is just work," she said quickly, "then I get it. I was afraid . . ." She didn't want to say it aloud. "Anyway, I know this year has been tough. And I know how focused you are on getting promoted. But if it doesn't happen this year, it's not the end of the world. The markets will be back up before you know it. Isn't that what you're always saying?"

Ted gave her a long look. "You're right," he finally said. "Just another big sell-off today. I came here to unwind and lost track of time." He sighed. "Anyway, I'm glad you're here. What would you like to drink?"

Maja ordered a club soda and lime from the bartender, and Ted gave her a searching look.

"Not pregnant," she said, reading his expression. "I just don't feel like drinking tonight. Actually, Ted, there's something that I want to ask you about."

For a second, Maja thought that Ted looked scared. Then he turned and downed the remainder of his beer, and when he turned back to her, his face was neutral.

Here goes, she thought. "I'm going to see the doctor next week," she said hurriedly. "I want to talk to her about the possibility of start-ing IVF. I know it's not ideal. It's a lot of money, and a lot of time. And more medications. I know that it's not what we planned on, and in the past you've been against it. But I want to give it a try." She held her breath. She wanted to add that it was her body, after all, but she knew that wasn't fair. They both had to be onboard for this to work.

To her surprise, Ted didn't immediately protest. Instead, he looked a little relieved. He signaled to the bartender for another beer. "I just don't want to see you disappointed again," he said. "I know how hard this has been on you."

"I can take it," Maja said. "I'm not ready to give up."

"This is really what you want?"

Maja nodded. "I want to have a family. With you. Isn't that what you want?"

"Of course it is." Ted seemed to be thinking. "How much are we talking about?"

"I'll have more information after I see the doctor," Maja said. "I'm guessing twenty-five thousand, to start, but insurance should cover some of it."

Ted gave a low whistle.

"I know it's a lot, but I think it's going to be worth it." She put her hand on his thigh. "I love you."

Ted pressed his lips together and nodded his head. "Okay," he said. "Talk to the doctor and see what she says. But I don't want to start any of this until we have the house back on track. It's just too much. If we're going to do this, let's do it right. Can we wait until the fall?"

"We can wait a few months," Maja agreed, feeling giddy with re-newed hope. She was anxious to get started, but she knew by the time she set up all of the specialists appointments she would need, it wasn't actually that long to wait.

"Let's go home," Maja said, and Ted followed her out of the bar, slipping his hand into hers as they went.

They were in a rough patch right now, Maja thought, but they were going to come out of it. Soon the house construction would be back on track, and the markets would eventually calm down—they always did. And most important, they were going to have another chance at having a baby. It would be expensive, but that was one of the upsides of Ted's job. It was stressful, and demanding, and it meant that she sometimes had to play second fiddle to his work. But it also meant that they had the resources to weather these storms. She and Ted were in this together, and they were going to be okay.

23

On Tuesday afternoon, Will picked Hunter up after school and they stopped by Wawa for cigarettes and snacks before heading into town to meet June and Rosie. On the way, Will texted Maddie, asking her to come. She hadn't been at school again today, and she hadn't answered his text that morning asking how she was doing.

When they showed up at the park, June and Rosie were already there, sitting on a bench and tossing stale bread over the fence to the ducks who waited expectantly along the river's edge below. June, as always, got straight to the point.

"I heard my parents talking about what happened at the school board meeting," June said. "I'm sorry about what my mom said to your mom. You know how she is."

"Your mom kind of threw Trip under the bus," Will said.

June shrugged. "She only said what's true. Trip *was* arrested for dealing pot."

"You know he wasn't dealing it," Will said, surprised at how annoyed he felt. "Besides, you're always the first person to volunteer me or Trip to buy the booze when you want it. Just tell your mom to leave him out of it, okay?"

"I said I was sorry," June said.

"What did the police say to you on Friday?" Will asked. "I heard they talked to a couple of kids."

"They were just fishing for information," June said, "but they didn't get anything out of me. I don't know how they got my name, but I heard that Olivia was sobbing her eyes out in Dr. Johnson's office, so I'm guessing she must have said something. I knew I shouldn't have told her about the party. She's a hysterical drama queen. I just felt bad for her."

"Did you ask her what she said?" Hunter asked.

"Are you kidding? I'm not saying another word to her. She can't keep her mouth shut."

"She was upset about Maddie," Rosie said quietly.

"That's no excuse," June snapped. "It's none of her business. Anyway, I told my dad, and he was seriously pissed, but he told the police to back off."

"You told your dad?" Will asked June, incredulous. "I thought we agreed not to tell anyone what happened."

"I didn't tell him everything, obviously. I said that we were hanging out at the rope swing, that there was a rumor that there was a party nearby, and we just stopped in for a minute. I told him that the cops were asking people about it at school. He didn't like that—the cops talking to students without parents present. He gave me a lecture about drinking and swimming in the river and all that, and then he spoke with the police chief."

Hunter looked worried. "Rosie, no one talked to you, right?"

"Nope. But I recognized one of the men who came to school. He eats at my dad's restaurant a few times a week. I thought that he was a cop, but he said he's a district attorney."

"That doesn't sound good," Will said.

Hunter frowned. "If the DA is involved, that means they're getting ready to press charges. What did he say, Rosie?"

"He said the police thought there may have been other crimes committed at the house."

"What does that mean?"

"I have no idea," Rosie said.

"Shit," Hunter breathed. "Look, Rosie, you said he comes into your dad's restaurant a lot, right? Do you think you could try to talk to him about it? Ask him how the case is going?"

Rosie was shaking her head. "I don't know," she said. "Wouldn't that be weird?"

"Just see what you can find out," Hunter said. "My dad always says that information is power."

"Okay," Rosie said uncertainly. "Maybe I'll overhear something."

"That's my girl," Hunter said, smiling and squeezing her knee. Rosie turned pink and brushed his hand off of her leg.

Only Will seemed to notice—June was busy looking at her phone. Will had been watching Rosie pine for Hunter for the last two years. She wasn't the only one. He wasn't sure if it was Hunter's money or the confidence that came from it that caused girls to fall all over him. Probably a little of both.

Will heard a car door close, and he turned to see a pale-green Prius pulling into the lot behind them. It was Maddie—her car always stuck out in a town full of SUVs and pickup trucks. She got out and walked along the path toward the benches where they sat.

"Let's drop the party talk for now," Will said quietly, and everyone nodded, seeming to understand. He waved to Maddie, and Hunter got up from the bench to make room for her next to Will.

Hunter passed around cigarettes, and they sat smoking and trying not to talk about the party, which was hard, because it was all that was on anyone's mind. Maddie was quiet, Will noticed, but at least she was there with them. Will thought about how she'd downed those two little bottles of vodka in his truck, and he tried to get a whiff of what she had in her water bottle without her noticing. Did it smell vaguely alcoholic, or was he imagining it?

Hunter was talking about the dorms at Princeton. "Make sure you put in a request for me as your roommate," he said to Will. "My dad can talk to the dean and make sure that we get assigned together."

Will nodded. Hunter still seemed sure that everything was going to turn out okay. But why shouldn't he be? Over the last few years he'd totaled his car, let his grades drop, and had even gotten caught with pills at school, and none of it had seemed to matter. His dad had bailed him out every time. Will wasn't nearly as confident. He didn't have that safety net.

Hunter's phone buzzed and he looked at it. "Speak of the devil," he said. "That's my dad. I gotta run." He kissed June goodbye and then leaned over the back of the bench to give Maddie's shoulders a squeeze. "It was good to see you," he said.

Maddie jumped at Hunter's touch. She turned around and stared at him with wide eyes, a frown forming. "Don't touch me," she said loudly.

Hunter backed away, surprised.

"Hey," Will said gently, standing up. "Hey, it's okay. It's just us. Okay, Maddie?"

Hunter looked flustered. "I'm sorry," he said. "I don't know what I did."

June finally looked away from her phone. "What did you do?" she asked Hunter, her eyes narrowed.

"Nothing!" Hunter said. "I just touched her shoulders. That's it."

Maddie was shaking her head, her face pale. Will started to put a hand on her arm, and then stopped, unsure what to do.

"I have to go," Maddie mumbled. Before Will could stop her, she took off toward her car.

"Wait!" June called out. She grabbed Maddie's bag, which Maddie had left sitting on the bench. "I'll go with her," June said over her shoulder as she followed Maddie to her car.

"What was that about?" Hunter asked, after they'd gone.

Will shrugged. "She's having a really hard time lately. We were hanging out the other day and she just ran off in the middle of our conversation."

"Has she said anything to you about what happened at the party?" Rosie asked.

"Not really," Will said. "She's not okay, though. I tried to talk her into going to the police, but she didn't want to."

"No police," Hunter said. "What are they going to do? You'll have to tell them everything. We'll all go down."

"I thought they never actually prosecute those types of cases anyway," Rosie said.

"You saw what Maddie's like, though," Will said. "I think she needs help."

Rosie nodded her head. "I'm not sure that was water in her bottle."

"We promised to stick together," Hunter reminded them.

"I know," Will said. "But if we're all sticking together, why does it feel like everything is about to fall apart?"

24

Maddie heard quick footsteps behind her, and she fought the animal urge to run.

"Wait!" June called out, and Maddie stopped. Her hands were still shaking.

June caught up with her and held out her bag. "What happened?" she asked. "Are you okay?"

Maddie took the bag, shaking her head. "June, I thought maybe I imagined it, but . . ."

"Imagined what?" June asked.

"That scent," Maddie said. Hunter's sickening scent of musk and sandalwood as he leaned over her was still in her nostrils and her mouth. And with the scent, a shadowy memory of Hunter, his arm around her, holding her up as he kissed her neck. The loud noise of the party and the feeling that people were watching them. Her head rocking forward and back as she tried to cling to consciousness.

It was all coming back to her. The ecstasy had overwhelmed her, but in the tidal waves of sensation there were brief ebbs, and in one clearheaded moment she'd slipped out of his arms and pushed through the crowd of kids. She'd lunged up the stairs and found a dark and quiet room in the back of the house where she thought she'd be safe. That's why she was alone up there, she realized. It should have been a relief to finally have at least one answer about that night, but it wasn't.

"The scent?" June prompted her.

She didn't have to say anything. She could just cry, or run away, or leave town and never see any of these people again. She didn't owe

June or anyone else any answers. But the way June was looking at her, she knew that June knew. June wasn't graduating second in their class for nothing. She'd guessed it.

"Hunter's cologne," Maddie finally said.

"Axe. It's body spray," June said, her voice tense. "Maddie, you have to tell me. Was it him?"

Maddie shook her head, hard. "No, no. He wasn't . . . he didn't. It was earlier. Downstairs. He was kissing me. I'm sorry, June. I barely even remember it. I went upstairs to get away from him."

June's face flushed. "Asshole. It's not the first time."

The two girls looked at each other. "Are you mad at me?" Maddie asked in a small voice.

"Of course not," June said quickly. "It's not your fault." She took a deep breath and seemed to regain some of her usual composure. "Are you sure you don't remember anything about the other kid?"

Maddie shrugged. The humiliation felt like a real thing, pressing in on her from all sides.

June sighed. "Look, no one wanted to say anything to you, but some kid took pictures. I don't know who he was. But if you want to go to the police, there might be evidence."

"Oh my god," Maddie said, looking horrified. "Are they . . . are people passing them around?"

"Not that I know of," June said.

Maddie couldn't tell if June was being truthful. But she didn't want to know. She made up her mind. "No. I don't want to go to the police."

"Are you going to tell Will?" June asked. "About Hunter?"

"How can I?" Maddie said, her voice thin. After all, she thought, she was the one who'd decided to take that pill. She'd let herself get completely out of control, to the point where a stranger had assaulted her. How could she tell Will that she'd also let his best friend kiss her? It was more than she could take. Had she done something to encourage him? She couldn't even remember. "Please don't say anything," she begged June. "I just want to put all of this behind me."

"I think you should tell him, but it's up to you," June said. "It wasn't your fault. Hunter is an asshole. I don't know why I put up with him. He's stoned half the time that we hang out. I'm done, though, and I'm so sorry he did that to you."

"I'm sorry too," Maddie said.

"You don't have anything to be sorry for," June insisted. "I know you, Maddie. You didn't do anything wrong. It was supposed to be a fun night."

"I wish that whole night had never happened," Maddie said, shuddering.

"Look, I know we all agreed to stick together and not talk about this, but you need to do whatever you need to do to take care of yourself. I won't say anything to Will if you don't want me to, but you should probably talk to your mom. And at least think about going to the police. What happened to you . . . it wasn't your fault. Don't worry about the rest of us. We can take care of ourselves."

"I don't know what I'm going to do," Maddie said. "I just want to go home."

"Okay," June said. "But let me drive you."

Maddie handed over her keys without protest.

When they reached Maddie's house, her parents were still at work. June followed her inside, even though she could tell Maddie would have preferred to go in alone. Maddie looked miserable, but June figured she would be unhappy with or without her there. And besides, being with Maddie helped her push away thoughts about Hunter. He hadn't just hurt Maddie—he'd humiliated her as well. June made up her mind. She wasn't even going to give him the satisfaction of a scene. He'd probably enjoy it, and aggrieved girlfriend was not part of her self-image. As far as she was concerned, he no longer existed.

When Maddie's mom arrived, June called her dad for a ride, and he told her that he'd pick her up on his way home from the train station. When he got there, she made a quick exit, hugging her friend and telling her to call. It had been awhile since she'd needed a ride from her parents and there was something comforting about her dad transferring his briefcase to the back seat so she could settle in next to him, NPR on the radio as always.

They drove for a few minutes in silence before her father turned to her and said, "Out with it."

"With what?" June asked.

"With whatever it is you're thinking about. You're never this quiet."

June smiled. Her father was her favorite audience, and it was true that she usually talked his ear off whenever she had time alone with him. But for once she wasn't sure what to say.

"The police didn't talk to you again, did they?" he asked.

"No," June said.

"You can tell me anything," he said. "Like I've always told you—when you have a problem, I can help you with a strategy."

It was true, June thought. She'd told him that she'd stopped by the party, hoping to leave it at that, and he'd taken her word on it. But she had a feeling that the investigation was getting more serious than she'd realized, and she hated feeling out of control. Her father had always listened to her, and he'd always been on her side. But what she was about to tell him was going to test that. She took a deep breath. "Dad?" she said. "I have something to tell you."

25

The young woman who sat between her parents in Chief Whitman's office had shiny black hair pulled into a bun. She was dressed in a pale-blue button-down shirt, a delicate silver chain with a cross around her neck. She looked like she was going to church. She didn't look at all like the June Jeffries who had tossed her hair over her shoulder and sneered at Detective Murray when he'd interviewed her at school. And yet that's exactly who she was.

Detective Murray had gotten the call twenty minutes earlier, telling him to report to Whitman's office. "I want to thank you again for your cooperation," the chief was saying to Mr. Jeffries when he got there. The chief looked at Detective Murray. "I think you know what to do here," he said, and Murray nodded. The chief shook hands with Mr. and Mrs. Jeffries, and then left the office.

Mr. Jeffries began to speak right away. "On my advice, my daughter has agreed to provide information about the house party that took place on River Road, three weeks ago. In exchange, we request that any charges against her be limited to simple trespassing."

It sounded to Murray like Mr. Jeffries had already come to a private agreement with the chief, which he wasn't happy about. But he also knew that at the moment they had very few names and even fewer good cases, with the possible exception of the O'Connor boys. If they were going to hold someone responsible for the damage at that party, they needed a witness.

"We will certainly take her cooperation into account," Murray said. He turned to June: "Why are you just coming forward now? It's been several weeks since the party took place."

"I decided that it's the right thing to do," June said. "There are a lot of rumors flying around, and I want to set the story straight."

So, Murray thought, her father had warned her that it was better to come forward, take a deal, and control her own story. It was a smart move. "What can you tell us about this party?" Murray asked her.

"I was only there for a brief amount of time," June said, her voice sounding practiced. "I was hanging out with friends in the woods, and I stopped by to meet up with my boyfriend, who was there."

"And who is that?" Murray asked.

"Hunter Finch," she replied, without hesitation. "I met him there around midnight. When I arrived at the house, it was a mess. When I realized that the house didn't belong to anyone there, I insisted that we leave."

"Can you tell me what you saw there?" Murray asked.

June gave her father a sideways glance, and he nodded.

"There were a lot of kids there," she said. "The kitchen looked like it was destroyed. The sink was clogged. I saw kids rip the cabinet doors off. They were launching bottle rockets outside. Like I said, once I saw what was going on, I insisted that we leave."

"How did you get home?"

"My boyfriend drove me home to his house." She glanced over at her father again. "We got there around one a.m. I slept on his sofa."

"Who planned the party?" Murray asked.

June shrugged. "I have no idea," she said. "But I do have a list of the kids that I recognized, in case that's helpful." She opened a folder on her lap and took out a typed list.

Murray took the list from her and looked it over. The first name on the list was Hunter Finch. She certainly hadn't shied away from naming her boyfriend. Murray wondered what he'd done to deserve that. He scanned the rest of the list, recognizing the names of a few kids that he'd spoken to—Brendan Sullivan, Olivia Park, and some kids who had been ticketed on the road the night of the party. Neither of the O'Connor brothers were on the list.

"What about Will O'Connor?" Murray asked. "I heard he may have planned the party."

"He's not on my list," June said.

"He wasn't there?" Murray asked.

"I-I don't know," June said. "I'm not sure."

"Bullshit," Murray said, surprising them. He shoved the list back at June. Mr. Jeffries started to stand up, but Murray gave him a warning look. "This is a criminal investigation, not a final exam, Ms. Jeffries," Murray said to June. "If you want to cooperate, we will take that into account. But we are looking at the possibility of half a million dollars in restitution payments that could be due to the victims here. So if you don't want to see your college tuition money going to court fees, you'll answer my questions. Was Will O'Connor at this party?"

"Watch your tone!" Mr. Jeffries said. "She said she doesn't know."

June was biting her lip, hard, but Murray had to give her credit. Most girls in her position would be in tears by now. Finally, she answered: "It's okay, Dad. He was there, but he didn't plan it."

"What about those big windows?" Murray asked. "Did he break them?"

"Who told you that?" she asked, but Murray didn't answer. "He might have," she said. "But I didn't see it. You'll have to confirm that with someone else." It sounded like she was giving him an assignment.

"Okay," said Mr. Jeffries. "I think that's enough. She's given you a list of names, and she's willing to plead guilty to simple trespass. Do we have a deal?"

Murray was quiet for a moment, and then Mr. Jeffries added: "And as far as I'm concerned, I don't think the chief needs to hear anything about your . . . outburst."

Murray let out a dry laugh. "Outburst, huh? Okay, you have a deal," he said. "I'll recommend that she plead to trespass. Thanks for coming forward, Ms. Jeffries. Our community depends on good people like you."

At the DA's office, Jake handed Donna a copy of the list that June Jeffries had supplied to Detective Murray. "Suspects in the house party
case," he said. "Can you add it to the file?"

Donna looked at the list and raised her eyebrows. "Hunter Finch,"
she read aloud.

"Do you know the name?" Jake asked.

"Well . . ." Donna began. "Dominic Finch lives up on Greenwood
Road." She looked at Jake as if this should mean something to him.

"Dominic Finch?" Jake repeated. "Do I know him?"

"Of Finch Properties? The property developers? He's a friend of
Hal's." She raised her eyebrows. "I believe Hunter is his son."

Jake conjured up a vague image of the name Finch Properties in
gold script engraved on wooden signs with the pompous names of
housing communities like Fox Chase Run and Wimbledon Green.
Hunter Finch sounded like it could be the name of another enclave of
houses built to look like faux châteaux. Somewhere in his notes was a
question about a rich kid who had been giving out, or maybe selling,
drugs. Was this the kid?

Jake started back toward his office, and then changed his mind and
walked to Hal's office instead. He knocked lightly on the door frame
and stuck his head in. "Hal, quick question. Do you happen to know
Hunter Finch?"

Hal took a few extra seconds to look up from his desk. "Why are
you asking?"

Jake wasn't sure what sort of answer he had been expecting, but
that certainly wasn't it. "Oh, no reason, really. The name came up in
a tip about the house party, but I don't have a face to connect it with.
Just ruling people out at this point." He decided to make the leap. "I
thought he might be related to Dominic Finch."

Hal looked put out. "Yes, that's Dom Finch's boy," he finally said.
He paused, and then continued in a warning tone: "Tread lightly
there, Jake. A family like that attracts a lot of attention. And jealousy.

I'd hate to see them get dragged through the mud for no reason. Focus on the O'Connor boys; that's a sure thing."

Jake kept his face, and his tone, neutral. "Got it, boss."

Back in his office, however, he immediately googled Dominic Finch, pulling up pictures of ribbon-cutting ceremonies and news items about massive real estate purchases. It looked like one of the kids who had destroyed the house was the son of a real estate developer. Now, that was a case. And if he made that case, that could mean real headlines, not to mention more public sympathy for the Jensens. June Jeffries was clearly playing her own game, but with her list of names, she'd delivered Jake a very promising hand.

26

"This is it," Detective Murray said, pulling off of Greenwood Road and stopping in front of an iron gate. He rolled down the car window and pressed the bell. A red light on a camera mounted above the gate blinked on. After a minute the gate swung open and they drove up a long lane, past a pond with the old springhouse still intact and across a wide lawn dotted with oak trees. The driveway wound through flowerbeds and up to a large stone house.

Jake Tillman let out a whistle. "Very nice."

"You think they have a butler?" Murray asked, only half joking.

Tillman laughed. "Remember what Hal said. We have to tread lightly here. We're just following up on a lead. We already have June Jeffries's testimony that Hunter Finch was at the party. If we can get Hunter or his parents to say anything that confirms it, we'll have a much better case."

"We're not going to get anything out of these people. I bet we don't make it past the front door."

"Twenty bucks?" Tillman wagered. "I bet they offer us coffee and tell us nothing."

"You're on," Murray said, and pressed the bell.

The door was opened almost immediately by a blond woman in jeans and an oversize white dress shirt. She looked at them warily, but her voice was polite.

"Good morning, Officers. How can I help you?"

"Mrs. Finch?" Murray asked, and the woman nodded. "I'm Detective Murray, and this is Jake Tillman, from the Hart County prosecutors' office. We're asking around about a property crime that occurred nearby a few weeks ago. Could we ask you some questions?"

For a minute Mrs. Finch looked like she was going to say no, but instead she gave them a tight smile and invited them in. "Would you like some coffee?" she asked.

"That would be great," Tillman said, flashing a smile at Murray as they followed her into the kitchen.

The kitchen was a tasteful balance of antique and modern, with exposed wood beams and sleek countertops. Tillman and Murray took a seat at the breakfast bar while Mrs. Finch worked the gleaming espresso machine. She set down the coffees and looked at them expectantly.

"You might have heard about a party that took place on River Road on a Friday, three weeks ago? Local kids, by the looks of it, but the property ended up sustaining major damage."

"I'm sorry," she said, shaking her head. "We didn't hear anything. The river is a few miles from here."

"Mm-hmm," Murray agreed, checking his notepad. "Mrs. Finch, I understand that you have a son? Hunter?"

"Stepson," she corrected him. "And you can call me Lindsay."

"Of course. Is he at home?"

"No, he's not. I'm not sure when he'll be back. I haven't seen him since he left for school this morning. It's a long commute."

"He doesn't attend the local school?"

"That's right, he's at Collegiate Prep, or at least . . ." She stopped, and she looked like she was going to say more, but she didn't.

"And how old is Hunter?" Murray asked.

"He's eighteen," Lindsay said.

"An adult," Murray said.

Lindsay gave a short laugh. "I guess so. He doesn't really seem like one, though."

"As I said, it looks like this party was mostly local kids, but we're just trying to be thorough here. Would you happen to remember where Hunter was on Friday, April twenty-fifth?" Murray asked.

"I'm not sure. He doesn't exactly ask my permission before he goes out."

Murray nodded sympathetically. "Teenagers," he said. "Would your husband know, perhaps? We could come back."

"I don't know." She looked nervous. "Let me look at my planner. Maybe that will jog my memory. I'd hate to bother Dom if I can help you myself. He's very busy, and I doubt he would know anyway."

"That would be great," Murray said, exchanging looks with Tillman as she went to find her purse.

She came back with an old-fashioned leather-bound planner, which Murray, as a committed pen and paper man, appreciated. She paged through it for a moment and then stopped, looking at the entry for a moment before she answered, as if she was trying to make up her mind about something.

"Hunter was here that Friday," she said. "He had two girls over, and they slept here. Downstairs, of course."

"That's great," Murray said, noting it down in his book. "And you had that in your planner? You're way more organized than I am."

Lindsay laughed. "No," she said, "but I do have a note the next day that I needed to take my car into the shop. Hunter borrowed it that Friday and got the side scratched up. He was supposed to take it himself, but of course he didn't."

"Teenagers," Murray said again, his voice even. "But I guess we've all been there. I remember scratching up my dad's car a few times myself. So, how did it happen?"

Lindsay shook her head. "He told Dom that he was kayaking on the river. There was mud in the car, so who knows?"

Murray nodded. "And just for our records, what were the names of the girls that were here?"

"June, of course. That's his girlfriend. June Jeffries. Honestly, I'm not sure about the other girl. They slept in, and I was upset about the car, so I didn't offer to make breakfast or anything. She was probably one of June's friends. They come around a lot."

"June Jeffries," Murray said, writing the name in his notebook. He looked at Jake. "I don't think we have any more questions," he said, "but we appreciate your time. And thank you for the coffee."

"I wish I could be of more help," Lindsay said, already moving toward the front door to show them out.

Murray was getting up to follow her when he stopped to ask one more thing, as if it was an afterthought. "And what time did you say Hunter came home with the car that night?"

Lindsay thought for a minute. "I think it was right around one a.m.," she said. "I fell asleep putting my kids to bed—they're still little. I woke up because I heard the alarm being turned off. I thought it was Dom getting home late from work."

"You've been very helpful," Murray said. "Here's my card, in case you think of anything else."

"You owe me twenty bucks," Tillman said as they climbed into the car.

"I don't think so, buddy," Murray replied. "I seem to remember that you placed your bet on coffee and *no information*. Seems like a draw to me."

"That's a detail!" Tillman laughed.

"It's all in the details." Murray grinned. "That's police work."

"He was there," Tillman said. "At the party. The timelines match up."

"Oh, yeah," Murray agreed. "He was there. We can add him to the list with the O'Connor boys—trespassing and criminal mischief charges, minimum. If we can get anyone to confirm that he was the kid who was selling pills, we might have him on distribution. Watch and see. Now that June Jeffries has come forward, kids will start crawling out of the woodwork. They'll all want to tell us how they were only there for a few minutes, but they know who did the real damage. They'll be falling all over themselves to turn each other in."

The first thing Hunter noticed when he got home was his father's car, a vintage Jaguar that he'd never once let Hunter drive, pulled up by the front door. His father was never home this early, and he rarely left his car sitting out of the garage. Neither one seemed like a good sign.

He slipped in the front door quietly, past the Edward Hopper oil that hung in the entryway, and was halfway up the stairs before his father's voice rang out: "Hunter! Kitchen!"

He glanced into the den, where Jack and Grace were building a tower out of magnetic tiles and listening to a kids' classical playlist. He waved at them and gave them a rueful grin, and they waved back, but they didn't get up to follow him into the kitchen, which meant that they knew he was about it to catch it for something.

His father and Lindsay were sitting at the counter, waiting for him.

He walked past them to the fridge and stood in front of the open door, not really looking for anything.

"Sit down," his father said.

He closed the fridge and pulled up a seat at the counter, keeping his mouth shut. There were a number of things that his dad could be pissed about, and Hunter wasn't about to give him any clues.

"Hunter. You're blowing it."

"Okay."

"Okay? This is okay with you? I got another call from the headmaster today. You're on academic probation. You told me this week that it was just history."

So it had happened. The dean of students had warned him a few weeks earlier that his average was getting dangerously low. His school had a strict requirement that students maintain a 2.0 or above grade point average, or they risked suspension or expulsion.

"It's the last semester," Hunter said, lamely.

"Exactly. This is the last semester, and if you don't complete it, you don't graduate. What about this don't you understand?"

"They're not going to do that."

"Why, Hunter? Why wouldn't they do that? Because I paid for the new faculty club building? I have news for you. That stuff only gets you so far. I can only pay your way if you aren't actively working against me at every turn. I'm pretty sure we used up all of our good will in the fall, when the school agreed not to make a report on your college applications about your disciplinary violation for selling Adderall."

"I wasn't selling them," muttered Hunter.

"Well then, what the hell were you doing with them in your locker? It took every ounce of influence I have at that school to make that go away. You have no idea how lucky you are. You've had *everything* handed to you, and you can't even pull a C average with what I think, frankly, is a pretty light course load."

"Maybe I'm just stupid," Hunter said. And then, for good measure: "Does she have to be here for this?" He hated the petulant sound of his own voice. What was it about these conversations that caused him to act like a spoiled child?

"Watch your tone," Dom snapped, and Lindsay flinched.

Hunter instantly felt worse.

"*Lindsay* spent the afternoon speaking with the police."

Hunter swallowed. It looked like they were going to hit every item on his list of fuckups today.

"Were you at this party?"

Hunter didn't even seriously consider trying to lie. "Yeah."

"Was it your party?"

"No, Dad, I just stopped by. I swear."

"Did you help destroy the house?"

"No. Come on. You know I wouldn't do that."

Dom leaned back in his seat. "Honestly, I don't know what you're capable of anymore."

"What did you tell them?" Hunter asked Lindsay.

"I told them that I didn't know anything about a party, and that you spent the night here with June and another girl." She paused. "And I told them that you brought the car home scratched and muddy."

"Why did you tell them that?"

"I don't know. It just came up. Look, Hunter, I wasn't about to lie to the police."

"If they showed up here," Dom said, "that means someone gave them your name. Whoever they've caught so far must be helping the police in order to keep themselves out of trouble. I'm sure whoever gave them the Finch family name scored major points."

"Not everything is about you," Hunter said.

Dom shook his head, disgusted. "This isn't about me? I'm a real estate developer, for Christ's sake, and you just destroyed a house. Or at least that's what they'll say. If this ends up going anywhere, the papers will have a field day with it. I have three big projects in front of the county *right now*, Hunter. How is it going to look when we show up for the land use hearings? This stuff is my bread and butter. These projects fund a lot of the bigger deals we're doing in New York and Florida. I'm already having a hard time getting the financing together right now. We're hemorrhaging money on the tax bills on some of these empty lots, and I really don't need any issues with the local stuff."

"Annnnd we're talking about work again," Hunter said, sarcastically.

"It's not just work, Hunter. It's our family business. It pays your school bills, and your legal bills," he said, sounding tired. "You are putting everything at risk. Our family's Princeton legacy. Your future. My business. We have a lot on the line here." He sighed and was quiet for a moment, then continued. "Look, I know that things haven't always been easy. Your mom leaving . . . I know how hard it was on you. But you need to focus on the future. And take some responsibility. I want you in the headmaster's office, first thing tomorrow morning, with a plan to get your GPA back up in time to graduate. I don't care what it takes."

"What about the police?"

"I'll put a call in to our attorneys, and to Hal Buckley, and see what I can find out. In the meantime, I don't want you discussing this with anyone. And no talking to the police without me or our lawyer present. Got it?"

"Got it," Hunter mumbled.

Dom looked at his watch. "I'm late," he said. "I need to get back up to Manhattan. Lindsay, walk me out?" He turned to Hunter as he left: "Don't forget to check in with the headmaster tomorrow morning. He'll be open to a plan. But you need to talk to him."

So his father had made some sort of deal with the school on his behalf. As usual, his dad was only giving away as much as he had to. But the news about the cops showing up at the house shook him.

"Thanks for stopping by!" he called out to his father's departing back, feeling a hot wave of rage, its power surprising him. He usually tried to care about what his father thought exactly as much as he figured his father cared about him. But Dom didn't hear him. He was busy kissing Lindsay on the cheek and sliding into the Jag, his mind already on other things.

Will saw Hunter striding across the orchard as he pulled up the driveway to the farm after school. He parked and pulled his backpack out of the bed of the truck.

Hunter was making good time across the field. As he approached, Will noticed that his face was flushed and his hands, shoved into his pockets, were balled into fists.

"Hey," he said, his voice clipped.

"Hi. What's up?"

"You wanna tell me?"

Will laughed uncomfortably and shrugged his shoulders, not sure if Hunter was kidding around or what. Will tried again. "What's up, man?"

"I'm just going to ask you straight out," Hunter said, staring at Will. "Did you give my name to the cops?"

Will just looked at him. "What the fuck, Hunter? Why would I do that?"

"I don't know," Hunter said, but it looked to Will like he had a few ideas about it. His voice had an edge, and his eyes were bright. His whole demeanor was different from what Will thought of as his usual rich-kid confidence, his wry smile and easy laugh. "You didn't actually answer me. Did you give my name to the cops?"

"No, I didn't. And fuck you for thinking that I would."

"What about Trip?"

"Trip wouldn't do that."

"Not to avoid jail time? Come on, Will. Think about it."

"Can you tell me what's going on here?" Will asked.

"The police showed up at my house and questioned Lindsay about the party."

"Shit."

"And Lindsay, always eager to please, helpfully told them that June and I brought her car home all banged up that night."

"But she doesn't know anything about the house, right?"

"Right. But someone told the police I was there. Someone is talking."

"Well, it wasn't me."

"Yeah? Because aside from you and Trip, I don't know anyone else who's talked to the cops. I know it wasn't June. She told the cops to get lost when they tried to talk to her at school."

"Hunter. First off, the cops have been asking questions all over the place. People are actually afraid to talk to one another at school. They think that if they say anything, someone might turn them in. And second, *everyone* knows who you are." It was the wrong thing to say, Will realized, as soon as it popped out of his mouth. Hunter hated having that pointed out.

"Well, someone is using my name to buy their way out of this," Hunter said, staring at Will.

Will laughed involuntarily. "Hunter, you're acting crazy. What the fuck?"

Hunter gave him a hard stare. "Just make sure you keep your mouth shut about me. And Trip too. Tell him. You guys brought the booze, and Trip is twenty-one. You know what that means? He'll be on the hook for all this if anyone finds out. I don't want anything bad to happen to him. He's your brother. But he's got to keep his mouth shut. I do not fucking need this right now."

Will felt his neck grow hot. "Is that a threat? Leave Trip out of this. *I* bought the booze, not Trip. He had to finish work, so I used his ID. I didn't say anything to the cops about you, and neither did he. You need to get your head right, Hunter. Besides," he added, giving voice to something that had been bothering him ever since the night of the party, "you're the one who gave the girls those pills. Maddie didn't even want to do it—you pushed her into it. Nothing would have happened to her if you'd left her alone."

"Are you serious right now? You're blaming me for that? We *all* took them. I didn't *drug* anyone."

"I didn't take any," Will said.

"Yeah, well, aren't you perfect?" Hunter spat. "But don't you dare tell the cops about the E. I will be seriously fucked if that comes up."

"What do you care, anyway?" Will asked. "You'll be fine whatever happens. You're not looking at losing a scholarship. Princeton isn't going to kick you out if you get in trouble for this. Your dad will make sure nothing touches you." He knew that this would piss off Hunter more than anything else, but he didn't care. Who did Hunter think he was, anyway?

"I'm just a spoiled rich kid, huh?" Hunter raised his eyebrows. "You know you want to say it."

"Hey, you said it, not me," Will shrugged. His mind was reeling. He couldn't believe that Hunter would accuse him of ratting him out.

Hunter started toward him, and Will intuitively raised his fists. The action seemed to snap Hunter out of his rage. He stopped short and stared at Will, suddenly deflated. "I thought we were better friends than this," he said.

"So did I," Will said. He could tell that Hunter wasn't really himself right now, but he was too angry to care. "Well, I'm sure that you have busy rich-kid stuff to do, so I won't keep you here." It sounded so stupid and childish coming out of his mouth that he almost laughed, which might have saved the moment. But instead he just stared at the ground. Hunter paused, then turned and walked away, back toward the woods that separated their houses.

27

Maja was standing in front of a giant American flag rendered on an eight-by-six-foot canvas. From the back of the gallery, it looked like any flag, but as you approached it you saw that the stars and stripes were made from an object collage of industrial materials like wire and circuit boards. It was a little on the nose, in Maja's opinion, but then flag art usually was. This piece had the advantage of ambiguity—was it a commentary on the role of corporate money in government, or a celebration of the strength of America's industrial past and future? In other words, it was perfect for the client standing next to her, who was looking for a statement piece to hang above the reception desk of his Flatiron-based tech startup.

The gallery had been seeing a lot of tech clients recently. For the first time since the dot-com crash back in 2001 had hobbled the budding New York start-up scene, they were beginning to outnumber the Wall Street firms who hired the gallery to outfit their offices in pieces that signaled success and taste. The financial firms that the gallery usually worked with had recently pulled back, but tech companies still seemed to be splashing money around.

The client leaned toward the painting, almost touching it with his nose. "It looks like the artist painted some of these wires to match the stripe color," he said. "Isn't that cheating?"

"Good observation!" Maja exclaimed. They'd been standing in front of the piece for ten minutes. Had he just noticed that? "I see that as a comment on assimilation," she said. "America is a land of immigrants, but there's always a tension between celebrating the individual and subsuming them into our culture." Or, she thought, it was just really difficult to find objects that fit neatly into the design. But the client seemed to like her take.

She glanced sideways at him. He was close to saying yes, she could feel it.

"How much?" he asked.

"Sixteen," she replied. She didn't need to add the "thousand"—it was assumed.

He nodded, thinking it over. Louis would be pleased—he was ready to move this out to make space for some new works. And Maja got a cash bonus on any sale over ten thousand.

She was about to point out that a certain actor had just bought one of this artist's pieces when Yasmine appeared at her side, holding her cell phone. "I'm sorry," Yasmine said. "But your phone rang three times. I thought it might be an emergency."

Maja looked down at the screen. She didn't recognize the number, but it had a 267 area code—Pennsylvania.

"Excuse me," she said to the client. "I'll just be a minute."

She stepped into the office and called the number back.

"Mrs. Jensen?" the voice on the phone asked. "This is your insurance adjuster. I'm at your house, but there's no one here. Are you on your way?"

"On my way?" Maja asked. "No, you're not supposed to be there until tomorrow!" She pulled her planner out of her purse and flipped to this week. There it was, written in for tomorrow.

"I've got you scheduled for today," the adjuster said. "Can you come by now?"

"I'm at work," Maja said. "In New York. Can you come back tomorrow?" She'd planned to take the bus down early in the morning, which was already going to be tight since she needed to be back at the gallery by two p.m.

"Afraid not," the adjuster said. "I'm fully booked up until next week."

"But we've already been waiting for three weeks!" Maja said.

"Sorry. You'll need to call your agent at Belltown and reschedule."

"Of course I will," Maja said. She took a deep breath. They were back to square one. She'd have to deal with this after work.

She walked back out into the gallery, ready to close the deal, but Yasmine was standing alone in front of the painting. Maja looked around. "Where did he go?" she asked.

"He said he needed to think about it," Yasmine said.

"Perfect," Maja said. "What a day."

When she got home from work, Ted was already there, watching a Yankees game on TV. She sat down next to him.

"The insurance adjuster finally came today," she said.

"Great," Ted said. "What did he say? How long will it take to get the payout?"

"I don't know," Maja said. "Because I wasn't there. I was here, at work. He was supposed to come tomorrow."

"Oh," Ted said.

"This is really hard to manage from up here," Maja said. What she thought, but didn't add, was *alone*. "Every time I contact the DA's office, all I get is a very polite secretary assuring me that I'll be the first person they call when they have any news to share. But so far I haven't heard a thing from them." She paused. "I think I need to go down there. Just for a week. It would give me a chance to meet with the new contractor and put together a list of all the materials we're going to need to replace. I can follow up with the police in person. And I'll be there when the insurance adjuster shows up. I got him rescheduled, thankfully."

"Sounds good," Ted said, not looking away from the game.

Maja sighed. "Okay, then. I'm going to book a room at the inn for the week. Maybe you could come down on the weekend? We could go to the stone yard and pick out new countertops."

Ted finally looked over at her. "You want to stay at the inn?" he asked.

"Well, yeah. I mean, I'm not going to camp out in the house."

"Right," Ted said. "But what about the gallery?"

"Louis isn't going to be happy," Maja said. "I'll ask for the week off to get everything started. If I have some downtime while I'm there, I can start putting in the new appliance orders and looking at tile. Honestly, I'm not sure I ever loved the bathroom tile, and now that it's being torn out, I'm thinking I might want to pick something different. What do you think?"

"I thought we were going to wait for the insurance payout," Ted said.

"Well, sure, but we still have to spend the deductible before the insurance kicks in. And some of the appliances might take time to arrive. I think it's better to get started now."

Ted sighed. "Could you stay with Aneeta and Adil?" he asked her. "I hate the idea of you being down there alone."

Maja thought it over. It was a lot to ask, but Aneeta probably wouldn't mind. "Did you want to go with me to look at tile? I can wait until you're down there."

"Not really," Ted said. "But do me a favor and don't use the Visa for anything else until I have a chance to pay it off."

Maja frowned. "I didn't know it was maxed out. I mean, doesn't it have a really high credit limit?" The card was a perk of working at Foxfield Barnes. It had come in handy when they were sourcing high-end appliances for the house.

"I didn't realize quite how much we were spending on everything," Ted said. "We went a little crazy. But don't worry, it'll just take a few days to clear. In the meantime, use this." He pulled out his wallet and handed her a credit card that she hadn't seen before, with her name on it. "I keep this line for emergencies," he explained.

"Emergencies?" she asked. "Are we in an emergency?"

"No, of course not. You know what I mean. Things are just a little tight right now, with the house and everything. And you know that they slashed bonuses in the last two quarters. It's just a weird financial cycle."

Maja nodded, feeling stupid. She'd also lost track of what they were spending on the house. There had been so many expenses, between subcontractors, materials, and city and county fees. She knew that they had already spent down most—all?—of the construction loan, and that Ted was putting things on his credit card. She had just assumed that he was paying it off each month.

"Are we in trouble?" she asked.

"No, babe, no," Ted replied, putting his arm around her shoulders. "I'm taking care of everything."

"Hey," Maja said. "That reminds me. Was there an issue with our last payment to John? The officer on the case asked me about it. I guess John told him we were behind. I said it must be a misunderstanding."

Ted frowned. "That doesn't sound right," he said. "But I'll check on it. Hey, it's late. Let's get some dinner. Chinese?"

"Sure," Maja said. "But do you want to go through the credit card charges first? I want to get a handle on what's already been paid for."

Ted looked at her. "It's been a long day," he said. "Can we do it tomorrow?"

Maja was also tired, and to be honest, she wasn't looking forward to having Ted look too closely at how much she'd spent the previous month at Design Within Reach when she was ordering the dining room chairs. "Good idea. We'll figure everything out in the morning."

She relaxed against Ted's shoulder and tried to put the business about the new credit card out of her mind. She wasn't sure what, exactly, everything was, but she was happy enough to put it off until tomorrow.

28

Maja was right—Louis wasn't happy about her taking more time off, but he grudgingly gave her the week. On Sunday night, she took the bus down to New Falls to stay with Aneeta. The following morning, the insurance adjuster showed up—on the right day this time—and walked with her through the house, taking pictures and making notes on the damage. He appeared to be just as horrified by the damage a party had caused as Maja was. Looking around and tallying up all the ruined items, she could see what Ted had meant when he'd said that they'd gone a little crazy.

If he'd been worried about what they were spending, she wished that he'd been more up front with her. But she couldn't really be mad at him. After all, she'd been the one to push for the ever-increasing array of luxury finishes: Carrara marble, a steam shower, a kitchen faucet that turned on and off with a wave of your hand. Her mantra had been, "If we're going to do it, let's do it right." To which Ted would jokingly reply, "And if we're going to spend our money, let's spend it all." Except now Maja was beginning to realize that he hadn't actually been joking, and she was embarrassed that she had left it all up to Ted and hadn't kept a closer eye on the budget.

That night at Aneeta's house, Maja was in an upbeat mood. She felt they were getting back on track. "Maybe this wasn't the worst thing to happen," she said to Aneeta. "I mean, now I can go back and fix all the little things that bothered me. I was never really sure about pale gray for the floorboards. I think I'm going to go with something warmer this time around."

But her good mood lasted only until the next afternoon, when an email came in from Belltown Mutual with a damage estimate attached. Every item was listed out separately, with replacement values and hour estimates she didn't totally understand. She scrolled through until she found the page with the total. She stared at it for a long moment and tried to do the calculations in her head. The insurance company had only assessed a little over two hundred thousand dollars' worth of damage. But her new contractor, and even the police, had put the estimate much, much higher. The marble in the kitchen alone, which all had to be replaced, had cost at least twenty thousand dollars, and that didn't include all the labor costs to remove the damaged pieces and install the new ones.

She picked up her phone and called her insurance agent. Cindy was patient with her, but Maja was still near tears by the time she got off the phone. It turned out that the adjuster had missed all sorts of things, misunderstanding how far along they were in the construction process. When Maja explained that they'd had to remove a lot of the damaged materials and fixtures to prevent mold from forming, Cindy clucked sympathetically. "You can certainly appeal the determination," she said. "You just need to hire an independent adjuster. And it helps if you have all of your receipts. Did you provide those to the adjuster?"

Maja was furious with herself. Why hadn't she put all of this together before? She felt a fresh wave of rage at the people who had done this to her. They had destroyed her dream, her home, and for what? A beer bash? It was infuriating, and she felt powerless to do anything about it.

She called Ted, and he picked up right away. "We're going to need to hire our own adjuster," she told him, "and I'm starting to wonder if we should get our own attorney as well."

"Let's hold off on hiring a lawyer. Look, Maja," Ted said, and then paused.

"Hmm?" Maja said.

"This is just an idea," Ted finally said, "but hear me out."

Maja had been looking at the damage estimate for the tenth time, as if studying it over and over would somehow change it. But the tone of Ted's voice made her give him her full attention. "What is it?" she asked.

"What if we sold the house," he said, his voice sounding odd. "You know, cut and run."

"Sell it?" Maja was incredulous. "Ted, that's crazy. Why would we do that? Besides," she said, hardly able to believe they were having this conversation, "it doesn't even have a functional kitchen or bathroom."

"I know," Ted said. "It's a stupid idea. I just thought, you know, maybe we could sell it as is. It's a great piece of property. A developer or someone might want to work on it. And then later, we can take the insurance money and put it toward another house when everything calms down. This is a lot for us to deal with."

"Ted, this is the house that we built. We can't just give up on this because it's hard." There was a catch in her voice. "I feel like I'm all alone here."

"Forget it. Just forget I said anything. It was a stupid idea," Ted said sharply.

Maja thought that he sounded like he was on the verge of losing it. She had a feeling that if she pushed him, they might really have a fight. The bad kind, with days of silence before they could reach an uneasy truce. And there was part of her that wanted it; that wanted to scream and blame and make someone else hurt as much as she did right now.

But instead, she took a deep breath. It was one thing to fight when you knew, in your heart, that the other person would still be there, next to you, when it was all over. Maja wasn't totally confident that that was true right now. Her marriage had always felt like a sure thing. The house, almost finished, felt like a sure thing. And now both seemed to be slipping through her fingers.

She kept her voice steady as she finally replied. "Ted, we're going to get through this. I know you're overwhelmed. I am too. But we can use the initial amount from the insurance company to at least get started with the new contractor. It doesn't feel like it, but we are making some progress."

Ted sighed. "You're right. We'll figure it out. Maybe we can apply for another construction loan to see us through until we can figure things out with the insurance company. I'll see what I can find out."

"Thank you," Maja said. That sounded a lot more like the Ted she knew: a problem solver.

"Okay, well, I have to get back to work," Ted said, and Maja thought she heard a catch in his voice. He'd told her not to worry, but his tone said something different. "I love you," she said, but he'd already hung up the phone.

29

When Maja called the DA's office on Thursday afternoon, Jake Till-man finally had some good news to share with her. It had been almost a month since the house party, and the Jensens' calls had become in-creasingly uncomfortable as the investigation failed to move forward. Jake had assured Maja that the police were making progress, but privately he'd started to think they'd be lucky to get minor charges to stick. The evidence they had was just too thin.

Detective Murray was right, though. All they'd needed to move the investigation forward, it turned out, was one kid to talk. In the beginning, when the police were asking parents to voluntarily come forward, no one had anything to say. They were sorry to hear what had happened, of course, and they hoped that the police were able to catch whoever did it. But it was a different story when, armed with June's evidence, the police were able to go to parents and say, your child has been named as a perpetrator, would you be interested in discussing a plea deal? That caused the floodgates to open. Over the last week, parents had been bringing their terrified kids into the station ready to strike a deal. They asked for leniency and were only too happy to give up the details of what had happened in exchange.

The picture that emerged was grim. Dozens of kids had made their way to the property, carefully carpooling or leaving their cars on the road to escape notice. They'd entered the house, knowing full well that they had no right to be there, and proceeded to tear it apart, piece by piece, as they cheered each other on. By the time the police heard these stories, they'd taken on a slightly mythic status with the kids: Will O'Connor showing up with a keg and throwing a hammer through a glass door, his brother, Trip, dragging a toilet through the hall and launching it off the deck. Hunter Finch, or as most kids knew him, Will O'Connor's rich friend, had handed out pills. The names of other kids they hadn't heard of yet started coming up: one who set a fire on the deck, and another who'd brought in spray paint to tag the walls. Two kids had sold lines of cocaine in an upstairs bathroom, and another brought the bottle rockets that had damaged the deck. It wasn't just a party that had gotten out of control. It was a party that was designed to get out of control.

Once Detective Murray had the confessions, Jake put together the charges and brought them to Hal for approval with an air of triumph. This was a real case, he thought. It would be covered in the papers. Not just the local one, but the Philly papers too, and maybe even on TV. It was his first big chance to make a name for himself as a prosecutor. Hal had shown little interest in the case after he'd told Jake to concentrate on the O'Connor boys, but Jake expected that, given the new evidence, he would happily sign off on the charges, which ranged in severity from summary trespassing to criminal mischief and corruption of minors.

What Jake didn't expect was for Hal to blow a gasket.

"What exactly do you think you're doing?" Hal barked at him, after spending an uncomfortably long time looking over Jake's work. "Felony criminal mischief? Intent to distribute? Didn't we sit here, in this office, and decide that we were going to keep the charges more manageable?"

"That was before we had over a dozen individuals come forward to give evidence," Jake said. "We're in a much better position now than we were then."

"We're walking a fine line, Jake. I know you didn't grow up around here, but try to put yourself in these kids' shoes. Sure, they've made a mistake and they must be held accountable. But I don't see any reason to totally derail their futures. What's important here is that we hold the people who planned the party responsible." He flipped through the charging documents. "The O'Connor brothers. Tell me what we have on them."

Jake sighed. There was no doubt in his mind that William O'Connor had organized the party, but Jake had been envisioning far more shared responsibility. To Jake's mind, the story that had emerged about the party was one of a community that had lost its way, a group of kids so out of control and privileged that they thought nothing of destroying a house. What Hal wanted was a convenient scapegoat. If everyone on Jake's list, from the daughter of a county supervisor to the son a wealthy real estate developer, faced serious charges, the town would have to acknowledge that they had a culture problem. If only the O'Connor brothers took the blame, it was easy enough to point to them and say, hey, every town has a few bad apples.

Still, William O'Connor was their strongest case. Jake opened his file. "We have the underage-drinking ticket that Detective Murray issued on the road, and June Jeffries's testimony that William was there. We also have the O'Connor name in the deposit book at Mason's Liquors, and Murray is pretty sure we can get a positive ID from Mr. Mason if we need it. And we have testimony from more than a few kids that it was William O'Connor who broke the first window, starting the destruction of the house. It's a pretty solid case."

"Not bad," Hal said. "Any physical evidence that puts him at the house?"

Jake shook his head.

Hal thought for a moment. "The more severe the charges, the greater the likelihood that he takes his chances at trial. You've got a good case, but it's not a slam dunk. See if Murray can dig up anything else."

Jake and Hal went back and forth, and eventually they agreed that the rest of the partygoers would be charged with trespassing or misdemeanor vandalism. As they finished up, Jake made one more push. "What about the Finch kid?" he asked. "We have multiple sources claiming that he supplied the drugs at the party. Are we really just going to let him off with a vandalism charge?"

Jake had barely finished speaking before Hal started shaking his head. "Did you recover any drugs?" Hal asked. "No? Then there's no case."

The charges were filed the next morning, and those named had until Monday to surrender to the police for arraignment. The DA's office sent out a press release, and there was a small item in the local paper listing the charges, as well as the names of all those who were over eighteen. Jake skimmed it as he sat in his office. There was a bland quote from Hal, saying that the perpetrators must be held accountable for their actions, but Jake couldn't help but notice that his own name appeared nowhere in the story, despite the fact that he was the one running the case.

30

On the morning that the charges were filed, rumors flew through the school about who was and wasn't being charged. Will hadn't heard anything before class, but he was pretty sure that there would be bad news waiting for him when he got home.

After school, he stood in line in the auditorium to pick up his graduation cap and gown and scanned the crowd, thinking about how many of those kids had partied on the booze that he and Trip brought to the party. One of his track teammates was standing in front of him in line. "I heard a lot of people talked to the cops," the kid said. "Right before graduation too. Sucks."

"Were you there?" Will asked. He was just making conversation, but his teammate drew back from him as if he was contagious. "Why?" he asked. "Looking for a name to give the cops?"

"No!" Will said. "No, I don't know why I asked. I haven't said a word to the cops about anyone."

"Well, I wasn't there," the kid said tersely. "I wasn't invited."

"Lucky you," Will replied.

At home, Will pulled up the driveway and sat in the truck for a minute. When he finally forced himself to go inside, his parents were sitting at the kitchen table under the glow of the fluorescent light, piles of paperwork spread out before them. The dogs were laying at their feet, heads resting on their paws forlornly. Will had expected some sort of explosion, but his parents just looked at him. Will sat down and tossed his bag onto the empty chair, and his graduation cap slipped out of the half-zipped bag. His father glanced at it.

"A lotta good that's gonna do you now," he said.

His mother put her hand on his father's hand. "Sean," she said, giving him a look. "That's not going to help."

His father raised his eyebrows, but he didn't say anything else. Both of his parents were looking at him as if they were waiting for him to say something.

"I'm really sorry," he said, because he couldn't think of anything else to say.

His father nodded, pursing his lips. "You're sorry," he said. "A child is sorry. A man takes responsibility for his actions."

"Sean," his mother was saying again, her voice strained. "We agreed that we weren't going to do this right now. We need to focus on what our plan is."

His father took a deep breath. "Well," he said, looking at Will. "What's the plan?"

"I don't know," Will said. He had no idea how to make this right, or even if it could be made right.

"No plan for this, huh? You have a plan to get beer, a plan to party, a plan to run all over town with your rich-kid friend, acting like you own the place. You don't, by the way, if that hasn't been made abundantly clear to you. Well, here's a plan. You can join up. It was good enough for me, and it's good enough for you. If they'll have you after this."

"I don't know if it's come to that yet," his mother said. "Can we talk seriously about this, please?" She turned to her husband. "First, I think we need a lawyer. We should at least consult someone. Will, you're being charged with trespassing and felony vandalism, among other things. You have to turn yourself in at the courthouse for arraignment. I don't think you'll have to . . . stay. Not yet, anyway." Her voice caught and her eyes welled up with tears.

Will swallowed. The thing he had been dreading had finally happened. Why had he thought he might get out of this? He stared dumbly at his mother, not knowing what to say.

"Do you understand what this means, Will?" his mother asked. "These are serious charges—if you're convicted, you could be facing jail time. And it's not just that. Everything is at risk—you could lose your scholarship, or even your place at Princeton, Will. Your guidance counselor called. It was her strong recommendation that you disclose this to Princeton yourself. She seemed to be unsure of whether the school would need to start contacting colleges, since it wasn't a school academic or disciplinary matter. But the fact that she called at all means that they are at least considering it. According to her, some kids have already pled guilty to minor charges, and she's getting a lot of calls from parents about this." She paused. "I don't suppose you could talk to Hunter's dad? Get his advice?"

"No!" Will's father banged his fist on the table. "Not going to happen."

His mom shrugged. "It's just a thought. But this is why we need a lawyer. It's not just Princeton we have to worry about. We could be looking at big fines, and the possibility of restitution payments, if Will is convicted."

"Did you do it?" his father interjected, looking Will right in the eye.

Will stared straight back at him. "Yes," he said quietly. And then he said it louder: "Yes. I was there." It felt good, after weeks of trying to pretend it hadn't happened, to say it out loud. "It was just a party." His father raised an eyebrow, but Will was on a roll. "I don't know where everyone got the idea that I planned it, though," he said. "It wasn't like some scheme that I had. We just showed up with some beer."

"You never think," his father said.

"Do you always have to think the worst of me?" Will asked him. "You don't know what it's like. I have to work twice as hard as everyone else. It's not enough that I got into Princeton. I had to get the scholarship too, just to be able to go, and work here every weekend. I can count on one hand the number of kids at school who have jobs. School *is* their job. So, yeah, once in a while I like to have some fun. Everybody does it."

"So you destroyed a house for fun?" his father asked.

"No!" He paused. "I did it for Maddie."

"I don't understand," Will's mother said. "For Maddie?"

Will let out a deep exhale. "This guy was all over her. She was passed out. I had to help her, so I broke the window."

Will heard his mother breathe in sharply. "Was Maddie hurt?" she asked.

"She's okay," Will said, even though he wasn't sure if it was true.

"That doesn't explain what you were doing there in the first place," Will's father said. "How did you get from one broken window to an entire house trashed?"

"I don't really know how it happened," Will admitted. "It was like everyone lost their minds." After a moment he spoke again, his voice sounding small. "It takes so much energy trying to hold everything together. Maybe . . . maybe it felt good, just for once, to tear it all apart."

To Will's surprise, his dad was quiet. He looked tired and old. The skin beneath his eyes was papery and thin, and the edges of the Gothic lettering of his SEMPER FI tattoo, peeking out from his shirt, were faded like old jeans. Will noticed how red and calloused his mother's hands were as she awkwardly fumbled through the pile of papers in front her.

"I'm really sorry," Will said. "I didn't mean for any of this to happen. I didn't mean to hurt anyone."

This time his father nodded, seeming to accept his apology.

"Do you think I should plead guilty?" he asked them.

His father looked grim. "Don't do anything yet," he said. "Your mother is right. We need to talk to a lawyer first."

"What about Trip?" he asked.

"He's going to need a lawyer as well. We'll have to fight the charge against him. If we don't, he'll definitely end up serving at least a year."

Will's head was buzzing, but he tried to listen as his parents told him what was going to happen. They would hire an attorney and start putting together the money they'd need to pay any fines or restitution that was ordered. They would make the first payment on his tuition, which was due this week, to hold his spot, just in case. And to make all this happen, they would take out a second mortgage on the orchard.

Will had always been vaguely aware of the financial balancing act that his parents performed to keep the farm going. The property itself was valuable, but it wasn't money they could tap without selling it. And there were always major projects that needed to be done: old fields ripped out and replanted, farm equipment upgraded, the barns and kitchen and shop maintained. Last year they'd had a stream flood one of the fields, and there had been major drainage work installed to prevent it from happening again. Some years the orchard made money spring through fall, when big crops and beautiful weather brought people out weekend after weekend, and some years everything seemed against them: late frosts that doomed their summer crops, and muggy summers that brought torrential rains seemingly every weekend, keeping tourists away. But either way, the bills and the farm help still needed to be paid. Will knew they took out loans to get them through big projects and lean summers. It was just part of the business. But even to him, a second mortgage sounded bad.

Will nodded, and his father got up without another word and walked outside. Will's mother was looking at him.

"You need to take some responsibility and try to make it right."

"I'll talk to Princeton," Will said. "I think it's better if I tell them the truth—that I've been charged but not convicted. And I'll talk to the scholarship committee as well."

"Okay," his mother said. "But I'm not only talking about Princeton. Making this right doesn't just mean getting yourself out of trouble, and making it up to your dad and me. If what I've heard is true, you did some very serious damage to someone's home."

"It wasn't just me," Will said reflexively.

"I don't know about anyone else. But I know you. And I know that you are better than this. Your father and I can try to protect you—that's our job. But you're the one who has to live with yourself. I really hope you can figure it out, Will."

Will looked down at his hands. She was right, as always. He had to figure it out for himself.

31

Dom Finch's study was a sunny room tucked into the oldest part of the house, where Dom always brought Hunter when he wanted to speak seriously with him. Today Hunter sat in the old leather arm-chair opposite the desk, feeling like a scared child, despite the fact that he now filled out the entire seat, his long legs sticking out and his elbows sinking into its worn padding, waiting for his father to speak.

Dom's voice was strained. "You have until Monday to turn yourself in for arraignment, Hunter. You're being charged with misdemeanor vandalism. That's a charge that carries a possibility of up to a year in jail. Since you haven't told me anything to the contrary, I'm assuming that you did these things?"

Hunter shrugged. "It's complicated," he said finally. "I was there. But so were a lot of people."

It was the wrong thing to say. "You are not like a lot of people!" Dom snapped. "You've been given so much more than other people, and you should hold yourself to a higher standard."

"I know," Hunter said. "I'm sorry."

"Well, that's not going to do us a lot of good right now. We're going to have to fight this. You're eighteen, Hunter. Your name is in the paper. Not to mention that this will be on your record if it goes forward. The optics are just terrible." He raked his hand through his hair. "You're going to plead not guilty. I have a lawyer lined up for you, Mark Greenberg. He'll go with you and guide you through the process. You'll meet him at nine a.m. on Monday morning, at the courthouse. I won't be there—it will only draw more attention. I talked to our PR people, and there haven't been any inquiries yet. Hopefully it will stay that way."

The optics, Hunter thought. It was always about work. But he kept his mouth shut. Now wasn't the time. "Is that it?" he asked. "Sounds like you have everything handled."

Dom looked at Hunter with contempt. "You need to grow up. This is the real world, Hunter. You've been lucky so far, but the party won't go on forever. You have to learn that there are consequences to your actions." He looked at Hunter closely, as if assessing him and not liking what he saw. "We're done here," he said, finally.

Dom was often angry or disappointed with him, but never dismissive. Hunter's success had been an interest they both shared, even if it did sometimes seem as if Dom was doing a lot of the heavy lifting. In his office, his father had sounded resigned, as if Hunter was a real estate investment that hadn't panned out, and the only thing left to do was to cut his losses. Hunter had to fix this. He just didn't know how.

He had to get out of the house. He borrowed Lindsay's car—again without asking—and headed for June's house. She hadn't answered his texts or calls all week, but she couldn't blow him off if he showed up at her front door. His father's words kept echoing through his mind: "We're done here."

At June's house, he banged on the front door. It swung open, and Mr. Jeffries leaned against the frame, his arms crossed. "Hunter," he said.

"Is June here?" Hunter asked.

"Yes," her father replied, but he didn't move.

"Can I come in?"

"No, you may not."

Hunter was surprised. June's family was always welcoming to him, maybe a little overly so. He knew that they liked the fact that their daughter was dating him. They tried to be low-key about it, but he could tell.

"Did you take her to this party?" Mr. Jeffries asked.

"Is that what she said?" Hunter snapped, a little surprised by his own rudeness. He still felt on edge from talking with his father.

Mr. Jeffries raised his eyebrows. "Is that any way to talk to your girlfriend's father?"

And just like that, Hunter could tell that in Mr. Jeffries's estimation, he'd gone from rich kid, category desirable son-in-law material, to rich kid, category troubled and destined to come to no good.

Hunter opened his mouth to argue, but Mr. Jeffries cut him off. "She's grounded, Hunter," he said, pulling the door shut.

Hunter was seething as he left June's house. He didn't want to go home, so he walked aimlessly through town and past the courthouse, which he crossed the street to avoid. He'd be there soon enough. Why had June been avoiding his calls? Even when she was busy with school she usually texted him back. He had a dark thought: Was it possible that she was the one who'd gone to the police?

When he passed Alejandro's Diner, he stuck his head in to see if Rosie was there. It was four o'clock, between the lunch and dinner rushes, but she was there, preparing the tables, laying sheets of white paper down and setting them with silverware and little glass vases of wildflowers. She had a white apron wrapped tightly around her waist and a dishtowel hanging out of the back pocket of her jeans.

He watched her for a moment. There were no customers at this hour, and she had the radio tuned to a station playing Rihanna. She was dancing as she worked, her long brown ponytail bouncing behind her. She was pretty, he thought. He'd made out with her once, a few years ago, and he occasionally flirted with her to make June jealous. But looking at her now, there was something so sweet and *normal* about her. He wanted to be part of it.

"Hey," he said, and she turned around.

When she realized that he'd been standing there for a minute, she blushed. "You scared me," she said. "Where's June? I haven't seen her all week."

He shrugged, not wanting to get into it. "Need help?" he asked.

"Sure," she said, handing him a caddy holding napkins and silverware. He followed her around as she laid tablecloths and helped her to set the tables.

"Not like that," she said, changing the positions of the fork and knife. "You've probably never set a table, have you?"

"The footman does it for us," Hunter said with a sly smile.

"You don't have a footman," she said, laughing.

"No," Hunter admitted. "But we do have a housekeeper. And she usually sets the table."

"Must be nice," Rosie said. "Hey, I heard about the charges. I can't believe they didn't get my name. A lot of the kids on that list got ratted out by other kids at school. Everyone is suspicious of everyone else. It's kind of a shitty way to end senior year."

"Who the fuck does that?" Hunter asked, his anger flaring, and Rosie looked surprised. "I'm sorry," he said, immediately. "I'm just pissed. Someone gave them my name." He paused for a second. "I took it out on Will."

"Will would never do that," Rosie said. "I'm sure."

"I know. I just thought maybe he was trying to get out of trouble. My dad put the idea in my head. It's ridiculous. I shouldn't have suspected him. Honestly, it was probably Trip. He's the one facing the suspended jail sentence if he's convicted."

"Maybe," Rosie said doubtfully.

"Have you seen that lawyer again?"

"The DA? He's been in, but he hasn't said anything about the party. I've noticed him looking at me a few times. I'm scared that maybe he thinks I was there."

"Maybe he likes you," Hunter said, playfully.

Rosie blushed again. "That's gross."

"No it isn't," Hunter said. "He'd be crazy not to."

Rosie looked back at him for a moment, as if she wanted to say something, and then she turned abruptly and went behind the counter. She started to refill the saltshakers.

"Rosie," Hunter said, sitting on a stool at the counter. "I know it's a lot to ask, but if there's anything that you can find out from him, it could make a big difference. Or maybe you could say something to him? Try to get him to understand? My dad says that the

DA's office has a lot of discretion on the charges. There's a lot riding on this."

"He's not going to tell me anything," Rosie said. "I mean, why would he?"

Hunter thought for a moment. "What about his phone?" he asked.

"What about his phone? What am I going to do? Steal his phone and, like, read his emails?"

"Why not?" Hunter said. "You girls do it all the time to each other."

"Okay, that's just nuts. First of all, it's probably a crime. And second, what could we do with it, anyway?"

"You're right," Hunter said. "It's a stupid idea. I just wish I knew who gave them my name. Then I'd have a better idea of how to fight it. I have no idea how much they know. Anything you find out could really help me."

Rosie looked at him, then turned her head toward the kitchen. "Alright, I guess I could try."

"Thanks, Rosie. That's a really big help," Hunter said. "Can you bail for a few minutes?" he asked. "Let's go walk around. I feel like I can't sit still."

"Sure," Rosie replied. "I just need to be back by six." She went into the kitchen to tell her dad, and when she came back out, Hunter noticed that she'd let her hair down, and it looked like she'd put on lip gloss. He slung his arm over her shoulders. "Fits just right," he said, which he always said to June, and she pulled a little closer to him as they walked out into the warm afternoon.

32

Tuesday was locals' night at Canal House, the brew pub in New Falls. The town didn't have much of a craft beer scene, and Canal House was no exception. Their house ale had a great-looking can but mediocre taste, and on locals' night the special was a shot and a beer—not the house ale, but a bottle of Yuengling. Trip was on his third round, but the bartender, Joe, was a friend, and he didn't keep too close of an eye on it. Trip's tab was always more of an estimate than an exact reckoning.

By six o'clock, Trip's friends started to roll in. They were mostly guys he'd grown up with and who were still hanging around town for one reason or another, working at restaurants or making a half-hearted stab at the nearby community college. They sat around the horseshoe-shaped bar, downing beers and watching the Phillies beat up on the Braves on the wall-mounted TVs. The mood grew rowdier as the hits—and the beer bottles—piled up.

Canal House was filling up. Some guys in work boots and T-shirts were playing pool, and a couple of girls who looked like they may or may not be old enough to be in there were drinking cosmos, an even worse choice than the house IPA. A band was setting up on the small stage near the end of the bar. Trip had gone home with the singer, a brunette in heavy black eyeliner, last time they'd played. He couldn't quite remember her name.

"The Phils are going all the way this year," declared Andy, Trip's buddy from high school.

"No way," said Trip. "They'll blow it. They're peaking too soon."

"I'll put fifty bucks on it," Andy said.

"Sure," said Trip. "I'll take your money."

"Don't bet against the home team," Joe warned, refilling their shot glasses with Jim Beam.

Trip tipped his back. "It's worked out for me so far. Why change a winning strategy?"

Joe turned to take drink orders from one of the guys who'd been playing pool, and Trip stood up to go to the restroom.

"Hold on there!" Joe said. "Where are you going?"

"The john," Trip said. Standing up gave him a head rush.

"Sorry, buddy, I'm afraid not," Joe said as he mixed drinks for the pool players.

"What?" Trip said, thinking Joe had misheard him. "I'm going to the bathroom."

"Not in here, you're not," Joe said, grinning. "The boss said I was on strict orders to keep you out of there. He said he doesn't want his toilet ending up on the deck."

Andy started laughing. "Trip, man, everyone knows you're not house-trained! Didn't you take a piss in the dishwasher at that house?"

"Okay, very funny," Trip said.

"Take it outside," Joe said.

"You want me to go in the parking lot?" Trip asked.

"You won't be the last one tonight," Joe said with a wink.

"I'm going outside . . . for a cigarette," Trip announced. He pushed through the doors as the band started playing. He knew his friends were just kidding, but he wasn't in the mood. He'd come to the bar tonight precisely because he didn't want to talk about the house party. Since he and Will had been charged, it was the only thing his parents talked about at home. They'd hired a lawyer but it wasn't looking good. If he'd been thinking straight, he would have left that party and gone to the bar as soon as they started playing Katy Perry. He hadn't even been having that good of a time. It was just inertia, he guessed, that had kept him at the beer pong table until he'd run out of opponents.

Outside, he pulled out a paper and started rolling a cigarette. He

heard the door open again behind him. "I'm not bumming you another cigarette," he called over his shoulder, thinking it was Andy.

"I've got my own," said an unfamiliar voice behind him, and Trip
turned around. One of the guys who'd been playing pool was standing uncomfortably close to him, and Trip took a step forward as
he turned around. The guy behind him was wearing paint-stained
khakis and a Carhartt hoodie. "I thought I recognized you," he said.
"Trip O'Connor, right?"

"We know each other?" Trip asked.

"Well, I know who you are," the guy said. His voice wasn't friendly.
"You're the asshole who trashed the house."

"What's it to you?" Trip asked.

"What's it to me? Oh, nothing. Just a job. Just putting food in my
kid's mouth. Or not, thanks to you and your friends."

"Hold up," Trip said. "I don't have anything to do with your job."
He looked at the guy again. He had a faded amateur tattoo on his
hand and small silver earrings in both ears. He looked familiar, and
suddenly Trip remembered him. He'd been a few years ahead of Trip
in high school. Trip remembered that he'd been in a band. Now it
looked like he was working construction.

"I heard you were at that party," the guy was saying. "But I guess I
had to see you to believe it. What the fuck, man? You guys destroyed
that house. The house I spent the better part of the last year building."

"So? What do you care?" Trip asked, looking him up and down.
"It wasn't your house."

The guy shook his head. "I worked for John Williams for three
years, and now I'm out of a job. I've got a daughter. I'm trying to save
up for my own place. And thanks to you, all I got for my trouble was
the police coming around, and my boss accusing me of leaving the
garage opener out and telling me not to bother coming back. All I
could get this week was two days painting houses, which doesn't pay
shit. Did you think about that while you were partying it up with a
bunch of teenagers? That there were hardworking people around here
you would hurt? But I guess you can't make anything out of your own
life, so you'll take everyone else down with you."

Trip felt the Jim Beam he'd drunk pulsing through his dilated veins. He was catching it from everyone, and he was sick of it. And this guy had hit a little close to home. "You're a big man, huh?" Trip asked. "If you think you're gonna get anywhere in this town working construction, you're as stupid as you look. You'll still be saving up for that town house when your daughter has kids."

As he spoke, Trip tried to push past the guy and back into the bar. But the guy stepped in his path and caught him on the shoulder. A few of the guy's friends had come outside and were standing by the door, watching them. Trip started to raise his fists. The guy had twenty pounds on him, but Trip didn't care. Maybe he wanted a beating. They looked at each other for a long moment, and then the guy stepped aside.

"You're not worth it," he said. Then he turned and walked back into the bar with his friends, leaving Trip standing alone on the sidewalk.

"I know," Trip said to no one in particular.

33

At first, Rosie didn't notice when Jake Tillman sat down at the counter. She had a lot to think about. There was the party, which was all anyone was talking about. She still couldn't believe that she hadn't been named, but she knew that it could happen at any moment. Now that the charges had been announced, people were desperate to get themselves out of trouble in any way that they could. She'd had more than one conversation at school with kids she barely knew who were clearly trying to feel out whether she'd been at the party or not. It felt icky. Even her dad had asked her about it. She hated lying to him, but she'd denied being there right to his face.

Then there was Maddie, who basically stopped hanging out and returned all of Rosie's texts with one-word replies. By now, the whole school knew what had happened to her. There had even been a name floated of the guy, some kid from New Jersey, who was apparently bragging about it, the douchebag. At least no one had mentioned Maddie's name to the police, so she hadn't been hassled on that front.

But more than either of these things, there was Hunter to think about. She knew that it was wrong to like him. He was her best friend's boyfriend, even if June seemed to be keeping her distance from him, and everyone else for that matter, after she'd gotten in trouble for the party. Liking your friend's boyfriend was such a stupid stereotype that Rosie blushed every time she thought about it. And yet he was exactly what she did keep thinking about. His hand on her knee at the tree house in the woods; his eyes watching her as she set the tables in the restaurant; and mostly his arm around her shoulders as they strolled down the main street in town, as if she belonged to him and it was the most normal thing in the world.

She shivered at the thought, and then looked up as a customer cleared his throat. It was the district attorney, and she nearly dropped the silverware she was holding. "Sorry!" she exclaimed, too loud. Gathering herself, she picked up her pad. "What can I get for you?"

"Ham and cheese on a roll, please," he said, and Rosie thought that he was looking at her weirdly. Was it because she was acting strange, or because he knew that she was at that stupid party?

"Chips or fries?" she asked automatically.

"Chips."

She poured him an iced tea without being asked. "So," she said awkwardly, thinking of Hunter, "I guess you found the kids who trashed that house?"

"We brought some charges. Nothing too major."

"You don't sound very happy about it," Rosie said. "Will there be more?" She knew this was dangerous territory, but the thought of being able to tell Hunter something useful made her bold.

He gave her a searching look. "Someone at the party may have been selling or distributing drugs. I'd love to see some solid evidence on who exactly that was."

Rosie pretended to be busy sorting the forks and knives. He's talking about Hunter, she guessed. This was exactly what Hunter was looking for. Her heart started racing, and she held her breath, waiting for the DA to go on. But before he could say anything else, her dad came out of the kitchen. He greeted Jake—they'd become pretty friendly, Rosie noticed—and cracked them both beers. "Hey, you gotta come out and see the new bike!" her father exclaimed, and Rosie rolled her eyes. Her father was apparently having a midlife crisis, and had purchased a long-desired used motorcycle. Rosie thought that it was silly, and slightly scary, but she did love how much her dad loved it. Jake put his phone down on the counter, took the beer from her father, and followed him outside.

Rosie stared down at the phone. It was a BlackBerry, sort of official-looking, and still lit brightly by a half-composed email on the screen. She hesitated for only a second before she grabbed it, slipping it into her apron pocket. She ran into the bathroom and locked the door behind her.

She wasn't sure what she was looking for. Hunter had asked her about the phone, but he hadn't been too specific. Her hands shook as she opened the email inbox and began to scroll through it. Nothing stood out to her, and she realized with embarrassment that of course the party wasn't Jake Tillman's only case. There were all sorts of emails—it would take her hours to go through them.

She stared at the phone as a half-formed idea came to her. She pulled down her tank top so her bra was exposed. Then she held out the phone, leaned over, and pursed her lips like June did when she sent pictures to Hunter. She looked at the screen. The photo was low-resolution, but it was actually kind of hot. She entered her number in Tillman's phone and texted the picture to her own phone: U look hot. My favorite pic. Then she pulled her phone out of her back pocket and texted him back: Hey sexy. See you after work. Go get those bad guys. It sounded kind of dumb, but she wasn't sure what people usually said in these texts. She went into his phone, opened the text, and added herself as a contact, under a nickname, Rosalita.

Her heart was beating hard. She looked at herself in the mirror and pursed her lips again. She looked good. Is this how June felt? Powerful? She thought about taking another photo and sending it to Hunter, but she couldn't bring herself to do it.

There was a firm knock at the door, and Rosie almost screamed. In an instant, she realized how stupid this was. What was she going to do—blackmail him? It was insane. Hunter wasn't going to be impressed; he was going to think she was weird.

"Just a sec," she called out as she jabbed frantically at the unfamiliar phone. It took her a minute to figure out how to delete their text conversation from his phone. She was trying to delete her contact when the knock came again. Forget it, she thought, shoving both phones back into her pockets, and opened the door. It wasn't Tillman, or her father. It was a lady with a toddler, who was doing the potty dance. "Sorry to rush you!" the woman called out as she passed Rosie, and Rosie just nodded, relieved.

When she returned to the counter, Tillman was back in his seat, eating his sandwich and chatting with her dad. He hadn't seemed to notice that his phone was missing. She dropped a napkin, and then bent down to pick it up, holding the phone as if she'd found it lying behind the counter. "Is this yours?" she asked him, her voice unnaturally high.

"Sure is," Tillman said, not noticing her discomfort. "Thanks!"

"No problema," she muttered, close to tears. She needed to get ahold of herself. She asked her dad if she could go home to do some laundry, and he let her go. "I got a good one," he said, winking at Tillman, and Rosie shuddered.

What was happening to her? Crushing on her best friend's boyfriend. Messing around with *the district attorney's phone*. She hardly recognized herself. Soon someone would give her name to the police, and her dad would see what kind of person she really was. She walked home quickly, determined to actually do her laundry, and her dad's as well.

If I don't tell anyone about this, she thought, it will be like it never happened.

34

The face of the girl behind the glass was impassive. She wore a sweat-shirt with the hood pulled up over her long blond hair, and she stared intently at the table in front of her as she spoke. Her parents, on either side of her, seemed to pantomime her emotions: her mother, pale and crying, and her father, with his fists clenched and his eyes darting around the room, looking for a target for his fury. Detective Murray sat across from them, taking notes, while a younger female officer named Nisha Boyd conducted the interview.

Jake joined the huddle of people watching the scene through the two-way glass, and he noted with surprise that Hal Buckley was already there. Dressed in tennis whites, with his hands shoved in his pockets, Hal cut an odd figure at police headquarters. Chief Whitman was beside him, along with a woman who performed victim psych evaluations. Hal shot Jake a look, but he didn't say anything.

Jake had gotten the call from Murray only two hours earlier when he was in one of the northernmost towns of Hart County, trying a DUI who'd been too stupid to plead out. According to Murray, a girl had been brought into the station by her parents, claiming an assault. Murray thought that it might be the assault from the party but that was all that he'd been able to say before he was called into the room. As soon as Jake finished, he hightailed it back down to New Falls.

Chief Whitman turned to Jake to fill him in. "Her name is Madison Martin. She claims she was assaulted at that house party. She doesn't remember very much, but she's firm it happened. The parents brought her in after the school guidance counselor called and told them she'd been missing a lot of school. Apparently it all came out during the meeting."

The Chief flipped a switch, and sound filled the anteroom. "So the last thing that you can recall is that the boy was on top of you, and you couldn't get up?" Officer Boyd asked gently.

"Yeah," the girl confirmed. "He was trying to take off my underwear." She glanced at her father and her big eyes looked miserable, but she kept going. "I wanted him to stop, but I couldn't make him."

"And why couldn't you make him?" Boyd asked.

"Well, he was on top of me and I . . . I was pretty messed up," she admitted, her voice small.

"Can you tell me what you mean by messed up?"

Maddie's father tightened his fists but didn't say anything.

"I had a few beers," Maddie said quietly, and then, when Boyd kept looking at her expectantly, "and some E. Ecstasy."

"Okay. And did he manage to remove your underwear?"

"No. I don't think so. After a certain point, I can't remember anything else. I'm sorry. But a lot of people saw. They were . . ." Her voice trailed off, and when she spoke again, it was almost a whisper: "They were watching through a window. Everybody saw. Everybody knows." Her voice cracked.

Maddie's mother cut in: "That's when the boy broke the window. To get her out."

"Which boy was this?" Boyd asked, and Maddie's mother looked over at her daughter.

"Will O'Connor," Maddie said, her voice flat. "He broke the window and then he beat the kid up. I don't know what would have happened if he hadn't done that."

"And you saw this happen?" Boyd asked, gently.

"No. But everyone is talking about it. Someone took *pictures*. It's disgusting," she added, her voice now growing stronger.

Maddie's father banged the desk with his fist. "If everyone knows about this, why haven't the police done anything?" he demanded. "You're too busy chasing down kids for drinking beer at a party, and meanwhile my daughter is assaulted, and no one here knows a thing about it. I heard the police were there that night, giving out tickets on River Road. Why didn't you bother to break up this party? Too much trouble? You'd rather collect your fat paychecks—my tax dollars—and sit in your cars drinking coffee. If you'd done your damn jobs, none of this would have happened! You better believe the papers are going to hear about this. And my lawyer." He was on a roll, and Jake could tell from experience that his righteous anger was giving him relief from other more painful emotions. "And whose house was this, anyway?" he asked. "I think it's pretty negligent to leave a big house like that just open to whoever might find it. That's an attractive nuisance, right? Have the police looked into that? And do they know how these drugs are getting into the hands of children?"

Chief Whitman flipped off the audio with a grimace. Hal turned to Jake. "This girl wasn't charged, correct?"

"That's right," Jake confirmed.

"And she won't be now," Hal said. "We can't have kids coming forward with sexual assault allegations and getting charged with trespassing."

"Of course not," Jake agreed.

"I just want to make sure we're on the same page," Hal said. "I'm not sure that our focus here has been up to standards. I seem to recall that you and Detective Murray were informed of a possible assault weeks ago?"

Jake's face reddened. He wasn't sure why he was catching the blame here. If anything, he had fought for a more serious investigation and charges in the case, and Hal had blocked him at every turn. "That's right," Jake said, carefully. "But it was just a rumor. Nothing concrete."

"And what about this kid, Will O'Connor? Wasn't he the one who threw the party?"

"That's our theory. He's being charged with misdemeanor trespass and vandalism. This doesn't change that. It's one of our strongest cases."

"It's not going to play well if it turns out that Will O'Connor was breaking windows to prevent a *rape*," Hal mused. "None of this came up in the investigation?"

Jake shook his head. They'd looked into it, but they hadn't found anything definite.

"Do we have any leads on who assaulted this girl?" Hal asked.

"Not yet," the Chief replied. "The girl doesn't know who he was. But if we can find the pictures she's talking about, we'll have our guy and our evidence."

"Get those pictures," Hal said.

"What about the father's theory?" the chief asked Hal. "That we buried this in the investigation? There's nothing to that, is there?"

"No," Hal said, "There's nothing there, liability-wise. But from a PR perspective, it doesn't sound great." He sighed. "When you have the transcript, send it over to my office. We're going to treat this with kid gloves."

Hal went directly back to the office with Jake, not bothering to change out of his tennis clothes. "I'm going to take a personal interest in pushing this case forward," he said as he opened the door.

It's about time, Jake thought.

When Jake arrived at the office the next morning, before he'd even sat down at his desk, Hal strode over. "Put your jacket back on, and follow me," Hal said. "We're having a press conference. Got to get out in front of this thing."

This was the first that Jake was hearing about a press conference. "What thing?" he asked, but Hal was already halfway down the hallway. Jake followed him into one of the conference rooms, where a crew of the usual reporters from the town and county papers and local news websites were waiting expectantly. Hal stood at a podium at the front of the room, and he motioned for Jake to stand beside him. Donna followed them with a coffee cart and closed the door.

"Morning, folks," Hal said, turning on his full charm. "Thanks for coming in early. Please, help yourself to coffee. Now," he said, getting serious, "I know that there have been a lot of rumors going around regarding the Jensen house party case, and I want to set the record straight. Our office and the police department have been handling the case with the utmost seriousness and attention. What we have here is wanton, willful destruction of private property, and we will absolutely be holding *all* of the culprits responsible. I know it's your job," he said, winking at the reporters, "to stir up a little controversy. That's how you sell papers and get those clicks. I get it. But our police force has been thorough and sensitive in their ongoing investigation, and we'd love to see that in your fine papers as well.

"I'd also like to thank Assistant DA Jake Tillman for his hard work on the case." Hal nodded in Jake's direction without looking at him. "No one can fault Jake here for taking the young ages of these kids into account in his charges. I think we're all sensitive to the fact that kids make mistakes. But from now on I will be handling the matter personally, and any questions can be directed to me. We may be dealing with young people here, but we can't let our concern for the futures of these kids cloud our judgment or prevent us from addressing the culture of wealth and entitlement that can lead to these shocking outcomes."

Jake couldn't believe his ears. Hal was laying this at *his* feet? Jake was the one who had argued for accountability, and *Hal* had sat in this very building and warned him to tread lightly and to wrap everything up as quickly as possible. Now that it looked like the case might be too big to dispose of neatly, with the assault accusation upping the stakes, Hal was shifting all the blame to him. Jake stood there, livid, as Hal finished up his statement. He couldn't concentrate on the words.

Hal's shortsighted handling of the case had only confirmed to Jake that Hal was halfway out the door already. A case like this could make your career, and Jake had seen it as his ticket to the corner office—as soon as Hal finally took the leap to full-time golf and tennis, of course. But now Jake saw that chance slipping away. He realized that he'd been wrong. Hal still relished the game. And worse, he was making Jake look incompetent at his job.

Jake hardly noticed when Hal concluded the conference, and he followed Hal back down the hallway numbly. He hadn't said a single word the entire time. At the door to his office, Hal clapped a hand on his back. "Professional hazard," he said, by way of explanation. "Got to let them know that we're all over it before news about the assault breaks. Thanks for being a good soldier."

"We're all on the same team," Jake said drily. "Right?"

35

Jake sat very still in his chair. Hal had thrown him under the bus. This was his case, and he'd handled it well. Or at least as well as possible, under the restrictions that Hal put on him. While it hadn't shaped up to be a spectacular, headline-generating case that would make his career in New Falls, he had hoped that it would give him a little name recognition in town.

But the tide had turned, and Hal Buckley had left Jake hanging out to dry. It was one thing for the DA's office to go easy on a house party, especially since the victims were from out of town, and unlikely to stir up much local protest. For the police to have missed an assault, however, was a much different issue. Hal may have been more interested in playing golf than grinding out indictments, but he wasn't stupid. This would generate real attention and outrage, and Jake and Detective Murray would look like the bozos who had been so busy justifying trespassing tickets that they missed the assault of a teenage girl. They'd have to come down hard now, and explain why they hadn't before. Jake, it seemed, was their convenient explanation.

It took Jake a few minutes to find Alisha Shah's contact info, and while the phone rang, he crossed his fingers that she still had the same number. They'd dated for a few months in college, and he'd followed her career covering local politics in the *Philadelphia Inquirer*. She had a knack for crafting stories that showed the human side of city policy debates.

She picked up and answered in a brisk, professional voice. "Alisha Shah, who's speaking?"

"Alisha, it's Jake. Jake Tillman." He suddenly wasn't sure that she would even remember him. It had been awhile.

"Jake!" she cried out, her voice more relaxed. "It's been ages! How are you? Are you still in town?"

"I'm okay," he replied. "I'm living in the suburbs. No wife or kids, though." Why did he say that?

"Me neither," she said. "So, what can I help you with? Hopefully not the wife or kids thing," she added, and they both laughed.

"Actually," Jake said, "I think I might have a story for you. Do you have a minute?"

"I always have time for a story," she said. "Do you mind if I record our conversation?"

Jake paused. He was having second thoughts. This is not how you handle setbacks at work, he told himself. He knew that, but he didn't care. He got up, closed his office door, and turned on the rotating fan that he used on hot days. "This will have to be off the record," he told her. "It's about work."

"Well, now I'm intrigued. Did I hear you're at the DA's office?"

"That's right, in Hart County. And we've got a case that deserves a little more attention. I'm not telling tales out of school—all of the facts are in the court documents—but I'm not sure anyone's understood the *story* here."

"That's where I come in," Alisha said. "Why don't you start at the beginning?"

With one eye on his office door, Jake began. He told her about the extent of the destruction at the Jensen house; the way the parents had shielded their kids; and the light plea deals his office had accepted. Reminding her that this was all off the record, he told her how the DA played golf and tennis with many of the fathers, and how he'd encouraged Jake to go after the less-connected kids whose futures weren't quite so bright. Jake could hear the whisper of Alisha's pen as she took steady notes. But it wasn't until he got to the part about Dominic Finch's kid that she really began to sound interested.

"Well, what do you know?" she said. "Dominic Finch is a name I've heard before. He's been in some hot water down here for exploiting loopholes in the affordable housing rules for new developments. You say his kid was at this party, destroying a house? That's rich. You know, Jake, I think there might be something here. But your office isn't going to look too good. Why did you call me?"

"I'm gonna catch it on this case either way," Jake said. "What I'd like to see is some justice for the Jensens, and some accountability from the perpetrators. The Jensens haven't received a single apology from any of these kids. Can you believe it?"

"I'm afraid I can," Alisha said. "I've got a niece and nephew that age, and as far as I can tell, they're basically sociopaths. Of course, my sister thinks they walk on water. Okay, thanks for the tip, Jake. I know that this is off the record, but I'll have to call you for an official comment."

"That's fine," Jake said. "But the person you'll really want to talk to is Hal Buckley."

"I'll follow up. And do me a favor, Jake? If you're planning on running for anything—say, district attorney—promise to give me the exclusive. It sounds to me like there might be an opening soon, and you seem like a guy on the make."

Jake smiled, but he kept his voice light. "I don't think I'm quite there yet," he said. "But you'll be the first to know."

Alisha's article appeared in the *Inquirer* two days later, under the headline THE POWER TO DESTROY. It was the first installment in a series that promised to examine how wealth and privilege affected arrest and incarceration rates, as well as educational outcomes, for the greater Philadelphia area's youth. The article featured before and after pictures of the Jensens' destroyed house, and a list of the charges in the case, including the charge against Hunter Finch. Within hours, the DA's office was inundated with calls from reporters at papers and news programs all over the tri-state area. The next morning, two network news trucks had set up shop in front of the courthouse, and the reporters were getting the local take from people in nearby coffee shops and parks.

Everyone in town had an opinion, and they were only too happy to share their thoughts in TV-ready soundbites: *This town is full of kids with too much time and too much money; That's what you get when you allow private development along the riverfront; The cure for affluenza isn't fines, it's prison; This is a really nice town—have you seen the farmers market?*

When Hal Buckley arrived at the office, still in his polo shirt from his morning round, one of the reporters ran up to him with a microphone. "Were you just playing golf with the parents of the accused?" the reporter asked. "Do you live in a Finch Property house? Do you still believe that these are good kids? Do they deserve a second chance?"

By the end of the day, Chief Whitman had hauled Detective Murray into his office. "It's a shitshow down at the courthouse. Reporters everywhere," he said with contempt. "They want headlines? Let's give them headlines—but on our terms. I want an arrest in the assault case, Murray, and soon. And talk to Jake Tillman. See if he can beef up any of those charges in the house party case, and make sure that the evidence is airtight. If you don't have it already, find it. We need to look like we're taking this seriously. There might be plenty of people in this town who were happy to have these cases neatly disposed of. But I'm sure as hell not having the newspapers say that the police department was one of them.

36

~

"You have to come out to lunch with us," Aneeta said. "You're famous now!"

Maja gave her a look. "More like infamous," she said. "I can't believe the newspaper printed my picture. Now everyone in town will know who to blame for their kids heading to the county jail instead of to college."

"Do you really think they'll do jail time?" Aneeta asked.

"I don't know. Honestly, I don't care," Maja replied. "As far as I'm concerned, they can lock them up and throw away the key."

"Amen," Aneeta said, picking up her purse. "Come to lunch. My friends want to meet you. And don't worry about the newspapers. It's a good thing that they're covering your case." She winked. "It will keep those kids from breaking into any of our houses!"

Lunch was at a restaurant set in a converted nineteenth-century train station. Maja sat with Aneeta and her friends at a table set into an alcove. Lorraine had kids who played soccer with Aneeta's sons, and Naomi was a real estate agent whom Aneeta knew through her house-flipping business. Sun poured in through the windowpanes as they sipped iced tea. "This is really charming," Maja said.

"Isn't it great?" said Lorraine. "When I was a kid, this building was a little general store. They sold old-fashioned hard candy, and I used to beg my parents to come here."

"You grew up here?" Maja asked.

"I did. I went to college up in Boston, but I ended up back here.

After you've lived here, it's hard to find anywhere that compares. You should have seen this town back then. It was a lot funkier, but it was great."

"It's pretty nice now," Maja said. She'd been making an effort this week to try to refocus on the positive. They'd walked down Main Street on their way to lunch, passing a pottery studio and a gallery selling Impressionist-style oil paintings of the river. She'd noticed an empty shop with a FOR RENT sign in the window. It was small, but it had great light, and a prime position right on Main Street. She'd filed this information away, thinking that she'd find the listing later and send it to Louis. She still hadn't given up on her idea of trying to talk him into opening an outpost of his gallery in New Falls. Although right now, when she was missing so much work, was probably not the best time to bring it up.

"I'm glad you can still see the bright side, after everything that happened," Naomi said. "I read about the case in the *Inquirer*. I can't believe that Dominic Finch's son would destroy a house. His father must be beside himself."

"Shhhh!" Aneeta said, drizzling just a little of her dressing, which she'd ordered on the side, onto her salad. "No house party talk."

"No, it's fine," Maja said. "I'm just glad that the DA's office finally brought charges. For a while, we weren't sure it was going to happen."

"From what I read in the paper, I think Hal Buckley should step down," Lorraine said. "How can we trust him when his campaign was funded by the families of the people he's supposed to be prosecuting?"

"I saw him on the local news saying he believes in second chances," Naomi said.

Lorraine snorted. "Sure he does. But only for people who've already had all the chances in the world."

"Well, I think this is the wake-up call this town needs," Naomi said.

"I hope it is," Lorraine said. "New Falls used to have a real sense of community. Now it feels like everyone just grabs whatever they can for themselves. Farmland turned into houses, *another* field house being built at New Falls High, while community services for people who really need them go begging. And no one seems to care. As long as the football team is well funded and there's a cute farmers market on Sunday mornings, they can tell themselves that this is a good place to raise kids. But it doesn't surprise me that those kids thought nothing of breaking into your house, Maja. They've been raised to take what they want."

Aneeta glanced over at Maja and put a warning hand on Lorraine's knee. "Don't scare Maja off before she moves in," she said. "We need fresh blood down here!"

"I'm sorry," Lorraine said sheepishly. "I'm only trying to justify sending my kids to the Montessori school when I could send them to the local school for nothing. Pay no attention to me."

Maja was grateful when the server brought the check, and she grabbed it. The other women protested, but Maja stayed firm. "I hope we can do this again soon," she said, and they agreed to meet up for lunch when Maja was back in town.

The server brought the check back, but instead of laying it down for Maja to sign, he leaned down and said, "I'm sorry, there's an issue with your card."

Maja double-checked to make sure it was the new card Ted had given her, and it was. "Can you try again?" she asked. "There shouldn't be a problem."

The server was back a minute later. "Do you want to try another card?"

Maja checked her wallet, and then realized she'd tucked her bank card into the pocket of her shorts that morning when she'd walked out to get coffee. "I'm sorry," she said to Aneeta, her face red with embarrassment. "I'm not sure what the issue is. I'll pay you back this afternoon."

"Don't worry," Aneeta said, already handing her credit card to the server. "It's my treat."

As they said goodbye at the door of the restaurant, Maja couldn't wait to get away. The immediate embarrassment of having her credit card declined was giving way to a larger sense of unease. Was the credit card already maxed? She wasn't sure how that could have happened, when Ted had promised her that he was freeing up space so they didn't have to wait to put in orders for the new appliances. It was possible he'd already ordered them, but that wasn't like Ted. Especially not now, when he seemed to be totally consumed with work.

Aneeta was going to pick up her boys from school, and Maja walked back to her house alone. She called Ted's cell, and when he didn't answer, she hung up and dialed his office number, which went to the firm's voice mail. She tried his cell again, and this time she left a message, her voice sounding high and strange to herself as she recounted the problem with the credit card. She wanted to call the credit card company, but although her cards had her name on them, the accounts were technically Ted's, and it was always a pain when she contacted customer service because she didn't know his passwords and pin numbers.

When she got to Aneeta's house, she grabbed her ATM card and walked to the drugstore a few blocks away. She was worried there was something she didn't know about the credit card accounts, and her stomach felt queasy.

In the drugstore she took out cash to pay Aneeta back, and then went to pick out a shampoo. She'd forgotten to pack her own, so she'd been using handfuls of the kid shampoo that was kept in the hall bathroom and wanted to replace it before she left. She couldn't remember exactly what scent they used, and she surreptitiously opened a bottle to check its smell. It was overpoweringly sweet, like sipping from a leftover cosmopolitan in the middle of the night when you thought you were reaching for a glass of water. Maja shoved the bottle back onto the shelf as she fought a wave of nausea. Then she stood very still, trying to think.

It's just the scent, she thought. Too sweet. Or her anxious, unsettled stomach. It couldn't be . . . she didn't even let herself finish the thought. But it persisted, like the slightly metallic taste in her mouth.

For the last few years, she could have told you off the top of her head what day of her cycle she was on. Now she realized that she'd lost track of it during the commotion about the house. Should she have had her period by now? She counted back. It had been at least a month. She felt a slight flutter of hope, but she tried to tamp it down. It was the stress, she told herself, messing with her cycle. She and Ted hadn't exactly been in the mood very often this month. Was it even possible?

There was only one way to know. She left the shampoo on the shelf and picked up a pregnancy test from the family planning aisle.

Back in the apartment, she went through the familiar motions. There was no way she was pregnant, she thought as she waited for the test. She hadn't done any of the things that she was supposed to do. She'd been sleeping terribly, and she'd been drinking coffee and the occasional glass of wine. She hadn't meditated. She'd been eating greasy takeout instead of the fertility blogosphere—approved diet of avocados, lentils, and salmon. And yet she felt a spark of hope. What if this was it? It didn't matter, suddenly, that they were starting over with the house, and money was tight, and Ted had been in a bad mood *for weeks*. None of that would mean anything if they were finally going to have a baby. She was so lost in thought that when the timer on her phone went off, she almost screamed.

She picked up the test and looked at it.

There, on the white applicator, were two lines. The second one was faint, but it was there.

Had she jiggled it too much? Could the color have bled from the control line? She put the test back on the sink and pulled out the instructions with trembling hands. In her nervousness, it took her a moment to find the ones in English. But there they were, next to a picture that looked just like her results: "A faint line on the pregnancy test indicates a positive result."

A tingle of adrenaline ran through her body. At first, she was cautious. She had performed the same series of actions dozens of times, always with the same result. This was an anomaly; it must be a mistake. She looked at the test again. The line was growing stronger. She felt annoyed that she hadn't bought one of the value packs while she was at the drugstore. Of course, she hadn't thought she would actually be pregnant. But as soon as she had the thought, she knew it was true, and she said it aloud.

"I'm having a baby."

37

Maja took a second pregnancy test that night, and another one the next morning. Both came up positive. After so many negative tests over the last few years, she wasn't sure if she'd ever get tired of seeing that double pink line. She called her obstetrician after the third test. The receptionist had insisted that Maja didn't need to be seen so soon, her voice conveying that she had little patience for hysterical first-time mothers. But she'd finally relented. It just so happened that they had a cancellation for that afternoon. Could Maja make it in?

Maja was on the next bus back to New York. As it snaked its way across New Jersey, Maja leaned her head against the window, watching as the highway laced together with others, growing wider as it funneled the multiplying traffic toward Manhattan. The city skyline suddenly sharpened through the haze, forming a strange oasis in the swampy expanse of industrial New Jersey.

Maja could have focused on any individual tower that formed the city's outline and instantly called to mind what that corner looked like, what food trucks could be found nearby, or which bars and subway stops formed its base. A lifetime spent in the city had made the map of the island as familiar to her as the contours of her own body. But it suddenly looked strange, as if it had changed in some way while she was staying with Aneeta. It was like running into an old boyfriend unexpectedly on the street—the conversation veering between intimacy and the small talk of strangers.

Maja couldn't believe how emotional she felt. She'd only been gone for a week! The city wouldn't have changed. It would still be warm and crowded, the way it always was in early June, the subway ripe with the scent of sweaty skin and the sidewalks speckled with water droplets from overworked window AC units. If anyone had changed it was her. No real New Yorker would be this sentimental about the city in the middle of a heat wave. It must be her hormones, she told herself, with a little thrill.

Maja didn't call Ted to tell him she was coming home a day early. She wanted to give him the good news that night, in person. The pink line on the last test had been so bold and insistent that she couldn't help wondering if she'd been pregnant this whole time. Had she somehow botched the test she'd taken last month? She thought back over the last few weeks. She'd been exhausted and sensitive, but she'd chalked that up to the problems with the house.

She remembered the morning that she'd gotten the call from John, right after the disappointment of the negative pregnancy test. She'd felt as if she'd hit a wall. It seemed like everyone else around her was moving on or up, creating families or careers that suddenly seemed to be taking off, and she was being left behind, trapped in an endless version of her twenties, even as she got closer and closer to forty.

And now, this thing that she had wanted for so long, that she had dreamed about, and planned for, and which felt at the end like it might never happen, was finally falling into place. It put the trouble with the house into perspective. They'd hit a stumbling block, not a wall. It might take time to sort out the issues with the construction and the insurance payments, but they would get through this and come out on the other side with everything that they wanted.

If all went well with the obstetrician, she was going to surprise Ted at the apartment after work. They could go out to eat, maybe sit at one of the sidewalk tables at their favorite Italian place if it wasn't too hot.

When the bus pulled into the city around eleven, Maja saw that she had just enough time to drop off her suitcase at the apartment before her doctor's appointment. Inside, the foyer was dark, and there was a pile of take-out menus that had been slipped under the door by delivery guys. She rolled her eyes. Ted must have been stepping over them all week while she was away. As she bent down to pick them up, she paused. To her surprise, she heard sounds coming from the direction of the living room, and she thought she smelled cigarette smoke. "Hello?" she called out, leaving the door open behind her, just in case. At first, she thought that perhaps the windows had been left open and the noise was coming from the street. But then she heard a rustling sound, like newspaper, and a cough.

In the kitchen, she was surprised to see a sink full of dishes and a pile of dirty take-out containers on the counter that was usually scrubbed sparkling clean. The trash can was full, and there was another bag of trash sitting next to it. A glass on the counter was filled with cigarette butts floating in dingy gray water. The room smelled stale and sour.

"Hello!" she called out again, trying to sound calm. Ted was never at home this time of day, and he'd given up smoking when she had. "Is someone here? I'm calling the super."

"No, don't," a voice called out.

It was a relief to hear Ted's voice. "Ted?" She walked down the hall. "Is that you?"

She entered the living room, and there he was, standing awkwardly next to the sofa. He was wearing track pants and a T-shirt. A newspaper was spread out on the sofa, and an empty beer bottle sat on the floor next to him, along with an ashtray.

"You're smoking again?" she asked, stupidly. Of all the questions running through her head, why was that the one that had popped out? She tried again: "What are you doing at home? It's Friday."

Ted sat down on the sofa, elbows on his knees, and put his head in his hands.

"Ted!" Maja said, her voice sharp. "What's going on?" As she said this, she realized that they hadn't had a real conversation all week. They'd talked, of course, but it had been rushed—just quick updates on the construction and the problems she was having with the insurance company. Now something was obviously very wrong, and Maja had a queasy sense that she had been purposely avoiding finding out what it was.

Ted didn't look at her, but he finally lifted his head from his hands. He picked up the newspaper lying next to him, refolded it, and handed it to her. It was a copy of that day's *New York Post*, with its signature bold white headline:

FOX ON THE RUN!

Big bank Foxfield Barnes begs for bailout on bankruptcy fears.

Foxfield Barnes, brought to the edge of bankruptcy last week by risky mortgage security plays in the midst of a global credit crisis, will be acquired by J.P. Morgan in a last-minute deal. J.P. Morgan scores a sly deal for Fox, paying a paltry $2 a share for the struggling firm, which was trading at just over $20 a share last week. One year ago, Foxfield's shares sold for $150. J.P. Morgan takes control of the firm's brokerage business and its Wall Street tower, valued at over a billion dollars. The deal saves Foxfield from filing for bankruptcy and causing a domino effect of failures on other banks. It remains to be seen how many of Foxfield's employees, who own one-third of the company, will retain their jobs.

Maja skimmed to the end of the article, but the details of the deal only half made sense to her. What was clear was that something very, very bad had happened.

"I had no idea things were this grim," she said. "The firm is being sold?"

Ted finally looked up at her. "Sold for scrap," he said. "It's a bloodbath out there. We're the first, but we won't be the last." He sighed. "Not that it matters. Just because everyone is fucked doesn't mean we're not fucked."

"Have they said what's going to happen?" Maja asked, her mind racing. "Will you go work for J.P. Morgan?"

Ted looked at her for a long moment. "No," he said, finally. "Maja, I was laid off."

"Already?" she breathed, her heart beating hard. "That was so fast."

Ted gave a short, bitter laugh. "I wasn't going to tell you," he said. "I thought I could find another job, and then I could just tell you that I changed firms. Use the signing bonus to pay back what I owed. Move on somehow. But I was kidding myself. There aren't any jobs to find right now."

Maja looked around the apartment. Ted didn't look like someone who had just had a shock. He looked resigned. Suddenly she understood. "When?" she asked.

"Weeks ago. Not long after we heard about the house party. Our department was the first to make cuts. Which is insane, because the guy who came up with these bullshit trades is still there. It's a fucking joke," Ted spat.

Maja was stunned. Tears sprang to her eyes, and she fought a rising sense of panic. "You didn't tell me. I don't understand. Why didn't you tell me?"

"How could I," Ted countered, "with the house a wreck and the bills piling up?" His words sounded almost like an accusation. "I just couldn't. How could I tell you that it was all gone? I had to try to fix it."

"What do you mean it's all gone?" Maja asked, feeling sick.

Ted didn't meet her eye. "The money," he said. "Everything. Did you read the article? $2 a share. They might as well have set it all on fire." He spoke mechanically, staring out of the window. "I knew the stock would take a hit—the whole market is down—and all of the contingent stock disappeared when I was laid off. But I didn't know it would be that bad. Almost everything we have was tied up in the firm's stock. We have about eight thousand shares, Maja. Last year, that was a little over a million dollars. Today that's fifteen grand."

The numbers were breathtaking. Maja knew their money was bound up in Foxfield's stock, but it had never occurred to her the stock could suddenly be totally worthless.

"We have other savings," she said. "You're going to find another job."

"Maja, we are leveraged to the hilt," Ted said. "Have you ever looked at what we spend every month? We have the rent on the apartment, the construction loan, furniture for the new house, and a hundred small bills that add up—the gym membership, the beach house we went in on for August. There haven't been cash bonuses in six months—we were already stretched pretty thin when this happened. The credit cards are maxed out." He sounded slightly hysterical. "And the health insurance," he added. "Do you know what that costs without the firm subsidizing it? You might as well know, I put it on the credit card this month, along with everything else. You have no idea, Maja."

She hated the way he was saying her name, as if she was a dense child. "I didn't know," she said. "I mean, I knew the bills for the house were adding up, but I guess I just figured it would all sort itself out in the end. We were so close to being done."

"It's so easy for you," Ted said. "You waltz around the gallery, making almost nothing, but you get to live like you sweat it out on Wall Street."

"Whoa! That's *not* fair!" Maja cried. How could he say that? He'd always encouraged her to stay at the gallery. He liked being the one who made the money. "I never asked you to work in finance," she said, her voice shaking. "This is your life too. This is what you wanted."

Ted looked at the space between them, where the newspaper and the beer bottles lay. "This is not what I wanted," he said. "But you're right. That wasn't fair. I shouldn't take this out on you. It's all my fault."

Maja's mind was reeling. "So we're broke. And you've been doing what—drinking beer all day?" She had a chilling thought. Ted had lost his job weeks before she'd gone down to New Falls. "What were you doing all day when I was here?"

"You really want to know?" he asked her. "I went to coffee shops. I walked around. I hit up all my contacts for job leads. You have to understand, Maja. I thought I could fix this. That I could just come to you when I had a new job, and you wouldn't have to worry. But no one is hiring." His burst of anger had passed, and now he looked like he was going to cry.

Maja tried get her thoughts straight. "But what about that night two weeks ago, when we sat at Reilly's, and you told me we could start IVF? You must have known then that we didn't have the money."

"I couldn't bear to disappoint you," he said. "You're already dealing with so much. I did want to be able to give that to you. I'm sorry, Maja."

Maja sat down on the sofa. "Okay," she said. "Okay, we can solve this. I can ask for more hours at the gallery. And what about my investment account? I know it's not a lot, but maybe we could liquidate it and use the money to see us through, at least until the construction is done, and you find another job?" Maja had been surprised to learn that she inherited fifty thousand dollars when her parents sold family property in Poland after an uncle passed away. Ted invested the money for her in the stock market, and it had done pretty well. She'd always thought of it as a nest egg for her future children. A gift to them from the past.

Ted turned around and slid down the wall until he was seated on the floor. He looked up at Maja. "It's gone," he whispered. "Sold off, like everything else we were holding."

At first, she didn't believe him. "No, that can't be," she said. "How? Those stocks belonged to me. How could you sell them without telling me?"

"It was all invested under my name," Ted said. "It just made it easier to manage."

That wasn't what Maja meant by her question. "But why didn't you tell me?" she pressed, a real prickle of fear, like electricity, running from her scalp down to her neck.

"I'm so sorry," Ted was saying. "I used the money from that account to cover some private trades that I made on margin. I was trying to trade our way out of this. I thought that if I could make a quick turnaround, we might be okay." He was almost whimpering now. "But it didn't pan out. All markets have winners and losers. This time, we're the losers."

Without even thinking about it, Maja was backing away from him. "I don't even know you," she said slowly. "I can't believe you would lie to me about something this big. *For so long.* You let me just go on, thinking everything was fine, *for weeks.* I've been writing checks to the new contractor that I don't even know if the insurance company will fully cover!"

"I thought I could fix it."

"But you can't," Maja said, her voice flat.

"It's too big to fix," Ted said, sounding almost like he was talking to himself. "This isn't just me. It's everyone. We got greedy, and now there's going to be a reckoning. And not just on Wall Street. They're going to feel it everywhere."

For a long moment there was silence between them, as Maja tried to make sense of everything she'd just heard.

Then Ted spoke. "I'm so sorry, Maja. I love you. I just wanted to make things right. But I messed everything up. You should probably divorce me. All I wanted to do was give you a good life, and I can't."

His voice sounded small and scared, but Maja felt repugnance rather than sympathy. She couldn't even bring herself to look at him. She picked up her purse and keys.

"It's not the money that I'm angry about," she said, her voice shaking. How could he not see that? "You lied to me. We should have dealt with this together. I probably *should* divorce you. But I can't." Her voice broke. "I'm pregnant, Ted. We're going to have a baby."

Ted's face, already pale, stared back at her. He seemed unable to speak. A thousand thoughts were going through Maja's mind, a thousand things she wanted to say. But she felt like she was speaking to a stranger. She took one last look at him, trying to see the man she'd married, and then turned and walked out.

38

Maja felt numb as she made her way uptown to the obstetrician's office. It was bizarre to be going through the normal motions of swiping her card at the subway turnstile, checking in with the receptionist, and sitting in the waiting room, staring blankly at a magazine, as the realization sank in that her marriage—and her life as she knew it—had fallen apart without her even realizing that it was happening.

The nurse took a urine sample and led Maja into a room where she changed into a cotton gown. Her doctor, an older woman, came in, looked over her chart, and then, for the very first time since Maja had become a patient at the practice, called for the nurse to bring in the ultrasound. After a few minutes that felt much longer to Maja, the doctor turned to her with a smile, delivering the news that she'd longed to hear: "Congratulations, Maja." She consulted the screen again. "Looks like your due date is the end of January. That's quite a New Year's present for Ted!"

Maja opened her mouth, but before she could say anything, she burst into tears. The doctor patted her hand. "Happy tears," she said. "It happens all the time. I'll have the nurse schedule your follow-up appointments. Bring Ted in next time! We'll be able to see the heartbeat. Smile, Maja, you're at the beginning of everything!" Then the doctor followed the nurse out, and Maja was left alone to get dressed.

Back out on the street, Maja stood on the corner, trying to decide what to do. She wanted to go home, but she wasn't ready to face Ted. She needed time to think things through, for the baby's sake, if nothing else.

She started walking downtown, taking some comfort in the familiar rhythm of dodging and weaving through the crowds of people along Madison Avenue. She had one repeating thought: How did I get here? She'd thought of her marriage as ideal. She'd smugly looked down on their friends who bickered and picked at each other, or who seemed more interested in their own careers than in their relationship. She and Ted, she thought, had crafted the perfect balance, and she'd prided herself on how nicely they'd arranged things. He paid the bills and she kept their lives interesting. Maybe she'd relied on him too much to manage their finances, but that was his profession, after all. And the truth was that she'd always thought of it as Ted's money. He wasn't totally wrong: she'd liked maintaining the artifice that she'd never sold out. Even if she wasn't painting anymore, she still worked in the arts, and she liked to think that it was just a detail that she was married to a Wall Street guy. She hadn't wanted to look too closely—either at their finances, or at how much she enjoyed perks and privileges of Ted's job. It was so different than how she'd grown up, always having to consider the cost of everything before anything else, her parents making constant trade-offs between what she wanted and what they could afford. It had felt good, for a little while, to leave those calculations behind. Just like it felt good to assume that her relationship was on unshakable footing.

It felt naive now, but she'd never seriously worried about her marriage. She loved Ted, and the only flirting that she did was of the professional type, necessary in gallery work. The secrets that she kept were minor, and had to do with how much she paid for a certain pair of boots, or which of his friends made passes at her after too many drinks. They were secrets she kept for the sake of smoothing things along. She'd never imagined that Ted was capable of harboring a secret so big, and so disastrous.

What if now, just as everything was coming together—when they were about to have a child, and the house of their dreams—it was too late? Maja thought about what her doctor had said: "You're at the beginning of everything." She wanted to believe it.

When she finally looked around, she realized she was almost back at her apartment. She'd thought of heading out to her parents' place in Brooklyn, or returning to Aneeta's house to lick her wounds, but there was no running away from this, no pretending that it wasn't happening. That's what Ted had done, and it had only made things worse. With a sigh, she turned toward her building. They weren't going to celebrate, as she'd hoped, but she still had to go home.

39

Rosie's European history class was watching part of a miniseries that took place during World War II. The classroom lights were off, and no one seemed to be paying much attention. She pulled out her phone, flipped it open, and texted Maddie, who hadn't been at school all week. Rosie knew that Maddie had finally told her parents what happened, and that they had taken her to the police station, but she hadn't heard much from Maddie since.

Hi, she texted. How are you doing?

To her surprise, Maddie texted back almost immediately: Been better.

Rosie was worried about her. Just when the talk about her at school finally died down, it started back up again with the police report. Officers had been back to the school to question students, and this time there'd been no complaints from parents. Rosie wasn't sure if she would have been able to go forward with it, if she'd been in Maddie's shoes.

Rosie, Maddie texted, the police are looking for the pictures from the party. They said they need them for evidence. Have you seen them?

Sorry, Rosie replied. Haven't seen them.

She hesitated, and then texted again: I can ask Brendan.

For a minute there was no reply, and then: He took them?

No. But I heard he had them on his phone.

Maddie didn't reply right away, and Rosie was staring at her phone, wondering if she should go to the bathroom and call her, when she sensed someone standing just behind her shoulder. She turned, and there was Ms. Grady, staring down at her screen. Before Rosie could react, Ms. Grady reached down and plucked the phone out of her hand. "Rosa!" she whispered. "I'm very surprised at you! You are supposed to be taking notes on the show."

Rosie was mortified. She never got in trouble. Then she felt angry. She had actual, important things going on in her life, and she was supposed to pretend to be interested in a bunch of grown men playing war? No wonder everything had gotten so messed up. Adults were always focusing on the wrong stuff. "That's private," she snapped. And then said, sheepishly, "I'll put it away."

Ms. Grady looked like she was trying to decide something. She sighed. "I'm sorry, Rosa, but I need to take this to the office. You know the rules. You can collect it there after school." Now the whole class was staring at her, World War II forgotten.

Fine, Rosie thought, her face burning. So what if Ms. Grady had seen Maddie's texts? Maybe the principal would haul Brendan and his dumb friends into the office and get the pictures, and she wouldn't have to do it herself.

She slouched down in her chair and forced her attention back to the TV, wincing along with everyone else as the hero narrowly avoided stepping on a land mine.

Detective Murray received a call from the high school office and turned his car around, checking his mirror and pulling a U-turn on River Road that made gravel spin out from under his tires. It wasn't necessarily an emergency, but getting to drive like that was a perk of the job.

The secretary, growing accustomed to his visits, showed him directly into Dr. Johnson's office, where the principal had a bright pink Motorola flip phone sitting on his desk.

"I thought you'd want to hear about this," Dr. Johnson said. "Ms. Grady confiscated the phone during class, after she saw that the student was communicating about pictures of the party."

"Who is the student?" Murray asked, pulling out his notebook.

"Rosa Mendoza," Ms. Grady said. "She's a good student. I was surprised she was texting, to be honest, but they all get antsy toward the end of the year."

The name didn't ring a bell for Murray. He thought quickly. He would need to show probable cause to legally search the phone. "Did you actually see these pictures?" he asked Ms. Grady.

"No," Ms. Grady admitted. "But they were definitely being discussed. I brought the phone in to Dr. Johnson as soon as my class wrapped up."

Murray only hesitated for a moment. He thought it was unlikely the girl would just give him permission to search her phone. He knew he was crossing the line, but he decided to take a quick peek. He opened the phone and the screen lit up. Neither Dr. Johnson nor Ms. Grady objected. In fact, they were looking at him expectantly.

The text conversation that Ms. Grady had seen was still open, and Murray's pulse quickened when he saw the name Maddie. Madison Martin was the girl who'd reported her assault, and although any pictures from the party would be helpful, what Murray really needed were the pictures that she'd told them about. With photographic evidence, they'd have a much stronger case. Since she hadn't come forward right away they had no physical evidence, and the witnesses were a bunch of drunken teenagers, many of whom were facing charges themselves. It wasn't a lot to go on.

Murray scrolled eagerly through the thread, but he saw right away that they hadn't actually exchanged pictures, only discussed rumors that a kid named Brendan had them. Was it the same Brendan that they'd questioned about the party? He would check in with him. He was about to hand the phone back to Dr. Johnson when he decided to see if there were any texts with this kid Brendan. In for a penny, he thought, in for a pound.

He scrolled down through the list of conversations, which seemed to be between the same few girls, looking for Brendan's name, but it wasn't there. But buried in the mountain of text exchanges— where did they find the time?—was a local number that didn't have a name attached as a contact. Murray paused. It looked familiar, but he couldn't quite place it. He weighed the odds of it being important enough to do this the right way, with a warrant, and quickly decided that it was most likely nothing. He opened the message.

It was a picture of a girl in her bra, with the usual abbreviated texts that accompanied those kinds of pictures. Sexting was becoming more and more common, Detective Murray thought, even among teenagers. U look hot. Hey sexy. He reread the last line twice: Go get those bad guys. Now, that didn't seem right. Who were these texts with—Batman? He looked at the number on Rosie's phone again, and then pulled out his own phone and typed it in. Up came the contact info for Jake Tillman, Assistant District Attorney.

Murray held both phones in his hands, trying to make sense of what he was seeing. He was aware of Dr. Johnson and Ms. Grady watching him. "Did you find something?" Dr. Johnson asked.

"Possibly." He tried to quickly sort through what he knew. A student at New Falls High is exchanging pictures and texts with Jake. Not many, but these might just be the ones she forgot to delete. He'd worked with Jake for several years and shared plenty of beers with him after work. Did this fit in with what he knew about Jake? Absolutely not. Did that mean it wasn't true? Of course not.

Murray had always prided himself on his sense for people's strengths and failings. His father had gone into police work because he liked the power: the gun, the authority, the chain of command. But Murray had followed in his father's footsteps because he liked solving puzzles and figuring out what motivated a particular crime or criminal. As a detective, Murray was constantly confronted with all kinds of facts: important and irrelevant, contradictory and consistent, and easily proven or taken on faith. It was the same with people. He'd put away charismatic businessmen who committed hit-and-runs, and helped clear good-for-nothing drunks who really were sleeping one off when a beating occurred. The key to the job was the ability to sift through information and find new patterns to fit changing facts and impressions. And yet, the simplest explanation wasn't always the right one. It was a balancing act that required a sense for how to slot the facts in the right way, without distorting the truth to fit them.

Murray looked at the picture of the girl again. "The girl who owns the phone—does she work at Alejandro's?"

Dr. Johnson seemed surprised by the question. "Yes, that's Rosa's father's restaurant."

A framework of facts began to come together, despite Murray's resistance to the idea. Jake often ate at Al's—Murray had been there with him several times. He searched his memory, but nothing odd about those meals occurred to him. But there was something. Of course. It was the first day that they'd come to the high school to speak with students. Jake had waved to a girl in the computer lab. That must have been Rosa. He could check that, to some extent, but he felt fairly sure Rosa wasn't among the students who were charged. Murray swallowed. What he knew of Jake was that he was a solid, hardworking guy. Murray would hold his judgment, but he was going to have to investigate.

Dr. Johnson was looking at his watch and clearing his throat. He was ready to move on. There was a knock at the door, and the secretary poked her head in. "Rosie Mendoza is here," she said. "Should I send her in?"

Dr. Johnson and Ms. Grady looked at Detective Murray. "Yes," Murray said. "And can you please call her father? I'd like him to accompany her to the station with me."

40

They had no choice, Hal Buckley and Chief Whitman agreed. It was upsetting that it was one of their own, of course, but that made it even more important to play this one conservatively. Jake Tillman would have to be put on leave, pending the outcome of the investigation. Afterward, he could quietly resign. He'd never really be able to come back to work. Not after this, even if it did turn out to be some sort of mistake, which, they agreed privately, was unlikely.

The girl was distraught when they questioned her, and denied everything, all the while sobbing and unable to offer any other explanation for how the texts had ended up on her phone. Her father sat beside her, looking clammy and trembling with anger. Apparently he'd been friendly with Jake, which made the whole thing worse for him. They kept the questioning short. She was eighteen, after all, and technically of age to consent. "He didn't do anything!" she kept insisting. "Like hell he didn't!" her father yelled. The DA had to explain they were investigating it not as a crime, but as a professional ethics violation.

Jake, under questioning, looked honestly shocked, and then, as it sunk in, outraged. When they didn't let up, he'd become flat and monosyllabic, and Hal had informed him the case was being handed over to the bar association's discipline committee. Later, in the bathroom, Hal heard him throwing up. It wasn't dispositive, however. Plenty of people fooled themselves into justifying their bad behavior, believing that they weren't capable of evil motives or actions, and that if it felt right, it must be right. Perhaps that's where Jake's initial rage had come from. When Jake's phone was examined by the office tech support, and a deleted photo of Rosie Mendoza was recovered, it seemed clear Jake was lying. She was listed in his phone as Rosalita, a childhood nickname according to her father. It turned Hal's stomach.

Hal suspected, but couldn't prove, that it was Jake who had alerted the city media to the story. They'd been digging around ever since, and one of the city papers had managed to turn up an old photo of Hal and Dom Finch sitting together at a fundraiser. The DA's office was getting calls and letters every day now from concerned citizens who wanted to know how their tax dollars were being spent, whether old cases against them could be reopened in light of the leniency those kids had received, and even, in some cases, calling for his resignation. To Hal's mind, the kind of man who would sabotage his own department that way was the kind of man who was capable of anything. Even sleeping with a young woman—a teenager—whose friends he was trying a case against.

Hal had always suspected Jake was gunning for his job. As if some upstart from out of town was ever going to be able to replace him. Hal wasn't retiring anytime soon. Why should he, when there were plenty of hungry young lawyers to do the grunt work while he tried the winners and attended the dinners? Jake had gotten too big for his britches, and looked at one way, this whole sordid business with the high school student was as good an excuse as any to show him the door.

With Jake both out of his way and occupying the spotlight, Hal could work quickly to wrap up the Jensen case and be done with this whole mess. He'd been DA long enough to know the media's attention was short-lived. He made a note to himself to get in touch with Dom Finch's attorney. No, scratch that, he would just give Dom a call himself. Dom wouldn't mind the breach of protocol—he was a businessman who knew how to get things done. His boy, Hunter, was going to have to take a plea. There was no other choice, given all of the attention. It would be better for the kid, and for Dom's business, if this wrapped up quickly. Hal would offer a short stay in county, as well as a stint of community service, as a sign of the kid's contrition.

Hell, Dom was in the construction business. Maybe he could be convinced to put the house back together himself. That would generate some positive press for everyone. The Jensens had been increasingly frantic in the messages that they left, and Hal wanted them off of his back. If they could rebuild their house, they could put this all behind them and so could he. Dom Finch wouldn't like it, but he would take the deal. He'd know a good offer when he heard it.

41

Will's mother always said bad news comes in threes. Nonsense, his father would reply. But then she would try to prove it, pointing out three celebrities dying in quick succession, or one of the farmhands calling in sick on the same day that the tractor wouldn't start and she left the jam on the stove too long, scorching the pot. It's easy to find bad luck if you're looking for it, his father said. So don't.

Usually, Will agreed with his father, but today he was feeling more superstitious. In the morning the bank called to let them know they hadn't qualified for a second loan against the farm. In addition, their agent reminded them the three-year low interest period on the current loan would expire in two months, and they should be ready for the increased payments.

Their attorney, Ed DeLeo, called next, and Will's mom put him on speakerphone. He'd just come from a conference with the prosecutor's office. "The news isn't great," he said. "The prosecutor's theory is that Will planned the party and provided the alcohol. I think he might have gotten off on lesser charges, but the media is all over the DA's office since that story broke, and they need to put on a show of taking this seriously. It's up to Will, of course, but my recommendation is that we fight the charges. If he's willing to plead, they're currently offering thirty days of jail time, probation, and a significant restitution payment. But I know that the big concern here is Will's college plans, and if he pleads, that could be an issue. The fact that they're offering a pretty light plea deal makes me think their case may be a little thin. For instance, we can always argue Will never had intent to trespass, that he believed the party was being thrown by the owner of the house. Of course, that carries the risk he could be convicted and could do a year or more in jail. Still, there's a chance he walks on this one.

"Trip's case is a harder call," he went on. "If he wasn't facing the suspended sentence, I'd suggest he plead out. Furnishing alcohol to minors is usually just a fine. But if he pleads to either corruption of minors or vandalism, it will trigger his suspended sentence from his last arrest, and he'll be looking at a year or more in jail. I suggest we fight it and see if we can call their bluff."

When the kitchen phone rang a third time, it was as if Will had been expecting it. He'd already heard from Princeton. He'd decided it was best to be up front, and he'd informed them he was facing a trespassing charge, keeping the details vague. They issued him a perfunctory response: *Princeton takes student safety extremely seriously, and the status of any student convicted of a crime will be reviewed on a case by case basis.* He wasn't convicted yet, Will thought, so there was still a chance he could go. He didn't want to think about what "reviewing his status" would mean if he was convicted. But there was one more call he was waiting for. He knew the Union Club Scholarship Committee would be contacting him to respond to the information he'd provided about the pending charges.

Will beat his mother to pick up the phone and carried it to the yard.

The Union Club representative on the other end of the line sounded almost as nervous as Will was. "We've reviewed your case," he said. "We appreciate your honesty and transparency in alerting us to your current situation. Of course, you know many of our club members are local business leaders, public servants, and officers of the law. Our members consider the recipients of our scholarships to be representatives of the Hart County community in the wider world. As such, I'm afraid that in the current circumstances, we will have to rescind our scholarship offer. We wish you the best of luck."

Will almost laughed. How would luck help him pay for Princeton? "I see," he said, feeling numb. He kept the phone to his ear for a minute after the rep hung up, buying time before he had to face his mom.

"Well?" his mother asked. "What did they say?"

"They're taking back the scholarship."

Linda sat down heavily in her chair. "How can they do that?"

"The police commissioner is on the committee," Will said.

"What are we going to do?" she asked him.

"I don't know," Will admitted. "But I'll take care of it. Don't worry."

"You sound like Trip," she said, biting her lip.

"No, I don't!" Will snapped. Before he knew what he was doing he had banged open the screen door, just as his brother had after the lawyer's call an hour earlier, and run halfway across the orchard. He couldn't spend another moment seeing himself through his mother's eyes.

Will almost expected to run into Hunter at the tree house, but of course he wasn't there. They weren't children anymore, with hours to waste running through the woods. Things with Hunter had been weird since almost coming to blows in the driveway. They'd exchanged only a few cursory text messages since then. But Will was hoping to see him—he needed to talk to someone, and one fight didn't change their friendship.

He climbed the hill behind the tree house and walked across the lawn to the Finch home, then went up to the kitchen door and peered through. He used to just let himself in, but he felt awkward doing that now.

Dom and Lindsay were standing on either side of the kitchen counter, facing each other. Will thought Hunter's dad looked angry, but then again, he often looked that way. Will tapped on the glass and they both turned to look at him, startled.

Dom opened the door. "Come on in, Will," he said. He looked like he was about to say more, probably ask him about Princeton, but then he appeared to think better of it. "Hunter just ran some documents down to the post office for me," Dom said. "But he'll be back in a minute. Why don't you wait in the den? Lindsay can get you some iced tea if you like."

Lindsay snorted, and both men turned to her in surprise, but she just stared back at them.

"I'm okay," Will said quickly. "I don't need anything. Thanks, Mr. Finch, Mrs. Finch."

He walked through the dining room and into the room they used as a library and den. It was lined with bookshelves that reached fifteen feet high. A ladder on rollers slid across the floor to give access to the upper reaches of the shelves. Will browsed the books, pulling out the ones that caught his eye and flipping to the copyright pages. There were first editions of Steinbeck and Faulkner, and even a pristine first printing of Hemingway. Dom had shown some of them to Will before, waxing poetic about his days reading literature at Princeton. Will wondered how many of these he would have to sell to fund a year of college. Probably not too many.

From the kitchen he could hear the sounds of Lindsay's and Dom's voices, at first muted and then clearer. When he heard Hunter's name mentioned, he slid the book he was looking at back onto the shelf and passed quietly into the hallway.

"He wasn't going with us anyway," Lindsay said.

"Just because he wasn't going with us doesn't mean I can just leave him here," Dom replied, his voice impatient. "Who's going to manage the attorneys?"

"Well, I don't know," Lindsay replied, her voice uncharacteristically sarcastic. "They're representing Hunter, so maybe he can manage them? He's an adult. He should take responsibility for his actions."

This was the second time in the last hour that Will had heard that, and he gave a dry laugh without thinking. All of a sudden they were adults. It's funny that no one had treated them like adults before all this. In the kitchen the voices were suddenly quiet. Will stayed still, and soon they started up again, apparently satisfied it was just the old house sighing.

"Being eighteen is different than being an adult," Dom said. "But I'm not trying to defend him. I'm just saying this is not a good time for us to spend a month on a yacht in the middle of the Aegean Sea, where I won't be able to keep an eye on things."

"So now you're keeping an eye on things," Lindsay replied, her voice reckless. "That's great. I've been dealing with this all year, trying to keep it together here while you're at work eighteen hours a day, but now you're keeping an eye on things. And that means the kids and I will be stuck here, in this creaky old house, all summer. When we were supposed to be traveling."

Again, Will couldn't help himself. He laughed. Not a funny laugh, but a you've-got-to-be-kidding-me laugh. This creaky old house? Old, yes, but it was a *mansion*. With a tennis court. And a pool. And a first edition of *A Farewell to Arms*. It wasn't exactly the kind of place you were stuck in. It was the kind of place that, if you got it, you stuck to it with all of your might. Christ, it had air-conditioning! That alone made it the ideal summer house, as far as Will was concerned.

He didn't need to be worried about being overheard this time. Dom was laughing as well, also in a way that implied he didn't think it was very funny. Then he sighed. "Lindsay," he said, "you know there is nowhere I would rather be than drinking wine with you as the sun sets over Mykonos. But this just isn't the time. The whole real estate market has gone to hell. Houses are sitting, already built, empty. There's a whole condo project in Miami that I may have to foreclose on. I'm laying off project managers and sales teams. The Brooklyn project is in jeopardy. There are crews of construction workers that I may not have work for until six months from now. Maybe longer. I don't know. And on top of all that, my son has just been arrested for trashing someone's house. It's in the papers, Lindsay. Think about the optics. How does it look right now if I fuck off to Greece for a month to work on my tan?"

There was a long silence. Will felt his face growing warm. He was thinking about his mom, sitting at the kitchen table in their cramped kitchen, shuffling through the bills as if she might be able to perform a magic card trick and make a few disappear.

Lindsay sighed. "How about the Hamptons? It's no farther from Manhattan than we are here. You can tramp up and down the filthy

Brooklyn waterfront as much as you like. I don't care. But I'm not spending August here."

"Done," Dom said, as if he was closing a deal. "But that filthy Brooklyn waterfront is going to make us a mint. See if you can find a last-minute rental on the beach. Any house you want, I don't care what it costs. But Hunter is coming with us."

"Fine," Lindsay said, the negotiation finished.

Will tugged at the collar of his shirt, feeling hot. This was Hunter's life, he thought. He'd known that, of course, but somehow he hadn't really understood it until this moment. The Finch family's biggest problem was whether to vacation in Greece or the Hamptons. Dom's words looped through his head: "Think about the optics." And that was the difference. It felt like the whole world was coming apart. Everyone he knew was looking at losing admissions or scholarships, or facing jail time. Will's parents couldn't even get a loan. They were making impossible choices between keeping the business going, paying a lawyer, or sending him to college. People's real lives were on the line, but not here in the Finch house. Here, they only needed to think about how things looked, not how they were. Because for the Finches, everything would always be fine, no matter what. That's what having money meant.

Lindsay and Dom were still talking, but Will didn't hear them. Blood was thumping in his ears, and his face burned. He turned and walked back into the library. Without really thinking about what he was doing, he made straight for the bookshelf and pulled out the Hemingway he'd been paging through. He lifted his shirt and slid it under the band of his jeans, against his back.

The angry pounding in his head drowned out all other thoughts and feelings. He'd held it together for so long. He'd worked hard at school, on the track team, and at the farm. He'd been a good friend. He hadn't envied Hunter's life. And none of it had mattered. He was going to lose everything.

Without a second glance he went back into the hall and turned toward the front door. He heard Dom's voice calling his name, but he didn't care. He was so angry he could hardly see straight. He pulled open the door, stepped onto the terrace, and ran smack into Hunter. The impact caused the book to come loose and fall onto the stones.

"Will!" Hunter said, surprised. A smile was spreading across his face, but it hung there, half-formed, as he looked at his friend's glaring eyes. "What's up, man?" he asked. When Will didn't answer, he tried again. "I'm glad you're here. I'm sorry about the other day." Will was silent, and Hunter followed his gaze down to the book that was now laying on the ground between them.

Hunter leaned down and picked it up. He looked at it for a minute and then looked at Will, understanding. His eyes were narrow now too. He pushed the book at Will. "Take it, then," he said coolly.

Will hesitated for a second, and Hunter pushed it against his chest, setting Will back on his heels. "Take it," he repeated. "I don't care."

"I bet you don't," Will said, shoving the book back into Hunter's hands. "Why should you?"

"You're just like everyone else," Hunter said. "Jealous of what I have. I didn't ask for any of this."

"You never had to," Will spat. "You just do whatever you want, take whatever you want, and no one seems to mind."

"Is this about Maddie?" Hunter asked, his face flushing. "Because it's not true."

"What?" Will said, not understanding. "What are you talking about?"

"Never mind," Hunter said.

"What did you do?" Will asked. A thought that had been bothering him for a few weeks, and which he'd tried to push to the back of his mind, came rushing out. "What did you do to Maddie?"

"Nothing!"

"Yeah? Why did she jump away from you at the park that day?"

"I don't know!" Hunter said. "She's crazy, I guess. Messed up."

"She's not crazy, asshole," Will said. The pieces were coming together. "Where were you the night of the party, Hunter, when we couldn't find Maddie?" he demanded.

"I told you," Hunter said. "I don't remember. I was fucked up."

"You weren't so messed up that you couldn't get yourself out of there before the cops showed up," Will said quietly.

"Are you accusing me of something?" Hunter asked.

Will thought about the words that Brendan had spat at him the day Will had given him a beating in the locker room. He'd said that he'd seen Will's friend all over Maddie at the party. Will hadn't wanted to think about what it meant. It had been easier to assume that Brendan was just trying to give him a hard time. But now, thinking about it, Brendan's words made sense.

"Is that why Maddie was hiding upstairs that night, all alone and stoned out of her mind?" Will said slowly. "Were you trying to get with her?"

"Will," Hunter started, but Will didn't let him finish.

"I've seen you flirting with Rosie," he said. "Touching her when June isn't looking. I can't believe I never said anything. It wasn't good enough for you, was it, having June? You had to have Rosie as well, and Maddie?"

"Will," Hunter said again, his voice pleading. "Look, I didn't know what I was doing. I'm sorry. I am."

So it was true. Now he understood why June had stopped speaking to Hunter. Was he the last person to know? "You have everything, Hunter!" Will yelled. "You couldn't have just left her alone? She didn't even want to get high that night. You want everyone to be as fucked up as you are, don't you? Well, you messed up everything."

"I know," Hunter said. "I know I did. I don't know what's wrong with me." He looked close to tears. "You're my only real friend, Will. June isn't even talking to me anymore."

Will was shaking his head. "That sucks for you. But we are not friends," he said. "Not anymore. I'm about to lose everything that I worked for. Maddie is drinking herself into oblivion, as far as I can tell. I can't feel bad for you. You have a whole team of people to help you. I only have myself. Stay away from Maddie, and stay away from me. I don't want anything to do with you. Ever again."

Will pushed past Hunter, ran back across the lawn, and slipped into the trees. When he was sure Hunter hadn't followed him, he slowed down. He yelled in frustration and took a swing at a tree, scraping the new skin off his recently bruised knuckles. Even alone in the woods, his face burned with anger and with shame. He couldn't believe he'd been so blind when it came to Hunter. And he couldn't believe he'd almost stolen that book. He didn't like who he was becoming.

42

Will pulled his truck into the parking lot of the county services building and cut the motor. He sat for a moment, looking at the east end
of the building, where the new police headquarters sat. Couldn't be
helped, he told himself. He swung the truck door open and went
around to the back, where he had bins full of sports equipment that
he'd collected over the last few months from local families. It was his
senior year service project: collecting gently used sports gear for the
county's camp program. The low-cost camp was a bit of an afterthought when it came to county funding, since unlike the school, it
mainly served working-class residents. He remembered being in the
program himself, using his brother's old glove to play baseball. Trip's
glove was already a hand-me-down when he received it, and by the
time it passed to Will, it was coming apart at the seams. When Will
got to middle school, he saw the equipment many of the other kids
were working with: fresh bats and gloves every year, the latest pads
and football cleats, and lacrosse sticks that barely saw playing time
before they were discarded for new and better models. He saw this
wealth of abandoned gear sitting in his friends' garages, and it occurred to him that he knew where it could be put to better use.

He dropped the gate on the truck bed and started to pull out the
bins. He was halfway done when he felt someone's eyes on him. He
scanned the parking lot and saw the detective who'd questioned him
on the track field leaning against the wall of the building, watching
him. Will felt a rush of annoyance. "You like the show?" he asked the
detective, sounding more like his brother, he thought, than himself.

The detective smiled and straightened up, as if he'd been waiting to be asked. "Need a hand?" he asked.

"It's for the kids," Will muttered, wishing he'd kept his big mouth shut. "For the camp program."

The detective was next to him now, pulling bins and bags down from the bed of the truck and carrying them over to the door of the community center. "This is nice stuff," the detective said, looking over what Will had collected. He picked up a pair of batting gloves with the tag still on them from the top of one of the containers. "Looks new."

"Uh-huh," Will said, working as fast as he could to get this over with.

"Where'd you get it?" the detective asked.

Will knew what he was thinking, "It's my service project," he snapped. "I collected all of it from local families. I didn't steal it, if that's what you're thinking. People around here have way more than they need."

The detective nodded, giving him that. Then his eye wandered from the sports equipment to the truck. He walked over to the rear tire and ran a finger along the tread. "Looks like you still have your snow tires on," he said. "It's June."

"What?" Will said, following the detective's eye. "Oh, no. I keep those on all year. They come in handy on the farm, with the summer rain and mud."

The detective was looking right at him now, a slight smile on his face. "Good on gravel roads too," he said.

"I guess," Will answered, not really understanding his meaning.

There were two more bins in the bed of the truck, near the cab. Will and the detective each leaned in and reached for one. Will lowered his onto the asphalt of the parking lot, but the detective stopped with his bin halfway out of the truck. He reversed course, crawling into the bed of the truck. He picked up something, but Will couldn't see what it was.

"You park this truck in a garage, Will?" the detective asked.

Will was caught off guard by the question. "No," he said. "Why?"

"No?" the detective asked. "Then what's this for?" He held up a sleek black remote with two buttons on the front.

"I . . . don't know," Will said. But in the few seconds that it took for him to get those words out, he remembered exactly what he was looking at. It was the garage door opener from the house on River Road. He had the faintest memory of seeing a kid toss it into the bed of the truck as they carried in the cases of liquor and beer that Will had brought. He'd forgotten all about it, and it must have lodged in the tangle of bungee cords and tarps that Will kept back there. He looked up and locked eyes with the detective.

"Why don't you follow me?" the detective said, turning and walking toward the entrance to headquarters. And Will, realizing that whatever good luck he'd been counting on had just come to an end, took the last of the sports equipment over to the collection bin and followed the detective into the station.

It hadn't gone down the way Will imagined. There were no handcuffs, and he wasn't led to a holding cell. It was more like being brought to the principal's office: the officer sat him down on a chair next to his desk and let him call his parents, even though he was eighteen. He hadn't known his lawyer's phone number.

The detective, who reintroduced himself as Detective Murray, recited Will's rights for him, but didn't bother to question him right away. To Will, whose entire body was coursing with an almost painful nervous energy, Detective Murray seemed oddly calm. When Will's parents arrived, his father was wearing an old suit that Will had only ever seen him wear to funerals. For some reason, this scared him more than anything else.

When their lawyer, Ed DeLeo, arrived, Detective Murray led them to a conference table. The District Attorney arrived last, nodded to Ed, and introduced himself as Hal Buckley.

Pleasantries finished, the DA laid out the situation: Originally, Will had been charged with misdemeanor trespassing and vandalism. But the discovery of the garage door opener in his truck changed this. The DA's office was now recommending that Will be charged as the organizer of the party, with a felony criminal mischief charge and a vandalism charge that would rate as a felony because of the amount of the damage, well over the five-thousand-dollar threshold.

"But I wasn't . . ." Will broke in, before his lawyer shushed him. He was going to say that he wasn't the only one who caused damage, and Detective Murray seemed to read his mind.

"With the evidence that we have against you, we can hold you responsible for a much greater portion of the damage," Murray explained, looking down at the garage opener that lay on the table between them in a plastic bag. "We have witness statements, and we have physical evidence. You're not getting out of this one."

"I'm assuming you've confirmed this is, indeed, the garage opener from the house in question?" Ed asked.

"It matches the description," Detective Murray replied. "And we'll be sending an officer over to confirm. We're also going to check Will's tire treads against the tracks found at the scene. But I think we all know we're going to get a match there, and this is a small department. We're working with a limited number of officers, and it's just as much in our interest as in Will's here to strike a deal."

The DA took over: "Here's what we're proposing: Will pleads to felony vandalism and agrees to assume responsibility for fifty percent of the total damage restitution payments. He does three months in county jail, and twelve weeks of community service. In return for his cooperation, we'll drop the criminal mischief charge. If we bring full charges, he's going to be looking at a year in jail, at least, and possibly up to three. And we can't guarantee the division of the restitution payments. That will depend on how many other perpetrators plead or are convicted. And of course your family will save the cost, time, and publicity of a court trial."

Will couldn't believe what he was hearing. He tried to concentrate on what the DA was saying, but his brain was stuck on the words *felony* and *jail*. He knew he was supposed to keep his mouth shut, but he couldn't help himself. "It wasn't my party!" he said, looking between his parents and the police. "I didn't mean to destroy anyone's house. I was only trying to help my friend. There were so many people there—why am I the one sitting here? I bet it makes you guys feel good to haul my family in here. It's easy to blame me, right? Did you go after anyone else half as hard as you've gone after me and Trip?"

"That's enough!" his lawyer barked, and Will stopped abruptly. He looked down at the garage opener sitting on the table in front of him. How had this one night come to be the defining event of his life?

While the grown-ups around him went back and forth, Will thought about a tubing trip they'd taken down the river last summer. He'd missed the main channel of the wing dam and had instead gone over where the water crested the low concrete arm of the dam. It was only a short, exhilarating slide down, but at its base the usually placid surface of the Delaware turned back on itself, creating an eddy where the water flowed briefly upstream, pinning Will and his tube back against the dam. The force of the water wasn't strong enough to pull him under, but the constant circular churn of the river made it impossible for him to move forward either. He was stuck there, pushing helplessly against the base of the dam, until his brother, Trip, paddled over in his kayak and pulled him out.

He'd had a similarly powerless feeling ever since the night of the party. From the moment he'd thrown the hammer through the glass door, he'd been stuck reliving that night over and over; until his waking and dreaming mind converged into one endless loop of hope, then fear, then despair; unable to move forward or change course. Now, at least, he had an answer: He had to take the plea, and he wasn't going to Princeton in the fall. He was going to jail.

"Will!" His mother had apparently said his name a few times. He looked over at her blankly. "What do you want to do?"

Will opened his mouth, but he didn't know what to say. He felt like there wasn't enough air in the room. He looked at his lawyer, who didn't look too happy. "Can we have a few minutes here?" Ed asked the DA.

When Murray and the DA stepped away from the table, Ed leveled with them. "It's not a bad deal," he said, "all things considered. With a three-month sentence, Will could be out in thirty days."

"What about the restitution payment?" his father asked, and Ed looked through his file. "That's going to be steep," he said. "The last total figure I saw was over five hundred thousand dollars. But the final individual amounts will be decided by the court."

His father shook his head. "A small fortune. Down the drain."

"It's a lot of money," Ed agreed. "But you don't want to spin the roulette wheel on that. If they're going to apportion the payments, Will could be on the hook for much more if it goes to trial and the judge wants to make an example out of him. Not to mention the possibility of Will doing a lot more time. Three months sounds long, but in the grand scheme of things, it's not. Will can serve his time, get out, and move on with his life."

"But not college," his mother said quietly. "Not Princeton, anyway."

Ed shrugged. He'd gone to state school, and it had been good enough for him. "A smart kid like Will is going to make opportunities for himself," he said to reassure her.

His mother closed her eyes and rubbed her temples. When she opened her eyes again, she seemed resigned. "Will, you're going to have to make your own choice here. I can't tell you what to do. Those days are long over. All I can tell you is that if I was in your shoes, I would want to take responsibility for my actions."

Will looked over at his father, who looked grim, but didn't say anything. They were telling him to take the plea, he knew. Do the right thing, his mom always said. And instead, he'd made bad decision after bad decision. He took a deep breath and nodded at his attorney, not trusting his voice. Ed nodded in return and called the DA and Detective Murray back over to the table.

They were about to sit down again when the police station seemed to come suddenly to life. A chorus of emergency service calls crackled over the police radios on officers' belts and desks. Detective Murray stopped in his tracks to listen as the call went out: *All available units. River Road and Taylor Road. Submerged vehicle.*

Both officers who'd been sitting in their cubicles stood immediately and headed out to their cars. Detective Murray looked at Hal Buckley. "You can take this from here?" Hal nodded, and Murray spoke into his radio. "Officer in charge, here," he said. "Number of passengers?"

"One female driver observed; other passengers unknown."

"Can I get a vehicle description?" Murray asked, picking up his car keys.

"Green Toyota Prius." And then: "Fire and EMT on their way."

"Maddie!" Will yelled. Before he knew what he was doing, he'd leaped from his seat and was following Detective Murray to the door. "I think that's my friend."

"Whoa there," Murray said, surprised. "Where do you think you're going?" He turned Will around toward the table. "Your plea deal expires today. Get it done." In the next moment, Murray was out the door.

"Mom!" Will said, ignoring his lawyer and the prosecutor, who were waiting for him to sit down. "That's Maddie's car. I have to go down there."

"Will," his mother said, sounding tired. "You don't know that. It could be someone else."

"It's a Prius," Will said, sounding desperate. "You heard him. Female driver. It's her. Please, Mom. You know things haven't been right with her."

His mother looked torn. Then she stood up, nodded at his father, and grabbed her purse. "I'll go," she said. "But they probably won't let me anywhere near it. You have to stay here. I'll call if I have any information."

His mother followed the officers out, and Will was left with his father and the two attorneys. He tried to concentrate on what was happening to him. But all he could think about was Maddie, downing vodkas in his truck and crying in his bed. Had she driven off the road?

His father was looking at him. "Can I have a few words with my son?" he asked the DA, who nodded. "Alone," he added for their lawyer's benefit.

"Now that your mother's gone, I'm going to give you some advice. I know I usually leave that sort of thing to her, but I'm gonna speak, and I want you to hear me out.

"Your mother is a good woman. And she's not wrong. But it seems to me that you're going to bear a lot of responsibility for things a lot of other kids had a hand in. I don't know if there's a good answer here. And I know they're saying that you have to take the deal right now. But I don't like being put on the spot like that. My bet is that if you come back tomorrow and you want their deal, it will still be good. I think we should go home tonight and think about it. Like I said, I don't know if there's any way out of this. But let's at least take tonight to talk it over." He sighed. "You're a good kid, Will. I know that you didn't mean for this to happen."

Will hadn't expected this from his dad. He'd expected yelling, or maybe silence, but not this. Understanding. "Will you tell them?" he asked.

His father stood up and signaled to the attorneys. "We're going home," he announced, not feeling the need to elaborate.

"This is a good deal!" the DA exclaimed, clearly surprised.

"We'll think about it," his father said, leading Will out of the station. In the parking lot, Will saw the bins of sports equipment still sitting outside of the community center door.

His father followed Will's gaze and put a hand on his shoulder. He shook his head. "No good deed goes unpunished, does it?"

"That's another one of Mom's sayings that you always tell her isn't true," Will said.

"Well, this time," his father replied, "I think she had it right."

43

Hart County General Hospital was a gleaming new building where the doors slid open as you approached and nurses in colorful scrubs pushed computer trolleys between the rooms. Will, in his baseball cap and jeans, felt conspicuous walking down the corridor with a bouquet of flowers from his mother's garden clutched in his damp hand.

His mother had called his cell phone before he'd even gotten home from the police station. "You were right," she said. "It's Maddie. They're taking her to the hospital."

When Will had heard the words "submerged vehicle" in the police station the previous day, he'd pictured Maddie's car sinking into the rushing current of the river, the muddy water quickly engulfing the windows as she banged helplessly against the glass. They'd been shown a video at school meant to prepare them for just such an emergency. There was a series of steps that you were supposed to follow for self-rescue: unbuckle your seat belt, open the window before the water level rises above it, and escape through the window. They made it sound so simple, but all Will could think was that, in the terror of the rising water, how could you stay calm enough to remember the steps?

Maddie hadn't driven into the river after all, but instead into the canal that ran along River Road near town. The canal was only five feet deep, but Maddie's car had slid down the steep embankment, landing hard on its nose in the water. The driver's window had smashed, filling the front seat with water, but somehow Maddie had managed to climb through the back seat and out of the trunk. When the police arrived, she was sitting on the back bumper, leaning against the embankment, bleeding but alive. She'd saved herself.

Will found the room, on the second floor, and peered through the window in the door. June was sitting in a chair next to Maddie's bed, and she caught Will's eye. She stood up, gave Maddie's hand a squeeze, and came out into the hallway.

"She'll be happy to see you," June said. "But she's pretty tired. She broke two ribs, and I think they gave her something for the pain."

"I don't want to bother her if she's tired," Will said, feeling awkward. He'd never visited anyone in the hospital before. He felt like he was pretending to be mature enough to handle something that was actually way beyond his experience.

"It's fine," June said. "Don't be nervous. Look, Will, I'm glad that I ran into you. I've been wanting to talk to you." She took a deep breath. "I was the one who came forward to the police and gave a statement. I wanted you to know."

"What?" Will said. "But you were the one who said that we all had to stick together and stay quiet."

"I know," June said. "But my dad insisted that I tell the police the truth. Or a version of it, anyway. I tried to protect all of you. I didn't give them Maddie's name, or Rosie's. But they already knew that you were there, Will. I tried to deny it, but they had other kids who'd given your name. I told them that you didn't plan it, for what it's worth. I'm sorry. My dad forbid me from talking to anyone about it, but I'm tired of lying to everyone."

"I get it," Will said, surprising himself. "It doesn't even matter now. The police found the garage door opener from that house in the back of my truck."

"Are you serious? Why did you have it?"

Will shrugged. "Someone must have tossed it in when we were unloading the beer. I didn't notice it. Anyhow, now the police are saying that I organized the party. They're charging me with a felony."

"That's crazy," June said. "You have to fight it."

"My lawyer told me to take the plea deal."

"What about school?"

Will just shook his head. He couldn't talk about it yet.

"June," he said, after a moment. "Can I ask you what happened between you and Hunter?"

"We're done," June said. "I couldn't trust him. And yes, I know how that sounds after what I just said to you."

"Was it because of something that Maddie told you?" Will asked.

June paused, then said, "She didn't want to say anything to me. But I guessed anyway."

Will nodded. He'd been right about Hunter.

"Everything got so out of control," June said. "For what it's worth, I think you did the right thing, breaking that window."

"But we never should have been there in the first place," Will said. I think I blew my chance at Princeton. He looked at June. She was wearing a black silk T-shirt, and an expensive-looking leather bag was slung over her shoulder. She looked sophisticated, like she was already in college. "What about Penn State?" he asked her.

"I only got a trespassing ticket," June said sheepishly. "It wasn't a big deal."

Of course everything had worked out for her—that was never really in question. Her father was a lawyer and her mom was the head of the PTA. They might not have been rich like Hunter's family, but they were rich enough that things like this wouldn't touch them. They were rich enough to be safe. He'd never thought too much about how different their lives were. All this time, his family had been one fuckup away from disaster. How could he not have seen it?

June looked uncomfortable. "Will you keep me posted?" she asked. "If there's anything I can do . . ."

"Sure," Will said. "Thanks." None of this was her fault. It was just the way things were.

June left, and Will pushed open the door to Maddie's room. She gave him a weak smile and a wave, and Will waved back, standing near the door. An angry-looking red cut along her cheekbone stood out against her pale skin.

"It's okay," she said. "You can come all the way into the room."

Will sat down in the chair next to the bed and dropped the flowers on the table. "Maddie," he said, and then he couldn't think of what else to say.

She pushed herself up in the bed, grimacing as she did it. "Ribs," she said. "I never thought about them before I broke them."

"How did it happen?" Will asked.

"I lost control," she said. "I told the police that a deer ran across the road and I swerved."

"But that's not what happened?"

Maddie shrugged. "I missed the turn."

Had she been drinking? Will wondered. "Maddie," he said. "I know you don't want to hear this, but I'm really worried about you. I want to help, but I don't know what to do."

To Will's surprise, she didn't get angry with him like she had the last time he'd tried to talk to her seriously. "I know," she said. "I know you've been trying. I thought if I pretended I was okay, it would be true. In a weird way, I think totaling my car was a good thing." She touched her cheek. "I mean, this might leave a scar. But maybe it will be a reminder. I can't go on like this, pretending to be okay. It's not working."

"Did you do it on purpose?" Will asked, feeling suddenly angry.

"No, that's not what I meant. I can't keep thinking about it all the time. Worrying about what everyone else is thinking. My parents want me to stay nearby next year, but I can't move forward here. I need a fresh start. I just want to go somewhere where I don't know anyone and never look back. I thought maybe I could try to find a program in California. I know it's late in the year, but the guidance counselor said she might be able to help."

But what about me? Will wanted to ask, but he knew enough not to say it. This wasn't about him. "What did the police say?" he asked instead.

"They called yesterday morning. They found the guy—that's why I was so upset. They said I have to decide whether to press charges. My parents want me to, but I don't know. Part of me just wants to move on. But the police said that since they have the pictures, there's a good chance he'll take a plea, and there won't have to be a trial or anything like that." She paused. "I know I'm not supposed to think this, but I still feel a little bit like it was my fault. I'm the one who took the ecstasy. I made myself a target."

Will shook his head. "It wasn't your fault."

"I could have drowned," Maddie said, talking almost to herself. Her voice sounded drowsy. "I could have drowned in the canal. How stupid would that be?"

"Pretty stupid," Will said, taking her hand. "Look, Maddie, if you need to get away from here, you should go," he said. He only wished that he could do the same. But any hope of that had been extinguished when the police had turned up the garage door opener in the back of his truck. He wasn't going anywhere.

Maddie's eyes were closed now. Her breathing slowed, and he was pretty sure she was asleep. "I'll miss you, though," he said quietly.

He sat by her bed for a few more minutes, thinking. He made up his mind. He would take the plea deal. It would mean, he knew, losing out on Princeton. But it was better than risking a year or more in a jail cell, an idea that had seemed unimaginable to him a few months ago. When his sentence was finished, he would get away from here too. He couldn't bear the thought of staying in town, nursing old wounds and drowning himself in beers at the local brewery, like his brother. He wouldn't be heading to the Ivy League, but he could start over somewhere. One party, he thought, was all it had taken to derail everything. He wasn't going to get away with it, but he knew he would eventually move past it, scars and all.

44

Trip O'Connor stubbed out his cigarette on the ground next to the hay bale he sat on and rolled another. He had to make a decision, and this time there was no easy answer. His lawyer had been clear: He should fight the charge, or he would serve his suspended sentence along with additional time. The more difficult question was how they were going to pay the lawyer, while still keeping up with the mortgage on the farm. Trip didn't need a fancy college degree to know that the math just didn't add up.

But the question that really bothered him was what was going to happen to Will. Trip loved to tease him, but the truth was that Will was a good kid, and he'd worked hard for what he wanted. It wasn't easy to watch as Will prepared to move on to a different kind of life, college and all of the opportunities that it would open up for him, without feeling as if he was being left behind. It would be worse to watch his brother get stuck here, though; to watch all of his effort come to nothing. And after the police had found that garage opener and hauled Will in, that looked like what was going to happen.

Trip had been sitting in the barn all afternoon going over all of this in his head, and he knew what he was going to. What he had to do. But now he had to actually pull the trigger. And that had never been his strong suit. It wasn't like he didn't know all the things he should have done. The SATs he should have shown up for. The community college courses he should have taken. The weed he should have stuck to just smoking and not selling on the side. He hadn't had some kind of grand plan to fuck up his life. He'd just always done whatever was easiest, from one moment to the next. And in the end, it had added up to this.

Christ, he could use a joint right now. The lawyer had warned him off of smoking pot, saying that a clean drug test might help cut down on the time he might eventually do. He wanted it so bad that he could smell it, a damp and funky singe in his nostrils.

He sat up. He was actually smelling smoke. He jumped to his feet and saw that his last cigarette butt had ignited the dry hay beneath him, and it was now smoldering and spreading through the bale. As he stamped the fire out with his boot, he had to laugh. He had lit a literal fire under his own ass. It was time to go and do what needed to be done.

Trip didn't have a dress shirt, so he grabbed one from his father's closet and slipped it on before he climbed into his truck. He was heading downtown to the courthouse, but first he had a stop to make.

In the driveway of the Finch house he pushed the intercom button and the gate swung open for him. By the time he pulled up the drive, Hunter was already waiting for him on the steps that ran along the terrace in front of the house. Trip stuck his fist out and Hunter gave it a bump, eyeing him warily.

"What's up, man?" Hunter asked.

"I need a favor," Trip said, sitting down on the steps next to Hunter.

Hunter gave a dry laugh. "Oh, yeah?"

Trip looked at him. "Is something wrong?" he asked.

"Will didn't say anything to you?" Hunter asked.

"Will hasn't been in a talkative mood lately."

"That's for sure. The last time I saw him he stormed out of here without saying more than ten words to me, none of them nice. And he almost took . . ." Hunter paused and then seemed to decide not to finish his thought. "Anyway, some shit went down. I don't think I'm going to be seeing too much of him."

Trip was surprised. "I thought you two were inseparable. Heading off to Princeton, arm in arm," he said sarcastically.

"I'm not going to Princeton," Hunter said. "I'm out."

"You're kidding me. Can they do that before you're convicted?"

"I'm going to take a plea, but it doesn't really matter," Hunter said. "My spring transcript was a mess. My GPA was 1.9. I shouldn't have even graduated, but my dad pulled some strings. Princeton wasn't having it, though. They said I can apply again next year, but I don't know. Anyway, who cares, right?"

"Will cares," Trip said. "He's looking at doing a year if he's convicted. If that happens, it's the end of Princeton. All for a stupid party."

Hunter nodded but didn't say anything.

"So what happened between you and Will?"

"I messed up," Hunter said with a sigh. "That night at the party. I made a pass at Maddie. It was so dumb. I don't even know why I did it. I was bored, I guess. And drunk." He took a deep breath. "And I'm afraid that's why Maddie went upstairs by herself, where that guy must've followed her. To get away from me."

"Shit," Trip said.

"Yeah," Hunter replied. "Like I said, I really messed up. Maddie won't come near me, and I don't think Will is going to speak to me again." He looked over at Trip, but Trip just shrugged. "So, what's the favor?"

Trip hesitated. He'd been counting on Hunter's help, but now he wasn't sure. On the other hand, Hunter would probably want to make it up to Will.

"I'm going to try to get Will out of this," Trip said. "I'm taking a plea. I'm going to tell the cops that Will was never there, that it was just me everyone saw. They've got this crazy idea that he organized the whole thing. They're hot for someone to blame—like there was one person who was responsible. If Will ends up getting convicted, it's going to kill my mom. He's her golden boy. I have a feeling that I'm not getting out of this one anyway, not with that suspended sentence hanging over my head. The least I can do is take the fall for Will."

"I thought you told them you were just there to pick up Will."

"True. But I can't see them turning their noses up at a confession." He looked at Hunter. "Especially if you back me up."

"Me?"

"I need your help. When the cops ask, just say that it was me. That people get us mixed up all the time."

"You want me to lie to the cops?" Hunter asked.

"I don't know if they're even going to buy it. But, yeah, I guess I'm asking you to lie to the cops."

Hunter was quiet for a moment and then said, "Why the hell not? Will's the closest thing I had to real family. I know this probably won't make a difference to him, but it's something."

"Thanks, man," Trip said, standing up. "And one more thing."

"Besides lying to the police?" Hunter asked sarcastically. "Maybe I could forge something for the FBI?"

Trip ignored him. "Between the lawyer, and the court fines, and everything at the orchard, I don't know if our parents are going to be able to make up the difference for school. If I come forward, my family is still going to be on the hook if the judge orders a big restitution payment. If there's anything you—or your dad—can do to help, it could make a big difference." He knew Will and his parents were all too proud to ask for any favors, either money or influence, from Dominic Finch. But Trip didn't feel weird about it. What was the point of having rich friends if they couldn't help you out?

"Lucky Will," Hunter said. "Everyone looking out for him. Must be nice."

"Don't give me that poor little rich boy horseshit," Trip said, ribbing him. "I could say the same thing about you. Besides, it sounds like you owe him."

"Think he'll forgive me?"

"I don't know," Trip said, truthfully. "But it's still the right thing to do."

"Lying to the cops is the right thing to do?" Hunter asked, raising his eyebrows.

"No, but looking out for your friend is." Trip stood up to leave.

"Okay," Hunter said. "I've got your back. And I'll talk to my dad. I can't promise anything, but I'll see what I can do."

⚭

At the courthouse, Trip was directed to the second floor. He knew he should have at least called his attorney, but he also knew the attorney wasn't going to like the way Trip was going about this. He reasoned that he could fill him in afterward. Plus it would mean less hours that they would be billed for.

At the desk a fiftyish lady with dyed-blond hair looked at him over glasses pushed halfway down her nose. She didn't seem to like what she saw. "Mmmmm?" she said, letting her expression ask the question.

"I need to see Hal Buckley," Trip said.

"Do you have an appointment?" the secretary asked, without bothering to look at her computer screen. She knew he didn't.

"I'm Sean O'Connor," Trip said. It felt weird, as always, to use a name he associated more with his father than with himself.

Recognition dawned on the secretary's face. She pushed her chair back. "Follow me. This way," she called over her shoulder.

"Mr. O'Connor," Hal Buckley said as he pointed to a chair for Trip to sit in. "Is your attorney present?"

"No," Trip said. "I wanted to talk to you myself. I'm going to take the plea. But I need to clear up some confusion first."

"I'm listening," Hal said.

"My brother, William O'Connor. He wasn't at the party. I don't know why people are saying that he was, but he wasn't."

Hal Buckley leaned back in his chair. He crossed a leg over his knee and knitted his hands behind his head. "Well," he said slowly. "That's not what we've heard. Our theory is that he planned this thing."

"You heard that from a bunch of kids who were drunk that night," Trip replied, feeling steadier than he expected to be. It had to be the adrenaline. "Those are your witnesses?"

Hal just raised his eyebrows and kept looking right at Trip. "And what do you say?" he asked.

"I planned it," Trip said, surprising himself. He wasn't sure if he'd meant to go that far. But what was the difference? "I admit that I planned it. I bought the beer. I found the spot. But Will had nothing to do with it. People get us mixed up all the time."

"Is that right?" Hal asked, still looking at Trip. "Your brother didn't, say, break a glass window to keep a girl from being assaulted?"

Trip was surprised, but he stuck to his story. "Sounds like whoever did that is a brave kid," Trip said. "But it wasn't Will. He was only there to pick me up. He was worried I was going to violate my parole. He says anything different, he's just covering up for me. You can't blame a brother for being loyal."

Buckley gave a short laugh. "Loyalty must run in the family," he said. "But you're going to have to give me some details. As I recall, you told the detective you were never at the party."

Trip thought for a moment. He remembered standing on the deck of the house when something white came flying from a window above and crashed a few feet from him. It was the lid of a toilet tank. He'd jumped back as the kids around him screamed their approval. "Throw it out!" they chanted. "Shoot the shitter!" Trip, still feeling the adrenaline of the fight he and Will had with that little punk, had taken it as a personal challenge. He ran up the stairs and joined the kids rocking the base of the toilet back and forth. There was a wrenching sound, and then a pop. He and another boy had dragged the toilet across the floor, leaving a deep welt in the wood floors, and then stood with it at the edge of the balcony before tossing it over. "Did you happen to find a toilet on the deck?" he asked the prosecutor.

Hal picked up a file from his desk and looked through it, nodding his head. "Well," he said, "it just so happens that you may have come to me at the right time. We'd like to get this all cleared up. But we must have the facts straight. Anyone going to back up your story? I don't need it changing again a week from now."

For once, Trip thought, he'd done things the right way. Planned ahead. It was just too bad that the first time he'd managed to do it was when he was planning for his own funeral. He took a deep breath. "Sure," he said. "Hunter Finch. He'll tell you. Will wasn't there."

Hal looked at him for a long moment, and Trip held his gaze. Then, suddenly, Hal rocked forward in his chair and slapped his palms on his desk, startling Trip. "Okay then," he said. "I've had enough of this case. It's a goddam three-ring circus. Have Donna get your attorney on the line. Let's wrap this up."

45

Trip parked his truck in front of the house. Will was sitting outside on the bench under the kitchen window, his head tilted back against the wall, but his eyes alert. Trip rolled down his window, and Will put a finger to his lips, silencing him. Will pointed, and Trip followed his gaze to a green Jaguar pulled up next to the O'Connors' cars.

Will walked over to Trip's truck and leaned on the door.

"What's up?" Trip asked.

"Mr. Finch is here," Will said. "He wanted to talk with Mom and Dad alone. I've been sitting here, trying to hear what they're saying."

"And?" Trip asked.

"It sounds like he's offering to buy a piece of the orchard and lease it back to them. He said something about it being win–win. That he just wants to preserve the character of the farmland behind his house."

"And they're listening?" Trip asked.

"Yeah."

Trip nodded then said, "Hop in, let's get out of here."

Will got into the passenger seat and Trip swung the truck around and headed back down the dirt road, past the U-pick blueberry bushes, and out onto the road.

Will looked at his brother's dress shirt and slacks. "Why are you wearing that?" he asked. But Trip ignored him and turned up the music, Tom Petty playing on the classic rock station. They drove for a few minutes without speaking, winding down toward River Road. When they reached the river, Trip made a left and started heading north, away from town. "Let's go to the Rock," Trip said, and Will nodded.

They parked the truck in a pull-off on the side of the road. There were no other cars there, a good sign. Trip grabbed a can of beer from under the front seat and slipped it into his back pocket. A break in the trees marked the entrance to an unofficial trail. The brothers started up the trail, gaining ground quickly through the woods. It was humid, and between the heavy air and the elevation, both boys were breathing hard by the time they reached the clearing.

Will heard it before he saw it: the roar of water rushing through the rocks before it tumbled over the edge, forming a waterfall that poured into a deep pool below. A large, flat rock ran alongside the creek and jutted out over the falls. The boys stepped carefully out onto it. From here they had a clear view of the river valley below them stretching south, past the whitewater section of the falls near town.

Trip inched out to the edge of the rock and looked over at the pool.

"Deep enough?" Will asked.

"Looks good," Trip answered. "There's been plenty of rain this spring." He pulled the can of beer from his pocket and stuck it into a shallow section of the stream to get cold.

They'd been coming to this spot for years. Will remembered the first time Trip brought him here, when Will was twelve and always trying to tag along with Trip's older friends, eager to impress them. Don't think, Trip had told him. If you wait too long, you'll get scared and you won't be able to jump. Trip had gone first, to show him where to leap. Will followed, closing his eyes at the last second. With the sound of the kids cheering behind him, his left foot touched rock and then his right foot found nothing but air. He let out an involuntary whoop, and then there was silence as he plunged into the cold water. The next second he was bobbing back to the surface, the sound of the falls behind him and Trip's smiling face close to his own, his strong arms pulling Will toward the edge of the pool.

Trip plucked the beer out of the water and popped the top. He took a long sip and then passed the can to Will. "I took the plea deal," he said, looking out over the valley. "I went in today and talked to the DA. It's done."

"Do Mom and Dad know?" Will asked, and Trip shook his head

no. Will's heart sank. He'd known that Trip was probably going to do time, but until this moment, part of him still hoped that somehow they were all going to make it out of this. That the lawyer they were struggling to pay was going to have some kind of magic answer.

"I tried to protect you," Will said quietly. "I never said anything to the police."

"I know," Trip said. "But it's not your job to protect me. I shouldn't have asked you to."

"Do you think I should plead too?" Will asked.

"Nope," Trip said. "You just sit tight. They're going to drop the charges against you."

Will stared at Trip for a moment, thinking that he heard him wrong. "What are you talking about?" he asked. "Why would they do that? They know I was there. They're charging me as the organizer."

"I admitted everything," Trip said, still not looking at him. "I told them that I bought the booze and that I tossed the garage door opener in the back of your truck. I said I put out the word about the party. I told them that you were a good kid, that you were only there to pick me up. That anything else they heard was just kids at school who were jealous of your success. I told them you were covering for your fuckup older brother. That you were afraid I was going to jail."

Will was stunned. "And they believed you?"

Trip shrugged. "I don't know if they believed me, but they liked my story a hell of a lot better than any of the stories they'd come up with. Think about it. In their version, they're going after a high school athlete, a soon-to-be Princeton man, who only broke the windows to save a girl from being raped. Nobody likes that story. Now, in my version, they've got a well-known area lowlife who led a bunch of nice kids astray by buying them booze and luring them into an empty house for a party. That's a good story. That's a story that doesn't scare off their campaign donors and golf buddies."

Will was quiet for a long time. He couldn't reconcile all of the thoughts that were racing through his head: hope and disbelief; fear that Trip was telling him the truth, and also that he wasn't.

"Thank you," he finally said. "I can't believe you did this for me. But I wish you'd said something first."

Trip stood up and stripped off his shirt. He turned to Will with a wink. "You can't think about it too long," he said. "If you wait, you'll get scared, and you won't be able to jump." With that, Trip turned and trotted toward the edge, his bare feet slapping against the rock. At the last second he took a flying leap, soaring out into the sky. "Team O'Connor!" he yelled, and then, a second later, he hit the water and disappeared beneath the surface.

When Will and Trip got home that evening, the house was dark and their parents' bedroom door was closed. Will wanted to know what they'd said to Dom Finch, but he had other things on his mind. He still couldn't believe what Trip had done for him. In the moment, it had felt like a massive weight was lifted from his shoulders. The afternoon spent leaping into the waterfall pool, climbing back up, and doing it again had exhausted his body and calmed his mind. But on the car ride home the unease that he'd felt for the last month crept back and settled in across his sternum, like a too-tight shirt. His mother's words echoed in his head. Making this right didn't just mean getting himself out of trouble. The DA may have bought Trip's story, but it wasn't actually true. He had to do something to make up for what he'd done.

The next morning, he opened his laptop and began to type out a letter. At first, he struggled with what to write. Trip was sacrificing so much to keep him out of trouble. He didn't want to throw it all away. He'd been so preoccupied by his own problems—whether he was going to get caught, how it would affect his chance at college, what was going on with Maddie. It was as if he hadn't been able to see clearly what he'd done. Now that Trip had come forward to take the blame, he finally felt the full force of the part he'd played. He hadn't meant to destroy a house, but he hadn't thought twice about showing up at someone else's home to throw a party. He knew he shouldn't have been there; he just hadn't cared. He'd felt invincible. Now he felt anything but.

In the end, he decided to admit what he'd done and apologize to the Jensens. Whatever Trip had said to the prosecutor, the truth was that Will had taken part in the destruction. None of his excuses would change the fact that a family's house had been destroyed. And so he simply told them what he'd done and asked for their forgiveness. *I didn't mean to hurt you,* he said, *but I know that I did.* When he was done, he printed it in the office behind the farm shop, signed his name, and placed it in an envelope. He felt an odd mix of resignation and relief. It would be up to the Jensens what they did with the letter, but the important thing was that he'd written it.

His mother was sitting in the kitchen when he went to grab his keys, and she asked him where he was going.

"There's something that I need to do," Will said. "I've been thinking about what you said. About figuring out what I need to do to live with myself." He slipped the letter into his back pocket and headed out to the driveway. She stood at the door and watched him go. Before he got into the truck, he turned back to her. "What did Dom Finch want yesterday?" he asked.

His mother's face clouded a bit. "He wants to help," she said. "I think . . . I think things might work out." It didn't really sound like she believed it. "Anyway, it's a way forward, for all of us. Nothing is free, right? The only question is, is the thing you want worth the price you have to pay?"

46

Rosie sat at a table at the back of her dad's restaurant, her laptop open in front of her. Her screen had gone blank several minutes earlier, but she was still staring at it as she methodically nibbled away at what was left of her fingernails. She glanced over at her father, who was behind the counter dealing with a busy lunch crowd. He met her eyes, and then quickly looked away.

She should have been working the lunch shift. Her plan for the summer had been to work as many hours as she could to save up spending money for college in the fall. But after the police called her father in to inform him about what they termed the *relationship* between her and Jake Tillman, her father had forbidden her from working in the front of the house. He seemed to think that he was to blame for what happened because he had had her work behind the counter. Rosie, who couldn't figure out how to tell him that nothing had actually happened, found it difficult to argue. In fact, she was finding it difficult to talk to her father at all, and he seemed to feel the same way.

Still, her father insisted she hang out at the restaurant with him during the day, even if she wasn't working, so she could "get everything ready for college." He wasn't more specific, and again, Rosie didn't want to argue, so she'd spent the time scrolling through course catalogs and event listings while the hard knot in her stomach wound itself tighter and tighter.

As she saw it, she had no good options. If she said nothing, she would destroy that poor man's career, if not his entire life. Did he have a girlfriend? She didn't know the first thing about him. Of course, when he was going after her friends, she'd thought of him if not as an enemy, at least as an obstacle. But she also knew he was just doing his job. He had only been kind to her, and he hadn't deserved this.

No matter how hard she tried, she couldn't understand what had made her do it. It had been a moment of madness, a stupid wish to impress Hunter. She'd tried to fix it right away by deleting everything from his phone. It hadn't occurred to her that her phone might be searched, or that nothing digital ever really disappears. What she had done was so at odds with her usual behavior that she worried that even if she did confess, no one would believe her.

Her mind whirred like an overheated processor, going over and over the same series of uncomfortable thoughts, unable to come to any conclusion. What would happen to Jake Tillman? What would happen to her if she told the truth? What was going to happen to all of the kids who had already entered their pleas, guilty or not?

There was also the possibility that what she'd done was a crime. She didn't know, and there was no one she could ask. Hunter had come to see Rosie after he heard what happened, but in what Rosie viewed as a darkly humorous turn of events, he seemed to be suspicious of her. *I asked you if you could find anything out from him*, he'd said, accusingly. *Why didn't you tell me you were hooking up with him? You could have helped us if you wanted to. Is that why you were the only one of us who didn't get charged?*

Hunter had sounded disgusted, as if it wasn't even a question. She'd been so hurt that she immediately burst into tears. Part of her had wanted to scream, *I was just trying to help you!* But she didn't say anything. She didn't think she could trust him to keep her secret.

When she saw Jake's face staring at her through the glass door of the restaurant, she stared back, thinking it was nothing more than the ghost of her agitated thoughts. Then he pushed open the door and slipped into the restaurant behind a group of women. He stopped in front of her table and she sat motionless, unable to look away from him. For one second, she thought that she might be mistaken, that her mind was playing tricks on her. But as different as he looked, it was definitely him. His dark suit and crisp, white shirt had been replaced by a ringer T-shirt for a band that she hadn't heard of. He hadn't shaved, and his eyes were bloodshot behind smudged glasses. His jaw was clenched and his hands were shoved in the pockets of his jeans.

She didn't move, or speak. All she thought, as she watched the anger build in his face, was that *something* was going to happen, and whatever it was, she wanted it to happen. Even if he screamed at her, or hit her, or *killed* her, it would be better than the state of suspended animation in which she'd been living.

He took a step toward her, and she flinched and raised a protective hand. But he was only slumping into the chair across from her. It was as if his anger had been the only thing holding him up and giving him shape, and now it was gone. He put his elbows on the table and cradled his head in his hands. He took a deep breath and looked back up at her, his hands extended toward her. "Why?" he asked, his voice hoarse.

It wasn't what she expected. "I don't know," she mumbled. "I'm sorry."

But he didn't hear her, because at that moment her father brushed past her elbow and grabbed Jake by the shoulders, nearly knocking him back in his chair. The buzz of the busy dining room came to an immediate halt. Before she could say anything, her father was clutching Jake by the front of his shirt and pulling him up to standing, holding Jake's face close to his own. The image of her gentle father lifting a man like he was a fifty-pound bag of flour was so bizarre that it felt like a scene from a movie rather than her real, suddenly unrecognizable, life.

"I don't care what the police say," her father was hissing, his spittle hitting Jake's face. "You're a sick bastard. She's a kid, and you need to stay the hell away from her."

"Dad!" Rosie yelled, pulling at his arm. "Stop it! Stop!"

He turned to her without letting go of Jake, who was struggling to find his feet. Her father's face was red and he was sweating. Rosie was afraid that he was going to have a heart attack. He was too old to be doing this. She was literally going to kill her father. "Dad," she said again, her voice pleading this time, and tears springing to her eyes. "Please. It's not his fault. It's my fault. He didn't do anything."

Now was the time. She should just say it, the truth. Jake craned his head around to look at her, even as her father was dragging him to the door. She opened her mouth, but nothing came out. She couldn't do it here, not in front of all of these people. In a second, the moment had passed.

"Rosa! Kitchen. Now," her father yelled to her over his shoulder. He pushed Jake through the door, and Rosie quickly darted toward the kitchen, desperate to escape the stares from the customers. Alex, one of the line cooks, stood by the counter watching her father, a baseball bat held discreetly at the side of his leg. In case my father needs backup, she thought. This is insane. I have to stop this.

As she slid past Alex, she heard her father address the dining room in a voice of strained cheerfulness: "Okay, people, the show was free, and so are the cookies! Alex, get these fine people some cookies."

She pushed through the swinging door, took the kitchen in three steps, and went out the back, the screen door slamming behind her.

At the bottom of the steps she stopped and sat down.

She heard the door open and her father came out and sat down next to her without looking at her.

"Are you okay?" he asked.

"Did you call the police?"

"Not yet, but I will. I wanted to check on you first."

"You can't. It wasn't his fault."

"Of course it's his fault. He's a grown man. He's a . . . predator." It seemed to pain her father to say this.

"No," Rosie said, feeling her stomach drop to her feet. "He didn't do anything. I mean, he really didn't do anything. I took those pictures, Dad. He had no idea they were on his phone."

Her stared at her. "I don't understand what you're saying," he said.

"Dad," she said. "I really messed up." And she began to tell him everything. About the party and the house, about what had happed to Maddie, and about how scared they all were of getting caught. She told him about Hunter, and how he had asked her for help. She'd thought it through so many times that it was like reciting lines from a play. "And then," she said, "one day he left his phone on the counter and I grabbed it. I hadn't planned it out in advance. I just did it. I guess I was thinking we could use it somehow, maybe to blackmail him? It was crazy. As soon as I did it, I realized how crazy it was. I deleted it from his phone. I didn't know that it could still be found. He had no idea. It was me. He really, truly didn't do anything."

"Rosie, I can't believe you did this. I thought I raised you better than that. You told me you weren't at that party."

"I know, Dad. But I couldn't tell you. I didn't want to disappoint you." A few tears had slipped down Rosie's face, but now she began to really cry, like she did when she was a kid, gasping for breath and tasting salt in her mouth.

"You've done nothing but lie to me. I thought we agreed to always be honest with each other," he said, shaking his head. "This is bad, Rosie. We have to figure out what to do. You messed with some powerful people." He shook his head again as if he couldn't believe it. "Jake Tillman is a *district attorney*. Did you think about that? I tell everyone how responsible you are, but now I feel like I don't even know you."

"Don't say that, Dad," Rosie said miserably.

"I thought I was doing the right thing, raising you out here," he said, his voice catching. "After your mom died, I thought maybe we should move back to the city, be closer to family. But you had your friends, and I had the restaurant. I don't know. Maybe it was a mistake. It's been hard, doing this on my own . . ."

"Dad," Rosie said. "Please. This isn't your fault. And I'm going to fix it. Somehow."

"It's not going to be easy," he said.

Rosie swallowed. "What do you think I should I do?" she asked.

"I wish you'd asked me that before all this happened." He cleared his throat. "You need to come forward and tell the truth. After that, ask for forgiveness. I'm not sure what else you can do, but you can't destroy someone else's life to protect your own."

"There's been a lot of that going on around here," Rosie said in a small voice.

"Maybe," her father said. "But not in my house."

47

∞

Hal Buckley asked Detective Murray if he'd be willing to give Jake the news in person. It wasn't really his job, but Murray had been worried about Jake ever since he'd been put on leave. When Jake opened the door, Murray stood there with a sheepish grin on his face, which faded when he saw Jake. Jake was in boxers and an undershirt, clearly two days away from his last shower. Jake started to shut the door, but Murray put his hand out, stopping him. "I've got good news," he said.

Jake just stared at him for a moment then turned silently and walked back into his apartment, leaving Murray to follow him in and close the door.

"It's been awhile," Jake said. He poured a cup of coffee for himself, not offering anything to Murray, and sat at his kitchen counter. He looked at Murray expectantly.

"Sorry, buddy," Murray began. "But you know how it is. With everything that was going on, I needed to give you a little space."

"I haven't heard one word from you," Jake clarified. "But you're not the only one. It's been complete radio silence from the office. Except for one call from Hal, letting me know he'd accept my resignation if I wanted to move forward right away." Jake shook his head. "Move forward to what? You think I was sleeping with that teenager. You think I'm the kind of man who would do that? A creep?"

"Hey," Murray said, holding up his hands. "You have to understand how this looked from their perspective. You're handling a case against a bunch of kids from the school. Then it looks like maybe you have a thing going on with one of them. And, lo and behold, she hasn't been charged with anything. It could have blown up the whole case. Taking leave was the best thing you could do, while it all got sorted out."

"That's a nice way to spin it," Jake said sarcastically. "There's just one problem. I didn't do it. I barely know that girl."

"Well, yeah," Murray agreed. "It turns out that's true."

Jake stared at Detective Murray.

"That's why I'm here," Murray said. "She came into Hal's office today, said she made up the whole thing."

Jake's mouth opened slightly, but he didn't say anything.

"She said she did it to try to get her friends out of trouble. I don't know how she thought it was going to help. Batshit crazy, if you ask me. But the father supported her story."

Jake let out a long sigh, leaned forward, and rested his forehead on the counter. For a minute he didn't say anything. Then he raised his head and looked at Murray.

"Did you really think I did it?" he asked.

"No," Murray answered, without hesitation. "But I had to look into it. Jake, I'm sorry that I was the one who found those texts. I wish I'd never seen them. But once I did, I had to report it to the court. That's the job. It's not personal. For what it's worth, I hoped like hell it wasn't true. I hope you and I are still good. My wife wants you to come over for dinner."

Jake was shaking his head. "You're going to have to give me a little time on that," he said. "What happens to Rosie Mendoza?"

Murray shrugged. "She never actually filed a false report. But if you want to press charges . . ."

"No thanks," Jake said quickly. "I don't want anything else to do with them." He looked down at his hands. "This case—these kids— they're like a tornado, picking up everything in their path, smashing it up, and spitting it back out."

"And leaving some people untouched. Like a miracle," Murray added. He told Jake about the plea deals that Hal had struck with Trip O'Connor and Hunter Finch. "He wrapped it up nice and neat," Murray said. "Trip O'Connor takes the blame and the Finch family pays the bill. Everyone else gets minor charges and community service. Very tidy."

"You gotta hand it to Hal," Jake said. "He knows how to work the job. You can tell him I said that."

"You can tell him yourself," Murray said. "He wants to see you."

An hour later, Jake sat in Hal's office. He'd showered, shaved, and put on a dress shirt. But the stress of the last few weeks was still apparent as he walked through the office, all eyes on him. His jaw was clenched and he kept his eyes on the floor, not meeting anyone's gaze. It was excruciating, like a perp walk. He had to remind himself that he hadn't actually done anything wrong.

Hal greeted him at the door, made a public show of patting his back, and motioned to a chair. Hal started off saying all of the right things: He was glad to see Jake; he'd never believed it was true; he hoped Jake was holding up okay. Jake smiled grimly, nodding along. Then Hal got down to the real business.

"Well, Jake," he said, leaning back in his chair. "What are your thoughts going forward? Of course, you're welcome back at the office, now that this is all cleared up."

It was an expert lawyer's question, Jake thought. Leading, but only slightly so. It implied Jake was not, in fact, welcome back at the office, without having to actually say so. It wouldn't look great for the DA to accuse him of something he didn't do, and then run him out of his job after it turned out he was innocent. But that was, Jake could see, exactly what Hal intended to do.

"I've enjoyed my work here," Jake said, noncommittally. Everything he had worked for—his career, his reputation—was slipping away. He wasn't going to make it easy for Hal.

Hal nodded thoughtfully. "You're a good lawyer, Jake," he said. "But this is a small town. As DA, I take an interest in the careers of all of the lawyers here. I'd hate to see you get stuck trying DUIs for the next twenty years."

They were negotiating, Jake could see, but for what? If Hal wanted him out of here, he could just as easily bury him in trial prep and traffic court, keeping him behind the desk and away from the court-house until Jake couldn't take it anymore and quit. He'd seen it done before. It was rare for anyone to be fired at the DA's office; they had other ways of showing you the door. "I'm capable of a lot more than trying DUIs," Jake said.

"That you are," Hal said. "And nobody in this office can say any different. No one here holds this whole business against you. But all that news coverage was tough. The press can be brutal, can't they?" Hal looked right at Jake as he said this.

He knows, Jake thought. Somehow, Hal knew, or at least suspected, it was Jake who had called the city papers about the Jensen case.

Hal was still speaking: "As I said, no one here holds it against you. But this job requires the utmost public trust. And respect. In a town like this, rumors live a long time. Unfortunate, but I guess that's just the price we pay for living in such a beautiful place. It's not like city life. You grew up in Philadelphia, didn't you?" Hal asked, without waiting for an answer. "Plenty going on there. No one pays as much mind to gossip; they're too busy. Speaking of which," Hal went on, looking through a pile of papers on his desk and picking up a business card. "Yes, here it is."

Hal gave Jake an appraising look. "It just so happens I have a friend up in New York. We went to law school together, back in the day. He's at the SEC now, pretty high up. It turns out they're going beg-ging for good trial attorneys right now. All of this fuss with the bank bailouts and the subprime mortgage market. What they've got on staff is a bunch of egghead analyst types. They're going to need real bulldogs to prosecute these cases. He asked me if I knew anyone who might be looking."

He handed the card to Jake. "Why don't you give him a call?" he suggested. "There's a lot of interesting work going on up there. It could be a good place for a man to make a name for himself. Of course, I'd hate to lose you here. But if you were set on leaving, I'd be happy to put in a good word for you."

Jake looked at the card. So this was the deal on the table: If Jake offered up his resignation, Hal would fix him up with a job in New

York City, out of Hal's way. Jake had to admire the man. It was a shrewd offer.

Jake hesitated for only a moment. "Make that word to your friend pretty good," Jake said, "and I'll give him a call." Jake was just as eager as Hal to put all of this behind him. Leaving the DA's office would mean starting over, but it seemed like a new start was exactly what he needed. "Hal," he said, "working with you—it's been a real education. I'll get you my letter of resignation this afternoon."

"We'll miss you, Jake," Hal said, continuing their pantomime of good humor. He got up and walked Jake to the door. "Come visit anytime. It's a wonderful place to spend a weekend. When you're not knee-deep in police reports and unreliable witnesses, you can really see what a nice town we have here."

Jake slipped the business card into his pocket, only half paying attention to Hal. His thoughts were already on the future. Moving to New York seemed like exactly the right play. He couldn't even remember at this moment what had attracted him to small-town life in the first place. "Maybe I'll see you around, Hal," he said. "But not too soon."

48

The helicopter touched down at the Downtown Manhattan Heliport, and Hunter followed Dom onto the tarmac and into a waiting town car. It was a quick ride over the Williamsburg Bridge to the construction site in Brooklyn.

"There it is," Dom said, rolling down the window as they crossed the bridge. He pointed to a stretch of desolate land that bordered the East River. Hunter followed his gaze, taking in the fifteen acres that his father had snapped up in a deal that had fallen into his lap as the mortgage crisis had taken down smaller developers and speculators. The new property connected two other parcels that Dom had purchased a few years earlier, giving him dominion over a breathtaking swath of land along the river. Right now it was just empty lots and weed-filled patches of grass, with stretches of chain-link fence protecting nothing worth stealing. But one day it would be a fortress of silvery apartment towers, green lawn, and outdoor cafés that would spill out of ground-level retail spaces. Hunter had seen the renderings. Finch Properties was slowly transitioning from sprawling suburban subdivisions, on which they'd built their fortune and reputation, to more urban high-rise buildings, meant for a younger demographic. The economy would bounce back, eventually, and when it did, people would want to live here, in shiny new apartments with million-dollar Manhattan skyline views.

"And there's the crown jewel," Dom said. He wrapped his arm around Hunter's shoulders and pulled him forward in the seat, to see better. There, at the end of the stretch of empty land, were the ruins of an old factory, long defunct. It was eight stories tall, built in grimy but solid brick, and Hunter could just make out the pale ghost of a massive white slogan painted across the walls. A single brick smoke-stack rose from one end, and the windows that dotted the facade were high and arched. On the lower floors they were boarded up, but the upper windows were empty, providing a glimpse of clear blue sky. It was nothing but a shell.

Hunter had been nervous about this trip. Things had gone off the rails so quickly: first Collegiate Prep threatening that he might not graduate, and then the pressure to take a plea in that stupid house party case. The newspapers had focused on his role in the party—it made for a great story, and his father had been eager to offer up Hunter's guilty plea as a way to bring the media cycle to an end. It seemed like every conversation he had with his dad started or ended with yelling, by either one or both of them. And then, finally, getting word that he was out at Princeton.

When he finally told his dad, he expected that Dom would hit the roof. That he'd disinherit him, or punch him, or finally send him to live with his grandparents—his mother's parents, in their dingy and brooding home upstate—like he'd been threatening to do for years. But his father surprised him. He'd been quiet and resigned. He said all the things a father should about disappointment and consequences, but it didn't seem like his heart was in it. It was as if, after years of trying to keep all of the plates spinning, the fact they'd come crashing down was more of a relief than a surprise. At least he didn't have to keep fighting gravity.

Dom was too distracted, both by the problems of the mortgage crisis and by the opportunities it was creating, to concentrate on prob-lems of Hunter's that he couldn't fix. The next morning the family packed up for the Hamptons. Lindsay had found a big house right on the beach, its former tenants presumably another casualty of the market crash, and the Finch family left New Falls, and their problems, temporarily behind.

The town car pulled up in front of the refinery building and Dom and Hunter stepped out. Dom shielded his eyes and looked up at the facade.

"This one will be different," he said. "Lofts. Just like Soho in the eighties, but with better amenities. I thought about tearing it down. There's enough room here for another tower. But then I thought about what you said, Hunter. That what people like about Brooklyn is the cool factor. The old warehouses. The bohemian feel."

"I'm pretty sure I've never said the word *bohemian* in my life," Hunter interrupted. "I said people like the warehouse parties. Raves."

"Right," his father agreed good-naturedly. "Well, you would know parties," he added with an uncharacteristic wink, surprising Hunter with his ability to joke about it. It actually seemed like his father was enjoying this. "These lofts will give the whole project authenticity," Dom went on. "We'll use some elements from this building in the high rises—exposed beams and brick, poured-cement floors. It'll tie the whole thing together. Plus the city is going to love that we're pre-serving the refinery facade."

"It sounds great," Hunter said, perfunctorily. He just didn't get the same thrill out of real estate that his father seemed to get.

"I'm glad you think so," his dad said, ignoring his tone. "Because you're going to help me put it all together."

Hunter looked at him, confused, and his father continued. "You're out of options, Hunter. If you want to stay under my roof, you're go-ing to have to do something. Look for a job, if you want, but I can tell you there aren't going to be a lot of better offers for a kid who barely made it out of high school."

Hunter looked at the ground, and his dad took a deep breath and started again. "This is a chance for you to learn the family business, from the ground up. You'll start off working construction."

"Dad, I don't know anything about construction or real estate."

"I bet you know more than you think, Hunter. You proved it to me when you brought me the idea of offering to buy the O'Connors' orchard fields. You knew I was concerned about them selling to a developer and us losing the privacy behind the house."

"I was just trying to help out Will," Hunter mumbled. But Will hadn't spoken a word to him since the day they fought. Hunter had talked to his dad about the O'Connors' financial problems, and he'd kept his word to Trip, coming forward to the police to back up Trip's version of events so that Will's charges would get dropped. Hunter would be serving a week in county jail, scheduled during what would have been his Thanksgiving break from college, and he had been ordered to do three months of community service with Habitat for Humanity in the meantime. The Finch family was also taking over the rebuilding of the Jensens' house. But he knew in his heart that his friendship with Will might be over. He hadn't meant to hurt Maddie, but the fact was that he had, and he'd hurt Will too.

Will, whose friendship Hunter had finally understood was the one thing that he'd actually earned, unlike the many things that he'd been given as Dominic Finch's son. And he'd blown it all up and lost one of the only real things that he had. "The O'Connors probably wouldn't have sold out to a developer anyway," Hunter said. "They're not that kind of people."

"It was a clever idea," Dom said, ignoring Hunter's dig at real estate developers. "Don't undersell it. The biggest part of this business is knowing when to strike. My deal with the O'Connors benefits everyone. They get to keep the orchard business going on very generous lease terms, and they get the cash that they need from the sale. I keep the property behind ours intact, which is valuable to me. You saw an opportunity, and you brought it to me. I was impressed."

Hunter hoped Will and his family saw it the same way. But he was pretty sure they didn't.

"Anyway, with everything that's happened this year, I don't think you have many other options. What you need is some hard work for a change. You're going to be on the construction crew and learn how it all comes together. You know what Mark Twain said?"

"Yeah, Dad, I know: 'Buy land, they're not making it anymore.' "

"See?" Dom said. "I told you that you know more than you think."

His dad was right: he wasn't going to get a better offer. He thought about Will, heading off to Princeton in a few weeks. Without him.

But there was no point in thinking about it now. Will had worked hard for it. And here Hunter was, once again, being offered an opportunity—even if it was just a job on a construction crew—that he probably didn't deserve.

He'd brought this on himself, he knew. He'd been reckless before. He'd cheated on girlfriends and tests, and smashed up his car. But he'd never done anything like this. He thought of the cop, last year, seeing his family name on his driver's license and letting him off on the speeding ticket. He'd felt invincible in that moment, and at the same time like nothing mattered. It was like punching in the dark, his fists meeting only air. Until one hit finally landed, and everything had exploded. He wasn't invincible. And more important, he saw now, the people around him were as fragile as he was. He'd hurt Will, and Maddie. And June. He hadn't meant to. He wasn't even really thinking about them. And he'd even, he thought, managed to hurt his father by blowing his chance at Princeton.

He'd lost his friends, but here was his father, still trying to help him, still extending a hand. He was going to take it.

49

The weather was as gloomy as the news. For the past two weeks, Maja and Ted had shared the apartment in strained silence, barely meeting each other's eyes, trapped inside by the rain. Ted stared at the reporters on TV and scanned the newspapers as the reverberations of Foxfield's collapse were felt throughout the city. The headlines were apocalyptic: PANIC GRIPS CREDIT MARKETS. FOXFIELD COLLAPSE SENDS SHOCKWAVES AROUND THE WORLD. JOB LOSSES HINT AT VAST REMAKING OF ECONOMY.

Talking heads on TV reported on the bailouts of major mortgage companies, as they tossed around the term *subprime mortgage* as if it had always been part of daily conversation. The stock market rose and dipped wildly, seemingly on a whim. On the news, people stood outside their locked-up homes, their kids and furniture lined up on the curb and foreclosure notices on the door. The *New York Post* summed it up in one word: MELTDOWN!

Ted looked like a shadow of himself, and Maja's heart hurt for him. But each time she wanted to reach out and comfort him, the shock of what he'd kept from her would hit her again. She couldn't find a way around it; it was just too big. But she also blamed herself. Ted was right about one thing: she hadn't wanted to know. She'd wanted everything to work out so badly that she'd refused to see what was really going on.

When she wasn't working at the gallery, where she'd been picking up as many extra hours as she could, she and Ted tried to be civil as they worked together to get their expenses down as much as possible.

They went through their purchases one by one, canceling anything that wasn't strictly necessary for the rebuild, and delaying or setting up payment plans for custom orders that were already in progress. They could keep paying their construction loan for a few more months, but their lease on the apartment was up in September, and it would be difficult to get the money together for a new place if the house wasn't ready, which was looking unlikely.

Working through the problems with the house kept Maja from thinking endlessly about her problems with Ted, or what would happen to them when the baby came. She saved that for her long, sleepless nights. They'd been on the verge of getting everything they wanted: the house and the baby, a picture-perfect life in a picture-perfect town. And now, despite finally being pregnant, she felt like it was all just beyond her reach. She knew women who were divorced. They survived, she told herself. But then again, most of them at least got to keep the house. It looked like she might lose her house and her husband. They just couldn't seem to find their way back to each other.

They'd been able to get started on gutting the flooded areas of the house and rebuilding the kitchen with the initial payment from their insurance company, but they'd run through that money quickly, and the insurance company hadn't gotten back to them yet about the independent report they'd submitted. It seemed criminal that they were able to drag out the process so long, but apparently it was all there in the fine print. Getting desperate, they'd tried applying for a second loan, but it hadn't come through. "Nothing personal," their broker told them. "No one can get credit right now."

Their contractor was making noises about moving on to another project, and Maja was starting to think that they might actually have to put the property up on the market, when they finally got some good news about the case: Finch Properties was offering to take over the work.

The call had come in from Hal Buckley. "Dominic Finch wants to personally send out a construction team to get your house back in tip-top shape," he said. "They do excellent work—you can see their houses all over New Falls. You'll still have some restitution money coming in from the other families, but believe me, this is better. Mr. Finch personally assured me that they'll spare no expense."

Ted was skeptical at first. "He's buying his kid's way out of trouble," he pointed out. "Who cares?" Maja replied. "The damage is done. What we need to focus on now is how we get it repaired. If Dominic Finch wants to rebuild our house, fine. Great, even. We've got less than seven months until this baby comes. We don't have any time to waste."

Ted looked at her as if he was seeing her for the first time in weeks. "Seven months," he said. "Wow."

"Yeah," Maja smiled. "Can you believe it?" Once she started smiling, she couldn't stop, even though she knew she looked a little goofy.

Ted smiled back. He was looking at her the way she'd imagined he would in the daydreams she'd had of telling him he was going to be a father. Just for a moment, she glimpsed a real spark of joy, something she hadn't seen in him for months. But in the next moment, he was frowning again, his eyes looking past her.

He can't let himself feel this, she realized. He doesn't think he deserves it. "Ted," she said, "I have an idea." She felt desperate to recapture that moment of connection. "Let's go down and see the house. It's been weeks since we were there together. We can bring sleeping bags and camp out."

Ted just looked at her. "It's raining," he said. "We don't have a car."

"We can rent one," Maja said, feeling reckless. It was another expense, but so what? The Finch family was going to fix their house. This was worth celebrating. She suddenly felt an intense desire to be there, in the place where they had planned to start their family.

Normally Ted would have argued with her and insisted they do the practical thing and stay where they were. And Maja would have gone along with him, knowing he was right. But today he just nodded okay.

An hour later they were in a tiny Hyundai, the cheapest car they could rent, heading down the highway with flashlights and sleeping bags in the back seat. It reminded Maja of camping trips they'd made upstate when they were dating. There was something comforting about sitting in the steamy car with Ted, listening to the oldies station as they drove. For weeks they'd felt like strangers. Now, at least, they were talking.

"I'm sorry," Ted said, staring at the road ahead. "I know that I keep telling you this, but it's true: I was so ashamed of what was happening. I got in over my head, and then it all spiraled out of control so quickly. I didn't mean to hurt you."

Maja nodded. "You should have told me," she said. "But I also should have been listening. I was preoccupied with the house, and with trying for a baby. I should have known that something was going on. I guess I didn't want to see."

"Maja," Ted said. "You know that even if we're able to do the work on the house, we still owe a lot on the construction loan. If I don't find something soon . . ."

Maja pressed her lips together. She knew he was right. "Can we hang on a little longer?" she asked. "Something might come through."

"It's a long shot, and I wasn't sure if I wanted to say anything to you," Ted said. "But Adil might have something for me at J.P. Morgan. It's a back-of-the-house job, in Hoboken. They need people for the team that's going through all of the mortgage securities they bought from Foxfield. It would be sort of like being the coroner at your own autopsy, and I'd be taking a pay cut. But at least it would be a job."

"That's great," Maja said. "I'm surprised. The last time I talked to Aneeta, she seemed a little standoffish."

Ted gave a dry laugh. "People usually feel bad for you when you lose your job," he said. "I guess it's a little different when they think you've taken the whole economy down with you."

By the time they pulled into New Falls, it was almost dark. They let themselves in and walked through the house. It smelled good, like new paint and freshly cut wood. The chaos from the party had been cleared out, and the restoration contractors had done a thorough job of excising the warped boards and cracked tile, setting up a solid foundation for the work that would come next.

In the kitchen there was a small pile of mail, mostly advertising and credit card applications. Near the bottom was an envelope with their name handwritten on the front. Ted picked it up and opened it.

"What's that?" Maja asked.

Ted took a few minutes to read it through. "It's an apology," he finally said, handing her the letter.

Maja read it and then looked up. "This is an admission, right? William O'Connor. I have to check, but I don't think his name showed up on the final list of charges."

Ted nodded. "That sounds right."

"This is evidence. We should hand it over to the police."

"We could do that," Ted said. "Or . . ." he began.

"Or?" Maja asked.

"Maybe we could just accept it as an apology."

"Ted," Maja said, her voice incredulous. "After everything that we've been through?"

"He's just a kid," Ted sighed.

"A teenager," Maja corrected him.

"Listen, I wouldn't have said this a month ago. But the house is going to be okay—Finch Properties is taking care of it. And there's going to be insurance money, and restitution. It's going to come together. What no one has given us is an actual apology—until now. Can we at least think it over?" He looked at Maja. "People make mistakes," he said with a wry smile. "I guess I hope asking for forgiveness means something."

Maja read through the letter again. Ted was right, it was a real apology. What would it really cost them to accept it? "Maybe you have a point," she said. "I don't know if I can live here if I feel like we're still angry, and still in conflict, with everyone around us. This could be a start."

"We give the kid a chance?" Ted asked, and Maja nodded.

"I love you, Maja," Ted said. "The rest of it, I can do without. But I never want to lose you."

Maja slipped her hand into his. They were standing in front of the lone glass door that hadn't been shattered, and Maja could see their reflection in the window, superimposed on the empty house. She'd thought that having a child and building their dream house would make them happy: a perfect life as a series of checked boxes. But now she saw that happiness might be more like the river in front of her; ebbing and flowing, the banks and trees giving way and gaining ground so they didn't break under forces outside of their control. She knew they would face other challenges and surprises that she couldn't yet imagine. She was happy here in this moment with Ted, though, and it felt like enough.

It was still drizzling, but the air was warm, and they stepped out onto the deck. They took off their shoes, and walked out together onto the wet grass. The river ran swiftly past the house, full from the rain. Maja rested her head on Ted's shoulder, and the promise of the baby she carried felt like a real presence between them. Ted seemed to feel it too, and he pulled her closer toward him.

"This is our first night at our new house," Ted said.

Maja laughed. "It isn't quite how I imagined it."

"It's okay, though, isn't it?" Ted asked, sounding a little surprised.

"It's good," Maja said. "We're here together."

50

In August the river was opaque, like milky coffee, from the summer rain that swelled its waters with muddy runoff. North of town, the water lapped against the boat launch, warm and inviting. The kids began arriving in pickups and Jeeps, backing down the launch just to the water's edge to unload tubes and kayaks. By eleven in the morning there were nearly twenty people there, all local kids.

Will plugged an air compressor into his car lighter and began to blow up floats and inner tubes. They filled coolers with ice and beer, and stocked the dry bags with snacks and cameras. The girls tumbled into their tubes first, and the boys pushed them toward the center of the river, then hopped into their own tubes and followed them out. Once they were all on the water they lashed some of the tubes and the cooler rafts together with rope.

This far north of town the river was wide and flat, and the banks were crowded with trees. Up ahead they could see the lacy metal structure of the pedestrian bridge that crossed the river at the state park, with a massive American flag hanging from the center, rippling softly in the breeze. In an hour or so they would come to a point where the river would be dotted with bands of other tubers in matching yellow floats from a company that catered to day-trippers from Philadelphia and New York, but for now they had the water to themselves.

Will rummaged through the cooler and pulled out cans of beer, tossing one through the air to his brother. He cracked one for himself and lay back in his tube, his eyes closed. He let his hand trail in the warm water. He finished the beer in two long gulps, and slowly began to relax. He looked forward to these tubing trips every year. Out on the water, whatever was happening onshore didn't seem to matter. The river determined the pace, and all he could do was let it carry him along.

June and Rosie had tied their floats together. Despite everything that had happened, they'd stayed friends. Everyone knew June had come forward to the police, but she'd managed to spin it to her advantage, in the way that only she could. The story that went around was that she'd been dragged in by her father and had no choice. "I did my best to protect all of you," she'd said, and everyone agreed it had only been a matter of time anyway. And by that time, Rosie had—for once—stolen the spotlight from June with her confession to the District Attorney's office. In the end, there'd been no official punishment for what she'd done. The DA's office had seemed as eager as she was to put the whole thing behind them. But her father had insisted she stay at home this fall. Instead of Penn State, she'd be taking classes at Hart County Community College and living at home, where her father could keep an eye on her.

Trip brought up the rear of the flotilla in a green kayak. He'd brought a fishing rod, and he had it gripped between his knees, the line trailing out behind them, while he carefully rolled a cigarette. "You got a fishing license?" someone called out to him, and Trip said sure, right here, and reached into his pocket, pulling out his middle finger. Everyone laughed, and Will laughed too.

Will downed another beer. If you'd asked him two months ago if he'd ever be out on the river with his friends like this again, he wouldn't have bet money on it. Everything had seemed to be doomed, his friends guarded and suspicious of each other, and his mother crying in her room at night, and in the shower, and any other time she thought no one was watching.

It wasn't like nothing had changed. There was the thing that Will spent a lot of time trying not to think about: Trip was going to jail for a year. When Will left for Princeton in a week, Trip would check into Hart County Correctional. The thought terrified Will, but Trip seemed strangely nonchalant about it. Probably he was just putting on a brave face, but Will needed that, and he didn't want to dig too deeply. Send me books to read from school, Trip said, and Will promised he would, and then they didn't talk about it again.

They also never talked about the fact that the fields behind the house, with their acres of apple and cherry trees, no longer belonged to the O'Connor family. Their name was still on the gate, and his parents still ran the farm, but the land itself belonged to Finch Properties. Except for the house and an easement on the driveway, everything else had been sold. Even the eighty-year-old apple tree that Will's great-grandfather had planted, and which still stood at the entrance to the fields, no longer fruiting but spreading and shady. The money had been used to pay Trip's lawyer and his restitution, and Will's school bills, and the rest put aside to lease back the property and invest in the business. His mother put it simply: "The terms were very generous." And then she'd added, more defensively: "None of you were ever so sentimental about it when the land belonged to us." And that was the last time they discussed it.

And it wasn't just his family. Things also hadn't been the same between him and Maddie. After she'd gotten out of the hospital, he'd hoped things would go back to the way they were, but they hadn't. She rarely talked about the party, or the accident, but there was something about the way she would stare off into space in the middle of conversations that unsettled him. Her mind always seemed to be somewhere else. And soon she would be leaving town. A week after the police announced the assault case had ended in a plea deal, Maddie told him she'd been accepted to a fine arts program in San Francisco that started at the end of the month. "I have to get out of here," she said. "I need to move on, and I can't do that here."

Will pushed off of his tube and dove under the water, cooling off. He flipped onto his back, like a river otter, and floated for a minute on the surface. Above him the sky was bright blue, but at the edge of his vision the southern horizon was dark and hazy. He paddled over to Trip's kayak and pointed at the clouds.

"That looks like a thunderstorm," he said. "Was it in the forecast?"

Trip followed his gaze. "I didn't check," he said. "Seems nice enough right now."

Trip's words didn't reassure Will. "I don't want to get caught on the water if there's a storm," he said. "We've had some crazy lightning this summer. Especially with all the girls here. You know they'll freak out."

Trip looked up at the clouds again and shook his head. "Nah," he said. "It'll hold. We're going to have smooth sailing." He winked at Will.

Will watched the sky for another minute and then shrugged. There was nothing they could do about it now, unless they pulled the tubes over to the bank and walked all the way back up the road to their cars. "If you say so."

Will kept his eye on the clouds, but soon he was busy passing out beers and pulling the flotilla over to the rope swing that hung from a tree halfway down their route. They lodged their tubes against the bank and took turns climbing the tree and swinging from its branches on the squeaking rope, holding on until they were out over the deepest water, and then letting go.

Long after everyone else had grown tired and gone back to drinking beer in their tubes, Will and Trip kept going, their arcs going higher and their bodies twisting into flips and swan dives. Rosie called out scores, and the brothers were in a dead heat.

For his last jump, Will gripped the rope tightly and climbed to the highest branch, past the wooden steps nailed into the trunk by kids a generation before them. They never jumped from up here. He inched along the branch and then stood, wobbling, with the rope clutched in his hands. He looked down at his friends, waiting in the water. Then, with a whoop, he went soaring down and then out, like a bird taking flight. At the last moment he released the rope and dropped into the river with his arms raised triumphantly. When he popped back up, he looked over at Trip, who just shook his head with a grin.

"You win," Trip said. And then, helping Will back into his tube: "You always wanted it more."

"What?" Will asked.

"Everything."

When Will frowned, Trip added: "It's all good. You worked hard for it."

"I wouldn't be going if you hadn't taken the fall for me," Will said.

They pushed off from the bank and continued floating down the river. The sky grew darker, and the air was still and humid. June batted away a mosquito. "Is it going to rain?" she asked, frowning.

"Nope," Will and Trip said at the same time. "It'll hold."

The trees on the right bank gave way to a clearing. There, in front of them, was the house. They all stared at it, their conversation coming to a halt. They could see men working on the decks. As usual, Mr. Finch had turned a problem into an opportunity—in this case, keeping one of his construction teams working during the recession, while also keeping the case from dragging on and making more headlines that might be bad for business.

"It's actually a pretty cool house," Rosie said.

Will wondered what would have happened if he'd never picked up that hammer and sent it flying through the window. Or if they'd never even gone to the party in the first place. He wanted to say something that would make sense of everything that had happened. A reason for what they'd done, or an excuse. Why had they risked everything for a stupid beer bash? But he didn't have an answer. It was a party, and in the moment, it had felt like morning would never come. But they'd done real damage—to the people around them, and to each other. And yet, here they were.

They rounded a bend in the river and the New Falls Bridge came into view. They would pull their rafts out on the sloping bank under the bridge, before the river hit the rapids. The afternoon light reflected off the metal bridge, shining pale green against the purple sky. The wind started up, pushing their floats along faster than they expected.

Trip watched the currents change. "Let's start paddling over to the bank," he said.

"It's definitely going to pour," June warned, her eyes skyward.

"No, it won't," Will said. "This is the last tubing trip of the year. The weather will hold."

The group slowly made their way to the shore. When they reached it, they hauled themselves out of their tubes and onto the muddy bank. The wind was really whipping now, and they worked quickly, letting the air out of the tubes and carrying the coolers up the hill to the road. They formed a chain, helping one another up the steep bank and trying not to lose their footing on the slippery path. It was only five o'clock, but the sky was suddenly as dark as if it was night. When they reached the top of the bank, they let go of one another's hands and scattered to the shelter of the cars that they'd left parked in town. None of them thought to call out last goodbyes as they jogged away, and it wasn't until they were safe inside, wrapped in towels and warming their feet on the dashboard heating vents, that the first bolt of lightning split the sky, and the rain finally poured down.

AUTHOR'S NOTE

In 2007, I was starting my career as an associate at a law firm in New York City. Specializing in corporate tax, I had a bird's-eye view of the financial crisis that was beginning to unfold. Working late nights, I'd gaze out from my midtown skyscraper and marvel at the constellations of illuminated windows in the neighboring buildings, so dense that we formed a sort of sad corporate Milky Way. The sweeping views included the headquarters of the now-infamous Bear Stearns, whose collapse was a prelude to the larger banking crisis.

By 2008, the lights in the Bear Stearns building began to go dark, floor by floor. Their rock-bottom sale to JPMorgan Chase shook the stock market, wiping out jobs and retirement savings overnight. The reverberations were felt throughout the economy, and the other big banks trembled.

I wouldn't be there to see how many more lights went out as the crisis spread. The economy ground to a halt, and I was laid off by my firm. I was far from the only person to have my life upended by the recession—all over the country people lost their jobs, savings, and homes.

As one character in *The House Party* notes, all markets have winners and losers. The financial crisis affected all areas of the American economy, but the middle class may have been hit hardest of all. Americans have always been preoccupied with the idea of the middle class, and the values and aspirations it embodies. In *The House Party*, I wanted to explore how Americans perceive their class standing, and how those perceptions play out within their friendships, families, and communities. I chose to set the book in a small town on the outskirts of

Philadelphia because it presented a microcosm of America: multi-generational farmers and first-generation immigrants living side by side with real estate developers and investment bankers.

In a way, the book is an ode to the charming towns that dot both sides of the Delaware River in Pennsylvania and New Jersey. These towns, with their historic mills and canals, art galleries and ice cream parlors, seem like an unlikely setting for class warfare. On the surface, they offer spacious homes and good public schools. But the people in these bucolic towns are subject to the same forces that shape the country as a whole, and they aren't immune to the struggle, resentment, and tension that such a society entails.

By focusing my story in part on high school students who make a serious but not atypical mistake, I hoped to show how differently one event could shape the lives of people who see themselves as peers, but who in fact have very different resources available to them due to their families' wealth and connections, or lack thereof. High school students—teenagers just on the cusp of adulthood—are at a point in their lives when their futures can diverge widely based on their social class. In a place like the fictional town of New Falls, Pennsylvania, kids from many backgrounds attend the same public schools and play on the same sports teams. But what happens after graduation, or when they face challenges or adversity, can be a very different story. I wanted to ask the question: When a town that prides itself on equality and community is put to the test, how willing are the individual members to put the community's best interest above the safety and future of their own families?

Placing a high school house party at the center of the story made sense to me because of parallels I saw with the housing crisis, both resulting in violence and destruction. In each case, many individuals made small transgressions or thought only of themselves. But added together, these individual actions added up to a major disaster. On a case-by-case basis, it can be difficult to assign blame to any one person. But whether it's a party that's gone wildly out of control or a housing bubble inflated by false hope, the participants will eventually wake up to face a reckoning, and a very steep bill.

ACKNOWLEDGMENTS

Thank you to my wonderful agent, Stacy Testa, for your enthusiasm and for the insights that you brought to this book. Liz Stein, I am so grateful for your thoughtfulness and guidance. Having an editor who understands where you are trying to go and knows how to nudge you in the right direction is a gift.

Thank you, Marlene Zakes and Lynn Aylward, for reading my early drafts and loving them in the way that only people who love the writer can. Your energy kept me going. Al Zakes, thank you for your encouragement and advice.

Thank you, Sean, for everything. I couldn't do it without you, and I wouldn't want to. And thank you to Cal and Bea, who bring so much joy into my life. Please don't let this book give you any bad ideas.

ABOUT THE AUTHOR

Rita Cameron is also the author of *Ophelia's Muse*. She studied English at Columbia University and law at the University of Pennsylvania. She lives in San Jose, California, with her family.